I0654430

WAITING

VINCE ADAMS

Kindle Edition First published by Vince Adams Copyright © 2025
Cover Design & Glastonbury Tor photo by author

Reviews on Amazon.com or at this book's homepage:

www.vinceadamsconnection.com

…are welcome and appreciated. I'd love to hear from you!

ISBN: 979-8-9933111-1-1

Acknowledgements

This project was conceived in 1991 and had been tickling my mind in moments of idleness until 2016 when I had an opportunity to return to Glastonbury and committed to finishing King Arthur's modern story. It was then that I embarked on a nine-year adventure with tortoise/hare pacing. The book has ballooned and shrunk over the revisions with several fun (for me) chapters left on the editing room floor. Maybe later... But I'm excited to have finally typed "Thee End" and bring this work into the light.

The only person likely as excited as me if not more so was my wife, Cyndi, who alternated between biggest fan and erstwhile taskmaster ("tough love".) Thanks for your love and patience, Cyndi!

I'd also like to thank Beth Deehan, my very first draft reader who's love of the book kept me going so many years ago. She had the unique experience of reading it in installments, getting each new chapter as it finished. Thanks Beth!

On a project that spanned decades, there were too many people who influenced it to mention (or even remember!) but of note were my good friend, the author Larry Latourette, my brother Denis Adams (who taught me about "head hopping"), and my Lake Zurich writers group, Nick, Kendra, Tracy, and Larry, who came into this project late but helped me work out some of the more difficult chapters, especially with Nick's coaching on writing magical elements. Thank you!

While it feels a bit futile to thank Gildas, Monmouth, and von Eschenbach, they were nonetheless critical to shaping this narrative. Of modern works, I'd like to note that Geoffrey Ashe's "King

Arthur's Avalon" was singularly inspirational on that cloudy day when I first discovered Glastonbury in 1991.

Lastly, I'd like to thank my editor, David Taylor at thEditors, who was more writing coach than editor.

This book could not have become what it is without this generous support system.

Enjoy!

Chicago, IL
September 2025

Prologue

Three hours west of London is the small and historic town of Glastonbury. In its center stands a hill, the Glastonbury Tor, that stood watch over the Somerset plains as the land bridge to Europe washed away and the last woolly mammoth fell to hunters' spears. British history marched in its shadow as the marshy waters that rendered the Tor an island receded and the Celts, Romans, Christians, Britons, Anglo-Saxons, and then Normans left their mark on the countryside.

While the rolling terrain of the region obscures the summit from much of the town below, the otherworldly nature of Glastonbury is always front and center. In ancient times, legend holds that Glastonbury was the mystical Isle of Avalon, the final resting place of King Arthur.

Decades after Arthur, St. Collen, a seventh-century warrior monk from Wales, wrote of a battle with the King of the Underworld on the Tor while he was living at the magnificent Glastonbury Abbey, the center of British Christianity until the sixteenth century. Other Glastonbury legends evoke Joseph of Arimathea and the Holy Grail. A more obscure myth surrounds the unholy mist and mirages that gather at the foot of the Tor, dubbed Fata Morgana after the sorceress Morgana, King Arthur's half-sister and the mother of his fabled nemesis, Mordred. The town claims to be more than meets the eye, and one doesn't need to spend much time there to believe what scholars call legend may actually be history.

The Tor continues its timeless vigil as Fata Morgana have been more frequent - the images within, more malevolent.

Chapter 1

A framed quote hung on the otherwise spartan wall to the left of Meghan Bonneville's desk at Bonneville Partners. *"The wrong we have done, thought, or intended will wreak its vengeance on our souls."* It was her evangelical father's motto - extolling his minions to consider their service as part of a greater cause - but it didn't define or motivate her. She alone grasped the hypocrisy. Normally, she could bury her disdain for him, his holier-than-thou crap, and his recent philanthropic excess, but lately it had annoyed her like sinewy gristle stuck between back teeth. Still, or maybe because of this background agitation, she'd done what she had to do, and soon it wouldn't matter. Her father had built this company on the backs of oppressed workers, trying to scratch out a living in the post-war years, and now thought he was balancing his karmic ledger. It was pathetic, and his upcoming Judgement Day had been weighing heavily on her mind as of late.

The thirty-two-year-old executive suppressed a chuckle at the fealty she'd feigned for so long. It was her time now. She couldn't recall when she'd decided she had to take a stand. *It was almost as if ... No; it was my idea, my plan, and it is necessary. He'll never touch another child again.* She'd covered the alternatives, playing her own devil's advocate. It was more than "just business"; all his victims deserved justice. *Now was the time.* Meghan shoveled loose papers on her desk into her shoulder bag and stepped towards the door.

"Goddammit!" she hissed and turned back to the desk. She grabbed a black marker, scribbled onto a green Post-it note, and slammed it in the middle of the glass over her father's quote. She took a step back and whispered, "Fuck him," then flung the door open and strode towards the elevator, towards her destiny.

The note on the frame, in angry capital letters, read:

CONSEQUENCES ARE FOR LOSERS.
-   Meghan Bonneville

As vice-president of acquisitions in one of London's most powerful financial institutions, Meghan thrived on ruthless negotiations. She was making the most aggressive play of her career this evening, and losing wasn't an option.

***

The daytime crowds in Hyde Park had dispersed to dinner plans as the gray October evening crept in. Cloud cover muted the setting sun's glow and absorbed the shadows of the trees. The joyless light mirrored the mood of a well-dressed family, walking shoulder to shoulder on the east bank of the Serpentine, the lake that cut the park in two.

Discreet observers further up the path would notice the agitated yet controlled gesturing of the older gentleman in the middle of the trio. The younger woman to his right, clad in a navy blue pantsuit with wide lapels on her waist-length blazer, was waving her arms either for emphasis or dismissal. Shoulder-length black hair framed her angular features, while heavy eyebrows, trimmed but imposing, divided her face as the Serpentine did the park. Completing the threesome was an older woman with short, impeccably layered silver hair, wearing an ankle-length dress, almost Victorian in style. She clutched her purse with both hands. Eyes downward, her head was pivoting side to side while she mumbled pleas to speak of something else, anything else.

"Was that a rat?" Meghan's mother whispered, stealing a glance at her husband.

Ignoring this, her father said, "Meghan, you simply aren't ready to move up in the company. You need to earn the respect of the leadership and, frankly, we both know you're failing at that. Being my daughter is not qualification enough. You are reckless and predatory, even in success, and this is not how we conduct business."

"You will not accuse me, of all people, of being predatory! Why…"

"No, enough! I will speak of it no more. And you are upsetting your mother. We don't even know who you are anymore."

Meghan stepped forward and stopped, forcing her father to clutch his wife's arm to prevent a collision. The foliage on this segment of the path grew close, amplifying Meghan's intensity, bordering on mania.

"Goddammit, *Dad*! The company is in free fall while you dabble in pet projects. It's like you've already checked out. We're losing market share AND standing. People are talking, and you're making ME look bad. You're a laughingstock, Dad, and no longer fit to lead. A relic. If you won't do what's necessary, and yes, predatory, when required, by God, I will."

If her father was going to respond to this challenge, a hand on his shoulder stopped him short. A masked man had stepped out of the bushes. When the senior Bonneville spun to confront this interruption, the hand clutched his jacket lapels, pulling him close. A gun was pressed flat against his maroon tie, the business end pushed into his neck, forcing his jaw shut before he could call out. Over his assailant's shoulder, he watched, wide-eyed, as another man from the shadows drew his wife away from him with an arm across her chest and a gloved hand over her mouth. Her eyes bulged with a desperate plea.

Meghan spun and attempted to bolt. She managed only a single step before the last man blocked her escape. He pulled a rough-cloth sack over her head and wrapped an arm around her neck. She felt sharp pressure on her right side.

"Yes, m'lady, this is a gun in your belly," a voice close to her ear barked loud enough for half the park to hear. "So, if you know what's best for you, you won't be makin' another sound."

"Look here, if you want money, I'll cooperate," her father's voice pleaded, his tone at odds with the bravado he attempted. "Just unhand my wife and..." A slap, open hand to cheek, ended that negotiation.

"Shut it, old man," his attacker growled. He made no demands.

"Someone call 999! We're being..." Meghan screamed before a surge of pressure on her neck reduced her to choking gasps. She thrashed to loosen this hold as her mind raced. The grip on her neck relaxed. "Dad, just do as they ask," she ground out.

Two loud cracks and the slumping sound of a body falling changed everything. She heard her mother's muffled scream from behind the gloved hand, then another explosion, this time, unmistakably a gunshot.

Meghan clutched the arm at her neck, attempting to break her captor's grip. "What the hell are you doing? You were just supposed to..." was all she got out before a blow to her head brought blackness.

Meghan woke to the uneven growl of an engine in need of care and the smell of whiskey-infused sweat. A trickle of light seeping through the weave of the bag still on her head, rising and falling with the waves of pain breaking on her consciousness, brought clarity to her predicament. The rolling of the car as it battled traffic, wielding lane changes like a weapon, informed her cheek was resting on a fleshy thigh; too close to the crotch to rule it out as the source of the odor. She could tell by the vinyl crackling beneath her she was on the bench backseat of a generational throwback.

Oh god, my head is killing me! Her hands weren't free to examine the damage. They'd tied her wrists together behind her back, her ankles secured as well. *It wasn't supposed to be like this.*

A hand she hadn't realized was on her shoulder began an unmistakable slide to grope her breast. That, more than the memory of her station and what had transpired that afternoon, vented the rage boiling beneath the surface.

"What the fuck do you think you're doing? Get your fucking hand off me!" She kicked at the door to drive her shoulder into that thigh. The hand returned to her shoulder, but laughter suggested it might slide back. She laughed even louder to project control. "Are you going to ransom me? Is that the plan?" She twisted to face her oppressors. "There's no way you assholes will get another dime out of me. In fact, if you don't untie me and let me out RIGHT NOW," she screamed. "…you can kiss what we agreed on goodbye."

A gravelly voice, close to her ear, hissed, "Shut it, princess. It was never about *your* money."

"Of course it's about the money. It's always about the money. I insist you take this disgusting thing off my head and…" A fist to her rib cage silenced her.

"You don't insist shit. We just need to get you there alive. Wasn't nuthin' about condition so there's a whole lot a' room for interpretation and improvisation," came a familiar voice from the front seat.

"Dylan, thank God! Look, Dylan…" she exhaled.

"Shut it, I said, for the last time." The hand that had groped her now drove a knuckle between the ribs he'd just bruised. The pain got his point across.

So, she lay still as she'd been told, wrists bound, head on a fat thigh, and, against her nature, suffered the minutes that followed in silence. Meghan was used to being in control, and she'd be damned if she wouldn't regain control. Her parents had paid for her childhood terror and for trying to hold her back. Now she'd make sure these losers paid too. She just needed some time to think. *Damn it all!* The throbbing in her temple made it so hard. She smashed her eyes shut to block the pain. The harder she tried, though, the worse it got. She was on the verge of losing it. *Damn it all! I will not give these assholes the satisfaction of tears. Get yourself together, Meg!* She needed deep breaths, but gulps of stale recycled air were all she could manage.

The change from a highway to surface streets caught her attention. A front window opened, and the breeze found its way into the bag. She gulped down the cool, fresh air. A forearm, likely belonging to the fat leg beneath her head, exerted pressure on her ear, just short of painful. Meghan understood the threat, clarity returning. She wouldn't call for help. *My god! How did this happen? It should have been over quickly.* These guys had never been a problem before, squeezing bankers for info, pressing competitors to step back from a deal, making roadblocks disappear. It was supposed to be quick. She hoped her parents hadn't suffered; she wasn't a monster. It's just that their usefulness had long since passed. The boys were then supposed to drag her, visibly struggling, past all the pensioners and pram pushers who frequented the park in the evenings, to a waiting car, and drop her near the river. She'd be "found" there, composed yet mourning, maybe with a black eye or a fat lip, though she hadn't been too keen on that prospect. She'd publicly insist that justice be served, and of course, under her leadership, the company wouldn't miss a beat. Strength with compassion, rising from tragedy - the PR would have been dynamite.

Corners were coming more quickly now. Stops and starts. *A city for sure, but what city? And did it matter?*

A quick stop, tires scraping on pavement, threw her into the well between the seats. The arm that only moments ago was pressing on her skull pulled her back up by the waist of her slacks.

"Look … look," she said. "Let's talk about this. Please!" She heard the clunk of the transmission being slammed into Park. "Dylan, are you still there? I'm sure we can come to an agreement. OK, I was bluffing about not paying. I'll pay, dammit, I'll pay. Please … talk to me. What do you want? What can I do? You did the job. Great job! I've got resources now. Fifty grand isn't enough? How about fifty grand each? Right? This can be big for you, too."

The door at her feet opened, and rough hands grabbed the cords at her ankles. With a single yank, they pulled her from the car and dropped her onto a cool, gritty surface. She landed on her hip and fell to her stomach. The pain didn't concern her as much as their total disregard for it.

"No … please! Anything! What do you want? Just ask! Goddammit, talk to me. Please." Someone shoved a balled rag into her mouth, which cut her bargaining short. The fabric tasted as vile as it smelled.

Hoisted by ankles and armpits, they jounced her up steps to the sound of hinges that had suffered the neglect of time. Footfalls changed from slaps to a deep, echoing pounding. A hint of spice trickled through the foul fabric. *Was it incense?* Her captors' pace quickened. Her body snapped taut in response.

Steps turned to shuffles, and without warning, they dropped her. The flesh on her exposed abdomen burned from the squeaking slide across a cold, smooth floor. Her bearers hadn't broken stride before letting go. The impact, however, freed the gag from her mouth.

Rolling to her side, in a fetal ball, she moaned, "Please, you don't have to do this. Please." Now crying, her battle to maintain control lost, "Pleeease!"

A sharp kick to her lower back was their answer. "I said shut it an' keep it shut."

She expected the gag again and the sour taste of the fabric, so the clumsy yanking at the knots caught her by surprise. She was being untied, but that wasn't necessarily good.

They pushed her onto her stomach. The prolonged pressure from an open hand on her back, punctuated by a vicious shove, told her to lie still.

"Keep your eyes shut too, you hear?"

I heard. They pulled the bag off her head.

"You keep 'em shut until you hear the door close, right?" *Right.*

She squeezed her eyes tight and waited - waited and listened.

The raspy hinges cried out again. A deep, resounding thud followed, confirming this must be a cavernous space. *The door was*

12

closed. Or was it? Was this a cruel trick? She didn't know what to think any longer. *No … lie still. Listen … listen.*

More waiting, immeasurable empty time. No air movement or vibration on the floor. Just silence, complete silence. Before that day, agendas, schedules, appointments … the clock governed her existence. Now she wasn't even sure if she'd been lying on this cold stone floor for minutes or hours.

She opened her left eye, squinting, praying that nobody was watching for this slight transgression. The cold floor under her face was … what? *Was it marble? Polished granite?* Flickering orange reflections danced in her limited vision. She opened both eyes. Only then did she realize she was shaking. *Cold? Dread? No, something else.*

Meghan pushed up to her knees, darting her head left and right to catch any sign of movement so she could prepare for the blow. A small shadow darted under the nearest pew. *A mouse? No bigger. Gone now, nothing else.* She was alone. She tenderly probed the side of her head where they had hit her. The pain was gone. *Adrenaline … It'll be back.*

With considerable effort, she pulled one foot under her still-shaking frame, then the other, and rose. Through blurred vision, Meghan saw she was in a small church, not a cavernous one. Provincial came to mind. She wiped the moisture from her eyes with her jacket sleeve. Her vision cleared. Light from outside oozed through thick, wavy windows at eye level, painting the room in a monochrome glow. The hint of color above those windows must be stained-glass. Run-of-the-mill candles, sputtering in the still air, caused the flickering she'd first noticed. She stood. The pulpit was on her right, with two columns of simple pews stretching before her to the rear of the room.

Turning her back to the nave, a massive door consumed her field of view. Taller than it needed to be, black iron straps, laddered from floor to vaulted top, bound the wide planks to their will. It seemed out of place … no, *out of time*, compared to the rest of the church. And something else … what? *Austere? Imposing? Foreboding?* Maybe that was it. This door forebodes. But what did it forebode?

Her hand was on the old wood. She couldn't remember taking the step towards it or reaching out. Like wrinkles on a face that had experienced life from the bottom up, the old wood had a deeply weathered surface. Doors had always fascinated her, evoked questions. Doors meant opportunity but also uncertainty.

A rumbling truck broke the silence. She snapped her head back to the main exit. *Run, Meg! Get the hell out of here and find the police. But ... the door. No, forget about the goddamn door.* She could always come back, back to wherever she was. *I'm out of here.*

But she didn't run. *There is no danger here, no reason to hurry.* "That's a ridiculous thought," she admonished herself. "Run!" The sound of her voice was off. *Acoustics?*

Your future lies behind this door. Let me show you a life truly free of consequences, little sister.

"Who … No … I …" Frozen in the moment, her legs couldn't resolve the conflict in her mind. Her fingertips continued to stroke the gnarled surface. She cocked her head as she concentrated on the old wood under her touch. It felt warm, reassuring, wise. It had seen the cycles of lives, of generations. Her breathing slowed. With heightened senses, she noted a calm, almost liquid feeling trickling from her cheeks, through her chest, and down her arms. Another half step closer, she brought up her other hand.

Her eyes and fingers explored the portal. She found heavy metal hinges, bigger than her palm. This substantial hardware ensured the door would respond, *ready to welcome, but also to entomb.* Eyes following fingers as they swept side to side, she found a cold iron handle. *A treble clef,* she thought, as her fingertips caressed it from top to bottom. The solidity, the firmness of the handle, the door, the opportunity, calmed her further. *Maybe it WAS the path?*

It now seemed absurd that she'd even considered running from this place and this feeling of comfort that enveloped her. The

14

journey - all that had passed before - now seemed like a dream. *She was meant to be here, only here.* Wrapping her fingers around the handle, she felt its solidity. Her index finger settled against the latch.

Open the door, she thought. She didn't dwell on what might be behind the door. Only that it must be opened, it longed to be opened.

Open the door, young one.

"Yes," she whispered. "Yes."

Of its own will, her finger squeezed. The metallic clank of the mechanism startled but didn't deter her. Her grip tightened, and she pulled. The door resisted. *Of course it did ... it was an old door, a heavy door, an important and substantial gateway.*

Consequences are for losers, little sister.

She gripped the ancient iron with both hands, set her feet, and yanked with all she had left. The hinges released from their teasing resistance with a snap, and the door swung towards her. Stepping back, she took in the portal, mesmerized by the emptiness. In that moment, she thought the vacuum of space couldn't vie with the blackness that confronted her.

The physical clunk of the door hitting its stop broke her trance. The light in the church had changed. She looked back at the windows. The ghostly glow from outside sources was gone, but the flickering flames within the church were more pronounced. She scanned the room. Unblinkingly, unbelievingly, she saw substantial sputtering torches where the candles had been.

Panic was rising. She smashed her palms into her eyes. *Think! Why was she still standing here?* Her hands drifted from her face. Eyes wide and mouth agape, she tried to make sense of what she was seeing. Before her, two hooded figures leaned across a table where there should have been pews. A trio of candles illuminated lined faces, their cold eyes fixed on her. These specters - women, she realized, glowering with thin lips pressed together - didn't mirror her look of surprise. Gaunt, stained faces, accentuated by the yellow candlelight, drew into tight lines of malevolence. *Towards me?*

She snapped her head back to the right and tried to re-establish normalcy - but nothing was normal any longer. Where the pulpit had been just moments before, a hunched, grizzled old man with a patchy beard and a pointed leather cap sat on a short stool. This troll of a man was bent over a half-barrel tub, scrubbing an animal carcass covered in - *what are those, maggots*? He was watching her as well, but instead of hate, she saw lust, hunger. His smile triggered shaking; vertigo distorted her vision.

Meghan's hand shot out to the door frame for stability and reassurance. *Why aren't I running?*

Nothing made sense. It couldn't be a dream, but it felt like a nightmare. She straightened up, hands dropping to her side, and turned to face the portal. It was no longer empty. Staring back across the threshold were two pinpoints of black despair, somehow darker than the void. They reflected her fear, her insecurities, things she'd buried so deep even she'd forgotten. Frozen in place, she watched as the spots grew. They filled and then consumed the doorway.

Images of plague, death, and rage flooded her mind. She felt the last shred of sanity draining into this void, and she had no power to stop it.

Then, she lost her will to try.

At that moment, the abyss contracted back to points, then to eyes, the face of a woman. She was tall and timeless. *Beautiful*, Meghan thought, draped in layers of dark, shapeless fabric, a hood concealing most of her head. From this specter, a thin white hand floated up to touch her cheek.

Through blood-red lips on an otherwise colorless face, the woman said, "Welcome, little sister. Now we can begin."

Meghan's world spiraled as she dropped to the floor at the feet of this apparition, asleep yet aware.

Chapter 2

B lasted weather!" Peter Pelling exclaimed as he paced in front of his desk, a laptop and two computer monitors rising from a chaotic blanket of papers. "The thunder is wreaking havoc on the signals." Autumn storms had been tormenting their town for the past few days. Today was shaping up to beat them all.

"Calm thyself, Peter," retorted the auburn-haired woman at the kitchen counter, just outside that makeshift office. She looked over to her father, Colin, who was reading the newspaper at the kitchen table, chuckling. *He looks good today*, she thought. Jennifer, Jenn to her friends, was fixing chicken with rice for her brother and father. *Another ordinary dinner on an ordinary day in what's become an ordinary life.* Jenn's hair, freckles, and bright complexion suggested Irish ancestry. The Pellings, more than most average-seeming British families, knew that wasn't the case.

Peter was her opposite in appearance and, by all measures, the most zealous in recent generations about their family secret. At eighteen years old, he was tall, whereas Jenn, nine years his senior, was average. He was thin and pale with a mop of wild, light brown hair that resisted even the most determined attempts to tame.

Family secret? More like generational dementia, Jenn reminded herself. Her parents had tried to pull her into this centuries-old fairy tale when she turned sixteen. An ancient ancestor had purportedly committed at least one Pelling to life in Glastonbury - for perpetuity. Family legend suggested it had been this way for over a thousand years. *A prank that took on a life of its own, most likely.* She caught herself chopping tomatoes a bit too aggressively as she thought through this ... again. "Maybe focus on your schoolwork, for a change," she called out to her brother, hoping to redirect her frustration.

"Patience, Peter," suggested Colin. "We're in for the long haul, and if you're a betting man, nothing is likely to happen tonight. No signs, apocalyptic events, or such. Don't forget how excited you got last week when the ladies' auxiliary wandered off the path in search of herbs on the hillside. Hah! That was rich!"

Nothing on the homework from Dad. OK

His laughing triggered a coughing fit that pulled Jenn a step in his direction, but he waved her off. It subsided as quickly as it had come.

One of these times ... With a heavy heart, she turned back to meal prep.

Nobody doubted where Peter got his looks. Colin was an older, grayer version of his son, but his blue eyes still burned brightly; brightest when they were telling stories about local history, factual or fantastical. Jenn wasn't sure he could differentiate between the two any longer as he leaned more toward the latter in recent months.

Peter had installed seismic sensors on the Tor, the ancient hill rising just beyond their back garden, capable of registering the faintest vibrations in the soil. Likely too few, he often told Jenn, but then, this was a pilot. Dad said funding would be available for more if they showed the data collected was reliable. However, nobody could be sure how many sensors they needed, or where Peter should place them. The handful of initial spots represented their best guesses for now, he said. *It didn't really matter*, she thought. She'd intentionally stepped out of these fantastical conversations, so it wasn't her problem. She was going to have a life, despite her family.

Over the centuries, the Pellings served as constables, teachers, artisans, and justices. Colin ran a bookshop he'd inherited from his father. Jenn had dipped her toe in the water of independence with a junior lecturer position at the University of Bristol's School of Economics, an hour north of Glastonbury. Her assignment was principally research, which allowed her to work from home but

18

offered the occasional opportunity to escape to civilization. While she was skeptical of their purported supernatural mission, she felt a strong bond with her family and their traditions. Loyalty and consistency were traits all Pellings seemed to share. As much as she craved more out of her life, more travel, more experience, more opportunity, maybe a man to explore the concept of happily ever after with, she had committed to remaining at her father's side until Peter was old enough to make it on his own. *Soon.*

Jenn had been self-sufficient by the age of eighteen. Life had thrust her into the role of lady of the manor at eight years old when Mother passed. This forced her to mature much faster than her friends. Peter, however, had the freedom to stay starry-eyed and brilliant. He was studying computer engineering, and with the support of a mysterious family trust fund, he had the resources to take his independent study far beyond his schooling. Her dad insisted the money was connected to their mission but would say no more. She'd need to insist that her father outline the specifics of this fund within the next few years. As much as she hated to acknowledge it, he'd be gone too soon. She was confident that the increased value of their property and other investments that went back decades generated this mystery cash, but it drove her nuts that he wouldn't just come out and say it. There was always another mystery.

The bookshelf in the office had become the permanent home of shiny black boxes with blinking green and yellow lights. "Servers and modems, Jenn," Peter would tell her. "We'd be in the dark without them." These servers managed the flood of data reaching the cottage in the shadow of the timeless Tor. The computers captured news and statistics from around the world. Augmenting these feeds were programs that processed and re-processed data, scouting for trends or, more importantly, disruptions of trends. Anything out of the ordinary would get Peter's attention. Her father had relied on dailies and the BBC over the years, but no longer had the energy for their quest and welcomed passing this role to his son.

He has increasingly been leaving the shop to his employees of late.

"Dinner in twenty-five," she announced. "I'm heading upstairs to finish a report. If you smell anything burning, figure it out yourselves." She smiled through the old admonition that preceded most dinners. *Tradition, repetition, consistency.* As Jenn climbed the carpeted spiral staircase to her room, she reassured herself: *Soon. My obligations will end soon.* Instantly, she froze. She didn't, and would *never*, wish for her father's passing. *I don't want this, but I can't stop it either.*

The trust assured her she would receive a significant stipend when she left home. In perpetuity, as she understood. Jenn could live comfortably in a somewhat better than modest flat in London, only a short Tube ride from the London School of Economics, her alma mater. Her former mentor had assured her she had a place at the college whenever Jenn could commit. *That would be soon,* she thought, as she dropped into her chair. *And I can join the consistently normal without having to give a nod to legend or fantasy.* Leaning forward, she rested her elbow on her desk and her chin in her palm. The red sky over the Tor, behind the storm clouds, was stunning.

She knew leaving would be bittersweet. She'd been born in this two-story cottage on the lower slopes of the Tor. From the ground floor, dense foliage obscured all but the top of St. Michael's Chapel, a figurative crown on the old hill. However, from the bedroom window behind her desk, she had an unobstructed view of the slopes, watching countless long-eared hares and a potpourri of visitors hike the winding paths. *How many generations of Pelling daughters had hiked those paths, wondering if their families were nuts?* She glanced back at the door of her room and exhaled through pursed lips. If pushed, Jenn would admit to feeling a certain energy permeating Glastonbury, although the academic in her would rise to the challenge and remind her it was just her imagination. Sometimes, that eccentric old coot who fed her father's obsession got to her too.

***

"No more stories for today, boys," said the ageless and stooped figure cloaked in grays and tans. He shifted his weight to his gnarled ash staff as he pulled himself off the barstool at Glastonbury's George and Pilgrims Inn. The day's light was fading as Lloyd hoisted the strap of his old leather satchel over his head and dropped it onto his shoulder. A jumble of grey hair, haphazardly parted in the middle, framed his time-worn face. Combed, it might have reached his shoulders, but as was his norm, the hair extended in every direction but down.

"But what became of the bishop's babies, Mr. Wyse?" the server asked from behind the bar as she scooped up the heavy coins Lloyd left for his beer.

"I'd be more concerned about your own babies, Mary," his voice a gravelly echo of more tales left untold. The barmaid let out a gasp, then hurried over to the two beer-sloshing, red-faced young men leaning more against each other than the iron and leaded-glass wall on the far side of the room.

Lloyd Wyse shuffled into the fading light of the setting sun. He hitched the strap higher and took stock of the comings and goings of the local citizenry. All was as it should be. *Slow and steady*, he thought to himself as he turned west on High Street. He relied on his staff for balance and to avoid random puddles in the ancient cobbles. A rumble of thunder behind distant clouds prompted him to glance upwards, where he caught the slow circles of a falcon, silhouetted against the pink and gray sky. With a smile and a wink, he picked up the pace.

Lloyd kept his head down as he walked unnoticed up the busy street. He'd mastered the art of invisibility long ago. Unremarkable browns and grays made up most of his wardrobe. He favored baggy pants, shirts, and jackets with a plethora of deep pockets. Short of a bright red scarf of long-forgotten origin for special occasions, he cloaked himself in the same forgettable ensemble on all his trips to town. His mid-neck beard was, that day, shorter than he liked thanks to an unfortunate stovetop incident involving sausages and distracting thought. It would grow back fast; it always did.

The George and Pilgrim's was his last stop for the day. No unusual visitors to town, a day like any other day. He'd best get home; a storm was coming.

***

Settling in at her small desk, Jenn could hear the familiar rattle of dishes and flatware. Hunger must have realigned Peter and Dad's priorities.

As Jenn tried to focus on her work and the rest of the family readied themselves for dinner, the digital signals from the hill changed. The seismic recorder captured a repeating pattern of three spikes. The storm had quieted minutes before.

Chapter 3

A thundering of hooves awakened Meghan.

She sat up in bed and turned to the source of the sound, an open window at her bedside - in a stone wall, not the billowing sheers in front of the bay window of her private room at the hospital in Whitechapel. Looking out across a brilliant green field - there was no London traffic, no London at all for that matter - on what may have been the sunniest day Meghan had ever seen. She could smell the grass, mud, and animals - a raw, earthy sense she'd never experienced in a dream; *for this must be a dream*. The sound of armored warhorses came in waves as heavily armed men drilled back and forth across the field. Underneath the male bonding and humor, Meghan could actually feel the seriousness. Men's lives depended on predictability, trust, and conformity. *How could I possibly know this? Any of it?*

An older man, dressed comfortably in cotton and a leather jerkin, fitted with rings and pockets, on a handsome but lighter horse, looked up at her and waved. *Can he see me?* She darted out of sight, unsure how she felt about that familiarity, then took in the room behind her. Where there should have been monitors and charts were tapestries and stone. In a puddle below the window, on the packed dirt floor, a young girl was staring back from the reflection. *I'm a child? I'm a child of the past*. Somehow, this didn't surprise her. Dreams never did. The girl in the water was ten or eleven, with sharp features, dark eyes, and long, straight, dark hair. What struck Meghan the most was how pale her skin appeared. It wasn't Meghan's skin. She was naturally ruddy, despite spending more time in boardrooms and restaurants than in sunshine.

Tearing herself away from the window, Meghan slowly advanced towards the only exit, an open door. Unlike the nightmarish portal in the church, this opened to a large multi-story, timber and wattle hall, awash in that same uplifting sunshine and the savory aroma of rich cooking. The breeze that blew through open windows was fragrant and fresh. Neatly dressed maidens buzzed about, laughing and chatting in the most carefree of manners. She could sense that this was a happy place.

As that thought crystallized, her world went dark. One by one, torches affixed to the walls in iron cages above her head burst alight and brought visibility back. It was nighttime, and this home was in distress. She ran back to the room she assumed was hers, a childlike impulse to seek familiarity.

"Morgan, where are you?" Her head snapped. Meghan froze as the name echoed in her heart - it felt both foreign yet achingly personal. Her name in this dream was Morgan, and she was a princess in a castle. "Morgan, please, we don't have time for your games."

Meghan followed the sound of the voice. Further down the hall, along wide, weathered wooden planks, was another open door. Through that door was a large bedchamber with a beautiful ebony-haired woman; her arms wrapped around two younger girls, further wrapped in sumptuous quilts and silks. A stone fireplace crackled gently and cast a yellow glow on the sparse furnishings and the figures on the bed.

"Come, dear," the woman called. Meghan saw she was struggling to keep a smile on a face, which was otherwise strained in fear. Something important was happening. "Your father is coming, and this will all be over soon."

Meghan-as-Morgan climbed onto the bed, and the narrow windows on the far wall informed her it was twilight, not yet black but certainly no longer sunny. Loud voices, men's voices, from the space she'd just passed through triggered her flee instincts, but she scrambled as requested into the communal embrace of her ...

mother? *Sisters?* The commotion was fast approaching. They were speaking too quickly for Morgan to make out a cohesive thread. A large man in mail and leather appeared in the doorway. This was the gentle-looking man who had waved at her from the lawn. He no longer seemed at peace but hard and ready for battle. Leather covered in plate and chain mail had replaced his comfortable riding clothes; a sword in a side scabbard with multiple daggers arranged about his torso. He handed his helmet to a younger man, *his name is Roderich,* as he stepped into the room.

"Igraine, they caught us in a trap. Scores of men came without warning. I'm afraid we didn't prepare for a siege. My options are limited." *Morgan's father? And Igraine was her mother?*

Igraine responded in a voice barely a whisper, "Gorlois, what will we do? You know what he wants."

"We will fight. And we will win, for we are right and Uther lacks honor. Such is the way it has always been and always will be," Gorlois said a bit too quickly. "The Lord Jesus will protect us as true believers." *Uther from the King Arthur stories?* Morgan looked at the hopeful faces of her sisters and was relieved to see that they believed their father. Whatever may happen to them, *or more accurately, whatever may have happened to them in their own time, clearly centuries ago,* they were strong girls who respected their parents. She sensed Morgan didn't share the same level of familial confidence. *Honor doesn't win battles; swords do. Wait! How could she have known this? Am I me or Morgan?*

"We will ride out the side gate and cut their head off. Uther is sitting back towards the trees. Our lookouts in the tower say he appears too confident for his own good. Once we've taken him down, the rest of the serpent should shrivel and melt away."

Gorlois strode further into the room, reaching the bed in one step. He hugged each of the younger girls with a kiss on the head. "Be brave."

He reached out and took a knee, holding Morgan by the shoulders, so their noses touched. The depth of his blue eyes was mesmerizing. *How can this man possibly fail? Fail his family, fail his home? If only I'd had a father like that.* She smiled up and said, "May the Lord be with you, Father." *What am I saying? Those words came so naturally, but I would never say that.*

Gorlois pulled her roughly to his chest. Tears were welling in his eyes. "Be strong for me, my oak tree." Then, dropping his voice so only Morgan could hear, "Be my strength for your mother if I don't come back. Promise?"

"I promise, Father." Morgan met his gaze and tried hard to look brave and confident.

Gorlois released her and stepped around the bed to Igraine. She reached one graceful hand up, and the lord of the house took it gently.

"I will be back by morning, my dear. I'll have glorious stories to tell." Gorlois glanced over to the girls. "And I shall share them with you at breakfast, my daughters."

He then pulled Igraine to her feet and embraced her deeply. "Come back to me, my lord," she said. "I will be waiting for you."

He kissed her mouth and pulled away, hesitating, as if there was one more thing he must say. Instead, he released her and stepped one pace backward, never losing eye contact with his love. Without further comment, he pivoted and marched out the door, accepting his helmet in stride. Morgan could hear a band of men hurrying down the hall, metal boot covers clanking loudly on heavy boards.

"Come, girls," said Igraine, and Morgan rejoined her sisters in their mother's arms.

Meghan slept as Morgan did, fitfully and with a foreboding that she would never see her father again.

Dark passages, locked doors, dimly lit rooms, stairs ... always heading down...

She woke with a start, struggling to orient herself as the night nurse assured her she was OK. Her vitals had spiked but were settling back down. Meghan accepted medication to help her get back to sleep and welcomed the creeping blackness.

Chapter 4

With renewed confidence that he'd make it home before the rain started, and he was usually right about such things, Lloyd turned on Chilkwell and treated himself to a pause outside the old Abbey ruins. "Oh, what a sight you were in your day, old girl," he muttered to himself. Lloyd paused again to rest at Wellhouse Lane and took in the wrought-iron gated entrance to the Chalice Well that some believed was a stopping point for the Holy Grail on its journey with Joseph of Arimathea. He allowed himself a knowing smile as the last tourists of the day hurried down the driveway. Then he hitched up his brown corduroy pants, reseated the strap on his shoulder, and began the slow uphill climb.

Few knew precisely where Wyse lived, and even fewer remembered when he had come to Glastonbury. The young folk assumed he'd always been there. Their parents might recall the first time they saw Lloyd walking about town. His shoulder-height ash staff, polished at the grip from years of use, was hard to miss. Beyond the staff and his tangled beard, nobody knew much about him. He never attended social activities, nor was he regularly seen with relatives or close friends … anyone.

Lloyd went to great lengths to cultivate this persona of a doddering, standoffish senior. If any townsfolk tried to get close, he'd start by ignoring them but wasn't above coldly dismissing them and sending them packing. When the old traveler reflected on his life, relationships were merely complications to be avoided. He was aware, at times painfully, that they couldn't last because, in the end, only Lloyd remained.

He had a mild distaste for the town's modern manifestation, a trinket capital for the curious. Occasionally though, as he had this day, Lloyd would regale patrons of a local pub with odd trivia from the town's ancient history. The old wanderer would light up with boisterous anecdotes from Glastonbury's days as a lakeside fishing village or as the unchallenged seat of British Christendom. In other words, he was an anachronism, just one more oddity in a town full of them.

On a straight stretch of road, about a quarter of a mile from the Chalice Well, he stopped. A tall, ivy-covered hedge was on his left, a clear view of the Tor's shallow slope was on his right. This random section of wall was indistinguishable from what lay in front of or behind him. He waved at a car he recognized and one he didn't before concluding that no other vehicles were likely to pass for a minute. Turning to the wall, he brushed foliage from a doorknob that was otherwise invisible from the road. The old green ivy-covered entrance opened inward. Lloyd stepped inside and closed the door. A car passing seconds later would never have known he'd been there. The entrance faded into the lush roadside greenery common in Somerset.

Lloyd placed his staff in a tall brass bucket, sorely undersized for the task, and put his bag on a small table by the door. He flipped on the overhead light and glanced around for anything that appeared out of place. The tells he'd placed and checked every day for the thirty-odd years he'd been back all seemed intact. His cottage was small, but he didn't need much. A life of constant motion conditioned him to make do with the basics. He'd furnished his home in a style one might describe as 'modern forest'. Old yet solid wood furniture and down-stuffed cushions contrasted with a state-of-the-art sound system. Bluetooth speakers and a laptop computer sat on his otherwise empty desk.

He leaned on the back of his sofa to pull off his boots, then retrieved an iPhone from a pocket of his baggy cords. Lloyd scrolled down through emails from lawyers and scholars, confirming that nothing required immediate attention. Swiping over to his music streaming app, he filled the space with soft blues classics. Letting the music wash over him, the old traveler felt revived and at peace. In time, he walked to the kitchen sink, above which was the only window on the ground floor. It was a circular portal with thick and murky old glass from which one could just make out the blurry splash of color from the roses lining his garden patio. He wrestled with what he expected to be the toughest decision of the day: go out back to check for storm and critter damage or take a nap. The nap was winning the battle.

Tucked off to the right of the small kitchenette was a low doorway to darkness. Stepping through, Lloyd began the climb up a circular staircase to his bedroom. He didn't need any light. He knew every step and turn by heart. As he began the second revolution, a glow from above, the only other window in his home, offered a break from the blackness. His destination - a small, wedge-shaped bedroom - contained a twin bed, dresser, and night table. The last piece of furniture in the room towered over the rest. Standing floor to ceiling and covering the small wall at the narrow portion of the wedge to his left was a wardrobe with massive doors and large brass rings. He'd fastened a small iron hook near the top of a side panel. A dark gray hooded cloak hung from it.

From his window, he had a clear view of the Tor, silhouetted against the darkening storm clouds rolling in from the east. He spotted a handful of hikers, oblivious to the encroaching rain, climbing the same winding path he'd walked countless times over his years in this place.

He opened the window halfway and then reached into his pocket. Wrapped in a paper napkin were chunks of sausage he'd saved from lunch. His hand had hardly opened when two falcons, with blue-gray heads and brown striped chests, landed gently on the sill and relieved him of the snack. "Yes, yes. Now off you go," Lloyd said and pulled the window down as the pounding of their wings faded.

The old man's thoughts went with the creatures, over the crest of the hill. They flew in a slow circle around a small neighborhood on the far side. While his home was invisible to all but the few that knew to look for it, he saw that the Pellings' cottage was bright, open, and welcoming, as it should be. He was due for a visit to check on Peter's technology and discuss plans to transition Colin's responsibility to his eager, maybe overeager, son. Jennifer would have been his first choice, he thought, as he laid his weary body down on the bed. He understood her need to wander, to grow into more, but not everyone had the luxury of choosing their destiny. Perhaps, one could argue, he chose his, but after all the years, it didn't feel that way.

He withdrew from his winged companion and stretched to full length, taller than his stooped posture would suggest, before stiffly lowering himself to the bed. *Ah, Memory Foam! What a marvelous invention ... if* only he could relieve some memories of his own as he slept. He sighed. *No, Lloyd, this is your burden to bear.* A burden that seemed less relevant year by year, in an era that no longer had any use for old wizards.

Chapter 5

Physically unharmed and remarkably stable, her doctors discharged Meghan the day after she'd experienced that strange vision of young Morgan. That evening, she attended an intimate yet hastily organized gathering at the Lady Chapel in St George's Cathedral in the London borough of Southwark to bid farewell to Sir Nigel and Lady Bonneville. They had no other close living relatives, so it fell upon Meghan to express the proper levels of grief in response to the condolences of the executives and board members of Bonneville Partners who deemed it politically expedient to attend. Her discreet monitoring of her diamond-set Rolex went unnoticed. There would be no celebration or dinner afterward.

Finally, back at her flat, she flippantly discarded sympathy notes about her parents and deleted voicemails from lawyers about funeral arrangements. None of this mattered to Meghan. She needed to know more about the strange girl and, more importantly, what the dark lady's promise meant.

The phone rang, but it didn't register. She sank into an overstuffed leather chair facing her floor-to-ceiling bay windows. The slow ripples of the River Thames in the distance hypnotized her. What memories does that old river hold? Could it explain these visions of antiquity? She leaned back and surrendered herself to the embrace of the chair and the imagery of the girl's memories. They'd been scratching at the door of her waking consciousness with the urgency of a story that must be told before madness overtook her. Now, in the privacy of her home and willing to learn, she opened that door as the child Morgan again, and her mind faded to black.

The darkness dissipated as a fog might break. She awoke in her mother's bed to the sounds of chairs being thrown, chains rattling, and footsteps echoing. Her mother and sisters were still curled up and asleep. When the footsteps stopped outside the door to her mother's chamber, she reacted ferally and leapt off her mother's bed, hiding behind a dressing screen. Meghan felt Morgan's fear grind against exposed nerves, stronger than her worst nightmare. It felt as real as being dragged into that old church.

But this felt more like a memory than a dream.

The fabric screen that sheltered her looked secure, at least safe enough for the young girl peering up at it. Small openings in the elaborate embroidery offered a view of the room. The patterns were beautiful, really. Then the door to the bedroom burst open, shattering this distraction.

Morgan saw her father stride into the room alone. Where were his servants? Where was his ever-present squire, Roderich, who always had a piece of fruit, a flower, or a joke for her and her sisters? His absence, more than anything, confirmed that things weren't right and may never be right again.

Her father stopped a pace shy of the bed and stared down at her mother as she slept. Dirt and blood streaked his face. His cape was missing, and his leather and mail were damaged. He had fought but lived. Meghan didn't know why Morgan was so apprehensive, but trusted the girl's senses.

Her father's thundering command broke the silence. "Girls, get up and go to your room!"

Her mother and sisters jumped and stared at their lord with the confusion and disbelief that often follows being woken abruptly from a deep sleep.

Igraine broke the silence. "My lord, you are safe! Is it over?" She unfolded herself from her yawning daughters and swung her legs over the side of the bed to greet her husband, to reassure herself that he was indeed alright.

Gorlois stopped Igraine with wild eyes and an outstretched hand. Something wasn't right. A combination of fear, longing, confusion, and anger on his visage suggested more had happened than the repulse of Uther's attack. She had seen her father after other battles. He was often tired, occasionally ecstatic, sometimes weeping, but never crazed. Without taking his eyes off Igraine, he pointed at Morgan's sisters. "Girls, go to your room, NOW!" He didn't ask about Morgan, and if her mother noticed she wasn't there, she said nothing.

The girls looked up at their mother, who nodded. They scrambled off the bed. The youngest, Elaine, stopped in front of her father and looked up, expecting an embrace, at least a smile, but got nothing. Confused and frightened, they ran out of the room. Gorlois broke eye contact with his wife and slammed the door with a boom that shook the few candles still lit. He paused, resting his forehead on the old wood. Then, as if having come to a decision, he returned to Igraine and pulled her to her feet. Morgan had never seen Father treat her like that.

Mother tried to speak words of comfort, but Gorlois smashed his mouth on hers in a kiss that seemed more like an attack, swallowing her face in hungry gulps. Igraine's hands flew up to her husband's chest and tried to push him away, maybe to catch a breath, maybe to protest, but his grip was too tight. His hand clenched the back of her head to stop her attempts at pulling away from his devouring embrace. The young girl watched in stunned silence.

Gorlois thrust Morgan's mother to arm's length, yet he didn't release her. His eyes, which until this point had never left her face, scanned her body, top to bottom, bottom to top.

Igraine used this pause and tried to bring her husband back to sanity. "My lord, I know you have needs, and I will see to them. But not like this. Please let the ladies undress and bathe you, then come to bed, come to me and let me caress away the horror of this night."

Morgan couldn't tell if he'd heard her pleas, but they didn't move him. His eyes hardened as he released her shoulders. With both hands, he grasped the front of her gown and tore downward. She shrieked as he ripped the loose white cloth off her shoulders and cast it to the floor. He pushed her onto the bed, naked but for a heavy gold chain that flew up into her face. He pulled the remains of the torn nightdress from her legs and threw them to the middle of the room. Her mother tried to roll away, but a hard slap to the face stopped her. To Igraine's horror, he fumbled with the clasps on his leather pants and dropped them.

Morgan's mother moaned, "No... No..." as her father pulled her to him.

Morgan leaned forward, terror-stricken but glued to the depravity unfolding. Her father's breathing was labored, and the animal sounds coming from his throat took on a more frustrated tone. Igraine's crying and struggling were not the experience he was expecting, and his muttering for her to be quiet gave way to almost pleading. He was in a hurry, and this was taking too long.

The vision quickened, and the sounds in her mind grew louder. Morgan watched in disbelief. Her father's eyes snapped shut, his pace quickened, and his voice took on clarity. "Yes ... come on!" The look on his face transfixed the young girl's attention. He seemed in pain, in fear - no longer enjoying this but enduring it. Beads of sweat were marking paths through the dirt, and spattered blood on his face. Exclamations gave way to shouts as his attack increased in intensity.

Meghan was aware she'd broken into a cold sweat, and her hands were clenching the arms of her chair. Yet, as Morgan watched from behind the screen, Meghan felt her terror turn to madness. She saw her father's face liquefy as he climaxed. The young girl leaned her face closer to the gap in the screen, not equipped to believe what she was seeing. Before her eyes, her father, Lord Gorlois, Duke of Cornubia, transformed into High King Uther of Dumnonia! Uther was in the room raping her mother.

Meghan understood that this was a dream, awake or not, and that anything goes in a dream. But this part felt as real as if it were playing out in her parlor, and something must be done. *I'm a grown woman. I can stop this!* She willed Morgan to act. Together, they would be unstoppable. Together. Uther finished with a shout like a cornered bear. Conflicting urges - fight or flight - overwhelmed Morgan. Fear and anger welled up like a knife in her gut as she frantically looked about for an escape. Looking backwards, Morgan saw a woman with shoulder-length dark hair, oddly dressed, crouching against the wall; instantly and terrifyingly familiar to Meghan.

"Go!" the specter screamed, then was gone.

In disbelief, Morgan stumbled backwards, lost her balance, and fell into the screen, knocking it to the floor. Exposed, she froze. Uther's look of shock gave way to malevolence towards the young girl cowering on her hands and knees - a witness to his crime.

Igraine never looked up from the bed. Meghan knew she'd retreated to a faraway place where her husband would never treat her like this. In this state, she didn't see her daughter scramble to her feet and sprint for the door. She didn't see the girl pull open the heavy door with both hands and squeeze through an opening just larger than her eleven-year-old frame. Morgan stopped in the doorway and looked back one last time in disbelief. Uther, back in the guise of Gorlois, had finally released his iron grip on her mother's hips and pushed off to right himself, throwing the woman farther into the bed. Igraine instinctively curled up in a ball, pulling the furs around her, and continued to cry.

Morgan could sense her mother's sobbing, more by her shoulders heaving than actual cries, as Uther struggled to pull his leggings on and gather up his gear. When her despair exploded into audible cries and then to the wailing of a woman who knew she'd lost everything, Morgan bolted to her lightless room and cowered. Only after the man's labored footsteps across the cavernous hall faded to silence was she convinced the immediate danger had passed.

As the echoes quieted, Meghan lifted her head to find she was back in her timeline, in her chair by the window. Looking out, she fixed her gaze on the river's timeless current as hate and a raging desire for vengeance enveloped her. Morgan's mother, her mother, had been raped, her father likely murdered, and somebody must pay. I know because I was there.

Catching movement in her peripheral vision, Meghan looked up to find the beautiful, pale specter from the church standing there, translucent but fully present. Morgan? No ... Morgana.

"Yes, little sister," Morgana whispered, so softly that Meghan had to focus intently to hear. "You now know why I waited ages to find you. You've witnessed what lengths men will go to, what atrocities men will commit, to slake their lust. And this man, this Uther, sacrificed an army and cloaked himself in black magic for an opportunity to rape our mother. Do you think him an aberration, a monster? No, young one, it just makes him a man; a man like any other. They would all be Uther if they had his power."

Morgana reached out to caress Meghan's cheek. "I have seen your thoughts, little sister. I know what you suffered at the hands of that man you called Father as your Mother turned her back. But you exacted justice, my dear, and together we can bring justice to the rest of the world. With my guidance, we can crush the established order of men, so no woman need fear what we have suffered. I can give you this power." Morgana placed her hands on the sides of Meghan's face. "Will you join me, Meghan Bonneville?"

"Yes," Meghan whispered and closed her eyes. When they reopened, she was acutely aware of the duality of her consciousness but saw the world around her with a singular purpose. She knew what they must do.

Chapter 6

A rthur! Wake up!"
The command pierced his soul like a flaming arrow. The wizard Myrddin had shouted this at Camlann just before his fight with Mordred. *Before I fell...*

Arthur Pendragon, High King of Britain, sat up, eyes snapping open. At least he thought his eyes were open. He could see nothing through the stagnant blackness. He pulled his elbows tight, shrugged his shoulders, and twisted to stretch, welcoming the popping in his back like an old friend. A quieter crackling greeted him as he rolled and twisted his neck to its extremes. Hands flat on the hard surface underneath his legs, he struggled to make some sense of this space. Cool, smooth stone; a slab. *Am I dead? Am I a spirit? Unlikely.* He rotated his head again, searching for light or a breeze on his face. *Nothing. But does a spirit feel the wind? Myrddin would know ... Myrddin!* He remembered being with the old wizard on a boat going ... Morgana! He rode Morgana's skiff to the island of Avalon. *I was wounded. I should be dead, but...*

Instinctively, his hands clutched his chest. *No pain. Mordred stabbed me here; of that I am sure.* He reached for his legs, flexed his feet, and registered the movement. He pulled his knees to his chest. The movement ignited dozens of tiny tears in time-frozen muscles. A clunk below his knees made him start - the sound of metal hitting stone. He reached out to the source of the sound, and his fingers wrapped around the hilt of a sword. The coarse leather wrappings of the grip and the cold stone pommel were instantly familiar. It was Excalibur, the ancient ceremonial sword of his father's family. Myrddin had thrust it into his hands during the battle with Mordred. This sword alone checked Morgana's attack. Pulling his legs into a crossed position, more to stretch than for comfort, he caressed the blade with his fingertips. "You saved me, old man," not sure whether he was speaking to the sword or the wizard. *Myrddin. He was with me. I remember his face close to mine, telling me to sleep.*

The old sword brought him comfort and clarity. Before this, before the blackness, his army had fought Mordred on the plains below Camelot, in full view of his home. *Guinevere!* If his army had lost the battle, surely Mordred's forces would have taken the castle. *No... No... think! What happened?* Resting the sword on his lap, he bowed his head into his hands. *What magic does this place hold?* Morgana's sorcery on the fields of Camlann came back to him vividly. *What had she done?*

Deep breaths pushed the questions he knew he couldn't answer to his subconscious so he could focus on the moment; action bolstered his confidence. He swung his legs over the side of the slab and probed for the floor with his toes. His feet touched nothing, so he swung the sword to find what his legs couldn't. The tip of the sword met resistance - a soft floor, not stone - inches below his outstretched toes. Mindful of how stiff his joints still were, he eased off the rock and came to rest on what instinct informed him was firm soil. Keeping one hand on the table and the other on the supporting blade, he took stock of his balance. "It's fine," he whispered. He dropped to a knee for stability and remained in that position while taking stock of his breathing, the muscles in his legs, the darkness, and the still air. When he was ready to move forward, he pushed to his feet, clutching the hilt of the sword with both hands.

Arm extended, he probed the surrounding space. Nothing. Again, he reached out with all his senses for the caress of a breeze, a sliver of light, anything to help point him to an exit. Realizing he'd been holding his breath while searching for moving air, he inhaled, stretching his chest, then released. He repeated these two more times to further settle his mind.

He lifted the sword up and explored the space in front of him. Nothing. He took a tentative step forward, using his free hand and his sword alternately to probe the blackness. An upward thrust to find the ceiling brought him a sharp pain in his shoulder. He jerked his arm down and probed the flesh. Bandages beneath his blouse crumbled at his touch. He felt scar tissue where there should have been an open wound. He swatted more than wiped the bandage remnants away. *None of this made sense.*

He reached up again, the pain more manageable. His sword tip met no resistance, no ceiling. Taking a few more steps forward, he encountered a stone wall. It was smooth and unmoving. He slapped it with his hand. No give. He brought up Excalibur's pommel, a lashed stone of legendary origin, and banged it against the wall in several places. Clack, clack, clack. The sharp sound confirmed that these walls were thick. *Had Myrddin entombed him, thinking him dead?* No, death held a particular fascination for the old sorcerer. If Arthur had lived, Myrddin would have known it, *which means this mustn't be a tomb but ... but what? An infirmary?* There must be a way out. He should at least be able to exit as he entered. If this was Morgana's sanctuary, she must have been free to come and go. *Go? Gone.* Morgana is gone, of that, he is sure. That baffling moment on the shore of this island, when Excalibur penetrated her chest, flooded his mind. Her physical being transformed into smoke, black smoke. *Curious.*

What evil claimed her soul in that final breath was not his concern. Magic was for wizards. He had more pressing problems. Emboldened by the growing clarity of his memories and feeling stronger and more stable by the minute, he continued his examination of the dark space. Using the tip of the sword to tap the floor for pits or steps, he walked along the wall, intermittently banging the stone with the sword's pommel at every step. Thud, thud, thud. It was cold and smooth, dry and flat. This was a room, not a cave. Continuing methodically, probing the ground and pounding the wall, Arthur repeated the cadence. Scratch left, then

39

right. Thud, thud, thud. He occasionally ran his flattened hand in large circles, seeking a discontinuity that might herald a door or other opening.

He found a corner, adjusted his direction, and continued. Two paces further, he found a smooth, straight, vertical seam. Dropping the sword, he explored it with both hands. The gap extended up and out to reveal the shape of a door, an exit. The rectangular shape was about as wide as his arm span. This would be the lake entrance, his point of entry. But there were no hinges and no latch. The reality that this door only opened from the outside threatened to crush him.

"NO!" he screamed, then "No…" more of a whisper than an exclamation. He collapsed against the wall, his cheek on cool stone. As his breathing slowed, clarity returned. There must be another door. Unless this was a prison cell, occupants must have another way out. He knelt, gathered up his sword, and continued his methodical circuit of the room. Another corner and another turn, the wall still frustratingly solid. Thud, thud, thud.

Five steps, six, seven … nothing. Twenty-one, twenty-two … there! The tip of the sword found an obstacle. Quick taps revealed a shallow rise. *A step!* He pushed ahead and discovered emptiness with more steps leading upward. His breath quickened again, but in hope, not despair, and he thought he could hear his heart pounding. *This was it!* He took to the stairway on all fours, the blade tip dragging and bouncing behind him. *Four stairs, five, six … his* pace quickened. The euphoria born of hope soon gave way to a sudden burst of pain as his head slammed into the terminus of the stairway. Instantly unsteady, he pivoted to sit. The faint fireflies that came with the concussion were almost welcome. They were the first semblance of light he'd experienced since waking, an event now distant as an eternity. He felt no moisture and tasted no blood on the fingers that explored the point of impact. *Deep breaths; this will pass.*

He turned back to the offending obstacle and reached for what he hoped was his way out of the darkness. His hands found a familiar texture. Wood planks, deep grain. Rising to his feet, he could feel the iron strapping. No hinges here, so they must be on the outside of the door. Sliding his fingers to the left, he found a latch. Yes! He could visualize the latch in his hands. One pull downward and a push outward, and he'd be ... *where would I be?* Maybe free, maybe another room.

There wasn't any other option though, so pull and push he did. The latch released, but the door didn't move. He rested his weapon on the stairs and put both hands to the task. Nothing, not even the slightest movement. Panic crept in as he put his shoulder against the door and drove with his legs. Still nothing. Pushing gave way to pounding with his right shoulder. Harder and harder, *this had to open.* The door was freedom. With one last lunge, pain shot through his shoulder again, and he fell back to the stairs. Anxiety rose from his gut into his chest and head. Primal instinct kicked in as he reached for Excalibur and started hacking at the wooden barrier to his release. He struck the wood again, again, and again until his arms could no longer swing the blade. Arthur examined his progress with his fingertips. The blade strikes were indistinguishable from the grain of the old wood. Feeling his hard-won sanity slipping, he pounded the stone pommel on the unyielding timber. Once, twice, three times.

"You will open; you must! I am the High King. By all the gods of the Britons and the Romans, you will yield!" And Arthur unleashed his fury, repeating that sequence until his voice, then his consciousness, failed, and he sank to the stairs, still trapped in the eternal darkness.

Chapter 7

The Daily Telegraph
London UK
Thursday, October 5, 2018

Authorities are puzzled over the gruesome stabbing of Conservative Minister Justin Reynolds, Parliamentary Under-Secretary of State at the Department for Digital, Culture, Media, and Sport on Wednesday, October 4. Minister Reynolds' wife of 34 years, Bridget, was apprehended at the scene and taken into custody in Devonshire. Upon failure to appear at an important ministry meeting today, Mr. Reynolds's staff dispatched police to his home, where they found Mrs. Reynolds sitting on the floor with the bloody murder weapon in her lap. She was staring at the wall with what one source close to the case described as "dead eyes." This same source stated that when confronted by authorities, she muttered, "Had to ... Had to," but was otherwise unresponsive. Authorities have reported that Mrs. Reynolds didn't flee or even deny stabbing Minister Reynolds as he slept last night. Since being taken into custody, she has said nothing.

***

D ear, you are truly an inspiration!" Cybil Kenny exclaimed, sitting on the front edge of her chair, knees pressed together and angled away from her host. "Why, I don't think there's enough Valium in the empire to get me through what's happened to you, but here you are! How long has it been, dear?"

"It's been a week since they killed Mum and Dad, then left me for dead, and three days since they sprang me from the hospital for

Mum and Dad's funeral, luv," Meghan said. At home in her Portobello Road flat, she coolly directed a servant with tea and finger snacks for her guests. The handsome young man in the pressed black slacks, white shirt, and gold embroidered vest flashed his winning smile at each as he presented a silver tray with small cucumber sandwiches and bits of salmon and watercress.

Susan deHavilland leaned forward over a knee-length pleated skirt that would have been age-inappropriate on a woman of half her years. "But, dear, so much loss for one so young. They shot your parents right in front of you, dear? Yet here you are..." She sat back and crossed her arms, confident that she had conveyed the implied question.

"I'm grieving, of course," Meghan said, reaching out to touch Susan's knee. "But they wouldn't have wanted me to slow down. No! Buck up and get to work, as Dad would say." Looking up, she said, "Dylan, fetch Mrs. Kenny and me glasses of that 2015 Château d'Yquem we've been saving." From her brown leather, high-backed chair in front of the fireplace, she moved to redirect the conversation. "Cybil," she said, leaning towards a flush-faced, heavy-set woman. "Be a dear and don't make me drink alone, will you? It's been a trying day." Cybil Kenny, who was known to keep a flask in her oversized Louis Vuitton shoulder bag, nodded confirmation a bit too enthusiastically.

Soft, cloud-filtered sunlight bathed the parlor, and instrumental jazz played in the background. Six women, whose ages ranged from mid-twenties to early-sixties, were chatting with ease on chairs that were arranged in a semicircle around their host.

Accepting her wine, Cybil cooed, "My Bertie says you've been positively mercurial at the firm since you've been back, dear. Don't you think you deserve a break?" Affirmation and support for taking a rest were forthcoming from a group of ladies who hadn't worked a day in their lives.

"An experience like the one I've survived makes you appreciate each day, each minute of each day," Meghan replied. "The gentlemen's club atmosphere, the misogyny, that my father had encouraged at the firm bred sloth and waste. No, my friends, I will seize every day from now on. Carpe diem, eh? No long game. We'll play as if tomorrow might be our last," she said, taking a sip of her sweet Bordeaux, dark eyes belying the smile behind the crystal glass. "And any man at the firm who takes issue with this new direction is welcome to seek employment elsewhere. I think we can find more qualified candidates within our female ranks anyway. Ones I'm more inclined to trust, like you, my friends."

Declarations of hesitant agreement filled the room. However, these were the wives of bankers, manufacturing executives, and top-level government officials. Her statement flew in the face of London's male-dominated culture. Their husbands would never approve of such a bold challenge to the status quo.

"Ladies, ladies," she called as she tapped her wineglass with long, dark nails. "Please, I'd love to chat all day, and there will certainly be time for that later. I have more wine over at the bar." She winked at Mrs. Kenny and smiled at her guests as they giggled and touched each other's arms in collusion. *It was only two o'clock.* "All of you have shared with me … no secrets in this group…" Meghan said, raising her hands for emphasis. "All of you have experienced pain from your controlling, oft abusive husbands. Now you understand why I said you weren't alone." The women looked around the room, and several reached out to hold hands as she continued.

"As you well know, and I fear all the UK knows…" Meghan bowed her head. "My suffering - the loss of my parents, then the theft of my freedom and my body to men who sought to control what they couldn't possess honorably - was all over the papers, the tele, and the Internet. However, as I listened to your stories and understood that you had to suffer equally degrading and demoralizing brutality at the hands of your husbands, your loved ones, in silence, I realized that your burden must be far greater."

All her guests were now rapt. Yes, they had suffered. None of them could deny their pain.

"Jacquie, your husband, Reggie, insists you wear the skimpiest of outfits when he entertains prospects and puts you on display. He might as well be offering your body to the highest bidder." She noted, without missing a beat, that Dylan had snapped to attention as his eyes explored the curves of Jacquie Mattson, the platinum blonde, full-figured wife of Reginald Mattson. Mattson was the CEO of one of the largest defense suppliers in the UK. She continued, "Susan, your husband beats you for arbitrary reasons when he drinks. Anna, your jealous Claude forces you to submit an itinerary for your personal time and suffer a chaperone because he must control your every moment. He's waiting in the car right now, isn't he?" Anna nodded, and Susan, sitting on the couch next to her, tightened her grip on Anna's hand as they shared a tearful nod.

"Ladies, I've asked you all to join this support group because none of you should have to live in fear, in shame, or feel like a concubine to the man you've married. I've experienced the power of group therapy in my recovery, and I want to share … I must share… this with you, my closest friends."

Susan said, over her half-empty glass, "That you would build a program to help others, knowing you'd have to relive your abduction repeatedly, is either madness or saintliness. I've not decided yet."

Meghan shrugged. "It has been therapeutic for me in ways I can't explain. Now, as I was saying, before you push back on the healing power of conversation, or tell me you've already got a sweet, and handsome … right Susan … therapist already," She smiled at Susan, who blushed but didn't break eye contact. "What I'm proposing is simply to tap into the power of the collective. We are stronger together than we could ever be on our own. While we may not win back our rightful place, our power, immediately, you'll know in your heart of hearts that all of us are with you in times of suffering, and we will stand with you in your hour of redemption." As she finished this sentence, she stood and walked to the center of the gathering. All the women sat spellbound; most were crying as hope filled them. With a warm smile and matching watery eyes, she stepped up to each woman, took their face in her hands, and whispered into their right ear. They settled into a trance-like state, their demeanor peaceful, as she released them and moved on to the next.

With no further need to deceive, she stepped back from the last guest, Jacquie Mattson, and surveyed the room with the cold visage of the sorceress. *It is for their own good, little sister.* She examined each to ensure they were in the proper frame of mind. Three young men, not as well dressed as Dylan, strode in from the guest bedroom and positioned themselves outside the circle. Turning around, she saw Dylan crouching in front of Jacquie, stroking down her cheek towards her breasts. His eyes were predatory.

The sorceress stopped him with a look. "Do you want her, Dylan?" Dylan pulled his hand back, dropped his arm, and stood up, stumbling backwards, as he attempted to extricate himself from that misstep. "Is she worth losing me, Dylan?" She stepped forward with a provocative yet threatening stare that dared him to choose otherwise.

He turned from Mattson, smoothed out his slacks, and shook his head. "No, Mum."

"Excellent," she said, "right answer." She took Jacquie's hand and guided her to her feet. Jacquie complied and shuffled, as if sleepwalking, with her to the bedroom. She looked back at the boys, waiting at attention behind the sleeping women, and said, "You know what to do, gentlemen. And be quick about it." She then closed the door behind her for a one-on-one with the pliant Mrs. Mattson.

Chapter 8

The news typically held little interest for Lloyd. He had seen it all and seldom found anything surprising. However, the news was still the best resource for world events, portending the crises he'd been expecting for so long, and that gray, rainy day offered an ideal opportunity to settle in with the Saturday Post and focus on life outside his small circle.

Splattered all over the front page was the latest in a string of murders that had London high society on edge. Lloyd could ignore a single incident, but not three. And not in one week. In each case, the wives of prominent figures killed their husbands without warning. Even stranger, the killers made no attempt to cover up their crimes or even run.

The paper said that authorities were looking into environmental factors. Since the women frequented the same upper-class venues, police were trying to find overlap in the meals or cocktails they'd ordered. However, Lloyd suspected the source of these women's behavior was intentional and psychological. The killers exhibited all the signs of mind control, a skill he was familiar with but had not seen in centuries. These were consistent with scenarios that had played out in his mind over his timeless wait.

Lloyd reached forward and retrieved a pair of scissors, the soft pillows of his sofa fighting him all the way. Sinking back into the cushion's embrace, he clipped the article he was reading, both the main section on the front page and the *Continued On* section several pages in. He also saved a background piece about the victims near the editorial section. He rose, leaning heavily on the left arm of the sofa, and returned the scissors with the clippings to his desktop for filing later. Now, another cup of tea was his priority. Some things are definitely worse in Britain and in the world these days. *OK, most things*, he thought. But the quality and convenience of tea bags were high on his list of civilization's successes.

He pulled down a box of black tea from a shelf above the stove and fired up a burner below an unremarkable red metal teapot. Grabbing a chipped ceramic mug off a wall hook, he willed his long, stiff fingers to open the bag.

"Oh, no you don't," he said to the string tab that had uncooperatively slipped into the cup. "That's better," he mumbled as he looked up to the rain-splattered, translucent back window. Leaning closer to the glass, the racing of blurry drops calmed him. He thought a few hours in the garden after the soft rain should clear his mind.

Encouraged by the soft, green glow seeping through the thick glass and the patter of drops on the low roof over the kitchen, his mind took the initiative and cleared itself. The knowledge he'd compiled over all his studies and travels was a blessing and a curse. Too many connections might obscure an insight that was just below the surface. An occasional soft reboot was required to fully analyze all the bits and pieces. His thoughts on the London killings needed this sort of processing if he had any hope of drawing a meaningful conclusion.

The shrill whistle of the teapot jolted him out of his musings. Unlike the usual, gentle return to consciousness he normally felt in these circumstances, Lloyd snapped alert, clutching the edge of the counter with white knuckles. *Something has happened.* A feeling he hadn't experienced in generations, ages, if he was honest with himself, shook him to his core. He spun about, feeling confused and unsure what to do or where to look. "The Tor, dammit! Something's happened at the Tor!"

"Curse these ancient legs," he said as he raced up the spiral stairs. Lunging for the bedroom window, he focused on the dark pyramid that was the Tor, silhouetted in the late-afternoon glow, sharpened by flashes of light behind clouds. He closed his eyes and let the obscuring layers of his countless burdens fade. Lloyd focused his thoughts inward; his breathing settled from near-hyperventilation to slow and steady … slow and steady. The moment he opened his eyes, he could feel the pounding, a repeating cadence of three pulses. It may have been there all along, but the beating of his heart would have drowned out any otherworldly sensations.

"Yes," he murmured, and then he cried it out loud. "YES!" slapping his hand on the windowsill. His translucent reflection in the window was that of a man markedly younger than just minutes before, gazing at the hill with a look bordering on rapture. The knocking and pounding were music to his ears. After lifetimes of waiting, it was happening.

Turning back, he crossed to the wardrobe and lifted the old gray cloak from its resting place. Cradling it, remembering journeys they'd made together, he tossed it over his arm and descended the stairs.

Stalling for time, uncomfortable with uncertainty, Lloyd walked to the door and slipped into his worn boots, not bending to tie them, trusting the ample shearling lining to cling to his feet. His mind's eye looked past the door to the gentle lower slope of the Tor. His destination, the back gate of the Pelling's cottage, was familiar enough to find, even in this weather. First, the message.

He flipped open his laptop, slipping the cloak on while waiting for it to come to life. The message he must now send had been first composed long ago. As generations passed, he adapted the language and style, along with the recipient list, but the import of this call to action never varied.

"Once sent, Lloyd, it can't be called back," he muttered. "I can't race after the letter carrier or rush to the post office and recover it. What if I'm wrong?"

Self-doubt was foreign to him, but appropriate in this case. This simple click would set in motion a chain reaction. He knew most recipients doubted this summons would ever come, that the oath binding them was real.

Would they still be checking, or had they lost faith, as Jennifer had? Would they come? Are they ready?

Lloyd had kept tabs on those tasked with this quest and knew there would be no abler or more loyal companions in the world. Knowingly or unknowingly, they'd prepared their whole lives for this moment. "Yes, they will come," he declared and clutched the mouse.

He solemnly moved it to the upper right corner of the screen and hovered over the 'Send' icon. With an imperceptible twitch of his long index finger, *click*; the world changed. In a single motion, Lloyd closed the laptop and spun towards the door. He removed his staff from the can, pulled his hood low over his brow, and stepped into the cold, blowing rain. The cloak rendered him invisible in the gray light.

Chapter 9

Rainy Saturdays meant card games for Jenn and her family; gin rummy was the go-to. She was doing her best to redirect the conversation away from legends and stories, but her brother and father's enthusiasm had been ramping up. "Peter, have you asked that Maggie Davies out for a coffee yet?" she asked.

"You know how busy I've been, Jenn, with school, the new tech, and all," Peter responded a bit too quickly, dodging eye contact.

"She's lovely and has clearly taken a shine to you. Trust me. You should never take a woman's patience for granted. She won't wait forever." *We all need to move on*, Jenn thought to herself. It was her time. She should simply declare this and get it over with. She couldn't support her father's quixotic quest any longer.

As if he'd read her mind, Colin said without lifting his nose from the playing cards in his hand, "And we know all about waiting forever, don't we, dear?"

Something inside Jenn snapped. It must have been audible, because both Peter and Colin dropped their hands to the table.

"I'm tired, Dad. Tired of the legends, both the ones you cling to as well as those the local clerics and crackpots keep alive. How many times must I hear that Joseph of Arimathea brought the Holy Grail to ancient Britain?"

"Impossible to disprove, Jenn," Peter said.

"That's my point, I guess. It's just the way the conspiracy nuts obsess over it. Or that when the same Joseph thrust his staff into the ground in front of the pile of rocks that became Glastonbury Cathedral, a thorn tree sprung up, and has thrived ever since as a symbol of the town's spirituality."

"OK, this is easier to disprove," Colin offered. "I've witnessed the removal and planting of at least four new trees in that spot. Tourists love it though, and what's the harm in letting them believe in a bit of magic while they visit?"

"Them? No harm, Dad, but *us*? You fantasize about King Arthur and that he's buried under that old hill and that WE are bound for all eternity to wait for him? Maybe there's a bit of harm in that belief."

"Someday you'll understand that this isn't a legend. It's history, dear, and we're part of it."

"C'mon, Dad, you've seen the report they published in 2002 after engineers used a ground-penetrating radar to ensure the foundation of St. Michael's Chapel was secure. The data didn't reveal any hidden chambers - only rock and dirt."

"And if you join Peter in our quest, our mission, Lloyd will explain that away. I'm sorry that isn't possible if you go forward with your plans to move out."

"Dad, I'm a scientist, trusting data to understand historical trends and cause and effect. I'm not one of the local mystics, storytellers, hippies, or opportunists who live and breathe the rumors of a fifteen-hundred-year-old king that may someday come back to life. Facts matter, and the facts don't support the supernatural." She saw her father's face fall.

"I'm sorry, Dad! I don't mean to … but … but Mr. Wyse. He believes he's Merlin. Sure, a harmless affectation, but he'd have to be a thousand years old; maybe thousands of years old. Why do you entertain his fantasy, and why do you always use him as a crutch when I ask for explanations?"

A lightning bolt struck close. Its crack and rumble rolled through the house, rattled the dishes, and cut Jenn's ranting off. She mumbled an apology and looked down at the forgotten cards.

Peter used it as an excuse to flee and check the instruments before Maggie Davies came back into the conversation.

Jenn dismissed him with a "Whatever" and rose to check on dinner, occasionally making eye contact with her father, wondering if she'd pushed it a bit too far this time. He just smiled and started gathering up the cards.

Peter walked back in with a puzzled look on his face. "Dad, could you come see this?"

Colin again smiled at Jenn. "Absolutely ... be right there."

She shot him a frustrated stare as he walked out with Peter, then turned back to the sink and looked out the window towards the Tor, then back to the kitchen door, window ... door... Finally, Jenn put down the potatoes she was about to peel, threw her apron on a chair, and stormed after her brother and father. They were in front of the computer monitors, playing and replaying a graph that resembled a lie detector's scribble.

"I see what you mean," Colin said. "It is irregular. Have you seen this pattern before?" They both glanced up to see Jenn looking over their shoulders, but continued their examination.

"See, right there..." Peter pointed out, "This is a classic lightning strike noise pattern. It matches what we recorded the other day." He glanced up at Jenn and clarified that 'noise' meant random vibration from the thunderclap. She rolled her eyes with a curt nod. It wasn't the first, or even the third time he'd lectured her on digital signals. "But here," Peter continued, "are patterns of three sharp peaks. They repeat at irregular intervals but are nearly identical when they occur. I've never seen this before."

"Something in the chapel has clearly blown loose in the wind and is slapping against the wall," Jenn offered. "I'm sure there's a simple explanation." As they watched, the spikes in the chart materialized, only they were stronger and repeated more rapidly.

"There it is again! Could it be?" Peter asked. Their father only raised his eyebrows and looked at them both.

Jenn was getting caught up in the excitement and immediately rebuked herself. "Look, the legend is that Arthur will rise when the realm needs him again. The Saxons are long gone. The French came and went, but no Arthur. Hitler nearly obliterated the world, and Artie slept through it. Now, there is no war, and the climate can't be fixed with a sword. I'm not loving where music is going, but that's hardly worthy of the second coming of a king that may or may not have even existed … is it?"

Peter and Colin listened patiently. They'd heard it before. Peter jumped up. "I'm going to check the hill."

"I'm coming with," said their father.

"Dad, you shouldn't…" Jenn planted her hands on her hips as the men rushed to the back door. "I can't believe this! It is pouring rain out there, dinner is almost ready, and you two are going to tromp around that old hill looking for what? A sign?"

Chapter 10

Neither acknowledged Jenn's admonishment, instead hurrying to grab boots, flashlights, and raincoats. Arms waving as they scurried around the house, they discussed possibilities and rehashed old theories. Then, in a flurry of movement, they were out the door. Peter glanced back and saw Jenn in the doorway, watching them from the warm light of the kitchen. After a moment's pause, he turned back to his goal, the garden shed.

"You know, I've planned for this moment my whole life," Colin said. "Now that we may meet King Arthur, the *REAL* King Arthur, I feel wholly unprepared. I hope I'm up to the task. I hope I don't let him down."

Peter pulled open the shed's door. "Please, Dad! I can't imagine how we could be better prepared. Jenn is probably right that this is a false alarm, but I think it's outstanding that we are doing it together. If nothing else, this will be great training, right?"

"Right you are, son." Colin reached inside his jacket and pulled out a checklist. He kept his tone measured, but Peter could see the note trembling in his hand. "OK. Two spades and two crowbars, check. We'll need to work fast, and we don't know what condition those old doors are in."

"I've got 'em, Dad. What else?"

"Check the backpack for the first-aid kit, electric torches, bottles of water, and energy bars … good?"

"All here," said Peter, "and the duffel has a tarp, blankets, boots, a scarf, and a jacket. I think we can pass on the stretcher and crutches. In this rain, they'll be useless."

"Agreed," Colin said, then reached out to his son's shoulder.

"How about the shotgun? When this was purely hypothetical, it was easier not to fight with your sister about it."

After much debate, Colin had removed a shotgun from the kit a few years ago and tucked it away in the kitchen pantry. Colin's father had been insistent that, when the time came, they bring a weapon to the hill. The logic was that if a 1,500-year-old warrior sprang out of a cave, there was no telling what condition his mind would be in. It was all well and good to assume he would pop out and ask for tea as if nary a day had passed, but he could just as likely be mad and swinging an enormous sword. The other argument for the gun was that the Pellings might not be the only ones watching and waiting. Lloyd had suggested as much. If the king came back, it was to confront someone or something. Colin and Peter might actually need to protect the warlord. These were all valid arguments, but Jenn, in an unusual moment of collaboration, had the final say. She wasn't comfortable with the idea of her little brother stumbling about the hill with a loaded gun.

"I think we should stick to the plan, Dad. In this rain and light, it's hard to imagine that old gun being of much use. I mean, how ridiculous would it be, after 1,500 years of waiting, we accidentally shot him because we panicked or slipped?"

After a few seconds of hesitation, Colin relented. They would leave the shotgun in the house.

Torches lit, tools, and bags in hand, Colin and Peter made for the back gate. Their yard opened onto a public access road that ended at a National Park Service (NPS) entrance to the Tor. An overgrown path through the bushes behind their property offered a discreet route to the hill with less chance of being observed. They took the National Park gate this afternoon. It was easier, and they didn't expect anyone would be out and about on such a stormy day.

Peter grasped the top of the gate and looked up at the hill, shielding his eyes and yelling to be heard over the downpour. "Do you think this is it, Dad? Are we really about to meet a legend, or are we as daft as Jenn thinks we are?"

Colin plunged his spade into the dirt and reached for Peter's shoulder to steady himself as he spoke into his ear. "Son, I don't know. And if tonight isn't the night, it could be tomorrow, or next year, or your children's tomorrow. Bloody hell, it could all be, what did your sister call it, 'Generational Delusion'? But I believe it, and I know you do too. Mr. Wyse has shown me things that defy explanation and, if today isn't the day, well, we'll show them to you. For now, let's you and I hike up our britches, climb that hill, and see what we see, OK?"

With a nod, Peter shrugged his backpack higher on his shoulders and climbed. Colin grabbed his duffel bag and shovel and followed.

The climb was easy at first because the NPS had maintained a path from the gate to the bottom ring walk. The wind wasn't too strong on this side of the mount, and the gravel offered decent footing. Peter reached under his coat and pulled out his cell phone and consulted the app he'd written to track the sensors. Shielding it under his jacket to keep the device dry, he nodded to his father.

A few hundred yards down the ring path, they headed up the hill on the slippery grass. Once they were close, the active sensors were easy to find. For as long as anyone could remember, a delicate, weathered tree had grown near the spot Lloyd had suggested. When not overgrown with thistle in the summer months, visitors to the Tor, both locals and tourists, had been tying ribbons to the branches of this tree. Jennifer postulated that a long-ago Pelling had tied a ribbon for fear of forgetting where to check in his advancing years, and it caught on. Peter preferred to believe that the collective subconscious of the region knew something here was exceptional and deserved to be decorated. For whatever reason, there it was, and here they were.

Peter checked his phone one more time. The sensors were still functional, but had been mute since they began their climb. He showed the screen to his father, then tucked the phone away. The men dropped their gear next to the ribbon tree and examined the area. Peter waited as Colin paced off three strides uphill from the tree and then four strides to his right. It wasn't science, but it was all they had. Yelling over the constant patter of rain on wet turf, Colin called out, "This is as good a spot as any to start, son. Bring the tools up."

Spades in hand, Colin said, "Ready?" Peter nodded, eyes wide with a grin that split his face, and the men drove their shovels into the dirt.

The first few strikes met soft turf. A point of discussion over generations of Pellings was whether they should attempt to uncover the doors Mr. Wyse had assured them lay under the grass. The arguments *for* were that it would both confirm that this wasn't a wild goose chase, and it would make access much faster and easier. The arguments *against* were that it might expose the secret to well-intentioned and maybe not-so-well-intentioned third parties. On top of that, they didn't want to risk providing an exit that an awakened Arthur might emerge from on his own and go wandering off in a world he wasn't prepared to understand. The latter argument held, which meant Peter and Colin had to dig.

Thump. Peter had struck wood. He snapped his face up, eyes wild. Colin froze, meeting Peter's gaze, then with a smile and a vigorous nod, encouraged him to continue. Peter made a second strike in the same spot to confirm. Thump. He stopped and looked up again, mouth agape. It took only a moment to understand what this meant, and Colin hurried to the spot. He maintained eye contact with Peter as he lifted his blade and struck. *Thump.*

Chapter 11

*T*hump.

Slumped against the door, head bowed, and hope fading, a sound snapped Arthur to full alert. More than a sound, he felt it in the shoulder pressed to the unyielding wood. He held his breath, frozen, afraid the slightest shift could mean missing another occurrence. Thump. *There it was again! It was real!* Something or someone was on the other side of the door. He turned to the wood and pressed both hands and an ear to the surface. *Please ... please. Nothing.* Then *Thump.* He felt this as a wake-up call to his soul. With a laugh and a yell, he started banging his fists on the door to signal his would-be rescuers. The thought forced Arthur to pause and reach down to feel the reassuring leather grip of Excalibur. Rescuers? Perhaps, but he couldn't speak of their intentions. He needed to be prepared. Resolved that his blade could neutralize any threat, he continued his pounding and yelling as the impacts resumed.

Arthur shook the latch and pushed the door with his shoulder. Then he heard it… "Hello." It was faint, but it was clear. Breaking into a grin, he slammed both palms on the door and yelled back, "Hail to you, I am here!"

***

After a moment's reality check, Colin and Peter doubled their efforts, digging and scraping to expose the door. Within minutes, their flashlights revealed the familiar pattern of deep wood grain. They had found the old door, strangely well-preserved considering the moisture and rot that should have turned it to mush over the centuries. Peter knelt to examine the surface when he felt the pounding from the other side of the door.

"Dad, feel this!" he yelled out over the white noise of the rain.

They could both feel erratic pounding through the boards and knew this was the time. Shovels back in hand, they worked as quickly as they could to uncover the rest of the opening. When they'd cleared the edges, they could see that the door was square, about four feet per side. Further digging and scraping uncovered a latch on the right side as they faced the peak. Minutes later, they stood in the rain, flashlights illuminating a long-forgotten gateway to a sorceress's lair.

Peter knelt back down and pulled on the latch. A shake of his head told his dad it hadn't budged. He dropped his spade and torch to get both arms and legs into the effort and heaved. Nothing. Peter yelled, "I'll go back to the rucksack for crowbars."

Colin stopped him with an outstretched palm and then pointed down to the door. "Look!!"

Peter saw it too… the latch was moving on its own. "Someone is trying to open it from the inside!" Peter dropped, put his face to the door, and shouted, "HELLO!" Then he pounded his fist twice.

Peter looked up. "He said 'Hello' back!! I'm sure of it!"

Colin had no reply. Lloyd warned them that communication might be tricky. The wizard said he'd done his best to prepare Arthur for re-entry into the world, but Colin was the one unprepared for this simplest exchange of greetings. The realization that they had just heard the legendary king's first words in 1,500 years was overwhelming.

Fortunately, the magnitude of the moment that had frozen the father had only renewed the energy of the son. Peter put his head to the door and called back, "Can you push? Can you help us open the door?"

"Aye," he heard in response.

"Smashing!" Peter replied. "I'll tap the door three times, and on the third tap, I'll pull and you push. Do you understand?" Again, to their continuing astonishment, 'Aye' came back through the boards.

The wind had picked up, driving rain into their faces. Peter leaned over to ensure Colin understood. "I'll grab the latch and pull. I need you to pound on the door with your shovel three times. On three, we open this sucker, got it?"

Colin nodded, stepped back onto the grass, and readied his spade over the door. Peter nodded. He was ready. Colin raised the spade with both arms, his expression reflecting the importance of what was about to happen. As lightning streaked through the sky behind him, his father loomed like a warrior from ages past, poised for a two-handed deathblow, looking majestic, knightly even. As quickly as that imagery came, it disappeared with the first impact on the door. One. Colin pulled the shovel back, paused, and struck again. Two. Peter adjusted his grip and shifted his weight to the balls of his feet. Three. Colin yanked the shovel back as Peter heaved.

The door burst open with a spray of water and mud. Peter fell back as the blackened wood flew away from him, almost taking his arm with it. Within that spray was the blurred figure of a man, momentum carrying him through the opening.

His hands grappled for a hold, to keep his face out of the muck. Scrambling backward and clutching at the turf to stabilize himself, he looked up. Peter watched as the bearded apparition lifted his head to the sky. He stood at least a head taller than the Pelling men. He had shoulder-length hair, soaked straight by the downpour, a Roman nose, and a close-trimmed beard. His eyes reflected black in the soft glow of moonlight leaking through the clouds.

"Fresh air, rain … this is incredible. The sweetest smell I've ever known."

Forgetting generations of protocol and planning, Peter asked, almost too softly to be heard over the storm, "Arthur?"

The once king of the Britons stared at him from the hole with a look of shock and wonder, a smile that spoke of unbridled joy.

He wore an oversized white shirt that clung to his body in the soaking rain. It hung over brown wool trousers laced up the sides. Dark stains spread across his right shoulder and across his abdomen.

Peter couldn't be certain in the gray light, but it looked like there might be tears within those stains. Legend held that Arthur suffered mortal wounds in his ultimate battle at Camlann, forcing Merlin to inter him at Avalon. It all fits.

Colin fell to his knees above the hole; his shovel had already dropped. Arthur hadn't noticed him, fixating instead on Peter as the two men took stock of each other and what this meeting meant.

Tears of joy mingled with the rain on Arthur's face. "Of course," he said. "Who else would it be?" He reached his hand to Peter, looked him in the eyes and said, "Bedivere, I knew you'd come for me."

***

One hundred forty miles to the east, in a pricey flat on Portobello Road, Notting Hill, London, the sorceress dropped the mug of tea she'd been sipping and shrieked.

Chapter 12

No, sir, my name is Peter, sir," he said, grasping Arthur's hand and struggling to his feet. Arthur came up the final step.

"Peter? You are not Bedivere?"

"No, your Majesty, my name is Peter…"

Before the king could process this, a voice came from behind, speaking too quickly and loudly. "And sir, I am Colin, Colin Pelling, Peter's father. We have been waiting a long time to meet you, your Highness. I mean, well, this is an incredible…"

Arthur pivoted to Colin and swayed. The adrenaline rush must have ended, and he was unsteady. The king looked from the older man to the younger and back, his face alternating between wide, questioning eyes and a defensive, furrowed brow. Arthur's movement slowed. His eyes closed, his head dropped, and he fell to his knees. Both father and son rushed forward to support him. Reacting, Arthur lashed out with his left arm.

"Get back!"

The rescuers froze. Colin deliberately extended his arms, palms forward, in a conciliatory gesture. "We're here to help you, serve you, your Highness. We have no weapons. You have nothing to fear."

Eyes still on the Pellings, "Fear? I fear no man! The insolence…" Arthur said, as he reached backwards, cut short by a graceless slip in the mud and tumble into the hole. Scrambling back to his feet, he pulled out a sword and took a two-handed defensive stance, frenetic gaze shifting from father to son and back.

"What witchcraft is in play here?"

Colin, however, kept his composure, and Peter raised his palms up to match his father's gesture.

"It's OK, my lord, Arthur. You have slept for many years. Bedivere was our father, our forefather, and he taught us of you and to wait for you. We're here to serve and bring you home. It's OK." He glanced again at Peter and nodded reassurance, then motioned towards the sacks.

Peter edged towards the tree as Arthur monitored his movement. He said, "We have a warm, dry blanket and dry boots, more appropriate for this weather." Both Arthur and Colin looked down at the king's feet, to his shapeless leather moccasins, now covered in sludge.

This simple gesture helped bring Arthur back to his senses. The talk of practical matters, footwear, eased the king's tension. Still in a defensive stance, Arthur's sword tip dipped.

Colin went on. "You must eat, my lord. We have water and food, simple for now, but we can catch you up later."

Peter had stepped back up with the bag and held out a heavy tartan-patterned blanket. "Please sir, allow me."

Exhaustion washed over Arthur's face. Father and son kept their expressions gentle, their stances neutral, to minimize the appearance of a threat. *Nothing I can't handle.* Arthur nodded and dropped his sword tip to the ground. Peter stepped up and placed the warm blanket over his shoulders. The king pulled it close with his free hand. "Thank you, lad."

Peter pulled a shining flagon out of his coat pocket and extended it to Arthur. The king accepted and examined it. This was unlike any skin or glass he'd ever held. It shared characteristics of both. He rotated it and shook it. The sensory feedback, the crackling sound, and the sparkling reflections captivated him. However, he didn't know what to do with it. He looked up and saw Colin smiling. "Are you mocking me, old man?"

"Of course not. I am sorry, my lord, you couldn't know." Colin reached out for the bottle in Arthur's hand with a nod. Arthur handed it to him, maintaining eye contact. Colin gave the bottle a quick twist, removing the cap, and handed it back. "You can drink from the opening now, lord."

Arthur raised the bottle to his lips, shifted his gaze back to Peter, and took a sip. The water was cold and clear. He drained it in seconds, squeezing the strange vessel as he would any skin of water or wine, to extract the last drop.

With a last look at the clear, shining empty bottle, he threw it to the ground. "Another! My thirst is great."

Peter picked up the bottle without comment, placed it in the bag, and offered Arthur a second flask, removing the cap as he presented it. The king took measured sips from this one. Peter then pulled a small package from his pocket and unwrapped it before handing it to Arthur. "Take this, Your Highness. It's small, but it will help. You need to eat, please."

"So much like my Bedivere," Arthur said as he took the offering. The first bite awoke a hunger to match his thirst. "Nuts and honey," he murmured. He devoured it and demanded another as well, wiping his mouth with his sleeve.

Peter unwrapped a second as Colin squatted down to rummage through the sack. "I will bring you to our home, Your Majesty, while Peter cleans up here. I really can't believe you … well…" Colin said with a broad grin that suddenly shifted to a look of concern. "Are you hurt? Can you walk?"

"No, old man, I am fit to walk. Lead on."

Colin flashed him a more measured smile, then pulled out a pair of boots. "First, let's get you into more appropriate shoes. Lean on me, Your Majesty, and slip your feet into these. It will make walking easier."

Arthur supported himself on his kneeling servant while Colin tied the laces. This gave him a moment to take in his surroundings. Colin could only imagine what must be tearing through his mind. Up the hill, a stone chapel sat where there had likely been nothing in his age. Down in the valley, the shallow lake with the docks was no more. He would see roads in the gray light of the storm and the glow of lanterns, whiter than they should be, Colin thought, in the windows of a large home at the bottom of the hill.

"Old man, the forests have been cleared while I've slept. Does not the warden check the growth of villages?"

Colin finished with the boots and, with a fatherly tap on Arthur's leg, stood back up. "Much has changed, my lord. I will explain this all in the fullness of time, but now, we need to go." Arthur didn't acknowledge the direction. His gaze swept the countryside while Colin gathered his scattered belongings.

From this position on the Tor, the town, modern-day Glastonbury, was behind him to his right, blocked by the summit. Hedge-lined fields and roads were all he could see from this vantage point. In these first crucial moments, where Arthur's grasp on reality would either hold or collapse forever, it was fortunate that this limited view minimized the shock of the modern world.

Colin's hand on Arthur's shoulder brought the king back to the moment. "My lord, we really must move." Arthur nodded, secured the blanket, and stepped forward onto the path Colin was directing him to.

"I'll meet you back at the house, Dad," Peter said. "I'll do my best to clean things up around here."

Colin turned on his torch to illuminate the ring path as they moved down the hill. Arthur walked without comment, entranced by surroundings that seemed both familiar and foreign. Following the well-maintained walkway, Colin signaled a stop in front of a small wooden gate.

"One second, m'lord. I need to make sure no one has seen us." He looked through the trees on both sides of the entry, then motioned Arthur to continue through to a short lane illuminated by a pole-mounted white light.

Arthur tried to keep his eyes forward, but his countenance said that nothing was right here. He was walking as if he were in a dream. "This is your home? This is more splendid than even the wealthiest of Roman dwellings. The sons of Bedivere must truly be great lords," he said. "Where are your animals? Surely a manor of such opulence would need livestock and horses to maintain it. And where are the smells!?"

Colin took a deep breath, as if experiencing his own world for the first time. He caught the faint, comforting scent of a hearth fire and cooking meat, but Arthur must have expected an overwhelming odor of waste and rot. He took another deep, clean breath.

As if Arthur had read his mind, he said, "The air is sweet, as in the middle of a forest or on the banks of a stream." His voice trailed off as he followed Colin through the second gate.

"We're here, my lord," Colin said, pulling him out of his thoughts. Standing in the entry before Arthur, arms crossed for warmth, a beautiful maid confronted him with penetrating eyes and a serious, questioning look.

"Oh my god," Jenn exclaimed as the soaking-wet men filed past her. "Quickly, please get inside."

Once out of the rain, she gestured to an interior door. Colin scrambled in, dropping the wet packs. Arthur's steps were more measured. Pulling his eyes off the woman and into the room before him, he struggled to take it all in. The space was too bright, too white. The oddly shaped lanterns glowed without flicker or the familiar greasy black smoke such intensity should require. "What strange magic is at work in this place?" he breathed.

"Such gaping and gawking are beneath your station, old friend. Please close your mouth and have a seat."

Arthur's head snapped to the voice, then he froze. Sitting at the table, cloaked in gray and sipping a steaming cup beneath a bushy white beard, was a face most familiar.

"Welcome, your majesty. It is so good of you to finally join us."

Chapter 13

Lloyd rose to embrace Arthur, who, eyes wide but mouth now set, hadn't moved since spotting the old wizard.

"Please, Arthur, come sit," he said and guided the dazed king to the table.

Jenn had stepped back into the room and was leaning against the kitchen counter, struggling to accept what she saw. Colin was stripping off his wet jacket while watching the reunion, 1,500 years in the making. "Dad, you're staring," she chided.

Colin nodded, the wonderment shaving twenty years off his face.

"Jennifer, if you wouldn't mind, could you please bring Lord Arthur a cup of tea? In fact, we could all use a cup of tea." To Arthur, he added, "And drink this down, son. You'll thank me."

Jenn thought she could use a shot of whiskey, but that could wait. Instead, she moved to the stove and began preparing for her guests.

"Colin," Lloyd asked, "if I'm not mistaken, there is a generous helping of leftover ham in the refrigerator. If you could be so kind as to make our new friend a sandwich, he really must eat."

Turning and reaching across the table, Lloyd took Arthur's hands and said in a soft voice, "There is much you want to know, and much more you need to know, but we have time. For now, you must eat. My spells have kept you whole across many years, but your body will soon realize it's awake, and its needs will be fierce. Eat, and while you eat, I'll share the basics. Then bathe and sleep, proper sleep. Your body and mind need to heal."

Jenn grasped the wisdom of this and looked over at Colin, who was slicing the ham with unusual precision and placing it neatly on a halved roll, putting way too much care into presentation.

"Let me do this, Dad." She stepped over to the counter and hipped her father out of the way. He didn't argue but leaned his head close. "He's real!" he mouthed. "It's happening!"

Jenn paused and reached for her father's face with a warm smile and a nod. "Dad, go get his highness a towel and dry clothes; I've got this." She saw tears in her father's wide eyes as he nodded and hurried away, looking back at Arthur as he slipped out of the kitchen. "Did they bring you anything to eat on the hill, Your Highness?" she asked.

Arthur watched Colin back down from his daughter and turned back to Jenn with an icy glare. "Yes, a nut and honey loaf, m'lady."

"A granola bar? Dad!" Colin shuffled out, head bowed, to find towels and the clothes they'd maintained per Lloyd's direction.

Jenn picked up the plate of ham and the tray of rolls and set them in front of Arthur. "Start with this, Your Highness, and I'll fix more." She pulled a handful of flatware out of a ceramic jar in the middle of the table and dropped it with a clatter in front of the king.

Arthur's eyes darkened, his chair flying back as he leapt to his feet. "You will not disrespect and abuse my favor with this lack of decorum. I will not be treated like a commoner in my nor any other land."

Jenn stumbled backwards, catching the counter to avoid a fall.

Lloyd leaned back in his chair with a wry smile forming on his face. "Arthur, shut up and sit down."

"And I will not stand idly by while a maid treats her father, one of such noble lineage, with such … such … cheek."

Lloyd reached out and grasped Arthur's forearm. "Jennifer, please excuse my befuddled friend. He knows naught of what he speaks. Arthur! Sit down, PLEASE."

The strain of the evening had numbed Jenn's reactions, but with blood rushing to her face, she stepped forward. "Now you listen to me, *Your Highness*. Don't you come into my home…" Lloyd's outstretched palm silenced Jenn. That was when she noted the sudden change in Arthur's face, from angry to lost.

Lloyd reached out to pull Arthur's chair back to the table and guided him again to sit. "Arthur, there is much about this age you must learn, but please lead with graciousness … and eat. Eat now."

Arthur held Lloyd's gaze as the enormity of that statement registered. Then he succumbed to centuries of famishment. He grabbed the knife and dug into the ham, ripping mouthfuls off, stopping only to gobble down a roll.

Reconciling that this would be a learning experience for all of them, Jenn went back to the fridge and reached for a gallon of milk, but thought twice. He'd probably need it, but she didn't know if it would require too much explanation. Did Iron Age kings drink milk? She instead pulled a pitcher from a shelf and filled it with water. After placing this and a glass on the table, Jenn retrieved a brick of cheddar cheese from the crisper and a few apples. Arthur welcomed the drink with a nod, food spattering from his open-mouthed chewing, never taking his eyes off the meal.

Watching this large, dirty man at her kitchen table eating two days' worth of food gave her a chance to reflect. She'd been wrong. King Arthur WAS under the Tor, and he is clearly real. They weren't waiting in vain. A mottled layer of filth masked his scarred face, so estimating his natural, pre-spell age was difficult. He wasn't a young man. Different legends placed him in his thirties; others suggested he died approaching one hundred years old. He might not even know. She hadn't given such nonsensical speculation much thought before.

Young or old, asshole or not, he was handsome, in a rough sort of way. As he dried in the warm kitchen, she saw his beard was a few shades lighter than his brown hair, almost blond. His hair … his hair was a wreck, but if the legend was accurate, he had been fighting and sweating in a helmet or something like that as recently as a few hours before he slept. She could forgive the mess and, if she was honest with herself, thought the battered look somewhat sexy. "Stop it, Jenn," she said to herself. Lloyd and Arthur glanced up. *Oops. That was out loud.* "Do you have enough to eat, *Your Highness*?" she said, folding her arms across her chest, chin down, eyebrows up. *Hide behind attitude,* she thought.

"Yes, m'lady, and call me Arthur, just Arthur. And please accept my apologies for the disrespect." All arrogance had drained from his face. He turned to the old wizard. "I suspect that I'm no longer king in this land."

"Yes, Arthur, thank you, Arthur … Arthur," she replied. She could sense her cheeks turning pink, feeling somewhat like a schoolgirl basking in the arrogant charm of the varsity football captain. Despite the inescapable confusion, he still exuded confidence and authority … an aura.

Oblivious to Jenn's creeping blush, Lloyd wished to keep the conversation moving. "Well yes, maybe introductions are overdue. Arthur, now that you've had your fill and while you still have your wits about you, it's best we get on with business. I suspect young Peter will join us momentarily."

On cue, the back door opened, and the small crowd in the kitchen paused for the sounds of a man unburdening himself of gear in the vestibule. Peter stepped into the room, energized and eager to talk. "I filled in the hole as best I could. I'll want to run sod up there tomorrow, but I think we're good for now. The storm's slowing, but there's no light to speak of. I…" He paused when his eyes met Arthur's. "Sorry, sir, for my poor manners." He attempted a bow, but his backside bumped the door jamb and propelled him a step forward.

This broke the tension, and stress-relieving laughter welcomed Peter into the room. Colin had returned in time for this. Jenn tried to stop herself because she was proud of Peter's attempt, but damn it all, they needed a laugh.

"It is all well and good, Peter. Apologies accepted, but unnecessary. I will forever be in your debt, yours and your father's." He stole a calculating glance towards the wizard, and Jenn observed a knowing nod. "There will never be a need to stand on ceremony around me. Thank you, Peter. Thank you, Colin, and," he looked at Jenn, "Jennifer, I believe Myrddin said?" using the only name Arthur had known him by.

"Yes, your ... Arthur, my name is Jennifer."

The room was silent as Arthur took this in. "Maybe you know, but my wife, the love of my life, was Guinevere, much like..." His voice trailed off.

"We know, Arthur," Jenn replied quietly, with no trace of her former attitude.

Arthur looked back at Lloyd. "Myrddin, I suppose she has passed, my queen, and my sons, Amhar and Loholt?"

"Loholt fell at Camlann, Arthur. Your queen and Amhar, though, died peacefully among friends. We'll get to that story, I promise. And as the legends have grown, the name Merlin has replaced my druidic appellation. A bit of life mimicking art, but that's neither here nor there. In this age, they call me Lloyd." Taking a last gulp from his mug and then slamming it down on the table for effect, he said, "Alright then, let's catch you up on the basics and then put you to bed. Please, everyone take a seat." Colin and Jenn both moved to the open chair next to Arthur. Jenn deferred to her starry-eyed father and grabbed another. Peter pulled up his rolling desk chair from the computer room. They were ready to listen to a story they knew by heart, told in a manner they'd never expected to hear.

Lloyd began, "Arthur, do you remember the battle with Mordred at Camlann?"

Arthur nodded. "Like yesterday, yet..."

Lloyd slapped his hands on the table and broke into a big smile. "Excellent, Arthur, your memory is intact. For you, it was yesterday. Well, my boy, that day, that battle, was one thousand five hundred years ago. You've been sleeping for over a millennium." All eyes were on Arthur as Lloyd allowed that to sink in. No person had ever been told that. Nobody could predict his reaction.

Arthur slumped back in his chair, fixing his gaze on Lloyd. He raised an eyebrow as if expecting him to admit to a jest. With that not forthcoming, he looked down at his hands and then looked up at the ceiling. "One thousand years," he whispered. "It was my birthday…"

"One thousand five hundred years," Lloyd corrected. His unrepentant lack of empathy was on full display. The wizard bobbed his head and waited for Arthur to react further.

In the silence, Colin stepped to the icebox and pulled out five bottles. Snatching the magnetic opener from the side of the fridge, he said, "Beer, anyone?"

Arthur looked up and smiled, understanding the sentiment behind the offer. "Yes, Colin, a beer sounds excellent," he said.

Colin opened and distributed the beers, then sat down. Lloyd offered a silent 'Cheers', and they all took a pull. "Arthur, do you remember the boat, Morgana, and the room?"

"Yes, Myrddin, I do. I struck Morgana down on the banks of Avalon and … well, she turned into smoke, and you put me … put me … well, to rest in her underground sanctuary." Arthur's head dropped to examine the label of the bottle, slowly turning it in his hands.

"Well, yes, yes. And please call me Lloyd. We will shortly insert you into the public, and it wouldn't do to prompt any queries regarding my identity. Now, without going into the details, few of which you'd understand anyway, I spent most of my energy conjuring a spell that would suspend you until I needed you again. Morgana has returned, and Arthur, and only you can defeat her. Did you bring Excalibur?"

Arthur cast his look about the room, rising from his seat, until he saw it standing against the end of a counter. "I did," he said, "but what could my sister want in this age? And why was it necessary that I be the one to confront her?"

"So many questions," the old wizard sighed. "I suspect her intention is to complete the conquest of Britain that began when her

army laid siege to Camelot in 537. As to why I still need you..."
Lloyd paused for a gulp of his beer. "That is a bit more
complicated."

"Excalibur! Of course!" Colin blurted out. "May I hold it,
m'lord?"

Arthur waved permission dismissively, and Colin jumped to his
feet more quickly than Jenn had seen him move in months.

Lloyd's hand on his arm stopped him short. "Colin, please. Not
now. There will be time for that later."

Crestfallen, Colin sat back down in a slump.

"Yes, thank you. Now, when you thrust that sword," gesturing
back at Excalibur, "into Morgana's heart, her devilish sorcery
allowed her essence, her soul as moderns might call it, to leave her
physical body. That was the black vapor you saw. I should have
foreseen that, but alas, was as surprised as you were. My initial goal
was to use the power of Avalon to restore your health right away,
but when I saw that turn of events, I needed to adjust my plans. She
couldn't stay in that state forever and would need to find a host to
survive. And find a host she would.

"However, there was no way for me to calculate how long it
would take for her to discover someone suitable because I didn't yet
know what dark magic she had used. I saw that you and your sister
exchanged something on the battlefield when you met her sword
with Excalibur, when all other weapons failed against her
enchantments. I guessed, and have confirmed, having had centuries
to examine the facts, that your shared blood, your mother Igraine,
will protect you from her magic, even if no other can resist it. Who
you are should give you the upper hand in a confrontation. You
understand this? Still following me?" All nodded, waiting for Lloyd
to continue.

"I couldn't foresee this eventual confrontation, so I couldn't be
sure that I would have the strength to stop her alone. As it turned
out, I depleted my magical energy when I conjured the two spells
for Arthur in that cave, both of which should be obvious to all by

now." He paused, expecting that this wouldn't, in fact, be obvious to any of them.

Jenn took the bait and asked, "What two spells are you referring to, Mr. Wyse, Merlin, please?"

"Why, first a suspended state, dear girl, and Lloyd is fine. I thought that was elementary. Clearly, it was not permanent, as evidenced by the fact that we're all sitting here in your kitchen. My spell, beyond the skills of any other wizard that ever lived, I can tell you, would waken Arthur only when Morgana had returned. That he is awake means she is back. Exactly where is still a mystery, but I suspect in London."

"The murders," Peter offered. "The crazy women who killed their husbands!"

"Yes, Peter, well said! That is my suspicion, but we'll get to that later." Lloyd sat back, ready to accept the praise and gratitude of all. Nothing.

"Annnnnd … What was the second spell?" Jenn asked, breaking the awkward silence.

"Well, didn't you find it strange, young lady, that you could speak to Arthur as if he'd stepped off a bus from Southampton?"

Caught up in the afternoon's excitement, she hadn't thought much about that. He was British, so of course he spoke English … but there was no English in Arthur's day.

Seeing the light of recognition in Jenn's eyes, Lloyd continued, "Yes, you see, in a flash of brilliance, I cast a spell that would allow him to converse in the language of the land when he woke. Granted, I fully expected it to be Saxon, or maybe French, but here we are speaking English together." He held his hands out in a 'you're welcome' gesture and beamed.

Arthur was the first to react. "Anglish? Saxon? Then we lost, and the Angles and Saxons conquered our island. All was for naught?"

"No, my son, but yes, Angles and Saxons did take Britain, at least as you knew it, then the French and then … well, it sort of became an amalgam of everywhere. You'll learn of all that later, but this country you protected became, for a time, the greatest power in the world, greater than the Romans, in fact. Sometimes, despite themselves, I might add. It certainly wasn't for naught."

"But you've remained, Myrddin," Arthur whispered.

"Yes, Arthur, I have remained. I depleted most of my magic to keep you safe, but am still, and I suspect always will be, by nature of the affliction, immortal. My story is your story, son, and we'll save that for a later date. What you need to know now is that I required your squire, young Bedivere, to swear me an oath. That oath was to ensure, by whatever means necessary, that his family and his descendants would watch for you to wake from your long sleep. This oath passed from father to son, mother to daughter, until today. Standing before you are the direct sons and a daughter of your beloved Bedivere. Colin, Peter, and of course, Jennifer Pelling."

The impact and the historicity of the oath Bedivere made fifteen centuries ago finally sank in for Jenn at that moment. None moved or spoke.

Arthur broke the silence again. He rose and bowed to each Pelling. "And I, Arthur, once king, am eternally in debt to your family, and I thank you for accepting me into it, as I fear I have none left to call my own. I afford you my protection and can assure you I will compensate you well once I have secured matters of state and my place in the realm."

The sadness in this last statement overwhelmed Jenn. A man out of time, with no proper place in the realm, or even this age. Now wasn't the time. He'd have to come to terms with it as events progressed. "Of course," was all she said, "Of course."

"Yes, yes, beautiful and well said, Arthur, but now I must insist that we clean you up and put you to bed. We'll talk in the morning. This has been more than enough for the night." He stood, stepped up to embrace Arthur one last time, and walked to the door. As he stepped out, he smiled and winked, saying, "And Arthur, there are more. They will come. Until tomorrow." He stepped into the evening air, pulling his cloak tighter around him to brace against the dropping temperature.

Chapter 14

Sweater weather had returned to London, but the crisp air didn't dampen the spirits of children in Green Park, both young and adult, kicking footballs, chasing discs, or simply enjoying what might always be the last sunny day of the season. The cheer of that early October day failed to pierce Meghan's grim mood as she strode from Buckingham Palace towards Wellington Arch.

Meghan had grown accustomed to Morgana's presence and took comfort in her companionship. She'd never had a friend who understood her as Morgana did, who gave her permission to hate. On this day, Morgana promised to share an important chapter in her story. One, she said, would solidify Meghan's understanding of why they needed to tear down the patriarchal society and rebuild it, by force if necessary. *This is for all our sisters, young one.*

Morgana, walking by her side, was as real to Meghan as any other person in the park. Other strollers would have seen a lone woman, head bent in deep thought and occasionally speaking quietly to herself. They might have noted Meghan's long black leather coat, steampunk knee-high boots, and tight black jeans. Her outfit wasn't out of place for the city or the times. For Meghan only, Morgana's garb was also monochromatic but of a different age. Her leather shoes were shapeless, and the oversized hooded cloak hid much of her severe face, head cocked to reflect their candid conversation.

"I didn't even try to hide my disgust and hatred for Uther," the apparition said. "I wasn't blind to the tension that permeated our fractured home and the pain I caused my mother. Yet I held back what I'd seen the night my father died, even when she gave birth to that atrocity, Arthur, who was nothing more than a changeling to me."

"Arthur? THE King Arthur was really conceived from that?"

"Fitting, don't you think? Man's greatest hero was a freak accident of violent lust. I withdrew from all things and sought dark corners, away from prying eyes, to plot my revenge. But in fact, my mind only sank lower as I realized how powerless I was; young and female in a world where we held less power than the lowliest male slave. I lashed out at my impotence in petty ways, but that was unsatisfying. And Uther knew it was simply a matter of time before he'd need to take action to suppress me. I'd seen, hadn't I?

"The usurper combed Brittania for a man to take me off his hands, away from Tintagel, to put me in my place. 'We must find a man to break you,' he would say, but I was no steed to be broken. I put my madness on full display for these suitors. None lingered. No man would own me. I'd rather die … and if that was my fate, I wouldn't be dying alone.

"When no man would have me, or to be precise, when I had driven them all away through one means or another, Uther knew he'd run out of options and time. His cruel solution was to exile me to an isolated Christian outpost in Isca. It's called Exeter now, little sister, where we first met."

Meghan stopped. "That church? Do you mean…?"

"Yes, little sister, and soon you'll know why our life together needed to begin there."

The walk continued. "You see, Mother and my sisters had adopted the cult of Jesus after Father's death. Not me though. I could see *that* God's love didn't extend to the wretched in our realm, and certainly not to me. Uther used this new god to manipulate Mother's pain and guilt. Her weakness sealed my fate, *but Christ's succubi penned my future*."

Color drained out of the grass, trees, and sky. For the first time since their first encounter, Meghan felt fear. Then, as quickly as it came, normalcy returned, and the walk continued.

Morgana exhaled loudly and continued. "Uther ambushed me

with this news as a contingent of soldiers appeared. They would escort me across the land that afternoon. That coward could barely hide his smirk as he told me, 'I would be a bride of Jesus since I will never be the bride of any mortal man.' I learned later that a sizable dowry and a promise of yearly stipends to ensure I would never threaten his sovereignty or peace again preceded my holy nuptials.

"'This is a lifetime commitment, my dear,' Uther said, still smiling. Then, to maintain the pretense of caring, stooped to kiss me. I shoved him with all the strength I could summon and spat in his face. A backhand blow to my face spun me as I fell to my knees. He then turned his back on me, forever in his mind. Yet, with clenched fists, I swore we would meet again, and mine would be the last face he saw.

"So it was that in three days' time, at eleven years old, armed guards escorted me into the crumbling Roman walls of Isca."

Morgana clasped Meghan's upper arm, bringing her into the memory. "You need to join me in this, little sister, to experience it as I did. Open your mind to me."

Meghan's vision swirled, and she would have stumbled had Morgana not guided her to a bench. Green Park was gone, and in the muddy ruts of ancient Isca, she watched the now familiar young Morgan step off a cart surrounded by four armed men with red leather jerkins.

Morgan looked neither left nor right, so Meghan stepped forward to join her. "Morgan, I'm here…" but the contingent walked past with no acknowledgement.

Taking in her surroundings, the dark ages church was neither elegant nor coherent. The austere façade rose from scavenged materials patched together over centuries. There were no straight lines to be seen, and layers of mud and mold obscured the surfaces. Maybe because of a heightened awareness in this state, or maybe because of the bleak, ghost-like appearance of all she saw in Morgan's consciousness, she felt that this might be the gateway to the underworld of the old gods, where no joy could penetrate, and no escape was possible. This was where Uther sent her to die.

Morgan's retinue stopped when the front doors opened, seemingly on their own, and a bowed, worn woman stepped out.

"I am Sister Agnes," she mumbled to no one as she shuffled forward.

Sister Agnes was a bent, bitter woman of indeterminate age. Her brown cotton garments were dirty and torn, sewn together from remnants of different styles and levels of wear, and her face showed years of trial and strife, deep-set wrinkles around a toothless mouth. She crossed her arms and cast her eyes to the ground as she approached the armed soldiers. This timidity didn't continue once the king's retinue had departed.

Shepherding Morgan into the building, Sister Agnes sent other bent women out to collect the offering that Uther's men had unceremoniously dumped in the cart path. This allowed Meghan an opportunity to assess their surroundings. The interior looked even smaller than she might have guessed from the outside. To the right of the entrance were three parallel logs, benches for group worship. The floor was dirt except for the small area in front of those black-stained trunks. There, the builders had set flat stones to create something of a paved floor abutting a wall that was bare except for a crude sculpture of Christ on the cross.

The body of Christ was roughly rendered but recognizable. His tortured face had monopolized the artist's time and effort. Meghan wondered how anyone could look upon that visage without revulsion. *What kind of pathetic god allowed themselves to be strung up?* Morgana gave Meghan a secretive half-glance. *During my time at Isca, I rejected this cult of Christ and recommitted to the old gods. I needed their strength.*

On the left side of the room were a handful of women, each more ragged than the next. As Meghan processed this world, all the women looked up in unison to meet her gaze. *Can they see me? No, they're looking at Morgan.* The princess's clothing was clean and opulent in contrast to their dirt and poverty. Her hair was neat and

81

pulled back in a jeweled comb, whereas the Sisters of Isca's hair was unkempt, greasy, gray, and thinning. She was not from this life or this world, and the sisters ferally resented her. They didn't hide it as Agnes guided her to the middle of the room.

One leering face was unlike the rest, and Meghan was instantly afraid. A gray old man in a peaked leather cap looked up from the small animal he was skinning over a half-barrel tub. He looked at Morgan hungrily and lasciviously. "I'm Drabach, m'lady. I take care of things 'round here for the sisters. If there is anything you need, you just call Drabach."

This old man was in her vision at St. Olave's. Meghan could not take another step, overwhelmed by the sight of this troll. She felt bony fingers on her shoulder. Sister Agnes was pushing her, not Morgana, towards the ancient door, the door that had changed her life.

Morgana's voice whispered from the depths of her mind. *I am here with you. We will do this together because you must learn of this place. From the horrors of this hell came the strength, the power, and the will to do what must be done, what WE must finish.*

Meghan clutched the handle, disengaged the latch, and pulled the door open.

Instead of blackness, she stepped back into the common area of the abbey, through the front door as she had upon Morgan's arrival! Vertigo blackened her vision, and she groped for the door frame. Seconds, *maybe minutes*, passed until she could step away from her anchor. She soon found Morgan, taller and older, now moving with the same lethargy as the prior inhabitants of this hellhole. Her once beautiful hair was now dirty and stringy, matching those who'd come before. Meghan couldn't even guess how long it had been since she'd brushed it.

Moving closer, Meghan could see that her hands and bare feet were red and calloused, but she could also see that the sunup-to-sundown labor had toughened her. Her eyes were still clear, darting side to side, missing nothing. Meghan hoped, no ... knew, she still dreamed of escape. She also knew that Morgan had no plan. With access to her soulmate's mind, Meghan knew someone watched the girl's every step. Morgan was the reason carts of provisions showed up every few months; thus, she was too valuable to risk losing, even though they spat on her and beat her.

Sister Agnes appeared at Morgan's side. While the others were drifting off in the waning light, Agnes was pointing Morgan to another pile of rotten, waste-covered hay that needed to be swept out.

"Please, Sister," she heard Morgan ask. "You must find me a bed up here, with the other sisters. You know what he's…"

A slap to the young girl's face stopped her fast. Morgan no longer gave the satisfaction of tears and knew better than to respond in any other way.

"I must do nothing, you whore of Satan. And I will not listen to your fabrications about our caretaker or any other member of this community. If you earn sisterhood, which is highly doubtful considering your arrogance and sloth, we'll reconsider. But until then, the cells underneath are better than you deserve." The older woman stepped away but turned back. "And down is where you'll go when you've swept out this corner. No lingering and disrupting the prayers of the devoted, or you'll experience the Lord's wrath as you've never imagined." She finally turned and shuffled away.

Meghan longed to comfort her young friend but knew she could only observe. She sank to the floor as Morgan finished with the mess, placed her straw broom in a corner, and made her way to that door, the portal where this all began. Taking a candle from an iron receptacle, Morgan opened the door and, after a long pause, descended. Meghan jumped up and hastened to follow, but as her foot touched the first stair, the door slammed shut and pushed a wave of air that extinguished the candlelight she was following.

Illumination returned as a weak torch, near the bottom of the stairway-bright enough to identify the end of the descent but not so much as to reveal the floor beyond. In the flickering light, the stairs looked like a beggarly constructed bridge where a misstep promised death. This bridge ended at an abyss, and into that emptiness, Morgan stepped. It took all the courage Meghan could muster, a veritable leap of faith, to venture off the last step and trust she wouldn't fall forever in silent darkness.

With that last step, violent, disjointed memories of Morgan's ordeal in this godforsaken pit accosted Meghan's consciousness.

How many nights had she longed for the escape of that infinite fall, a gentler, kinder fate than what was waiting for her in the shadows? Death would free her from his wet, dirty claws. Free her from the cruelty of the sisters, who beat her relentlessly before casting her into the darkness and the horrors they knew would be waiting.

As a macabre play for an audience of one, Meghan experienced the first night he came to Morgan in the dark, retching at his very real smell as he covered the girl's mouth and forced himself on her. Morgan tried to fight, but she was so small. Meghan lunged, but nothing she did brought her any closer to stopping this vile act.

"Now you'll be keeping our relationship just between us, Princess. The good sisters wouldn't listen, and even if they did, wouldn't care. However, I might not be as loving and gentle next time if I felt you betrayed our trust. Don't forget, Princess," he said as he left her, alone, bleeding and crying on the straw pallet that passed for a bed. The orange light faded.

After an eternity of absolute darkness, the torch sputtered to life again. Morgan was now lying on that filthy pallet, listening, smelling, trying to sense minute changes in the air that warned her of his approach. The young girl's terror was overwhelming.

A second flickering and spitting flame in a trembling hand announced his approach. After he'd taken her in the darkness, he needed more. He needed to see the suffering and fear. He started bringing an oil lantern with him, black smoke curling, playing, mocking her as he forced her to lie still and suffer his fingers everywhere. In this orange light, Meghan saw him as the beast he was, the form he hid in the light of day when the sisters were watching. Amid the random patches of hair covering his body, the grease on his chest and stomach bore the tracks of his scratching at the parasites who shared his living decay.

Morgan fought to abandon her physical self while he did the unspeakable things. She'd wake up dirty and reeking of his body, but could not remember exactly what he'd done to her. This, and Morgan's obsession with revenge, were the only ways the girl could keep her sanity and continue. With each defilement, she thought of the man, Uther. This monster was the evil in Uther personified, and each depravity bolstered her resolve the next morning. While that never made it tolerable, never relieved the terror, it stoked primeval flames within her, promising an eruption that would reshape this land forever.

Meghan curled up in a corner of the cell, shaking from her inability to avenge this poor girl's treatment. Her head dropped; her eyes closed. Her mind went black.

Chapter 15

"Dad, if you can spare our guest, he could really use some fresh air and a stretch," Jenn said. "I mean, Arthur, if you can tear yourself away from the differences between Malory and White's fictional accounts of your life and death?"

"But, Jennifer, we've really just begun," Colin said. "You see, Arthur, lines can be drawn back through Monmouth all the way back to Gildas, if you simply…"

Arthur pulled himself up from the sofa and said, "Yes, Colin … well, I think a stretch is best, and while I do appreciate the lesson, I must take my leave."

"Of course, of course. I'll draw up a few diagrams we can review when…"

"Bye, Dad," Jenn said as she guided Arthur out the front door. Peter followed with a sheepish smile.

They set off for the town center on that cool and overcast Thursday afternoon. Arthur, dressed in jeans and a plaid flannel shirt, caught the occasional eye, but as a handsome stranger, not as a Dark Ages warlord. "If anyone asks," Jenn told him, "you're a distant cousin from Cornwall, passing through while finishing your book on medieval Britain. Let Peter or me do the talking."

"Why the subterfuge? I walked openly among my people in a more dangerous time. I'm sure the common folk would welcome the opportunity to, well … welcome me."

"Right, I'm sure they would," Jenn said, with an eye roll that surely created a breeze. "But, as Lloyd said, we don't know where Morgana is or what form she's taken. Best she doesn't learn of your presence before we're ready, if you take my meaning."

Walking on, Jenn noticed Arthur absentmindedly dragging his fingers along the length of parked cars. "Pretty cool, huh?" she said. "Who needs horses?"

"But how do these steel chariots propel themselves, I wonder?" Arthur asked. "There is so much I need to learn."

"Peter, do you want to take a stab at this?" Jenn asked.

"Sure, you see, they have internal combustion engines that..." His voice trailed off. He could see that Arthur's attention had drifted to other things.

On High Street, the conversation turned to governance. "I will say, the town is wonderfully ordered and clean, but I don't believe this can be maintained without a firm hand watching over the people."

"But that's the beauty of a democratic society," Jenn said. "We all chip in because we're all equal and it's in everyone's best interest, not out of fear or mandate."

"True, the people look well-fed and content, but this equality is not the natural way of things. Some are meant to rule, some to fight, and others to serve. I mean, you said there is always a king or queen to ensure order is kept, correct?"

"There has always been a king or queen," Jenn said. "But the role is mostly ceremonial, I'm afraid."

"Ceremonial? That can't be true. From the mists of time, there are men chosen by the gods, obliged, if you will, to lead, and those destined to be led. The common folk lack the imagination, the wisdom, to make decisions for the greater populace."

"Pardon me, your haughtiness," Jenn snapped. "But this commoner knows we are now better positioned to build a world that works for everyone, not just a privileged few; and certainly not just men."

Arthur laughed off her outburst. "But, Lady Jennifer, you descend from nobility. In the absence of a true ruler, I'd expect you, and those like you, to step up."

Peter jumped in and said, "Just look around you, Arthur. These shops, these streets, these people, have collectively built a society that is generally free of sickness, desolation, and fear. I think we've done pretty well without a ruling class."

Jenn snorted. "Hah! We still have a ruling class. It's defined by money now, men with money to be more specific, not birthright and certainly not merit."

Arthur looked to Peter for clarification. "Surely, Peter, at least you understand this is…"

Peter put his hand up. "I think maybe you need to live in our world a few more weeks before we try to explain how complicated it's become." Casting a furtive glance at Jenn, he said, "In a good way, though."

The trio walked in silence until Arthur stopped at the windows of a shoe store. "This may be one of the greatest achievements of your age, Peter." He gestured to the hiking boots he'd been wearing since coming off the hill. "These shoes are incredible. I could walk for days with no pain. Even my most prized sandals tortured the foot."

Jenn laughed. "On the importance of shoes, my lord, we do agree."

For the rest of the walk, Arthur peppered Jenn and Peter with questions like a child. And, like a child, Jenn noted, he wanted to know more about what people thought of him. Some of the King Arthur lore and legends Colin had shared weighed heavily on his mind.

"Sure, Galahad was fair, but no more so than many," Arthur scoffed. "Most perfect? Hah!" Arthur then laughed about the fictional Sir Lancelot, but fell into melancholy when Peter let slip that stories were written about his wife's infidelity with this hard-to-pin-down character. "Guinevere was true and innocent," Arthur grumbled. "Why would anyone claim otherwise?"

As they turned into their neighborhood, Peter tried to recover by telling Arthur of a lasting local legend that he and Guinevere were buried as man and wife in Glastonbury Abbey. "Yes, that sounds like quite a farce, doesn't it?" he responded. "Although, as we all know now, they only missed the mark by a mile or so. It makes you wonder if someone knew something or if it was just a coincidence."

Stepping through the front door of the Pelling home, they heard a familiar voice from the kitchen. "It wasn't a coincidence, but I can assure you they didn't know what they thought they knew. A story for another day, I fear." The three explorers walked into the kitchen to find Lloyd, already on his second pint to Colin's first, sitting opposite the older Pelling at the table.

"Dad, what are you doing home so early?" Jenn asked.

"The lads are watching the store, dear," Colin replied, slowly levering himself up from the table to grab a beer for Arthur. "I think the circumstances permit some flexibility with the established order." After handing the drink to the king with a bow, he shuffled back and slipped into his chair.

Jenn looked from her father to the refrigerator and back a few times with a lowered brow, then huffed at his obliviousness and rose to grab a beer for herself and Peter.

Lloyd spoke up. "Sit please, all of you. I have much more to tell, and have always felt stories are best told over a pint. If you would please, pull up chairs and let me prepare you for what will happen in the next few days." Peter, Jenn, and Arthur gathered around the table and settled in. Lloyd had been unreachable over the three days since Arthur awoke, and they were bursting with questions.

"Arthur, if you recall, after Bedivere successfully transported you to the docks across from the island of Avalon, I bade him return to the battle."

"I was greatly fatigued, my old friend, but recall him leaving us. I didn't have the faculties to put more thought into it than that."

"Not to worry, you were mostly baggage at the time. I didn't need your input," Lloyd retorted and then resumed his tale. "His orders were to return to Camlann, find any of your captains who had a reasonable chance of surviving the day, and have them meet me in Aquae Sulis five days hence; that's modern-day Bath," he clarified for the Pellings. "I arranged a private room at the Bear Claw Tavern. Six of your captains, plus Bedivere, arrived that evening. They described to me how the battle ended. As expected, once we removed the two heads of that cursed force, Morgana and Mordred, it failed. Those who could run, ran. Your troops slaughtered many but spared men who pleaded for mercy if they swore an oath of fealty to you, Arthur. Spoil was plentiful, and the crows ate well."

He paused, looking at Arthur as the two silently shared memories. Colin broke the silence by asking, "Who made it to the Bear Claw that night, Lloyd?"

"Right, yes," he said. "Let's stay on point. Bedivere arrived first and said he'd spoken to many but didn't know who would come. You see, to many, with Saxons still active on our borders, whether Arthur was alive or dead wasn't important."

Arthur jumped up from his chair. "You say that my kingdom was leaderless, enemies were swarming, and my fate wasn't important?"

"Arthur, don't be a fool. The Saxons were going to prevail. You bought the Britons a few more years, but the outcome was inevitable."

"That is not so! Our victory at Camlann would have united the clans. Our ranks would have swelled and…"

"Listen to the history Colin shared with you, Arthur. ALL the kingdoms of your age failed, transformed, reformed, and failed again. You survived and are back. Your land, regardless of name or monarch, has survived and has become a world power. That is the important part." He stared Arthur back into his seat, not mollified but content, for now, to continue listening.

"Back at the Bear Claw, six of your men joined me in a solemn blood pact. Cai, Perceval, Bors, Morfran, Galahad, and, of course, Gawain, shared a meal with me."

Colin shot his arms into the air, pumping his fists with an ear-to-ear grin. "They *were* real, all of them. I knew it!"

Lloyd reached out for Colin's shoulder with a squeeze and continued. "I offered them a glimpse into the future that none but their blood would ever know. The price of this knowledge would be high. I shared with them my prophecy of Morgana's return and of Arthur's internment. I didn't discuss your location and asked them not to seek you. When you returned, they would be told where to meet you. That night, we came together as Keepers of the Realm. It didn't sound as corny then as it does now, but it was a great honor and a monumental task.

"Each man swore an oath to commit themselves, their fortunes, and their families to the support of their king when he needed them," Lloyd explained. "It might come quickly, or it might take generations. Therefore, they were binding both their immediate families and their descendants to the cause for as long as it might take."

Jenn sat back and folded her arms. "Are you telling us you expected a legend, a legend of an oath from antiquity, would survive, I don't know, sixty or seventy generations over six bloodlines?"

"I deemed it reasonable to expect they might pass the oath over a few generations. But to your point, I anticipated that distant generations, lifetimes removed from the origin, may need a sign of its credibility and solemnity. I'd prepared for this."

He leaned across the table. "I brought six knives to the tavern. Embedded in the grip of each was a piece of the King's Stone, the same stone that gave Excalibur its pommel." He looked up at Arthur as recognition seeped into his face.

"You kept that stone locked in your quarters at Camelot and, before that, in your cave under Tintagel," Arthur said to Lloyd. He turned to face the Pellings, who were rapt with attention. "You see, this black stone had been handed down from generation to generation in my father's family from the rulers of the land beyond memory. They brought the stone out only for coronations, along with that old sword, Excalibur." He gestured to the broadsword resting unceremoniously in the corner of a countryside kitchen. "It has been said that only kings crowned in the presence of this stone were destined to rule. It was something of a tradition, but I never assumed it was more than that."

"That 'old sword' and 'just an old tradition'," Colin spat. "Preposterous!"

Peter then started forward, eager to contribute. "But that must be the Stone of Scone! See, there is an old stone, although it's sandy red, not black, that is fabled to be a relic that bestowed the throne to the ordained ruler. It was just recently returned to Edinburgh. That's in Scotland."

Lloyd clarified to Arthur that this town was called Din Eidyn in the sixth-century land of Lothian.

"King Edward the First took this relic to England in 1296, and it has been at the center of every royal coronation since," Peter continued. "Is this the same stone, your King's Stone?"

"That is certainly what we wanted those fools to believe back then, and they were easy enough to manipulate. Strength and advantage were so difficult to maintain that any superstitious relic believed to offer an edge was coveted. No, Peter, as you noted yourself, the Stone of Scone is sandstone-colored, while the true King's Stone was black with red flakes; more like bloodstone as we know it today. In those ancient times, this stone was imbued with exceptional powers if one knew how to harness them, as I did for these weapons, but like so many important relics, it too is now lost." He paused again, looking down into his glass while everyone waited. He lifted the mug to his mouth, drained the remaining beer, wiped his mustache on his sleeve, and asked Colin for another. "Once again, an amusing distraction that I might entertain you with another day, but we need to get back to the Bear Claw Tavern.

"I enchanted those daggers with the power of the stone to bind themselves to one person at a time. This would be a direct blood descendant of the original owner if they followed the proper ritual.

I initiated each man that night and bound them to perform the same rites when a worthy son or daughter was ready to accept the responsibility. I composed a mystical-sounding oath to make it seem more real, but any words would do. The key was sincerity and the exchange of blood. Once the dagger was bound to a Keeper, it couldn't harm him or her.

"When, say, Cai for example, was ready to pass along the oath, he would drag the blade across his palm to show that there was no blood, then drag it across his heir's. The blade was always sharp and cut the initiate's hand cleanly. Cai and his child, or designate, would then grasp hands and speak the oath. When they released their grip, if the delegate was committed to the oath, the wound would have transferred to Cai's hand, and the dagger would have passed to the next Keeper. It was effective and achieved the proper purpose."

Jenn had done the calculations in her head many times. "Even so, over 1,500 years..."

"Even I couldn't have predicted it would take so long, my dear, but the magic of the stone was strong. To ease the path, the families of Keepers were endowed with a bit of unusual good luck, making them less likely to be fatally surprised or fall in a reasonably equal contest. This serendipity, if you will, also crossed over to their financial fortunes, ensuring that their lines would be well cared for and could contribute to the needs of the cause." He gestured into the adjoining room with all the computer monitors. "Who did you think provided for your family's well-being and all the toys Peter has accumulated? The trust fund you were so skeptical of, Jennifer?"

"I guess that all makes sense," she said, "but our family, Bedivere's family, was never held to this blood and dagger ritual. We have no knight's enchanted knife."

"But you always had me, haven't you?" Lloyd chuckled at a joke that nobody else acknowledged. "Your role was too important to be left unsupervised. I have always been here for your family and have overseen the passing down of the oath. I don't recall that I needed parlor tricks to convince you of the reality of our quest," he said to Colin.

"No, you didn't, Lloyd! No, you most certainly did not," Colin said.

Peter's face had been agape with a wide-eyed stare since Lloyd started this story. Jenn listened with her arms crossed in disbelief. She couldn't gauge Arthur's reaction by his expression, but he hung on every word.

"Maybe if you'd offered me a magic knife…" Jenn muttered.

"Your scientific mind would have only found another reason to doubt, Jennifer," Lloyd said. "Once you'd made up your mind, young lady, it was in the mission's best interest to keep you out of the loop."

Jenn's mouth opened, but she had no retort. She glared at her father, then at Peter. Her gaze fell on Arthur and softened. This wasn't about her.

Finally, the king spoke. "Can we please get back to the matter at hand?" To Colin, he said, "Or must we entertain all your daughter's whims while the rest of us sit idly by?"

Jenn's expression hardened again, but she couldn't decide whether his arrogance or his dismissal of her as simply Colin's daughter bothered her more.

Arthur continued, "So you are telling me that the heirs of Cai, Bors, Galahad, Gawain, Perceval, and Morfran are out there waiting to be summoned? That they will rally to me to combat Morgana, wherever or whatever she may be up to, correct?"

"Nearly so, Arthur, except that the line of Morfran died out around the turn of the last century. It was 1914, I believe, in Belgium."

"Yet the others live. Remarkable. Then how do we contact these modern-day warriors?" Arthur asked.

"This, my boy, has already begun," the wizard responded with a cryptic smile.

Chapter 16

With one e-mail, Lloyd's click, a machine awakened to a message nobody ever expected to hear. Maintaining this machine, keeping all the pieces whole and lubricated, consumed much of Lloyd's time. He'd learned to work behind shell companies and law offices over the past centuries to reduce his traveling. This was critical because the network had become global, spanning four continents, six countries, and many military and intelligence organizations.

He visualized the spread of the message as flaming paths across a kindling-strewn field, fire rushing in a line until it branched and then branched again. Conflagrations sprang up at the terminus of a branch, each in a glorious blaze, signifying the signal had reached its recipient.

***

The first explosion happened as the rising sun was waking the remaining men of the 2nd Ox and Bucks, The Oxfordshire and Buckinghamshire Light Infantry, a proud but decimated and exhausted component of the British Expeditionary Force's front line in the Great War. As Major Chance Lewis scrambled to gather his gear, the bombs and missiles started falling with hellish regularity. Major Lewis was determined to set an example for the younger boys in this now-godforsaken Belgian valley. There wasn't much he could do but try to stem the losses, both physically and mentally.

At ten o'clock, orders came to clear the German-held trenches at Nonne Bosschen. Outnumbered three to one in this battle, the BEF needed to make up for their lack of men with pluck and surprise. When the call to advance came, Major Lewis and company were on the left flank of the southeasterly movement. Within moments of the order to move out, Major Lewis signaled his men to stop. He had seen dark figures silhouetted against the snowy ground to his left; their flank was exposed. Grabbing the five closest men to him, the young officer led a charge into the surprised German force and, after what devolved into hand-to-hand fighting, ended the threat which might have doomed the greater attack.

Major Chance Lewis received the Victoria Cross posthumously for his gallantry in 1914. Merlin learned of his death when Morfran's dagger appeared in a deep pocket of his old gray cloak.

***

When Merlin and Prince Gawain arrived in Lothian after Camlann, they found a man ready to step into his place in history. King Lot had kept his land neutral in the conflict that Mordred had incited through the efforts of his sons, who had seen the treachery in their cousin. Therefore, he could receive and act on Merlin's news about the fall of the king from a position of strength. Merlin convinced Gawain to support the story that Arthur had died from Mordred's blow but that his body had been buried in secret to prevent desecration. Only Lot had enough power and respect to step up to the mantle of High King and bond the fractured British forces into a legitimate resistance to the ongoing Saxon invasion. Unknown to Gawain, King Lot swore an oath to Merlin for an equally important mission on this visit. He would accept responsibility for the Queen and her priceless consignment.

When the north finally fell, Gawain's family negotiated for the best conditions possible and remained in a position of authority for generations. Various colonial governorships in the expanding British Empire took the dagger to Hong Kong, India, and finally, in the nineteenth century, South Africa.

The whistle blew No Side on a hotly contested Super League Rugby match as Danie Swanepoel, the left half of the crushing Blue

Bulls second row, pounded the Sharks outside center into touch. Jumping to his feet, right hand pumping in the air, his twin brother, John, met him in a hug that would have crushed an average-sized man. John and Danie were both six feet six inches in height and a sausage away from three-hundred pounds. Their longish blond hair and green eyes, sporting fuller than usual lashes, softened their appearance, as long as you weren't carrying the ball. Nothing would soften that look. This was their last game with the Pretoria team, and they were determined to leave on a high note. Burying the Sharks, their Durban-based rivals, certainly qualified. John and Danie had shared everything since they were child terrors in the otherwise ordered home of Major-General (Retired) Petr Swanepoel. More inclined to battle in sport than warfare, they were both accomplished academics and had accepted associate professor positions in engineering at the University of Cape Town; John in Mechanical Engineering and Danie in the growing field of Mechatronics. Of course, this was the furthest thing from their minds as they exploded into the clubhouse and accepted cold beers from the staff.

"Boys," Coach called out, "I need to speak to you before the celebration gets out of hand." John and Danie looked to see Coach standing next to a smallish man in a wrinkled dark suit; a few days of unshaven stubble over an otherwise nondescript face.

The gossip and discussion among teammates would go on for weeks. None of them ever learned why, after leaving Coach's office, John and Danie showered, changed and hustled out the door with an unacceptable level of decorum. All agreed, though, that they both had the same look of joy, awe, and purpose as they took their leave.

***

Galahad and Bors left the Bear Claw together that fateful night after Camlann. They both took Merlin's prophecy to heart. Britain as they knew it would fall to the Angle and Saxon invaders. As they walked the streets of Aquae Sulis, they agreed to stay together and bind their families' fates as further assurance in the fulfillment of their vow to the sleeping king. They traveled to the land that would become France and established legacies that would be remembered as just and generous. Both their families embraced Christianity and funded the construction of stunning cathedrals across the French countryside. Family legend held that descendants of these Round Table warriors helped found and guide the Knights Templar in their early days.

On Friday, October 13, 1307, King Phillip of France shattered their lives as Templars and their eight-century family bond when he launched his purge on the mystic organization. On that day, consistent with the good fortune that seemed to follow both their families, Templar Knights, Dreu de Rochefort and Simon Martel, were passing through the outskirts of Lyon. Clothed in secular garb on a fact-finding mission for their leadership in Paris, they learned of the King's treachery and the near-instantaneous roll-up of their organization. Neither De Rochefort, as fierce and hulking as Martel was lithe and quick, could know they were spitting images of their Arthurian ancestors. Widespread Templar persecution meant that they could no longer remain together. Each would need to find their place in the greater world where they could lie low until the madness passed. The families of Bors and Galahad would not unite again for seven-hundred more years.

Mikol Muller was a former Austrian Army sniper and captain of the Austrian Olympic shooting team. He was now owner, lead instructor, and sole employee of Innsbruck Alpine Ski and Shoot. Muller trained his focus on a target six-hundred meters distant on the practice range he co-owned with three other independent consultants. His dark complexion and size, large for an expert skier, supported his unapproachable persona well. Therefore, even when it became apparent two men, underdressed for the autumn cold, were trying to get his attention, he turned his back and tuned them out. Instead, he focused on the Steyr SSG 69, standard Austrian Army issue, bolt-action sniper rifle and smoothly increased trigger pressure. Anticipating the recoil, he maintained his rigid position, watching the brightly colored wooden cutout through his scope. Only when he saw it fall straight backward, indicating a center shot, did he release his breath, close his eyes to compose himself, and stand. In no hurry to speak to strangers, he turned to face his visitors and waited for them to make their intent clear. The conversation lasted thirty seconds. Mikol grunted his understanding, packed up his gear and followed the men to their waiting Mercedes truck.

If one could script the opposite of Muller in every way, it would be Eric Martel. Five foot six inches of wiry muscle, fair-skinned with a wisp of a beard, carefully groomed to look like he hadn't shaved in two days, Eric was the privileged son of a storied Parisian family. The Martels stood out among other old and known aristocratic families in France for having had a place in all major historical events dating back to Charlemagne. The sons and daughters of Sir Galahad, the "most perfect" of all Arthur's knights, achieved notoriety as military leaders, explorers, and inventors. In the twenty-first century, the mantle passed to the most unlikely of the Martels, Eric. More interested in wine and women than empire building, Eric devoted himself to the banned world of mixed martial arts, or MMA. He self-funded training facilities while supporting efforts to legitimize the sport. Eric's generosity, speed, and fearlessness had made him a celebrity in the underground world of MMA. On top of fighting, Eric took personal pride in his mastery of knife and shuriken, or star, throwing. These more unconventional skills allowed him to sharpen his focus and, as an added benefit, earned him plenty of drinks at a dartboard.

Eric was sitting at his usual table at Le Palace Club near historic Montmartre in Paris after winning a fight in a blacked-out gym, tucked away in a part of the city tourists rarely visited. He was looking forward to an adventurous night with the two young ladies from Chicago, vying for his attention on a back-wall sofa in the darkened establishment. Even though authorities often looked the other way, the fighter knew what he and his colleagues were doing was, in fact, illegal. Out of habit, he monitored the two men in suits stealing glances at him as they moved closer. When they called out his name, he jumped to his feet, spilling the girls' wine glasses. "Qu'est-ce que tu veux?" Eric asked, eyeing the crowds he'd need to manage to access previously established escape routes.

"There is no need for concern," the taller of the two men said. "We need to speak in private, Mr. Martel, regarding your promise ... to your family."

It took a moment for Eric to comprehend the magnitude of this statement, but then his posture relaxed. He nodded to the messengers and turned back to the women, who were dabbing red wine off the only clean party clothes they had left. "Je suis désolé, mes amours," and flashed them the best smile he could muster. "Maybe another night." He then exited the club without looking back.

***

Cai, the hot-headed captain and Arthur's friend since childhood, was the least able to accept the charge Merlin placed on them. Every fiber of his being screamed to act. Under pressure from his comrades, he took the oath but stormed out of the tavern, confident there had to be a better path than hiding and waiting. He went north to build a future beyond the reach of Saxon incursions, hoping to find an opportunity to do something proactive. Eventually, his descendants broke from his fight-first mentality and found fortune in negotiation rather than battle, working behind the scenes when possible. Positioning themselves as peace brokers after the Norman devastation of the North, Cai's family built some of the wealthiest manufacturing centers with an emphasis on defense in the nineteenth and twentieth centuries. Close ties to the military establishment encouraged service from his progeny, although the Jones family offered more engineers than warriors to the Queen's cause into the twenty-first century.

Cynthia Jones, CJ, was a notable exception. Quick-tempered, passionate, and athletic, CJ had always excelled in sports but was never much of a team player. Rising swiftly through the Special

Forces, CJ, the loner, was a natural for the Special Reconnaissance Regiment, which favored traits enabling extended periods of isolation in the most dangerous parts of the world. Her dark complexion and straight black hair allowed her to blend in areas where terrorist recon was required. The irony that the badge of the SRR featured Excalibur, the legendary sword of King Arthur, wasn't lost on CJ, who took her family obligation seriously, almost religiously. Her only fear was the ability to pass it on. The marriage-and-family DNA seemed to have skipped her generation.

When she was summoned without explanation to command in Kabul after months of network building among the Afghans, instincts that had served her well as a covert agent told her that this was it. She remained standing to accept written orders from her lieutenant. The message was brief and to the point. It was time to go home. With a curt "Yessir," CJ pivoted sharply and walked out the door.

***

The responsibility he had solemnly accepted overwhelmed Percival, the youngest of Arthur's captains in the Aquae Sulis gathering. Brave, loyal, and fair were all common descriptions for the young warrior. Creative and self-reliant weren't. He followed Galahad and Bors to France, but it was his children who would brave the return trip back to their father's homeland and establish roots in the seaport towns of South Britain. Dynastically associated with the seas, Percival's descendants would build and captain the ships that brought the might of the British Empire to all corners of the world. The center of the family's fortune would shift to the New World when Lord Hugh Asheton accepted a commission and joined the British force sent to quell the native uprising in the American colonies. Finding himself between countries when fighting ceased, Asheton made a new home for himself in Virginia and built his fortunes in what his family had always known, enabling men to sail the seas.

Julius "Jules" Ashton, a former operative turned desk jockey, was enjoying a light lunch in a small Greenwich Village shop, known for its unique sandwiches, with his wife, Michelle. At forty-five years old, he stopped worrying about the lines circling his mouth and eyes, more visible on his rich walnut skin every day. His once thick black curls were now silver, short, and frustratingly farther from his brow. The move from naval intelligence to the CIA was easier than from a man of action to a man of administration. More importantly though, it was time to start the family he and Michelle had always dreamed of, and he needed to be home for that. His wife was in her second trimester but not yet showing. She was drinking lemonade to avoid caffeine and eyeing Jules' unfinished chicken salad sandwich. Jules was attempting to make a case for an ultrasound determination of the baby's gender when he stopped in mid-sentence, looking up to the cafe door. Michelle was used to sudden and often inopportune interruptions, so she didn't think that was out of the ordinary. "Excuse me, babe," he said as he dropped his napkin on the table and stepped around her chair. She replied, "Uh-huh," and reached to grab his sandwich the moment he turned his back.

She had concealed most of the evidence of the heist by the time he returned a few minutes later. His wife smiled up at him with the most innocent look she could muster, despite the smudge of mayo on the side of her mouth. His expression told her something was wrong. "Babe, I'm going to need to go to the UK for a few weeks. I need to leave right away."

Michelle protested; he promised there wouldn't be any travel with this job, but he cut her off with a soft hand on her arm. "It's not the job Chelle, it's that other thing." The sadness in his otherwise resolute face told her what the 'other thing' he was referring to was. He helped her to her feet, draped his coat over her shoulders and walked her to the waiting Land Rover without further conversation.

Five flights from four continents; one destination - the ancient city of London.

Chapter 17

Awakened by the silent screams of her soulmate, Meghan was no longer on the floor of Morgan's cell but in the main room of the abbey. The fading light of the blue hour rendered the dulled, shuffling sisters as shadows. She couldn't grasp how much time had elapsed. It was a new day, possibly a new year.

She looked about anxiously for her vision guide. As the other sisters dispersed, she saw Morgan, and she regained a link to her consciousness. Her companion, no longer a girl but a young woman, stood motionless, hoping to melt into the background yet expecting to feel his eyes on her any moment, defiling her, lurking, waiting. He was always there, intuitively knowing when she'd be alone. She'd smell his unwashed body and his sour breath before he stepped out of the darkness. She always froze, knowing that resisting or running during the day would only make the nights worse. These encounters - the pawing, the sniffing, and the tongue - would be over quickly because getting caught would complicate things. All the sisters knew about his depravities, but if they didn't see it, they could ignore it. Morgan could only endure, then go back to her chores or face another beating.

But Meghan sensed something was different. Everything would change this night.

She followed Morgan through the portentous door. A thunderous slam plunged them into soul-consuming darkness. Step by step, they descended into that dank space, reeking of urine and sweat, of that creature who cemented their hatred of men.

Wait ... not 'our', but 'my' hatred of men. We passed through the portal as one. I am Morgan again. She reached for the wall until

103

her disorientation passed. Ready to move, she took one step at a time. Holding her breath, she strained for any sounds, fearing the pounding of her heart would drown out the telltale signs of his presence; or worse, that it might waken the monster.

She was chilled to the bone but refused to shake; refused to show the beast anything that he might interpret as weakness. She listened. Another step.

She almost prayed to be left untouched that night, but she knew the Christian god didn't listen to her pleas. She was a slave to his brides, who offered her in sacrifice to the beast below.

But not tonight. She was so tired, but, tapping her pocket for assurance, this night would be different.

Reaching the bottom step, she crept to her cell with the same fear-bred caution she'd taken on the stairs. Her eyes had adjusted over the years to the near absence of light, and she could sense the tiniest shift in the air. One step from the entrance, she froze. She wasn't alone. Drabach was sitting on her pallet in the shadows, covering the small flame until he was sure it was her. Under his foot, she recognized the torn tail of the skinny rat she'd befriended - her only friend, anywhere. Its blood darkened the dirt.

"There's my Princess," he hissed through his toothless grin at her fallen face. "It won't do for you to grow attached to these creatures. Drabach is the only friend you need, the only one." He shifted on the pallet and said, "Now, come here. I have been waiting for you, my love." He reached out to take her arm, but Morgan snapped. A door in her mind slammed shut on the cowering victim she'd become.

She lashed out with her fists and her feet, kicking and scratching the wretched gnome. "NO!" she screamed as she slapped his hand away. "NO! You will not violate me tonight, or any other night. This will end." She'd never fought back before. Drabach dropped the torch, still glowing from the grease-soaked rags, and scrambled to a corner, mewling.

Morgan dealt him a vicious kick to the ribs, then fell on him.

She found his neck with the pointed end of a tin shard she'd secreted away in the pocket of her cloak. The trembling man became still. His ebony pupils obscured his bulging yellow eyes as it sank in that his death was imminent.

For Morgan, the adrenaline rush was unyielding. "You will die tonight, you swine," she whispered between gasps. "But I shall make it last, and I shall make it painful. The moment your heart last beats shall be the moment mine begins again."

"Please, Princess, have mercy. I'm a weak man, a terrible man. Please…" Drabach whimpered, then steadied his gaze, and played a card that would change Morgan's world. "Maybe I can help the princess? Yes, show her ways to get what she craves?"

Breathlessly. "What could you know about my wants? Speak quickly, because your life depends on it." *Don't let him talk. End his existence!* But curiosity stayed her hand.

His wide, terror-stricken eyes relaxed. She was listening. "I know you want to destroy this place. I can help."

Morgan didn't acknowledge that truth, but he was right. She didn't just need to be free of this hell. It must burn to the ground, with all the harpies who found pleasure in her suffering consumed in the conflagration. Revenge, not justice. In a whispered scream, clinging to self-control, she asked, "How can you help me?"

The pressure of the blade on his neck subsided, and the knee on his chest released. Morgan had stepped back but held the weapon pointed at his face.

He was a small man, and Morgan now had inches on him. He relaxed his clenched hands and attempted a toothless smile that came across as a grimace. "There, there, my Princess. Drabach meant no harm. Drabach will earn your love back, I will."

He had access and moved about unnoticed by the sisters. Maybe he could be the instrument of her retribution. "How will you earn my love, you filth?"

"Oh, I know things, about the Abbey, about the sisters … about magic…" He let that last one hang in the air between them.

Morgan took a half step forward. "What could you possibly know about magic? A dirty, depraved rat in a godforsaken place like this?"

Drabach sat back down on the edge of the pallet and patted a spot next to him, motioning for her to join him. She sat but swatted his hand away when he tried to touch her leg, thrusting the shiv towards his neck.

Fixing his gaze on the girl, Drabach continued. "I wasn't always what you see, my Princess, just like you weren't always like this." Morgan subconsciously touched her hair. "I served in Uther's castle, you see. Long before you were born. I served Lord Myrddin Emrys. I kept his chambers and wore fancy clothes," he smiled and dared another touch on her leg. "You know of the wizard Myrddin, princess," a statement, not a question.

She didn't respond to this latest attempt to touch her. Morgan's thoughts were spinning with this revelation. "Go on," was all she said.

"So Drabach took an interest in Lord Myrddin's craft, my Princess, and struck a deal with the powerful wizard. I would bring him … treats, and he would teach me things."

"What treats?" Morgan snapped.

"Oh, things he required for his works…" He reached up and touched Morgan's hair. "And things that a man needs from time to time, if you take my meaning."

Morgan pushed his hand away and stood up. "You brought him girls, is that what you are saying?"

"Oh, Princess, a man of his power has needs that we mortals can't understand. But teach me he did."

Morgan was disgusted but stood her ground. "What things did he teach you?"

"Important, dangerous things, my princess…" he said as he looked about the floor. A smile came to his face as another skinny rat crawled into the dwindling light of the torch. "Like this," he said, and as Morgan watched, the rat stopped in its tracks, then ran full

106

speed into the wall, smashing its head. It backed up and hit the wall again, and again.

Morgan couldn't take her eyes off the unfolding horror. Slowly, she sat back down and failed to notice Drabach's hand stroking her leg once again.

As she watched, the rat took one last run at the wall and slumped to the ground, dead. Within seconds, other rats tore its flesh until the remains bore no resemblance to the rodent it had been. Sated, they scurried back into the darkness.

"I … I have never seen rats behave like that." She turned her attention back to Drabach. "Can you do that with other animals … people?" Her voice dropped to a conspiratorial whisper at the end.

"I can control feeble-minded creatures, vermin, and the like. I have seen Lord Myrddin bend wolves, birds, and even humans to his will, but such things are beyond me, my princess," he whispered with as much smoothness as his toothless mouth was able. "But I'll teach you what I can, my love, and p'raps you will master the skills old Drabach couldn't." As he spoke, he gently pulled her back down to the straw. "I will teach you for treats."

She finally saw a path out of this place, this life, but could she pay the price? Was it worth it? Resolve and hatred forged a renewed strength in the young woman. Yes, she would do whatever it took. "Teach me," she said.

Drabach let out a low guttural laugh as he laid her back on the dirty straw bed. Meghan's consciousness failed.

***

She woke, still on the soiled pallet, still in Morgan's memories, but now apart. She sensed a change in her soul sister, who was standing, arms crossed. Physically, Morgan's cheekbones had become sharper. Her breasts and hips were a woman's, not a girl's. And, more than a change to her outward appearance; Meghan sensed newfound calmness, confidence.

The fiend was still there, on a makeshift stool across the small floor from his former student. A dozen fat, toothy rats had formed a protective crescent around Morgan. When Drabach shifted in his chair, they inched forward and hissed.

"If you have nothing more to offer, old man, then I shall consider our relationship terminated."

"Please, princess," he groveled. "You haven't mastered the art yet. Your wish was to control humans, and I can still help. Please."

Morgan fixed his gaze and leaned over to take his hand. "Still help? I think not." But as the words left her mouth, his consciousness flooded her mind - his thoughts, his memories. Images of his own abuse as a child and the decades of depravity it spawned were as vivid as her own past. His wants, needs, and fears revealed themselves as tools to control him, perhaps to kill him. *The touch ... that's the key to accessing humans.* She released his hand but found the access persisted. A wry smile, then a soft push, *Suffer.*

Drabach's face contorted, and his hands snapped up to clutch the sides of his head. "What? No!" His eyes smashed shut, but tears still emerged. He felt warm liquid trickling down his leg.

"You are a useless husk, and I've outgrown you. Leave me."

Understanding crept onto the man's face as he looked from his hand to hers. A soul-wrenching pain that drew a primitive howl cut his clarity short. He fell off his stool trying to shake her out of his head. He scrambled for the door on his hands and knees, pausing only to pound his head, unable to displace the growing agony.

Meghan followed him out to watch the debasement, but found herself upstairs, back in the main hall. *Vertigo again.* She reached back to the door frame to combat the swimming in her head caused by yet another unexpected transformation, but that door was no longer there. *Why would it be?* Taking a steadying breath, she collected herself and looked about. The sisters were clutching each other and fixated on something happening in the road. She jockeyed for a view, unnoticed but physically in the vision. A taller woman in front of her succumbed to base emotions and doubled over to vomit, providing Meghan the line of sight she needed. In the dirt, just feet from the window, a scarlet mass that had been Drabach was being ripped apart by his own hounds in a flurry of snarling and snapping, both matted with his blood. Meghan spun about searching for Morgan, spotting her alone and motionless on a log in front of the tortured crucifix, eyes raised and mouth set.

She wasn't the only one interested in Morgan's conspicuous lack of response. A grey, skeletal being in a torn, patched robe stepped forward.

"Do you understand what's just happened, you wretched thing? Have you lost your senses?" Her bony fingers clenched Morgan's shoulder.

The younger woman's head turned to confront her accuser. Wordlessly, she reached up and brushed her fingers across the intrusive hand.

The sister pulled her arm back as if it had been scalded. Still looking at Morgan but now with confusion instead of defiance, she stumbled backward, tripping over the rearmost seat. As she kicked out against the dirt to put space between her and her oppressor, she clutched the tin cross hanging below her neck. "No! I will not … I cannot…"

Other women lifted the terrified wraith to her feet and ushered her to the dormitory; casting looks back at Morgan ranging from fear to hatred. Morgan's only acknowledgement of the commotion she'd caused was a slight cock of her head. As it subsided, she stood, and the remaining clutch of shocked women parted to open a path to that ever-present door. Meghan followed her down into the darkness yet again.

Stepping off the bottom stair, the blackness parted, and Meghan found herself on the dirt road in front of the nunnery. The dark stain that had been Morgan's abuser-turned-teacher was now barely discernible in the intense sunlight. The disorientation Meghan had felt at these transitions of time and space had passed. *Have I finally gone mad?*

Many of the residents were outside as well, tending to the

meager gardens in front of the nunnery. Morgana was present, but the others had given her a wide berth. Meghan moved towards her spirit guide, but a growing cloud of dust up the road, heading their way, captured her attention. Few of the nuns noticed this, or if they did, showed no signs of concern.

Minutes passed, and the source of the dust came into focus. A team of two horses was galloping recklessly with an unmanned cart careening behind. She looked back to make sure Morgan had seen it, but the fledgling sorceress was instead fixated on the frail woman who'd confronted her after Drabach's demise. The object of Morgan's attention was standing stiffly with a lost look in her eyes and watching the oncoming calamity. Alternating her attention between Morgan, the out-of-control cart, and the unresponsive nun, Meghan almost missed it. Things happened so fast that no one could have intervened. As the pounding of hooves drowned out all other sound and the dust obscured its source, the sister dropped the few tools she'd been allowed and leapt into the brown cloud. In just moments, the racing vehicle had passed, and her broken body appeared within the dissipating debris.

Meghan turned her attention to Morgan, who returned her look and offered a hint of a smile, which vanished when she noticed others looking. Meghan's mind clouded over again, then cleared to reveal she was back inside amid their evening meal. Morgan was sitting on the other side of the common room, alone and unfazed by the unbridled fear and hate directed at her.

Movement on her right caught her attention. Sister Agnes, Morgan's chief tormentor, stood, dabbed her mouth with a rag, and walked purposefully to the large open hearth in which their meal had been prepared only moments prior. Without any declaration or hesitation, Agnes stooped, crawled into the fireplace and stood upright in the flames. The hungry orange and yellow fingers crawled up her rags, consuming her old, greasy garments in a sudden burst. Before the rest of the congregation, still reeling from the horror they'd witnessed outside, could comprehend what was happening, flames engulfed her body. Too late, several sisters bravely jumped into action and fought both the fire and their burning leader to no avail. Agnes resisted efforts to pull her from the blaze. Only when she collapsed could her black, crackling body be dragged from the smoking embers. In that moment, the grief-struck sisters looked back as one and saw Morgan, unfazed and with a self-satisfied look on her face.

Meghan's vision spun, faster and more chaotic than her consciousness could endure, and the blackness came again. Focus returned and revealed her standing alongside Morgan in front of the acting senior, who sat behind a desk that was no more than a plank on ancient stumps. The sorceress's arms were crossed over her chest, and her dark eyes glowered from beneath a hood, pulled loosely over her head.

"I've learned all I can here," Morgan stated without pretense of servility. "I wish to go." The white-faced sister nodded and composed a letter to the king requesting that he accept his daughter back with garbled and nonlinear descriptions of alternating piousness and depravity. The message was simple; Morgan could not stay.

Darkness again fell upon this vision, and Meghan awoke with a start. She was lying face down on the floor of her flat in front of the fireplace. She was still in the black outfit she'd worn in the park. However, the stench of smoke and sweat confirmed that she had traveled to a place and age beyond her reality and finally understood why she had to sacrifice everything to manifest Morgana's revenge. A tall shadow crossed her peripheral vision, then was gone.

Chapter 18

The television at The Coral Grotto - Covent Garden's latest hotspot - was broadcasting the sensational murder of another prominent local citizen. Nick Stearns, CEO of British Power, was strangled in his sleep. The alleged killer was his third wife and twenty-five years his junior. Mr. Stearns's past wives had since offered shocking stories about his behavior during their marriages, earning a bit of empathy for the suspect. Their housekeeper found Mrs. Stearns lying beside her dead husband in a near-comatose state at their Surrey home. Scotland Yard confirmed they had engaged the Joint Terrorism Analysis Centre of MI5, the United Kingdom's domestic intelligence service, to support their efforts.

Jacquie Mattson turned from the tele to Reggie, who was chatting up the coat check girl. As the thin cashmere cape, with fox fur trim at the collar and cuffs, slid off her otherwise bare shoulders, his head turned to his wife. All patrons, both men and women, watched the statuesque blond as she stepped into the dining room, and not just because she was the wife of a leading industrialist with regular coverage in the fashion section. There were more than a few under-table kicks, arm grabs, and sharp words from wives to husbands as Mrs. Mattson smoothed out her blue, off-the-shoulder, mid-thigh dress with long, slow strokes.

The maitre d' stepped up to the couple and said in a conspiratorial tone, "Mr. Mattson, we have seated your guests and have brought them drinks. Your requested bottle of Dom Pérignon is chilling table-side." He then led the Mattsons to a round table covered with a light gray cloth. Gentlemen in conservative suits occupied two of the four chairs. Both stood as the newcomers approached.

Mattson leaned across the table to shake hands. "Richard, Tom, thank you for joining me tonight. I am confident this will be the beginning of a profitable endeavor for all of us." Both guests nodded as Mattson spoke, but the stunning woman on his right consumed their attention.

Catching their stares and accustomed to this reaction, he smiled. "Oh, my apologies, please let me introduce my beautiful wife, Jacqueline." He stepped to the side and, with a slow slide of his right hand to her bottom, encouraged her to step forward. Both men came around the table to offer a hug versus a handshake. Both also lingered a bit too long in the embrace and in their eye contact. Many women would feel uncomfortable with this, but Jacquie took it in stride.

Mattson directed his guests to their seats, positioning his wife between them. When the server materialized at the table, Reggie directed him to pour each a glass of Dom. He kicked off the conversation by toasting their health, and "Of course to the lovely Jacqueline," the guests added. Jacquie dropped her eyes and accepted their well-wishes with a suggestive side smile.

"Please, gentlemen, you can call her Jacquie. She prides herself on a close relationship with my most important business partners, don't you, dear?" His eyes bored into hers and held the gaze until she broke it. Still smiling, she confirmed his request with a nod to each of the guests.

The conversation at the table turned to business. Other than poorly disguised glances at her cleavage, the men all but forgot about Jacquie. Consequently, the first sign that anything was out of the ordinary at the swank eatery was the sound of gunshots.

As she listened to Reggie drone on and on about Middle East contacts, the value of air versus ground transport, and financing cutouts on the continent, all expression on Jacquie's face melted away. The busy din of the restaurant faded. All she could see was her husband's face and his red and blue striped tie. She waited until the men's focus was on Reggie and slid a hand into her oversized clutch purse. In a smooth movement, she pulled a handgun out of her purse and emptied all seven rounds into her husband's chest, resulting in a tight grouping to the left of his tie. When a pull of the trigger finally yielded nothing but a hollow, metallic click, Jacquie rested the gun on the table, picked up her glass, and took a small sip. "Reggie says it won't do to gulp expensive champagne," she said moments before being tackled to the ground.

***

Back in the Portobello Road flat, Meghan sat at her substantial dark wood desk. Dylan was sitting across from her, basking in his favored position. With all his memories of the abduction erased, Meghan was still the boss, and he assumed the improved access was a reward for the snuff job they'd executed flawlessly on her behalf. They were both watching breaking reports on the television of the shooting in Covent Garden. Authorities were at a loss to determine where Mrs. Mattson could have obtained a handgun. While the news anchors speculated, Dylan chuckled. Meghan switched the set off with a wave of the remote and turned to face him.

"I sense growing urgency, Dylan, and need to speed up our schedule. What we seek must be known to one of these feckless bureaucrats, but we're running out of time. Something has happened, but I can't yet see it."

"We've got watchers here at the flat, men at your office and, let's face it, nobody in their right mind would walk into the clubhouse uninvited. I think you're becoming a bit paranoid, luv," he replied, slumping back in his chair, only to jump to his feet. "Christ! Was that a rat? Behind the plant?" He pulled a handgun from his shoulder holster.

With strained patience and a tone parents use on obstinate children, Meghan responded, "Sit down, Dylan. Pay that no mind. Now, before he expired, Minister Reynolds denied knowledge of our prize. Assuming he didn't lie to his wife about it, and I don't think he respected her enough to lie to her, we are no closer to the goal. And we haven't been able to find any other ministers or bureaucrats who have even passing knowledge of it. This means either the records have been lost or ... there are honorable men in the right places with wives we can't control... and that I doubt." She stood up and paced the room behind Dylan, forcing him to swivel his chair to maintain eye contact while struggling to monitor the floor near his feet.

"If we learn nothing that can help us from the group tonight, we're going to need to ramp up the chaos and make an overt demand. The growing fear in London is deliciously palpable, but that is not the end goal, not yet." A knock on the study door interrupted her.

Paul Knowles, a rising lieutenant in her ranks, opened the door enough to pop his head in. "Your guests are seated and ready, Mum." She waved him off and turned back to Dylan. "I want you to send someone to Glastonbury in the morning, someone respectable looking; maybe even Paul."

"Glastonbury, luv? What do you want in that backwater hippie town?" he replied with a smirk on his face.

"I'm not sure yet, but I feel that something is happening, and it's happening there. Have your man buy rounds at a few pubs and ask about anything out of the ordinary. Have any unfamiliar faces shown up or any old faces disappeared? He can stay through the weekend, but no longer. I want a report by six o'clock on Sunday evening. If another variable has been introduced, I need to know right away. Do you understand?" She didn't wait for his response as she stood, ran a hand through her hair, took a breath, and opened the door.

Chapter 19

It really feels like magic to me, too," Jenn said to Arthur. The double entendre was unplanned, but she feared her lingering looks might cross all language boundaries.

That morning, Arthur found Jenn engrossed in her phone, fuming about his dismissal the previous evening, and offered an olive branch.

"Jennifer, I fear I haven't treated you with the respect you deserve; that all women deserve, I suppose. For that, I am truly sorry."

After a moment of silence to ponder his sincerity, Jenn said, "Did Lloyd put you up to this?" She attempted to mask the rising heat in her cheeks.

Arthur pulled up a chair, laughing. "Actually, your father spoke to me. I'm not sure the old wizard is attuned to such sensitivities."

Turning in her chair to face him, Jenn smiled warmly. "Then, apology accepted."

"Thank you, Jennifer. Your father also suggested that instead of our daily lessons in town, a visit to the summit of the hill might offer a better perspective, of both the town and the age. With Peter engaged in errands for Colin, would it be inappropriate to suggest you and I venture out alone?"

"NO," she said a bit too quickly. "No … of course not," in a more measured tone. "That sounds like a brilliant plan. Why don't I pack a lunch, and we can … give me a minute."

An hour later, they sat on a stone at the summit of the Tor, in the shadow of St. Michael's Chapel. An empty picnic basket sat at their feet while they watched planes paint long white vapor trails across the cloudless blue sky.

"I mean, I can't explain the science behind flight any more than your miraculous revival."

"Shienshe, hmm," he mumbled through a mouthful of chicken, keeping his eyes on a northbound plane. He washed that down with an entire bottle of water and wiped his mouth on his sleeve before continuing. "We couldn't differentiate magic from science in my time. I doubt few besides Myrddin, your Merlin, even knew there was a difference. I do think we had real magic, though. As you've said, 'Here I am.' Dropping his gaze from the skies, he rooted through the basket to see if there was anything he'd missed.

Jenn pulled her heavy wool cloak tighter, a shield against the cool autumn winds, and the rude yet intriguing man out of time. "Yes, here you are, and your recovery has been incredible. Not that I have a point of reference, but I would have expected your body to require weeks to get to where we are today. It's remarkable."

"I give all credit to the excellent meals you've provided and the hospitality of your family. I'll be forever in your debt, m'lady," he said, standing to bow.

Jenn rewarded the gesture with a grin and a slow nod. "M'lord."

He sat back down and looked across the rolling green countryside with hedges and trees subdividing the world into manageable parcels as far as the eye could see. He said, mostly to himself, "Whatever 'forever' means anymore."

Her slap on his leg got his attention. She said, "Speaking of meals - and thank you, by the way - I have much experience cooking for men - we have a treat for you tonight." Arthur perked up and turned to face her with a broad smile.

"Since you're feeling better, and your appetite has settled to only twice that of a normal man..." They both chuckled at this. "We thought we'd take you out for dinner, a night on the town with a bit of extra-Pelling interaction."

Arthur responded to this revelation with a questioning look. Jenn had been adamant that he attract as little attention as possible.

She and Peter avoided stopping in any single place for long because modern references and slang terms tripped him up. After a moment, Arthur said, "Thank you, Jenn. That sounds wonderful." He stood back up and offered her his hand. "Shall we?"

Jenn took his hand and rose, then offered him a curtsy before they walked through the pointed archway of the chapel and down the shallow steps on the west side of the Tor.

A pleasant-sounding evening turned into an adventure for Arthur when Peter announced they should take the car to town instead of walking. "We'll need to pick Lloyd up along the way," he said as they walked out to the blue Citroën in the carport. "Dad will meet us there when he closes up the shop." Peter opened the passenger door for Arthur. "I wish we had a more appropriate vehicle to take the once High King of Britain for his first ride. Maybe a Jag or a Land Rover or at least a Merc," he muttered.

Arthur had no misgivings about the Citroën. He hopped into the passenger seat and bounced like an impatient child. Jenn climbed into the back, chuckling.

Peter dropped into the driver's seat and tried to help Arthur buckle in. "Just grab that metal clip near your left shoulder; no, the shiny one. Right. Now pull it across your body and insert it into this buckle, this box … with the red button…"

Arthur shifted to his left to look for the buckle as instructed, but his unzipped coat was covering it. "Why must we tie ourselves down?" Arthur asked, "This is a sturdy metal box! And I raced across rocky ground on horseback with no such restraint." He shifted in his seat and tugged at the unyielding belt.

"It's the law," Peter replied. "We all have to." He reached up and pulled his belt down to emphasize that point.

"The law!" Arthur said. "When I was king…" He left that thought unfinished and looked out his window, signaling the conversation was over. Peter reached over and snapped the clip in for him.

"The way Peter drives," Jenn loudly piped from the back seat.

"You'll wish you had two seat belts. You thought riding a horse into battle was dangerous." Jenn sat back, beaming with self-satisfaction, while both Peter and Arthur shot her a dark look, for different reasons.

Arthur broke first, giving Peter a reassuring smile and nod. "All right then, let's go!"

"Peter, where are we picking up Lloyd?" Jenn asked. "We can't exactly pull in the drive."

"You know Lloyd, Jenn. He told us to drive to the pub, and we'd see him along the way. Didn't ask when we were leaving either, but that's not surprising." Peter backed onto the road and sped west.

"What glory we could have achieved with a dozen of these metal chariots on the battlefield," Arthur said. "Have any of your modern generals considered this?"

"Well, yeah! And now they've got tanks with enormous guns … Right, so guns are…" Not sensing comprehension, Peter said, "So I think we'll cover this in more detail when we get back home."

Just after the A361 became Chilkwell Street, Arthur pointed off to the left. "There, sitting on a bench."

"Pop the boot if you please, Peter," Lloyd asked as the car pulled to the curb. The wizard deposited his ever-present staff in the car's trunk and slid into the back seat beside Jenn.

"King Arthur, is it?" he asked, winking at Jenn.

Arthur turned in his seat, with eyebrows furrowed in concern. Searching the old traveler's face for understanding, he asked in a soft voice, "Myrddin, have you forgotten me? Is it this garb?"

Peter put the car in gear and pulled off to a chorus of laughter as Lloyd clarified. "No, my boy, I can assure you that I, at least, have not forgotten you, nor will I ever, I suppose. The name of the dining establishment we'll be visiting today is called The King Arthur. I thought it might be an appropriate place to bring you up to speed on why everyone else in England *has* forgotten you."

The Citroën turned left onto Benedict Street and pulled up to a local favorite, The King Arthur restaurant. Arthur's eyes were unblinking as Peter pulled the car into an available space just in front of the pub. The king's face hardened as he took in the garish display of local Arthurian marketing.

"What luck," Peter shouted. "My driving skills paid off."

"There is no such thing as luck, Peter Pelling. At least not when you travel with me," Lloyd retorted as he scrambled out of the car.

Rolling his eyes, Peter jumped out of the front seat, leaving Jenn to help Arthur free himself from the safety belt, and heaved open the restaurant's bright blue door. "We should try to grab a table out in the garden as long as the weather is cooperating," he called as they gathered.

Jenn noticed Arthur was looking up at the green sign above the door, depicting somebody's guess at what he had looked like: dressed in red and holding Excalibur with two hands. His countenance wavered between outrage and loneliness. She was relieved to see a smile overtake his more destructive emotions.

"Doesn't quite capture me, does it?" he asked, posing for a moment under the sign and enjoying the laughs.

They entered the pub and walked past the neon-lit bar into the back garden. Colin had arrived early and was sitting at a wooden table near a blazing fire in a circular stone pit. "Welcome! Welcome, my liege," he beckoned as he pushed himself to his feet and offered Arthur an exaggerated, albeit unsteady, bow. "Please, m'lord … sit here. The warmth of the fire is delightful." He pulled a handkerchief from his pocket and dusted off both the seat and the table before offering the chair with a flourish.

"Daaaad! Low profile, remember?" Jenn hissed.

As the group was settling in, Colin caught the server in passing and asked her to bring a round of pints for the table.

"Will you be eating, then?" the server, a long-time fixture at The King Arthur, asked in a monotone while staring at the sky, arms crossed. With Colin's affirmative, she pivoted away and mumbled something about bringing menus with the drinks.

120

When she was out of earshot, Colin said, "Peter, run up to the bar and get us the first round, will you, lad?" Putting his hand on Arthur's forearm, "Winnie is about as fast as she is good-humored, so we'll die of thirst before those beers get here, if she even remembers."

Arthur sat with his hands crossed in front of him, taking in the place. "Is the music too loud?" Jenn asked.

"It's tolerable," he said, "but it's, I don't know … *complicated*? What joy do folk get from this noise? Surely you can't dance to this."

"They call it 'rock and roll' and I can assure you people dance to it," Lloyd replied. "I doubt you'd recognize it as dancing, though." He then slapped his hands on the table to get everyone's attention and said, "First order of business, dinner. The crisps are tolerable, but the salad is subpar," he proclaimed.

"Hey, I like the salad here," Jenn interjected.

Lloyd continued, unfazed. "I recommend the Potato Boats as an appetizer. They're hearty enough with sufficient flavor to suggest intentional preparation." Despite the thousand-year gap in their relationship with the old wizard, both Arthur and the Pellings could recognize when Lloyd had the floor.

"Arthur, you can't go wrong with any of the mains, the notable exception being the veggie burger. That is a violation of nature's laws. The steak is excellent on most days, but you've had steak. For god's sake, I remember you and your boys putting away whole cows at your feasts. Beef is still beef, and while a classic, hardly worth it for your first dining-out experience in this new age. Fish and chips or pizza. Fish and chips AND pizza. That is what we should order. Fish and pizza." He finished as he started, with a hearty slap of the table, then relinquished the conversation to other, lesser opinions.

"I hate to say it, but he's right," added Colin. "We can split a pizza, but you really should try the fish and chips. It's sort of a national specialty."

Peter caught the tail end of that as he passed the glasses around the table. "I'll stick to the burger, thank you. I don't fancy fish and chips like you all do."

The group around Arthur enjoyed a moment of silence as each enjoyed their first sip of cold beer on that crisp mid-autumn night. Jenn thought it was nights like these that made anything seem possible, like sitting for a meal with a legendary king from the mists of history. The waitress interrupted their moment of reflection, defying all expectations, and bringing their tray of pints in record time.

She eyed the mugs arrayed about the table. "Couldn't wait, could you?" Her nasally voice drew each word out longer than required. "I suppose you won't be needin' these menus either," she asked in the same tone.

"Actually, my dear," answered Lloyd for the table, "we have become so enthralled over our years of patronage by the cuisine in your never-changing offering that we can confidently select our favorites from the memories of cherished times, in your company, I might add, such that menus are superfluous."

All eyes were on Winnie, their mouths agape, as she shifted her weight from foot to foot, trying to determine if she should be offended. Still unclear, but giving in to her impatience, she said, "Fine, what'll you 'ave then?"

Orders in and privacy re-established, Arthur drained what remained of his first beer and took a pull from his second. Satisfied, he leaned into the table, clutching the cold mug with both hands and asked, "*Lloyd*, going back to what you said in the car, how is it that everybody seems to remember King Arthur, but nobody seems to remember ME? The stories I've been told, the paintings, statues - none of them are right. Peter and Colin have shown me other stories from my time, even before my time, so I know those histories have been passed on. How can it be that my life has been uniquely and completely replaced by such fantasies?" Everyone's attention shifted to Lloyd.

"Well, my son," he started, "it wasn't easy."

122

He took a long drink from his mug, letting that sink in. "What you must understand is that I couldn't have people come looking for you. Of course, in those early years, confusion and war were the norms, and nobody had time to think about you, Arthur. Kings came and kings went. People were more concerned about staying alive and feeding their families. A basic story of Arthur leaving this world on a ship into the mists was a sufficient deterrent to any would-be seeker. People really didn't start asking questions for a few hundred years."

"This makes no sense. I was the king and a well-loved king. This is the second time you've suggested my fate was inconsequential. How could the people, my people, simply forget?"

Colin tried to explain. "What you need to understand, m'lord, is that most Britons had no relationship with the king, with you. You were important to those who surrounded you, but most common folk took no notice when kings … well … came and went."

Lloyd picked up the thread. "And of those that surrounded you, the best who survived Camlann took an oath of secrecy. The rest accepted a change of leadership when Lot stepped in and carried on. It wouldn't be the last shift in command for most of them."

Arthur's head dropped as the reality of Lloyd's revelation sank in. He stared at his hands and fidgeted with his mug. "Was my life's work then, my struggles for peace in the land, also inconsequential?"

Colin gripped his arm. "No, m'lord, no. That you're here, you're back, should tell you that's not true. And we're with you. To the end."

Arthur covered Colin's hand with his. "I sense there is more to this story that transcends the real Arthur. Please carry on, Myrddin."

"Thank you. My first challenge to obscuring your existence was that monk, Gildas, because, well, he knew, didn't he? Between threats and a bit of sharing, he and I reached an understanding, and he expunged you from his history. However, over the following few years, academics started documenting the oral histories, and I couldn't rein all of that in. I traveled to the growing universities, which were mostly Christian institutions, planting seeds that I was an expert in sixth-century history. In fact, one of the earliest, well, fibs I told was that you were a staunch Christian. They were overjoyed that Arthur was a Christian king and ran with it blindly. It guaranteed me access and influence over their messaging.

"I traveled extensively in the centuries that followed and didn't settle down until the turn of the first millennium. Truth be told, I was inebriated for the first half of the twelfth century, after the Norman invasion. The French brought superior organizational skills and fantastic wine. British wine was garbage until then. I spent much of that binge in Oxford with a man named Geoffrey. He went by Monmouth as well, a cleric of sorts. We had many a conversation about the legends of Arthur, usually over a glass, and I fear I shared a bit too much as his Historia Regum Britanniae, the History of the Kings of Britain, came close to the truth. Fortunately, I had embellished enough to cast doubt on his story, kept Glastonbury out of it, and subsequently paid for my indiscretions by working to discredit it over the next few hundred years. I learned my lesson."

"So, you erased me," Arthur stated through gritted teeth.

Spitting beer through his mustache, Lloyd retorted, "No, Arthur, no. You're missing the point. Had I done nothing, you indisputably would have disappeared, become irrelevant like Cynan of Powys. Nobody remembers him, do they? Or Maelgwn of Gwynedd. People remember you, Arthur, but aren't looking for you. You were a hero, but you've survived to be a legend, a legend others will recognize and follow when you need them to."

The old wizard hadn't realized he had stood, and his voice had risen. Others in the beer garden had stopped to listen. Colin stood up and leaned in. "Best you sit back down, Lloyd. This conversation should stay between us."

Most people in the garden forgot the outburst as quickly as it had come. However, one hard-looking young man in black jeans and a leather motorcycle jacket, wearing sunglasses despite the sun having set an hour before, took notice. Jenn registered his lingering interest because he didn't fit in with the usual Friday night crowd. With nothing more suspicious than how he dressed, though, she lost interest and turned to the table. He was gone when she looked back.

"My gift to you, Arthur, and frankly to the world, is your anonymity." Lloyd continued. "You weren't real, so nobody will look for you or expect you. Morgana wasn't real, so no cult or church is waiting for her. I'm not real; none of this is real. Anonymity, my friends, is a weapon no king, prime minister, or president can buy, and it will be our greatest strength in the battle to come."

"And Morgana's," Jenn added.

"This is also true," Lloyd said, leaning in conspiratorially. "Listen carefully. This won't be an interactive history lesson that you simply wander through at your leisure. All your lives might soon be in danger. This improbable task force, seated at this not-so-round table, must stop a sorceress who's had more than a millennium to prepare." He sat back in his chair and sipped his beer. "Enough said."

"But not tonight." Arthur stood up and waited until he had everyone's attention. "I can't say I support this subterfuge, but without the identity or location of our foe, I suppose this is how it must be. For now, I think we should get one more round and return home." He smiled, "and I'm buying."

Jenn looked up, and Arthur was staring at her with a sheepish smile. "Right," she said, and fished a twenty-pound note out of her purse for the king.

"Thanks," he offered, then hesitated as if there was more he wanted to say. "I'll be right back," was all that came out. Jenn watched as he navigated the crowd, struck by the realization that she could never understand how alone he must feel.

Chapter 20

A clear pattern has emerged in the series of killings, now being labeled the #HimToo murders, inspired by the 2006 #MeToo movement in the US. Interviews have revealed that in each case, there had been ongoing abuse and humiliation perpetrated by the victims on their wives, daughters, or girlfriends. Twelve killings to date have been linked to this pattern. None of the alleged murderesses attempted to flee or even cover up their actions. Nor did they seem to even realize what they'd done.

"Sources inside Scotland Yard, speaking under conditions of anonymity, have told BBC One London that they are finding certain overlaps in the schedules and social calendars of the suspected killers but have not yet zeroed in on a relevant commonality."

Remote in hand, Meghan turned the volume down to a whisper and spun her chair to face Dylan. A brown rat with glowing black eyes crawled off her neck from behind her hair and wriggled into her lap. Now accustomed to these strange pets, he didn't react. He just swirled his rocks glass; more ice than whiskey. "We knew it wouldn't be long before they made connections," Dylan offered. "The clock is ticking on this game of cat and ... rat, luv."

She tapped the end of the remote on her bottom teeth as she thought through her next moves. "Agreed," she said. "We've worked over the wives and mistresses of all the ministers and other officials who might know of what we need and have come up empty."

"It has been fun though, hasn't it, luv?" Dylan interjected. She shot him a look that wiped the smile off his face.

"And the scumbags who still live are on to the game," she said. "I'm hearing of apologies, restitution, and lavish make-up gifts. It won't make a difference to the ladies we've recruited, but finding more recruits in my dwindling social sphere will be difficult, as the girls will be less suggestible. The fools believe their men have changed."

Men don't change, little sister.

"And men don't change," she said. "It's time for Phase Two. Where do we stand?"

Dylan stood, walked to the freestanding ladder-style bar, and refilled his glass from a crystal carafe. Turning back to his boss, all business now, he informed her, "We have five recruits fully programmed and ready to activate. Two others, Trinny Lees and Becky Green, are iffy, but I certainly would volunteer personal time, off the clock if you will, with either of those birds."

With a slow shake of her head, she announced. "We'll go with the five that are ready. I can't risk a response failure from Trinny or Becky."

A knock interrupted her instructions. Dylan stepped to the door, making a dramatic show of pulling his Glock from his holster and holding it high. He turned the knob with his left hand. Paul stepped in, folding his shades and slipping them into his jacket's inner pocket. Dylan eyed him with raised eyebrows, shifting his gaze to the pistol.

"You were going to shoot me, were you?" He laughed at Dylan, then stepped past him.

"You're late," Meghan said with a false pout on her lips, eyes dropping seductively as if she was waiting only for him. *Too easy*, she noted to Morgana, as she watched Paul puff up like a rooster, stealing a glance at Dylan to broadcast his success.

Yes, sweet sister. They are such simple creatures. Control comes easily to you.

Flushed with that small praise from her mentor, she snapped at Paul to regain her composure. "What did you learn? Out with it, young man."

"Besides confirming that I never want to live outside of London, it was maddeningly quiet until Friday night. I was making another round of the pubs near High Street and had just ordered a pint at some cheeky place called The King Arthur…"

"What was the name of the place?" She asked, immediately reprimanding herself for the display of anxiety. She set the animal in her lap onto the floor and sat forward.

"The King Arthur, mum," he repeated. "The whole place has tacky paintings, small statues, and cheesy Arthur shit from that Monty Python movie everywhere. Not our sort of place, trust me." He winked at Meghan and stole a glance at Dylan. "Anyway, I walked out to the back garden in time to see an old, bearded fella' yelling at a table of cowed-looking locals. Another old gent, not as old I guess, no beard, clearly felt the place was a bit public for whatever the bearded guy was saying and sat him back down."

Morgana felt a strange apprehension but fought to control it and reacted through Meghan. "What was the old man saying?"

"Couldn't make it out. Something about legends and heroes."

Meghan squeezed the remote until it nearly snapped in two. "Go on," was all she could say.

"So, I noticed this red-haired bird at their table was eyeballing me, and not in the way most ladies do, if you take my meaning." Since Meghan gave no sign that she thought this was funny, he went on. "I tried to blend and turned away for a bit. When I looked back, she was lost in the convo at the table. I snapped a few pics and headed back into the bar for more recon."

"You have pictures?" She asked, trying to check her composure.

"I do, but that's not all. I chatted up the bartender and learned that these were the…" he reached into his back pocket and pulled out a small spiral-bound notebook. Flipping up a few pages, he resumed. "The Pelling family. The second old dude, no beard, is the father and runs a bookstore off High Street. The redhead was his daughter, Jennifer…"

Meghan cut him off. "Jennifer?"

"Yes, Mum. The really old dude is a local character named, let's see … Lloyd Wyse. A strange old coot, the barman said. Nobody in town knows much about him, but he's also been around forever."

"Forever, he said?"

"That's what he said. Trying to look like I was just passing time, I asked about the other guy at the table, the big guy. He said that dude showed up a few days ago."

"Exactly when?" Morgana snapped. "What day?"

"I didn't press the issue, Mum. I was trying to fly under the radar, if you will. But people started noticing him with the Pellings earlier last week. They said he was a cousin from Cornwall or something like that."

"Did you get a picture of him?"

"I did at that." Paul pulled his phone out of his back pocket and began scrolling through his photos. "Wouldn't you know it, but as I was talking to the barman, the cousin himself walked up and ordered five pints. He was a big guy, moved like a rugger or a fighter. I got a few pics of him at the bar, then walked out before he took notice of me."

Paul spun the phone around and handed it to his boss. She swiped through the pictures, then back again. An eerie calm had taken over her face.

Morgana pushed to the forefront of Meghan's consciousness. *It does not surprise me to see Myrddin because that old fool WOULD stick around for this.* She zoomed in on the bearded face of the man at the bar. *And I'd know that face anywhere. How can it be that Arthur has survived? And how was this Pelling family involved? Coincidence? Possibly. Convenient pawns to be thrown away by the old warlock when he was through with them? More likely.*

Returning to Paul, she asked, "This cousin, did you learn more about him?"

"No, ma'am," Paul said, sensing it wasn't a moment for

informality. Meghan's eyes had grown dark, and her countenance serious. "I couldn't have known he was of interest. I asked a few others about him, but they didn't know any more than the barman. After that, I was keeping an eye out for other strangers in town, so didn't press it. Sorry ma'am."

"Was he carrying a sword by chance?"

"A sword, ma'am?" He cocked his head and furrowed his brow. "No, I didn't see no sword."

Nodding, she looked up from the pictures and graced him with a warm smile, Meghan's smile. "You did well, my boy. Splendid." Her mind was still racing. *This is a serious threat to our plans. Arthur's presence in this age is problematic. The senile old wizard has crashed back into my world with the only weapon that can stop me.*

"Maybe we can use this to our advantage. Coerce him into finding it for us," Meghan whispered.

"Finding what, Mum?" Paul asked, evoking a sharp look from Dylan. He knew better than to question these random utterances when they weren't directed at him. Meghan ignored the comment.

Possibly. We have time, and while they likely know of my return, they don't know of us. Otherwise, they wouldn't be wasting hours over fish and chips. We must act fast to eliminate my troublesome brother while I consider how to handle Myrddin.

"OK then, boys, slight change of plans," she said. "There's one more thing we'll need to deal with before we launch Phase Two."

Meghan leaned back in her chair. "Dylan, I want you to grab a few of the boys and pay a visit to Glastonbury." Before Paul could object, she added, "Paul, you were too visible over the weekend to return. I've got another job for you, my sweet."

She swiveled her chair to face Dylan. "I want that cousin taken out, first and foremost, however your talents or the situation best suggests. And find that sword. If he didn't bring it to dinner, then he probably left it in the home of that family ... what was their name, Paul?"

"Pelling, Mum."

"Yes, the Pellings. If the opportunity presents itself, kill them. Kill them all. The cousin and the sword are critical, though. You must not fail me there. Do you understand?"

"What's all this about a sword, ma'am? I mean, really?" he asked, tapping his gun.

"Kill the cousin and get the fucking sword," she hissed.

Her words struck him physically, like a cricket bat to the head. His swagger dissolved. After blinking away the pain, he said, "Yes, ma'am, I understand. When should I head out there?"

"Right away! And one more thing, make sure the old man, the bearded old man, isn't with him when you do it." Meghan cut off his objections with a raised finger. "No, that's significant. That son of a bitch ruined his first death. I can't risk it happening again."

"His first death?" Paul asked.

"Never mind that," she said. "Paul, I need you to start Phase Two. You know what to do. I'll be relocating to Exeter sooner than I'd planned. I'll need a car; something simple. The Aston will draw too much attention."

"Yes, ma'am," Paul responded. "I'll rustle up something suitable in the morning."

"NOW," she snapped. "For God's sake, tonight. I want to leave tonight." Recognizing the hurt puppy-dog look on his face, Meghan rolled back her tone. "Tonight … please."

Dylan cleared his throat to refocus her attention. "Want us to kill the old codger with the beard, too?"

She laughed. "Yes, more than life itself, but that may be more difficult than you can imagine." Propping her elbows on the desk, she looked within for guidance. *The threat that miserable old druid poses exceeds the hope that he might help us, albeit inadvertently. Let the boys try.*

Clasping her hands, she smiled and said, "Yes, kill the old man too, if you get the chance AFTER you've killed the cousin. But Dylan … send someone expendable to do that job."

131

Chapter 21

Following their dinner in town, the rest of the weekend was a crash course for Arthur in relevant history. Colin threw himself into this task.

"This here's my collection of movies and documentaries…" and "These shelves contain no less than two hundred books…" and "I've got these maps, some hundreds of years old…"

Jenn chuckled as Arthur grappled with it all, sharing smiles as they both knew this was more cathartic for her dad than informational for him. By Sunday night, Colin had exhausted his memorabilia, so they settled down in the living room in front of the crackling fire for a lower-intensity conversation.

Colin had insisted Arthur take his recliner, where the king then sipped a glass of red wine, while Peter and Colin relaxed on the sofa. Peter's feet rested on the coffee table, computer in his lap, as was so often the case. Jenn was sitting cross-legged on the floor by the fire with a knit blanket wrapped around her shoulders. Arthur was sharing stories of his time, events that would never have made it into a history book, even if Lloyd hadn't erased most actual references.

"So, the twenty of us, having ridden hard through the night, expected to ambush a Saxon raiding party that Morfran had heard tell of. We waited in a copse of trees past a rise in the road, hidden, arms at the ready. Cai, at the front of the line, gave the signal that riders were approaching. Seconds later, the horn blew, and we stormed out of the treeline. It was marvelous. I can't describe the feeling." He sipped his wine before grinning at his audience. "I have a harder time describing the faces of the three tradesmen and their boys clopping along on mules when they saw us. The vicious Saxons turned out to be a group of merchants with poles of skins on their carts, not pikes and shields. We had them circled before I could defuse the situation. The first man's mule threw him, and the others jumped to the ground and begged for mercy. Needless to say, Bors and Cai set upon Morfran with the most rigorous ridicule. When I stopped laughing, I offered to buy all their wares as compensation for the fright we caused."

The Pellings laughed with Arthur, Colin a bit more than was called for. In Arthur's day, Jenn thought, this sort of story must have been a hit at castle feasts. The shock of the greater situation and Lloyd's revelations Friday night had settled into the comfortable camaraderie of old friends.

"Arthur ... are you ready for tomorrow?" Colin asked. "Meeting the rest of the Keepers, getting down to business and all?"

Arthur took another sip. "I don't know what to expect, but this will be a gathering of elite warriors, so I'm confident I'll forge a winning team. Myrddin must have had his reasons for minimizing the import of my reign, but you will all see in the coming weeks why Arthur Pendragon was both feared and admired in the islands of Britannia and in Gaul. I am also thrilled about the drive across the country and seeing Londinium. When I made that trip by horse, it took the better part of a day."

"We'll be passing Stonehenge, you know," Peter said. "If time permits, maybe we can stop and ask Lloyd to share stories of the druids. I've known him my whole life, but it's only in this past week that I've accepted the fact that he's seen two thousand years of history here. And Arthur, your thoughts on this route, from your age, will be fascinating."

Jenn stood up and said, "Speaking of Lloyd, he asked that we be ready to travel at seven tomorrow morning. I'm heading up to finish packing and get some rest. Dad, are you sure you don't want to join us? Meeting the descendants of the proverbial Knights of the Round Table, at the Temple Church of all places? It really sounds like something you'd walk through fire to attend."

Colin smiled at this and put his hand on Peter's shoulder. "This is a young man's - and woman's - adventure," with a nod to Jenn. "And … well … the shop can't run itself, you know, and the tourist traffic is still good." Tourist traffic had slowed to a trickle weeks ago. This might be the first concession to his declining health that Jenn could recall. She turned to the task at hand before her father could read her face.

"Arthur, is there anything you need for this trip?" she asked. "We'll certainly have to buy you more clothes once we get settled into whatever Lloyd has planned for us. I hardly think we've given you enough for an extended time away."

"I'm sure Jenn could force herself to go shopping for you. I mean, it is London," Peter added, closing the lid to his laptop and dropping his trainers to the floor.

Arthur didn't get the sarcasm. "I'll be grateful for whatever assistance you can provide, Jenn."

Colin elbowed a good-natured warning to Peter about his tone and stood up. "Someone has to go first, I imagine. I'll get up early to cook you all a proper breakfast before you leave. Sleep well." He pulled Jenn to him and kissed her on the head. With a bow to Arthur, he grabbed his glass from the table and headed to the kitchen.

***

Lloyd walked through the back door the next morning at precisely seven AM. "Are there any sausages left for me?"

The four travelers were on the road in Colin's Citroën at half past seven. Lloyd, from the back seat, approved of a slight detour to Stonehenge but wouldn't allow a tour. "Not enough time to stop since they built that blasted visitor center and added all that fuss. We can stop on the side of the road, take a picture if you're so inclined, but we need to keep moving."

Peter had purchased a cell phone for Arthur before they'd left Glastonbury and shown him the basics. The Dark Ages king delighted in taking pictures and had to be coerced back into the car when Lloyd said it was time to leave the stones. He spent the next thirty minutes of the drive swiping through these pictures, and others from Glastonbury, with a satisfied smile and an occasional nod or chuckle.

Arthur put the phone down and watched, open-mouthed, as they approached London on the M4 from the west. He stared out at the blue and green glass high-rises, office buildings, and sprawl of the global metropolis coming into view. "Never in my wildest imagination…" Arthur whispered.

Passing Buckingham Palace, the once king asked, "Might we stop so I can meet the queen? There is much we might discuss."

"Probably a bit premature," Jenn offered.

On Fleet Street, Lloyd announced they were almost there just as the GPS in the Citroën informed them that a right turn on Old Mitre Court was pending. They turned onto an arched drive under a row of shops and came to a cantilevered gate. The white barrier lifted as they approached.

"More of your magic, Myrddin?" Arthur asked.

"Weight sensors, Arthur. There are devices under the road that…" Lloyd cut his reply short, realizing there was very little in that explanation that wouldn't then need further explanation. "Yes, Arthur, magic."

"I'll walk you through it later, Arthur," Peter offered. He pulled into the car park on the left and looked over at Lloyd. "Park anywhere?" he asked.

"Yes, son, it doesn't matter. They are expecting us."

Exiting the car, Arthur turned to Jenn. "The size and energy of this city makes Glastonbury feel more like home to me."

"Until you came, I had been planning to move here…" Her voice trailed off as she took in the entire courtyard.

They walked under a white archway, then through a tunnel beneath the Inner Temple building. Exiting into the light, the visitors faced the historic Temple Church. Lloyd paused the group to explain the significance of this location. "The Knights Templar, Arthur, were an order of Christian warrior priests who protected travelers, pilgrims they were called, to the Holy Land."

"The Christian Holy Land?" Arthur asked.

"Yes, Arthur, as you would know it. Ships that sailed from Cornwall, Cornubia, in your age, traded across the Mediterranean Sea to Egypt and the Holy Land, where they say Jesus was born. Now, I was in Britain at that time, so I can't comment definitively on him."

Jenn and Peter exchanged eye rolls. She sensed another lecture was coming and turned away, feigning interest in the gardens.

Since nobody bit, the wizard continued. "The Templar's mysticism came as close to the world we shared as anything since. I chose this temple in London as the place to meet your … knights, if you will, because our quest will be no less historic and may have an even greater impact on the world than those brave warriors did."

Arthur looked up at the austere walls of the Chancel and then down to the Round Church. "I like this place," he said. "I sense its history and can feel its permanence."

"The British Templars built it about five hundred years after you went to sleep, Arthur," Jenn said. "That's about two hundred years before the Abbey ruins you saw in Glastonbury."

"It is one of the oldest remaining structures in London," Peter added. "There are older walls from Roman Londinium, but only small sections. If we have time, we should go see that."

Jenn noticed that Arthur and Lloyd exchanged a slow, joyless look. "What was that look for?" she asked.

"The optimism of youth," was all Lloyd said.

Lloyd led them to the visitor entrance at the transition between the Chancel and the Round Church. A placard on the door said, 'Closed to the Public Today.' Unfazed, Lloyd pushed the unlocked door open, and they stepped in. Cast effigies of select Templars were to their immediate left, but what caught everyone's attention was the group of five men and one woman in the pews on the opposite side of the church.

Jenn first noticed two of the largest men she'd ever seen, twins by the looks of it, chatting behind the back pew with a smaller man who was somehow fidgeting and standing still simultaneously. Seated in front of them were an attractive, olive-skinned woman and a large, dark-haired, dark-eyed man, leg positioned in the aisle as if he was ready to bolt. The last, a lean black man, older than the others, sat to the left in front of the woman. He smiled more than the other two, but Jenn sensed he was assessing all those around him like Lloyd might. The two groups watched each other wordlessly.

The standoff ended when one of the enormous men in the back called out, "So, which of you is the king?"

Arthur walked forward. "I am, or was, King Arthur. Just Arthur now. Welcome."

"So, it's true," the woman in the pews muttered as she rose to her feet.

The descendants of Arthur's former band rose, the dark-eyed man more slowly. The king straightened up, lifted his chin, and nodded to each. One of the large men in the back clapped, but a look from his brother cut that short.

The wizard, all business, broke the moment with two sharp pounds of his staff on the stone floor. The acoustics in the old church amplified the impacts into cannon blasts. "We have all met Arthur now? All set? Excellent, then please, everyone, take a seat, please," he said in a tone that lent falseness to the gratuitous niceties.

Arthur stepped to the front, expecting to lead the meeting, but Lloyd stopped him with a look that sent him to the pews.

"Excellent. Well done. Very nice," Lloyd began again. "Now, I understand you've all come a long way, and I am sure you have questions. I've invited you to this historic place to underscore the reality of this quest. Much as the Knights Templar sought ancient wisdom, so will we be seeking to right long-forgotten wrongs. Evil from the sixth century has returned as I prophesied, though I was somewhat off on the timing. I rather thought it would have been ages ago, but never mind that. It is here now, and it's a threat to England

and the world. We'll be adjourning to a more suitable briefing location, but I thought this would be a proper and sober venue to introduce ourselves, sort of setting the stage, if you will. I'll start, although I doubt I need much introduction. I am Lloyd Wyse, originally Myrddin Emrys, and I've roamed this planet for about two thousand five hundred years." He let that sink in. "You would likely know me as Merlin, and while sequestered for this mission, you may continue to call me such. To avoid confusion, Jennifer and Peter, henceforth Merlin?"

"Right, so it was by my efforts that your ancestors pledged the oath that you are now fulfilling. I've visited each of you, as I did your parents and ancestors, although I'm sure none of you noticed. It is easy to miss a bent old man smiling from a park bench or across a crowded cafe. You'll need to sharpen your observational skills as we proceed because the enemy can assume any form."

"OK … that's me. Left to right, please, front to back, I suppose. Peter?"

Peter's eyes widened as they darted around the room. He looked at his sister, then ran his fingers through his unruly hair and stood. He gripped the pew in front of him, then pulled back and wiped his sweating palms down the front of his shirt. Clearing his throat, he shoved his hands deep into his pants pockets, then cleared his throat again, albeit more quietly. "My name is Peter; Peter Pelling. I am here with my sister, Jenn." He motioned to Jenn, who acknowledged him with a small wave and a tight-lipped smile. "I, uh, we, are the descendants of Bedivere. Our family has been watching the Tor in Glastonbury, the hill that used to be the Isle of Avalon, for Arthur, I mean King Arthur, to return." He looked at Arthur, who nodded encouragement. "My father, Colin, and I were there to help him out of the cave he'd been sleeping in. So … hello everyone."

He sat down but jumped back up when Merlin called, "PETER … Peter is a computer genius and will act as our central resource for information, data, and records. Thank you, Peter."

Peter smiled, nodded at everyone again, and sat, eyes down. He looked up at the older, dark-skinned man next to him, eyes pleading with him to pick up the ball … who instead turned to the woman behind them and said, "Ladies first."

She stood and nodded to Arthur. "My name is CJ, Cynthia Jones, Your Highness. I'm with the British Special Forces, anti-terror, based out of the Afghanistan war zone. I'm told our ancestor was Sir Cai. The legends say that you and he were close."

"He was like a brother to me, CJ," replied Arthur. "But what are Special Forces? Some form of cooking or other support unit? Perhaps nursing?"

Jenn felt the temperature drop from CJ's icy look.

"You aren't suggesting you intend to fight, are you?" He looked at Merlin quizzically. The old wizard smiled and nodded back towards CJ.

In a cool monotone, all prior deference gone, CJ continued, "Welcome to the 21st century, *Your Highness*. I'm solid in hand-to-hand, shooting, and infiltration. Yeah, I can fight. So, I say let's find this asshole, take him down, and get on with it before you exhaust my ladylike tolerance."

"The asshole is likely a 'her' as well, CJ," Arthur corrected, unfazed by her challenge. Then, in a conciliatory tone, "So a modern-day Boudica. Very curious. I guess we'll see. Thank you."

Jenn couldn't wait to learn more about this woman who wasn't afraid to put the warlord in his place.

With a friendly smile, the man who'd deferred to CJ pushed himself to his feet, using the pew in front of him for leverage, and turned to address the larger group. "My name is Jules, Julius Ashton. I live in Virginia, which is in the United States, and work for the CIA. I guess I can share that, since nothing said here will leave this group. My ancestor was Sir Percival. I was a field agent for much of my career, so I trained in many of the skills CJ has. I have worked with MI5 and MI6, so, in guessing at the skill sets the rest of you younger warriors might have, I may be of best use liaising with the local intelligence. Otherwise, I'm honored to be part of this and to fulfill my family's commitment. Thanks." Jules turned back around to Peter and repeated his thanks.

With a nod from Merlin, the unsmiling man on the right stood and stepped into the aisle, hands on his hips. "My name is Mikol Muller."

His accent and brooding looks reminded Jenn of the actor, Michael Fassbender, but even more brooding.

"I guess my ancestor was Sir Bors, but until now, I never really believed it. Maybe I still don't. We'll see." He crossed his arms insolently. "I live in Innsbruck, Austria, and I am a marksman. Long-distance rifle work is my specialty, although I shoot everything well. Das ist alles…" With a shrug, he sat back down and looked at Merlin, daring him to ask for more. Merlin smiled and looked over Mikol's shoulder to Jenn.

She stood up and said, "Hello everyone. As Peter already shared, I'm Jenn and am a descendant of Bedivere. Our family has been in the same small town in south-central England since Bedivere's days - waiting for Arthur. I'm a lecturer at a small college specializing in Historical Economics, which … well, you don't have to be a rocket scientist to figure out … is far less useful than computers," nod to Peter, "secret agent skills," nod and wink to CJ, "or marksmanship." She smiled down at Mikol, although he hadn't turned from his cell phone to listen. "I'm not sure what I'll bring to the mission, but I can't believe fate added me to this team for no purpose. I promise that when the time comes, I'll do my best." She directed the last bit to Arthur, who didn't return her earnest look, then sat.

"I am Eric Martel," the smaller man in the back row said, speaking rapidly as he jumped to his feet. "Sir Galahad is my ancestor, and I live in Paris, France."

"Yes, Galahad!" Arthur blurted out. "You look just like him, sir … Eric. Welcome!"

"Thank you, *monsieur*. It is an honor to be part of this adventure. I am a fighter, mixed martial arts, and I train in all manner

140

of hand-to-hand combat, including knife fighting, throwing, and improvised weaponry. Except for swords, I have not used swords, sir. Because of the precarious position of my chosen profession…"

"Like, that it's illegal in France," Mikol interjected.

"Correct, *monsieur*," he said, unfazed by the intended slight. "Due to that, I, at least, can be quite sneaky and stealthy, if that should be useful." He glanced back at the massive twins behind him with a smile. "One last thing, family history informs that I have Templar blood. I don't know if this will aid us, but thought it relevant since you, Lord Merlin, felt this sacred place might also be relevant."

Merlin leaned on his staff towards Eric. "It is true and relevant, Sir Eric. And as I recall, Galahad and Bors traveled together from Britain to France. I believe there are Templars in your family tree as well, Sir Mikol?"

Mikol looked up and held Merlin's gaze for a moment. "*Legenden*. Never put much stock in them. No point. Could be." He looked back down at his phone, ending that conversation.

"Yet here you are, *Sir Mikol*," quipped CJ with a half-smile.

"An oath is an oath. *Mein Vater* believed."

"Last but not least," said one of the oversized twins, the one who had attempted applause, as he and his brother stood up. "I'm Danie Swanepoel…"

"And I'm John Swanepoel," John added with a wave. He turned to Danie and gestured with open palms for him to continue.

"We're from South Africa, Jo'burg. We're related to old Sir Gawain by way of British colonialism. John and I are mechanical engineers, soon to be professors. Until we got the call, we were on the Blue Bulls Rugby team, so … what do we bring to the table? John?"

"Thank you, Danie. We're rather handy in a scrap, but I guess that's obvious; big, fast, scary and, as a bonus, are masters at solving problems. We'll pull our weight, no worries there." He and Danie fist-bumped, nodded at the rest of the team, and sat back down.

"Thank you and welcome, all," said Arthur, standing up with outstretched arms. "Before we adjourn to the meeting room Merlin has arranged, can you all please present your daggers and confirm that they are, in fact, yours? Our opponent is a master of misdirection, disguise, and manipulation. Trust nobody outside this group."

"Great advice," Mikol said. "So how can we be sure you're the real King Arthur?"

"I have NEVER had my identity questioned and…"

"Enough!" Merlin called. "Sir Mikol, please look at your dagger. All of you, take them out."

Merlin held his staff with both hands and bowed his head. Jenn thought she heard him whispering, and in the dim light of the Temple, the pommel of each dagger emitted a faint green glow. Nobody spoke.

"Now, if you are satisfied that I am who I say I am," Merlin said, looking back up, "then you'll have to trust that when, or if, you need proof of Arthur's authenticity, you shall get it. Now let's move on."

Jenn looked at Arthur as his knights stepped forward. She felt the smug look on his face was masking self-doubt after realizing he had no answer to Mikol's challenge. Everything he'd learned to rely on in his life was gone, except for an old sword and an older wizard.

Chapter 22

But you didn't go home, did you?"

The specter of Morgana looked out to the river from the bay windows. Meghan could no longer differentiate Morgana's ethereal presence from hard reality. In fact, reality itself had ceased to be a rigid concept in the woman's mind.

"No. I had business in the North."

"Uther?"

"Uther. I learned that he and Arthur were engaging the Saxons north of London, near what you now know as St. Albans." Morgana turned in her chair to face Meghan. "Reaching his tent was easy. Soldiers were trained to be compliant, just more sheep, really, and simply let me pass. When the old man finally stumbled in, he saw his queen, Igraine, sitting demurely at his table. Forcing myself to smile was the most troublesome part of this spell.

"I offered him a cup and motioned him to the seat across from me." The ghostly presence mimicked the offer to Meghan. "I never did master the voices of those I portrayed. No need. Men were so stupid that the right look made them senseless with anticipation. I could have brayed like a donkey, and he would have thrown himself at my feet.

"He sat watching me lustfully and drank deeply. My eyes encouraged him to finish the drink, then I let my disguise drop. Little sister, I can't begin to describe the thrill, the euphoria, of watching your enemy put the pieces together, realizing too late that the end was upon them."

"You poisoned Uther? How magnificent!"

"It was and in his last moments, I whispered, 'Do you recall my vow, old man? Look upon me and despair. I have plans for your bastard son, Arthur, as well, but his death won't be so discreet.' His eyes went wide, and his mouth opened soundlessly. Within seconds, the cup fell from his hand, and he slumped to the ground. Relishing the sweet vengeance, I walked out of his tent to begin my new life."

"But nobody knew that you'd gotten justice?"

"Not then, little sister. There were some who would need to know, but their time would come."

"So, where did you go after St. Albans? Did you go home?"

"I had no home any longer, so I wandered the island in search of necromancers and conjurers. I traveled to Hibernia and north of the wall, where the old ways were untouched by the Romans, and learned powerful secrets. More importantly, I learned there was a source of ultimate power that had been lost centuries before, and all the rumors and speculation converged on a single point. So, after years of wandering and growing in strength, I turned south. Travel with me one last time, little sister."

Meghan closed her eyes, anticipating the now-familiar veil darkening her mind. When it lifted, she was again descending a worn, stone staircase, but flickering orange light filled the terminus accompanied by the satisfying crackle of a welcoming fireplace. Instead of the rot and stink that had assaulted Meghan on that other staircase, she picked up notes of incense and applewood.

Morgan strode down those rough-hewn steps with clarity of purpose. Meghan struggled to keep up. In the warm light at the end of their descent was a cavernous space, its floor cluttered almost to capacity with tall piles of barrels and baskets that rose above the glow of the flames, into untold darkness. On a chair by the fireplace, in front of a table strewn with stone figures that Meghan thought might have been chess pieces, sat a deeply wrinkled soul with unruly white hair and beard. He reached up to his collection of figurines and laid flat a tall, thin, and dark one, then slowly turned to face the newcomers. "Morgan, you look well. Travel suits you."

"My traveling has just begun, Myrddin. I assume you know

what I've come for."

"Right to the point, I see. Come and sit by the fire with me and tell me of your life since you left Tintagel so many years ago. We have much to discuss, like how unexplainable death seems to follow in your wake." The old wizard rose and gently guided Morgan by the arm to the chair across the table from his.

Rebuffing his advance, she snapped, "If you know of what I've done and what I've learned, then you must know that I have seen your complicity in the events that brought us to this moment. I have no desire to speak with you, old man. Will you grant me the access I require?"

The old mage sat back in his chair, took a puff from a pipe he'd cradled on the table, shifted a short, wide statuette from the edge of the table to the center, and replied, "That is not meant to be."

Morgan fiercely waved her arm above her head and sent his entire collection crashing to the floor. "You love these mortals too much. I will not suffer the weakness and vileness of men any longer, knowing the power to rule them, to crush them, exists."

The wizard held her gaze for a moment with a hint of amusement in his eyes. He reached towards the scattered pieces and, with his own, more measured, sweeping gesture, reset all back to the table where they'd been. All except the black piece he'd tipped over moments before. Another puff from his pipe and a slow exhalation. "This is not your fate. Too much ill has befallen the world when one with access to this power attempts to control it. It doesn't know right from wrong, good from bad. No, it is best when it serves, not when it rules." Myrddin sat up straight and crossed his arms under his beard.

Morgan spun and reached for the now-dying hearth. Slowly, the glowing coals burned brighter until another crackling flame burst forth, reflecting in the wizard's tight-browed stare. She hissed, "If you send me away empty-handed, I'll return but with an overwhelming force. After tearing thousands of souls from their earthly burdens, I will take what could have been given without such loss. That will be on you, *Lord* Myrddin."

Myrddin examined the thin ribbon of smoke escaping from his pipe. Without turning to Morgan, he quietly said, "I think not. There is too much rage, too much hate in you. It could mean the death of this world."

"If I come to take it, do you think you can stop me? Or those that follow me?"

Now turning to face her, "Be careful what you suggest, child, because I can do more than stop you. Though your powers have grown over such a short time, don't forget that you are a neophyte compared to the lifetimes I've had to perfect my skills. As for those that follow you, I have full confidence in Arthur, as I had in his father, Uther. You will not amass an army capable of challenging the forces he can assemble."

Morgan stepped closer to the wizard, and the fire's intensity swelled. "Arthur? Please!" She laughed, "Myrddin, you vile, filthy old sow, it was a simple matter to ensure your Uther wouldn't return from that dalliance with the Saxons. I don't imagine that removing Arthur from the game board will be any more difficult." With a flick of her finger, one of the taller carvings, shining like white marble, leapt into the flames.

"What have you done?" he muttered, leaning forward and looking shocked for the first time in this encounter.

"I've righted a terrible wrong. I am stronger than you assume, and time is on my side. Know this: I shall return to you, not with my hand out but as your master, a vengeful angel who will bend this entire nation to my will. The reign of men will end, and their servitude to women will make the enslavement of the Israelites feel like a holiday on the Severn."

Flames in the hearth rose with her anger and expanded beyond the fuel they consumed. They caressed her, cleansed her; Meghan thought her face looked almost rapturous. Morgana reached out, and a tall, thin staff that had rested against the table in front of the wizard jumped into her hand. The fireball blackened the wood, then expanded to singe the carpet at Meghan's feet and the whiskers of Myrddin's beard before rapidly contracting to a point within Morgan herself. Absorbing this energy, she shot up the chimney in a plume of black smoke and exploded into an unsuspecting world.

Meghan remained. Not sure what to do next, she watched as the wizard absentmindedly patted smoking patches of cloth and facial hair. Moments passed, and he mindfully turned towards her. "You must go as well," he snapped with a backhand wave.

A silent explosion of white light blinded Meghan. When her vision returned, she found herself in the chair at home she'd entered this vision from, but the seat across from her was empty.

Chapter 23

Within an hour of leaving the church, the team assembled in a modern conference room at the Inner Temple, an office complex on the old Temple grounds. Merlin, however, had left them to attend to other business in the building. Arthur stood looking out the window, arms crossed over his chest, while Jenn tried to guess what must be going through his mind. The room was silent, and nobody was sure where to start.

Arthur turned away from the window and looked over his team. They were sitting around a long cherry wood table with crystal water glasses in front of each setting.

Peter settled into the chair at Arthur's right hand, likely oblivious to the symbolism that the spot entailed, and typed away on his keyboard. Bright though her brother was, she felt Arthur needed warriors, not geeks like her and Peter, to seize the day when that moment arrived. She was eager to be part of the team, but would have offered her spot for more South African behemoths in a heartbeat.

The wizard's return broke the silence. "What's this, Merlin? No round tables available, were there?" Danie asked with a devious smile.

Merlin moved to the open chair at the end of the table and smiled at the rugger. "No, Sir Danie, there were, but the rooms couldn't accommodate the likes of you and your brother. This was the only one with a wide enough door."

Danie and John, not the least bit self-conscious about their size, shoulder-bumped each other with matching grins.

"All right then, everybody," Merlin said without preamble.

"Shall we get started? Right. First, I'm sure you'll all have questions for Arthur and me about things that have no bearing on our mission, like the Round Table comment." He nodded to the twins. "Since that's out there, there was no Round Table per se. I made that up for a bard named Wace who, like you boys, was obsessed with details nobody else cared about. But you can discuss those sorts of things, Arthur trivia if you will, in the ample off-time you'll have at the beginning of the mission because, frankly, we haven't yet located our target, learned what form she's taken, or determined her intent. Things will move quickly once we do. I ask that we keep planning sessions, like this one, focused so you don't try my patience. Understood?"

Arthur leaned back in his chair, arms crossed over his chest again, and jabbed back at the wizard. "Understood, but is it true you can turn into a bird? Those last remarks bespoke an offended goose." He stared Merlin down with a smirk.

After an uncomfortable silence, Merlin broke eye contact and laughed. "OK, that may have been a bit over the top. My apologies, but the last group of warriors I addressed was much less sophisticated. Overgrown children, to be honest." He sat down and pulled himself to the table. "My point, though, is that I don't want the historic or fantastic nature of the mission's origin to dilute the importance, and frankly, the danger, of what we're tasked with. Is THAT understood? Thank you," he replied. "Let's begin."

"As a young girl, Morgan, as she was called at the time, resented Arthur, her stepbrother, from birth. King Uther genuinely feared for Arthur's safety. He had no choice but to send her away to an early outpost of Christian women that had sprung up in Exeter. This plan backfired when, as we later learned, she engaged in a nefarious relationship with an old man of druidic ancestry, who introduced her to the ways of sorcery."

"Why was Morgana so … I guess … antagonistic, Merlin?" Jenn asked, her voice sympathetic.

"That isn't important," Merlin snapped back. "We should stay focused."

Arthur turned to Merlin. "They deserve to know, my old friend. We may ask them to put their lives on the line for this quest. Nothing is out of bounds."

Merlin stood back up, ready to argue, but Arthur stopped him with an extended hand. He said, "I was conceived in trickery. My father, King Uther, fell madly in love with my mother, who was another man's wife. He then set upon their castle to take what he felt should be his. In the last moments of his successful siege, my father had misgivings about being accepted by my mother and conspired with Merlin in treachery."

"We've all heard this story, but I can't believe it's true!" Danie turned to the room, hands flat on the table in front of him. "Merlin conjured up a spell that made Uther look like the husband."

"Lord Gorlois," Arthur added, slowly nodding his head.

"Right, 'Gorwa' and had his way with the queen."

"Duchess, in today's vernacular," Merlin added.

Danie took no notice of the correction. "It was in that movie *Excalibur*." Danie then sat back, staring at Arthur, mouth agape. "What were you thinking, Merlin?" he blurted out. "While we wouldn't have had Arthur, we wouldn't have had Morgana the Witch either."

Merlin slammed his staff on the floor with a boom. Standing, he appeared to tower over the room, and his dark eyes bore into Danie. Though eight inches taller, one hundred pounds heavier, and maybe 2,000 years younger, the rugger sat down like a scolded, yet unrepentant, schoolboy.

"Britannia needed Arthur, and the world demands balance, so Morgana was always to be what she has become," Merlin said. "I knew not the circumstances nor the triggers, nor are they germane to this quest. I will not be challenged by infants, no matter how large." All eyes except Arthur's were on Merlin.

Jenn leaned forward in her chair, itching to respond, but thought better of it. There would be time later.

Arthur raised his head, stared out the window, and continued. "We believe that Morgan confronted Uther about his treachery, so she was banished." He reached for his glass of water and took a slow sip. "When Morgan came back so many years later, now Morgana, my father had passed. He simply fell ill, of all the ways for a great warrior to die, in a confrontation with the Saxons."

"Arthur…" Merlin said quietly.

Arthur paused, but Merlin looked down at the table and waved him on.

"I was then king," Arthur continued. "And knew she hated me. For the most part, she hated everyone. But my sister had become a stranger, so I put little thought into her. I had so much else on my mind."

"It was actually quite a relief when I learned she had taken possession of Avalon and stated her intentions to build a home there. With the Saxons checked, it was a time of peace and rebuilding in Britain." Arthur said, "I also commissioned a new home at the far eastern edge of Dumnonia, in a more strategic location. I called this castle on a hill overlooking the River Cam, Camelot, and moved my wife, the court, and the center of Dumnonia's power there. And it was there that Morgana showed her hand."

"We had been in Camelot for ten peaceful years. The only source of sadness was that I had no heir. I was preoccupied with this, but will not blame that for what happened. Morgana's skills at deception were flawless." He stopped for a bit. His voice had been rising, and he used that moment to calm himself.

"As I experienced it, my queen came into my chambers one evening, unaccompanied and unannounced. It struck me as odd, but I had little time or mind to put to the thought. She came to my bed in the flickering light of the fireplace and made love to me as never before. It was…" he paused in reflection. "Well … it was unexpected. When I finished, she leapt off the bed, pulled on her cloak, and made to leave. In the doorway, she stopped and turned back to the room. It then occurred to me she hadn't uttered a sound throughout the entire act. As that thought crystallized, she spoke. It was not my lover's voice, but my sister's! She said, and I shall never forget the words or the malice behind them, 'You will now have an heir, Arthur. I have taken you as your father took my mother, and you will soon learn to hate and fear the offspring of such a union as I have.'

"With that, she swept out of the room. I jumped out of bed, but when I ran into the hall, she was gone. I asked all I encountered, and none could recall seeing either the queen or my sister in the castle that night." His voice trailed off, and he turned to look out the window once again. "I finally understood the mistake that Merlin and my father had made when Morgana used the same treachery on me. Mordred was my penance."

John leaned forward and asked softly, "Was your wife alright, Arthur?"

Arthur turned back and offered him a tight-lipped nod. "Yes, John. I ran to her chambers next, and Guinevere was sleeping peacefully. She didn't know anything out of the ordinary had transpired."

Merlin retook the lead. "We know Morgana fled north, across the wall, to the Kingdom of Lothian, where her sister Morgause had wedded King Lot. She birthed the demon Mordred in their home and under their protection. The witch concocted a story that Arthur had raped her and that Mordred was the rightful heir. However, Guinevere was finally pregnant, and both she and Arthur denied all of Morgana's accusations. The kingdom expected the true heir shortly, and none were prepared to take Morgana's word over Arthur's.

"In Lothian, Mordred reached manhood under the patronage of King Lot and grew to have an undue influence over him. Reports informed me that when Lot did appear in public, it was as if sleepwalking, rarely speaking, at least not of anything of substance. Royal communication was through Morgana or, later, Mordred. I suspected this was more of Morgana's trickery, but she denied me access to examine the king. As he grew, Mordred sowed widespread distrust and enmity towards Arthur with other local kings who agreed to rise in treason to dethrone Arthur and place the crown on Mordred's head. For as long as could be remembered, all High Kings were coronated in the presence of the venerated stone, which was at Camelot. Morgana knew that taking the castle and the stone was key to having Mordred rightfully placed as the head of Britain. The battle at Camlann, in plain view of the castle ramparts, was their desperate attempt to seize control."

Silence met Merlin's pause as they waited for stories of the battle. When three knocks on the door broke the spell, even Merlin jumped. CJ and Mikol sprang to their feet, but the wizard, with a glance at his phone, motioned them back down, saying, "That would be lunch."

After the meal was served, the team seized the opportunity to talk about the legends they'd grown up with. Danie asked about the sword in the stone. "As Merlin shared, there was always that stone at coronations," Arthur replied. "From what Jenn and Peter have told me of this tale, that is the only connection I can make. Merlin, was this a product of your imagination?"

Merlin, caught shoveling an oversized forkful of beef in his mouth, waved the question with a shake of his head.

CJ asked about the Holy Grail. "The signature King Arthur story for me, growing up, was always the quest for the grail," she said. "Is there a shred of truth to that tale?"

"Of course not," Mikol spat, then winked at CJ.

Jenn waited for CJ to tear him apart for that. Instead, she laughed with all but her eyes.

Arthur smiled and dabbed at the corners of his mouth with his napkin. "I have enjoyed that tale myself, CJ. Jenn, Peter, and Colin showed me computer screens on this…"

"They're called web pages, Arthur," Peter said. "That's a term you'll want to know."

With a slow nod to Peter and a slower turn back to the room,

Arthur continued, "Thank you, Peter. Yes, web pages about the Holy Grail. But I can find no parallel in the actual events of my time, and certainly, it wasn't something I or my men would have had time or interest to pursue. Merlin was obsessed with magic vessels, weren't you? I would wager that you were behind this legend."

"Yes, yes, I may have suggested the grail to that lovely French boy, de Troyes, while we were both in the cups, if you will, ourselves. The story served a purpose at the time, as I was hearing of increased interest in the real Arthur and artifacts from that age. I needed to throw nosy scholars off the scent, and I knew de Troyes would eat it up. I didn't expect this one to take on such a life of its own." Another tap at the door signaled the staff was prepared to clean away the lunch dishes. All conversation halted until they had the room to themselves again.

"Arthur, can you walk us through those last hours at Camlann and the Tor, I mean Avalon?" Jenn asked. "I think this was an important turning point, and we should understand it."

Chapter 24

Camlann..." Arthur whispered. "I suppose you're right, but I'm not sure I know where dreams end, and memories start. There is so much I think I remember that makes little sense in plain thought." He leaned back in his chair. "OK ... Camlann." The ancient king expelled a long breath, then raised his eyes and began.

"We'd ridden hard from the south. You see, reports of a Saxon landing had drawn us away from Camelot days before, but when a rider caught up to us with news that Mordred was moving, we realized it had been a ruse. By the time we'd reached the field of Camlann, Mordred's troops had crossed the River Cam.

"We engaged the enemy and were making a good show of it. Through a momentary gap in the killing, I spied an enemy foot soldier breaking ranks and sprinting to the rear. His liquid courage must have finally run its course. I watched him elbow through the melee, and it looked like he might escape the field when a flash of red lightning struck. Not from the sky, mind you, but across the ground like an archer's bolt. He fell to the ground, a smoking heap ... and rats, from nowhere, everywhere, swarmed the charred body, feeding.

"I recognized Morgana as the source of this bolt, hovering at the back of Mordred's army. If I could reach her, this traitorous rebellion would end.

"I charged into the fray, and my army pressed our advantage. In this chaos, a path opened through the melee, so I ran for my sister, broadsword drawn, prepared to end this. Her two personal guards pulled swords and stepped into my path. I downed the nearest of her men, but unfortunately, left myself exposed, allowing the other to land a blow to my shoulder. It was checked by my mail, and it left him off balance. I struck him down, then confronted Morgana.

"We were finally face to face, separated by less than a sword's length when you, Lord Merlin, stepped into my field of view. I recall waving you off and then … then Morgana laughed. She laughed … and I attacked.

"The witch raised her staff to block my stroke, and it transformed into a sword. The impact knocked me back while she stood unfazed. My swing would have felled a man twice her size. I retained my footing and leapt forward. Our swords clashed again, and this time I was sent to the ground. Only then did Morgana advance. I recall being paralyzed by shock. It shames me now to think of it, but this was too much for me to comprehend. I could only watch, feet uselessly churning the turf, trying to catch a grip, as she raised her sword and then plunged it towards my heart. Just as it was about to strike, Merlin transformed it back into a staff with a bolt of white light."

"Perhaps my help was more welcome than you had thought, eh?"

Arthur grunted. "Perhaps. And perhaps you might have tried a bit harder because where the staff struck, my mail burst into flames. I watched the iron links and leather protecting my chest ignite with a sickening crackle, much like dry pine needles in a campfire. Morgana further pressed the staff into my body, causing me indescribable agony, and then began to raise it, and me, like a fork clearing hay. And like so much hay, in one smooth movement, I was flung towards Mordred, into the rocks near the river. I must have struck my head because my next memory was of Merlin's voice…"

"I said, 'Arthur! Wake Up!'"

"That's right. You helped me to my feet. Mordred was moving towards me, and I'd lost my sword. Then you handed me Excalibur. You said it was time I understood its true value. I recognized it as the ancient ceremonial sword of my family, although frankly, I'd forgotten it even had a name."

"I find that hard to believe, Arthur," Danie said. "It's literally the most famous sword in the world."

Arthur chuckled. "I've since learned that Danie. However, in my day, Excalibur hadn't seen battle in ages. My ancestors had mounted it above the great hearth in Tintagel, and it was only brought out for coronations or other celebrations. We can talk more of this over a meal, but frankly, I'd never thought much of this relic. It had lost its shine, but I hoped it still had an edge. Alas, I had no other option as Mordred was upon me. I squared up and faced my opponent, then realized, with Excalibur in my hands, I felt no pain. None.

"He said, 'Happy birthday, Father.'" Arthur's voice trailed off. "His first words to me after so many years of political maneuvering were 'Happy Birthday.' I hadn't thought about that until now."

Jenn reached out and touched his arm, which was answered with a half turn and a set jaw.

"It matters not. We fought, but it seemed that every time our swords met, he became weaker and less focused. Out of the corner of my eye, I saw Morgana making her way to our standoff. She wasn't laughing any longer.

"Mordred was circling me, struggling to keep his eyes open with violent shakes of his head. I tracked his movement and waited, also wary of Morgana's progress. With a howl, Mordred charged, blade swinging wildly. I launched a two-handed stroke that met Mordred's weapon with a deafening clash. Mordred's sword shattered, and he dropped it.

"I didn't hesitate. On my backstroke, Excalibur sliced downward from Mordred's shoulder, through his chest armor, and tore open his abdomen. 'No' was all he could utter, more of a whimper, as he stumbled back and collapsed to his knees.

"Suddenly, there was a blur of motion. Morgana inserted herself between Mordred and me, her staff held high. Unleashing a cry of fury, she swung it towards me. With reactions I thought no longer capable of, Excalibur rose to the challenge and met the Sorceress's weapon mid-air. There was no transformation of the rod, no red lightning, no explosion, or force. Only a crack as her pole split in two. The leading edge spiraled slowly over Merlin's head and landed unceremoniously in the river. Morgana backed off, true fear in her eyes. I advanced, ready for the killing blow. Morgana almost tripped over her prone son, wildly looking from side to side for aid, for ideas, for an escape. There was nowhere to go.

"I advanced and drew my sword back to finish her when I felt a pain in my chest that erased all other thoughts. The biting and tearing … Mordred, I assumed, had mustered an adrenaline-fueled surge of strength and thrust the shattered end of his sword under my rib cage, through the gap Morgana's burning staff had left. As I processed these memories in recent days, I now suspect he hadn't acted of his own volition."

Arthur sat, hands on the table and his eyes to the floor. "Our eyes met, our gasps for air, for life, matched. Then Mordred fell to his side and dropped the blade. I looked up to see Morgana beaming triumphantly. Here, my memories falter."

Merlin rose, and all heads in the room swiveled to the other end of the table. "Mordred's surge caught me off guard as well, but I recovered my wits as Morgana moved in. I knew more certainly than anything that I must protect Arthur's life, maintain balance. And to accomplish this, time was of the essence. You see, I normally preferred men to sort out their own problems. What's one king versus another in the eternal scheme of things, eh? But I knew I was as much to blame for these circumstances as anyone and could foresee even greater tragedy if the witch went unchecked. I transformed *my* staff into a sword of fire as I met Morgana's swing. We engaged in stroke and counterstroke, yet I drove Morgana back from Arthur's prone body. Suddenly, without so much as a turn of her head, she flung two stunned sycophants into my path, then turned and fled. I hacked the wretches down, but let her retreat. Tending to Arthur's needs was a higher priority … Although I'll admit there was a bit of admiration mixed in with my horror…"

"Stay on point, Lloyd," Jenn said.

"Sorry. So, Arthur was on his knees, head bent, holding his wound and gasping for air. Bedivere - your Bedivere - was at hand as always. I grabbed him by his cloak and bade him fashion a litter from spears, shields, and clothing. We had very little time … Arthur had very little time.

"Bedivere ran towards the bodies of the fallen as I, Myrddin the Great, Myrddin the Powerful, knelt next to the fallen king and searched my vast memory for ideas, not feeling so great or powerful at that moment.

"Within minutes, we had Arthur strapped to the makeshift litter and tied to his mount. Bedivere rode Arthur's warhorse, following me on my black stallion. We rode northwest with as much speed as I felt Arthur could bear. It was a thirteen-mile ride to the Isle of Avalon in Ynys Witrin. It was Arthur's only hope, and we had to get there before Morgana."

"I've dreamt of this," Arthur said. "Until now, I wasn't sure they were actual memories. There have been so many dreams." His voice trailed off.

Merlin allowed a few moments to pass as Arthur came back to the present. "We outpaced Morgana with enough time to hide in the cluttered docks on the shore of the shallow lake surrounding the Tor. I knew of her hidden entrance where the hill met the water on the southeast slope. That is where she would flee to and behind that door was Arthur's only hope. We advanced to the furthest dock, where I bade Bedivere unstrap Arthur from the litter, then we shooed the horses away and waited while I desperately cast incantations and fought to keep Arthur alive.

"When I thought I had done all I could, I pulled Bedivere close and said, 'Only Morgana can open the sea door. That skiff, floating out of reach of the pier, is her passage, and the door will open once the boat approaches. We just need to be on it.'"

Merlin chuckled. "Bedivere started blabbering about oaths, about how he would take that skiff, and lay his life down if his king needed him to. It was endearing, really. But I had to clarify that 'We' didn't include 'He'. I told him that once Morgana arrived, he needed to rush back to Camlann. His fate was not to fight but to wait and watch. I bade him return to the field and gather as many of Arthur's loyal captains that still lived. They were to meet me at the Bear Claw Tavern in Aquae Sulis…"

Jenn added, "That's Bath today."

"Yes, Bath, to meet in five days, at sundown. They must tell no one of this command and must come alone. The poor boy was crestfallen. He muttered nonsense about glory and objected to being an errand runner, forsaking his glory to others. Glory, glory…

"'You will have responsibility enough,' I told him. 'Just get them to the Bear Claw or I will find you and curse all your progeny to dim-witted irresponsibility as a reminder of your inability to follow simple orders.' Merlin winked at Jenn, who shook her head with a half-smile.

"There was no place in my plans for self-pity. Also, to be fair, I wasn't the sensitive, even-tempered, old wizard you see before you now." He paused, but nobody bit. "And this boy, truly still a boy, was the key to everything … as you now know, although even I couldn't foresee then what the end would look like."

Merlin sat and looked across the table. "He looked so much like you, Peter. Thin but wiry and strong … Right, so as commanded, he ran off just as Morgana approached the docks. There were only two guards with her. I turned to Arthur and assured him I'd get him to the boat by animating his failing limbs. He needed to give himself over to me for it to succeed, and we had no room for mistakes. Do you recall this at all, Arthur?"

Arthur shook his head.

"It doesn't matter. And after some time to reflect, I realized that the spell I used on Arthur to move him must have been what the witch used to control her near-dead son … as you now suspect, Arthur. Never mind that. There is still much to unpack. Mist rolled over the still water as Morgana approached. As expected, the small craft, with a coarse wolf's head carved into the prow rising above the mist, drifted to the narrow platform that had provided our cover. Silently, large wharf rats with glowing eyes materialized from the darkest recesses of the littered paths.

"We stepped into the open, not as Arthur and Myrddin, but as dirty, rag-covered dockworkers bound to serve her that night. Arthur slumped along before me, head down, feet shuffling as Morgana swept imperiously past us. In her wake, I reached for her attendants' heads and took control of their weak minds. Morgana was too agitated to notice.

"I picked up Morgana's packs and hauled them quickly to the boat. We stepped in, my staff now a pole, and I pushed us off. Morgana stood motionless up front as a heavy mist spread across the water. Within minutes, I felt more than heard the grasses in the shallows caress the bottom of our skiff. I could see through the swirling vapor that only a few steps separated the water from the steep hill and the door that was our goal.

"Morgana raised her reconstituted staff. I hadn't seen her recover the broken shard, but couldn't dwell on it with all that had happened that day, and began to chant in old Celtic. Torches on the shore burst alight, illuminating a hidden entrance, silently opening. That's what I needed to see. I rose and snapped my fingers. Both of Morgana's servants, sitting in the midsection of the boat, stood silently and threw themselves into the dark water. Morgana reacted to the splashes, recognition seeping into her eyes.

"I cast off my disguise and began reciting a spell I'd crafted for this inevitable confrontation, although that environment wasn't ideal. We were so close to her power base. Still, Morgana was immobilized and, as my words grew in power, began to decay before my eyes. Her skin wrinkled and became paper-thin; her eyes grew larger and sank into their sockets. To my horror, I couldn't maintain it; my strength began to wane, and Morgana began to recover. I was stretched too thin, you see, as so much of my focus was keeping Arthur alive. I'd overestimated my abilities, a rather foreign feeling,

161

I might add.

"Overwhelmed with fatigue, my arms dropped, and I slumped forward. The power shift was immediate. Morgana recovered in an instant, then leapt, flew actually, from the craft to the shore and turned to face us. She transformed her staff back into a sword with curses buried in unintelligible shrieks, then pulled the boat to shore with sheer will.

"Once we were grounded, she stepped up to me and raised her sword for the killing blow. I struggled to rise, to meet her, still hoping to best her with magic, but my muttered curses had no impact. I'd run out of options. Now, I didn't fear death, never have, and yes, I can be killed, but I did experience the regret of failure. Nevertheless, my fate was no longer in my power, and I surrendered myself to whatever the gods next had in store for me."

"Did she say anything, Merlin?" Danie asked. "I don't know, like a supervillain with a gloating monologue?"

"In fact, she did. She said, 'With your death, old man, the era of Myrddin and the reign of men in Britannia will end.' She said, 'I will take my rightful seat in Camelot and impose my will on these sheep you've fought so hard to protect!' Yes, now saying it out loud, this might just be relevant. But let me finish.

"A slow backswing to maximize the force of her blow - pure vanity, really, as a poke would have ended me in my state - turned out to be her downfall. Before she could begin her downstroke, Arthur lunged from his prone position and drove Excalibur through her heart."

Merlin closed his eyes for a moment, breathing deeply. Looking up, he said, "You must understand, this blow was Arthur's own doing … or maybe the gods intervened. Either way, I did not guide his body as I suspected Morgana guided Mordred's. The symmetry was beautiful, though. And I'm sure this was the only way it could have gone. Do you remember this moment, Arthur?"

Again, the king shook his head.

"Unimportant. So, Morgana's eyes snapped open and rolled

162

back in her head. Her mouth opened as if to speak, but no words came out. With the deed done, Arthur released Excalibur and dropped to the stale puddles on the boat's floor. The witch dropped her sword and grasped the hilt of Arthur's blade, still protruding from her chest. Before my eyes, she faded, losing her solidity as the torches inside the now-open portal on the hill became visible through her. The rage on her face was still discernible, but changed to disbelief as Arthur's sword dropped from her grip; her body now more vapor than flesh. She pointed a translucent hand at Arthur with a look of unbridled fury and hate. Suddenly, both arms, no more substantial than pre-dawn fog, snapped upright. She burst into a plume of black smoke and rocketed upwards, turning west until she disappeared over the hill."

"Where did you think she was headed?" Jenn asked?

"I believe she headed for Cornwall. Tintagel may have been a familiar touchpoint, but the ports were a more likely goal."

"Did you try to go after her?" Peter asked.

"I did not, young Peter, as I needed to tend to Arthur before he slipped away. In hindsight, a falcon had accompanied me from the battlefield, and I could have dispatched her to follow the apparition, but I was tired … so tired. I live with that regret to this day.

"So, no, what strength I had was spent guiding Arthur into Morgana's cell and laying him to rest. Then, with a heavy heart and crippling foreboding, I sealed the hill and poled the skiff back to the dock."

Chapter 25

As the sun sank below the London skyline, the shadows on the Temple Church contrasted the golden light striking the tower of the Round Church and accentuated the tragedy of Arthur's last days. Questions flew regarding Morgana's likely plans after Avalon. "I searched where I could," Merlin said. "But until she resurfaced recently, there had been no sign of her. I discussed this at length with the much-renewed King Lot when I brought Gawain back and personally cleared my caves at Tintagel Castle. Ruling those out, I was at a loss for other options."

"From your knowledge of her powers, what was her most likely plan to survive, having transformed to, I guess, *son esprit*?"

"Excellent question, Sir Eric, and one I pondered those first few centuries. A purely ethereal existence isn't sustainable. Her natural body had passed, so it couldn't be reconstituted. She could have lasted days, maybe weeks, in that state, but would have needed a physical body in time. It didn't need to be human, and frankly, the longer she was in that weakened state, attaching herself to a human would have been difficult. As I examined the papers and writings she'd left behind, I concluded that she'd uncovered the secrets behind attaching her core spirit, maybe essence, to people or animals. However, magic power, like any other energy you've discovered or developed in this age, dissipates over time, as mine has. Unless something or someone was able to energize her..."

"Like jump-starting a weak battery?" Jules asked.

"Yes, Sir Julius, like jump-starting a battery. Without that, I wouldn't have expected her to have the strength to control the consciousness of a human as she appears to have done, even after only a few hundred years of dormancy."

"Learning how she recharged might help us determine how to stop her, ya?" Mikol muttered.

Arthur slammed his palms on the table. "We know how to stop her, Mikol. It is the reason Merlin kept me around. I alone must strike her down with this sword." He motioned to Excalibur standing in the corner to his right. "And I must do it while she is weak, else we start the cycle over again." He leaned forward, his voice low and determined. "We must find her and crush her. I fear we've wasted too much time talking."

"And I," Merlin added, "don't have the strength to put an arrogant king back on watch, if you will, for a second time if we botch this up. I'd also need to be recharged, but I fear the source of my power is lost to history." He directed the next comment at Arthur. "So, we will talk until we're sure because, unlike two armies on a field, we can't win this with brute force."

Arthur leaned forward. "And you'd know that winning a battle is much more complex than brute force if you'd joined me against the Saxons instead of hiding in your cave, weaving your little webs!"

"My little webs…"

"Boys, please," Jenn said. "Is it possible that your source of power, as you called it, and the source that recharged Morgana, are one and the same? What was your source of power, Merlin?"

The wizard waved his hand to dismiss her question. "It's not important."

"How can you know that? We need to have…".

"JENNIFER … Jennifer." Merlin looked down at the table, then scanned the faces around the room. His face softened. "Look, I feared Morgana might try to use the power that fed me to come back, so I sent it far away. Since then, it has been lost. It would be a false path to pursue, and we have limited time to identify the person Morgana is working through and stop her before she can take her plans to fruition. That is what we must focus on." His countenance defied challenge.

165

The temperature in the room was dropping fast. Jenn's look to Arthur implored him to speak up, but it was Peter, though, who broke the ice. "It was the stone, wasn't it? The stone you used for the daggers, which you sent away. That was your source of power."

"Enough! My business is my business, and I am telling you, pursuing a link to my power, be it a stone, a flower, or a burrito, is a dead end. Let's focus on what we know, what is real, and what will allow us to finish our job."

Merlin had stood in the middle of that declaration, pushing his chair backward with a scrape, leaning in, and placing his palms on the table. Arthur also leaned forward, locking eyes with his old friend.

The king finally looked away. "As Lord Merlin requested, let's move past the discussion of his secrets unless further investigation warrants returning to them. Please, Merlin, let's continue."

Merlin stood back upright, more relaxed, fingertips still touching the table, but his face had softened. "Yes, right, thank you. So here we are, and what do we really know? The spell that put Arthur to sleep was complex. He would only wake if Morgana regained human form. That he is among us is proof enough that she has returned. I've concluded that she has hitched a ride on another, who feeds the witch her energy and shares her consciousness. Morgana's goal, however, will be to claim that body and displace him or her completely such that she is, in effect, reborn. It should be obvious to all that she hasn't reached that desired state of existence, so she's still vulnerable."

"Merlin, it isn't obvious to me. Why do we know she hasn't completely possessed another?"

"Simply this, Lady Jennifer - to reach that level of power, she would have had to super-charge, not simply recharge, using Sir Julius' analogy. To super-charge, she would have had to locate and possess a primeval source of power. You'd be surprised how many there had once been. Had she located one though, frankly, the game would be over. She wouldn't need to hide."

"So, the fact that we don't know who or where she is means that she still feels vulnerable; therefore, she must not have found this battery or whatever, right?" Peter asked.

"Exactly, which leaves option two, that she's found a receptive host and is working through them. Based on her history and loathing of men, it's fair to say she's chosen to ally herself with a woman, thus reducing our pool of candidates."

CJ laughed out loud. "Right, we only have to interrogate half the world's population. Let's get started."

Eric, pacing behind the chairs, chuckled in support. Mikol crossed his arms and shook his head, but the others dismissed the comment.

"Fine, sorry, continue, Merlin," she said, and slouched a bit in her chair.

"We know quite a bit more than that, CJ," Merlin added without reproach. "Peter, can you summarize what we've compiled?"

"Um, yessir," Peter mumbled as he cycled through open documents on his laptop. "I'm sorry ... it was right here..." His face reddened as his mouse movement picked up its pace.

Jules put a hand on the young man's arm. "It's OK, son, take your time."

Peter nodded to Jules, took a deep breath, and clicked his mouse twice. He smiled up at Jules and said, "Right. Has everyone heard about the #HimToo murders in and around London?"

"It's not like *we've* been living in a cave, kid," CJ quipped.

"Yes, well ... right," Peter said. "It is our theory that the mental state of the perps fits Morgana's historical MO of mind control, and the fact that all the victims are men of power or influence supports it. We believe that Morgana, or whoever Morgana is acting through, is a woman with high social status in or around London. It is also likely to be a woman on edge, maybe with grudges or a victim of abuse. Maybe both, where Morgana only needed to give them a little push. While still a large subset, it will be manageable after additional filters we have yet to apply, such as schedules, demographics, and target personae."

"The police," Jules offered, "would have likely come to most of those conclusions as well. They wouldn't trigger on the paranormal aspects we understand, but I don't yet see how that additional knowledge will lead us to Morgana more quickly."

"It may not give us an advantage over the authorities, Jules," Arthur answered, "but we don't see it as us versus them. We all want the same thing initially. That is why your ability to work with them will be crucial. Our goals diverge at the conclusion. We must get to her first. If she is simply caught and incarcerated, she'll have opportunities to disappear again, either whole or in spirit form."

"The firm that has managed our affairs for the past century has already connected with MI5, and they are expecting you, Sir Julius," Merlin said. "They only know that America has an interest in this case and that they must collaborate with you fully."

Jenn, who had answered a call while the others talked, leapt to her feet; the urgency of which nearly knocked her chair over. She walked to the window with her cell phone pressed to her ear.

"Merlin, wait," Arthur said, as Jenn turned back to the room. The color had drained from her face, and her eyes were wide and welling with tears. "What is it, Jenn?" he asked.

Staring past Arthur, Jenn gripped the table with two hands as she fell into her chair. Then, her eyes found her brother. "That was the Glastonbury police. Somebody broke into our home; they tore it apart, Peter," she said.

"Is Dad OK?" Peter asked.

"He's dead, Peter. He's been shot."

Chapter 26

Jenn looked at Arthur. "I ... I need to go back," she whispered between choked gasps.

He wrapped her hands in his. "Jenn, I am so sorry. This is all..."

She cut him off, eyes finding focus. "No," she snapped. "It's not your fault. Don't go there. And we don't even know it's related to..." She looked around at all the strange faces suddenly thrust into her life, "to this."

Peter rushed around the table and threw his arms around his sister, tears running down both of their faces. "Oh my god, Jenn ... How...?"

Jenn crushed Arthur's fingers, her eyes glued to his, then melted into her brother's embrace.

Merlin stood. "You both need to go home. I'll have a car brought around for you. We'll cover all costs and make sure the local authorities provide additional security. I am very sorry, Jenn and Peter. I greatly respected your father."

Arthur stepped back and crossed his arms. "I ... well..." was all he said.

Danie broke the awkward silence and wrapped them in a bear hug. Crouching to make eye contact, "We're so sorry. We will catch her, and she will pay."

John pulled the Pellings from his brother and guided them to the door. "You need to go. Let's get you on the road."

Mikol stood by the door, hands in his pockets, head bowed. Jenn looked up, and their eyes met. A somber nod was the best Mikol could offer. CJ, Jules, and Eric came around and offered their condolences.

Merlin ended a call and stepped forward. "A car and driver are downstairs. He's a security professional and will stay with you for as long as you need him. You'll be safe. I'll have your things brought to you later today. Focus on each other and your family. We will take care of everything else." He put a hand on their shoulders, met their upturned faces with a reassuring smile, and walked them out the door.

When they had left and the door closed, Arthur looked at Merlin, now sitting back down, head dropped, taking all this in. "What was that speech you made the other night on anonymity, Merlin? It seems we've lost that advantage."

"But who could have known?" John asked.

Merlin lifted his head. "I should have foreseen. As Arthur was conscious of Morgana's return, the reverse might have been the same. I'm afraid I put their family in danger without proper precautions, and the results were tragic. Centuries of waiting have made me a fool."

John stood up, followed by Danie. "Then let's head back to Glastonbury and find these bastards. This is a lead that could take us right back to the bitch."

CJ met their gaze. "John, Glastonbury is a small town, and strangers would stand out. The first rule of covert ops is to blend when you can, but if you can't, get out. It is highly unlikely they are still there."

"Speaking of security, if they knew where Jenn and Peter lived, they know what they drive," Jules added. "Pure speculation, but if they have enough access to murder ministers in their homes, they can get into the London CCTV camera system and track down Peter's tags. I don't think London is safe anymore, either."

"Yes, but unfortunately, this is a contingency I didn't plan for. I expected this to be our base of operations for the duration." Merlin stared down at his hands, retreating into his head.

"My family has a cottage up in Woburn that we can use," CJ said. "My parents are in the islands this time of year, so the place is mothballed. We could go there."

Holding up a Maps app on his phone, Jules said, "Woburn's about three hours north of the city, mostly rural." He handed the phone to Merlin.

Arthur came around the table to look at the map. "I like the remoteness and the fact that it's also not too far from here. That can work. But CJ, we are ten." Looking at John and Danie, he corrected himself. "Twelve. Will a cottage have enough space for this entire group?"

CJ sat back in her chair and crossed her arms. "Yes, your highness. I'm sure there will be plenty of room."

Chapter 27

The last leg of her run that evening took Meghan across the Exeter Cathedral Green, skirting the medieval church's grim Norman towers. Windowless and imposing, the tower spoke of days when people knew their place and respected their superiors. The sorceress reveled in this body's vigor, savoring Meghan's grueling runs. Still, she would trade this for some other powers denied to her, like the ability to see events from afar. Merlin had mastery of time and space, yet her time would come. *Faster!* Morgana pushed.

With St. Olave's in sight, Meghan lengthened her stride down the brick-paved alley, energized by the cool, early November air. She slowed when she reached the narrow walkways leading back to St. Nicholas' Priory, an ancient residence attached to St. Olave's. She'd left the front door unlocked, as she had nothing to fear in this quaint town of … sheep. *Yes, sheep. They are all sheep who wander, thinking only of base needs, waiting to be herded, told what to do, and where to be. They need a shepherd to guide them. You be that guide, young one.*

Stepping inside, she grabbed a cold bottle of water from the fridge and a blue towel she'd left over a chair. Mopping beads of sweat off her face, neck, and arms, she dropped onto the front sofa and gathered her laptop and cell phone. She saw a text from Dylan saying only, 'Skype me.'

Sitting back against the armrest with her right leg stretched out, she flipped open the laptop and clicked the blue and white icon. She selected Dylan from the Recent Chat list and took another gulp of water. Dylan accepted the connection immediately. "Is it done?" she asked without wasting time on pleasantries.

Dylan's face filled her screen, bobbing back and forth. He must have been sitting on a hotel bed, with a generic black and white print of leafless trees against a snowy background behind him. Meghan stared at her screen as the last drop of sweat fell from her nose onto the keyboard while Dylan adjusted his position.

"Well, Mum, we got to the house around nine this morning, and it was empty."

"And…?" Meghan responded, staring back across the Internet, not blinking, not smiling.

"Potts, Joe, and I entered the premises by the back door." Dylan glanced down to his right to check his notes. "Potts picked the lock. We didn't want to leave no trace of forced entry…"

"Get fucking on with it," Meghan hissed in monotone, resulting in even more shifting and squirming.

"We missed him, luv, the cousin. He skipped town earlier this morning."

She turned to her left and said, "He's gone." She clutched the sides of the laptop and willed him to follow that with a 'But…' and save the situation, save himself.

"Is there someone else…" Dylan said, blinking with a shake of his head. "Never mind. While we were tearing the place apart looking for intel, Joe signaled that someone was coming - the old dude that Paul talked about."

"Which 'old dude'?" She whispered through clenched teeth.

"Sorry, luv, the dad. Anyway, we grabbed him and pulled him into the kitchen. He didn't seem surprised but told us that the cousin had left earlier that morning. We asked where he was headed and if he was coming back, but the dude got a convenient case of amnesia, if you know what I mean." He paused, waiting for a response, anything to break that stare his boss was burning into his phone screen. "Well, I wanted to let him know who he was fucking with and smacked him. When he hit the ground, his shoulder popped open the pantry door. Listen, Mum, we were focusing on all the fucking computer gear they had and the rooms upstairs. Why would we have checked the fucking kitchen pantry?" He was speaking faster, no longer looking at his notes but taking nervous glances right and left. She remained silent. She had released her death grip on the laptop and brought her water bottle to her mouth, tapping it to her lower lip.

"Well, the son of a bitch pushed to his knees, head in the pantry, and jumped up with a fucking shotgun!" The cadence of Dylan's speech quickened. He held the phone to his face, and she could see it redden. Still, she waited before reacting to what looked to be disastrous news. "Before I knew it, fucking Potts popped two shots in his chest. Jesus Christ! He didn't have his silencer on because, you know, you can't tuck the piece away like that, and, well, shit. We took what we could and got the hell out of there before the fucking neighbors could figure out what happened." He stopped, staring into his camera, brows raised, eyes bulging, waiting for a reaction, any reaction.

"So, you missed the target and killed the only person who knew where he might have gone?" Morgana spoke the words through Meghan's unmoving lips. She captured the young man's eyes with a black stare, attempting to project her rage across the connection. She saw Dylan wince on the screen.

"Shit!" he said and dropped the phone.

She closed her eyes and took another draw from the water bottle to regain her composure. *That was unexpected.* As the heat drained from her face, she saw Dylan had the phone back in his left hand and was rubbing his temples with his right. "Sorry 'bout that, luv, crazy headache hit me. Gone now."

Cataloging that phenomenon for later use, she said, "Is there anything else, Dylan?"

"No, Mum. We went into town and checked the restaurants and pubs. Nothing. Asked a few people if they'd seen the guy, but nothing. We could hear sirens heading for the fucking hill, so we took off. Went north and holed up for the night."

Meghan had regained her composure and smiled. "Win some,

lose some, eh, Dylan?"

"Yes, Mum," he snapped, returning the smile, the smile he thought had charmed her skirt off just over a week ago.

"Come back to town then," she said. "Things are going to move quickly now. I want you to call a meeting at the center for Wednesday morning. Do you understand?"

"Yes, Mum."

"Good boy," she said, her composure restored. "I'll make my own arrangements to get there. We'll be launching Phase Two tonight. I'll have Paul take care of that."

"Yes, Mum ... and luv." Dylan was getting his swagger back. "I'd like to have a few of the boys head out to Exeter right away and make sure you're OK."

"Because you failed me today, Dylan? Because the one person who can hurt me still lives, Dylan?" Color and arrogance drained from the man's face again. She noted this even with the low-resolution video and dim lighting of his hotel room. She took no satisfaction from this. It was too late.

"Well ... yes, Mum. But ... shit, my head is killing me! You know, I didn't like you there by yourself from the beginning, right?"

"Fine, but I have affairs to attend to in the morning. They can meet me here around dinnertime." She slid her index finger on the touchpad down, putting the cursor over the red circle that would break the connection, but paused. "Please don't forget to call the meeting, Dylan. I'll take care of the rest."

"Yes, Mum, I'll..." but that was all Meghan heard as she tapped the pad and killed the conversation.

The next morning, Meghan was on the move, not waiting for Dylan's men. Coming into Glastonbury just before lunchtime, she headed to the Tor. Morgana wanted an opportunity to connect Meghan with her past again before events reached a climax. The old hill brought back memories, despite the Christian abomination on the summit where her home had stood. The modern city bore no resemblance to the dirty bedlam that Ynys Witrin used to be. She saw a sign for parking, two pounds. She pulled her Ford into the small lot and circled to a spot facing the street. Stepping out of the car, she saw a diminutive, hairy man in a black t-shirt walking towards her, a lost look in his eyes.

Meghan felt her hand rise to the attendant's face. His eyes bulged, and his face reddened.

"Morgana, stop this," Meghan whispered. "It isn't necessary, and we don't need the attention. Please." She regained control of her hand, and the confused man's face deflated. He still clenched the sides of his head. She fished a two-pound coin out of her purse and stuffed it into his pants pocket.

Morgana whispered, *Sheep*, and they headed up the street.

Meghan reached the park entrance, a gravel path leading to the hill. Out of the brush, a small brown and white dog confronted her, its tail was down and the hair on its neck raised. The growl was cautionary.

"Yo, shithead!" echoed from the homes to her left. The source was a shirtless, bearded man in sandals walking towards her. He paused his hunt for the mongrel when he saw the dark-haired beauty in front of him. With an involuntary suck of his gut, he said, "I think he's taken a fancy to you, miss."

She met his lustful look with dark, disinterested eyes and continued past the dog and up the path. With a faint flick of her wrist, the dog backed off and turned its menace on its owner. Screams of pain and disbelief punctuated his attempts to control the dog.

"OK. That was worth it," Meghan whispered to her symbiotic soulmate, suppressing a smile. *A distraction.*

Pushing through the gate, in the shadow of the timeless hill, Meghan stepped forward, closed her eyes, then gave herself over to Morgana's long-buried memories.

Like holograms in a film, Meghan saw cattle grazing on the steppes of the Tor. Looking up, where St. Michael's Chapel should be, was a neat, yet simple single-story abode with an open platform off the roof, what might in modern times be called a Widow's Walk, on the east side, offering a clear view of the Abbey or the skies over Glastonbury. Timber steps, accompanied by a rough-hewn railing, extended down the south side of the building, ending halfway down the slope. This was their destination. The ancient imagery faded, and Meghan set out onto the ringed pathway.

Thirty minutes later, she stood in front of the ancient entrance to Morgana's underground keep, confirming that the man-child Arthur and his feckless sycophants had violated it. "Had you left anything of value in this hole? Anything dangerous?" *Unlikely. I cleared most everything out before launching the attack at Camlann, expecting I'd be taking up residence at Camelot shortly.*

Distracted by the snapping of those disrespectful ribbons tied to the scrawny tree behind her, Meghan made a mental note to put a watch on the hill, then continued her climb.

Reaching the summit of the Tor, she took in the panoramic view. For all the centuries St. Michael's Chapel had seen, she knew it to be a historical infant in this region. She looked back at the slope she'd climbed and thought of Morgana's ascendancy to sorceress. This had been her home after she'd abandoned Arthur's court. Here she had initiated her plan that, although delayed for centuries, was finally reaching its culmination. The mid-autumn wind that whipped up the sides of the hill brought Meghan back to the present. A chill shook her, not from the breeze, but through clarity of purpose. Without further hesitation, she began her trek back down.

Chapter 28

So much left to do," Jenn muttered as she walked out of Goode and Sons. The gray stone of the funeral home and, frankly, of all the surrounding buildings only deepened her melancholy. Her assigned black Mercedes and its silent driver were waiting where she'd left them, but she turned right to walk a bit. She'd left Peter at the house to work on the cleaning, more like clearing, of the wreckage her father's murderers had left. Jenn had been rethinking her decision to leave Glastonbury but now knew that the house on Wellhouse Lane would never bring her peace again. The surety that Arthur's arrival brought about the evil that murdered her father had shattered the joy and adventure she'd felt when he came into their lives. Burying her father was an eventuality she'd not brought herself to consider. At least not until they'd had more of those long walks and father-daughter talks. *Godammit, not yet!*

Movement in her left periphery reminded Jenn of the black car creeping behind her down High Street. She stopped, and with a half-hearted wave, called the driver, more golem than man, forward. "Flowerly Yours," she declared more than asked, as she stepped into the back seat. The driver nodded but had already set his course for the flower shop they'd discussed and needed no direction.

Colin hadn't been a flowers kind of guy, so the arrangements were simple. Stepping out of the shop, she approached the driver's window. It slid open. "You know, I'm going to grab lunch and walk home. I could use some fresh air to, well … I'm going to walk home, OK? Can you meet me there? Maybe check out the place, you know, secure the premises if you will?" The driver did his best to smile, then closed the window and pulled away from the curb. Jenn

178

watched the car disappear, tucked her hands in her coat pockets, and headed down the street.

She paused in front of the Hundred Monkeys Cafe and scoped out the crowd. Jenn was thankful she didn't recognize any faces. The emptiness she felt sucked away any interest in conversation. She pulled open the door and stepped in. A fresh-looking young girl with braids looked up from behind the baked goods display and said, "Cheers! Sit wherever." Jenn grabbed a booth by the window, avoiding the handful of locals sipping coffee at the counter, gossiping about the latest. It struck her that, even a week ago, she might have joined in to catch up on who's who and what's what. Gossip was a cheap but effective remedy for days glued to her laptop in the ancient catacombs of the college. Not today.

"Bloody 'ell, Meghan Bonneville?" exclaimed a counter patron, cow-like legs straddling a stool that didn't look up to the task.

She couldn't help but perk up at the reference to an A-list celebrity in a local conversation. An overfed, younger man with an untrimmed beard and shoulder-length, unkempt hair was beaming at his audience. "Yessir, as close to me as you are, she was. She was loving up my pooch. Now, when she saw me, that was it, you know. She gave me her private number before hiking up the hill."

"No fucking way did Meghan fucking Bonneville even acknowledge the likes of you, you lying fuck," said the heavyset man who had first caught Jenn's attention.

"You bet your ass she did," the braggart continued. "And she's even hotter than on the tele. Yessir, she is. So hot she drove Keegan nuts, she did. It was like he was possessed."

Possessed? Shaking her head, Jenn pulled out her phone and lost herself in the latest round of texts, Facebook messages, and e-mails of condolence for her murdered father. She'd have to share that unlikely story with Peter. Posh Meghan Bonneville hiking up the Tor? *Hah! They could both use a laugh.* "Possessed," she chuckled as she watched lengthening shadows consume the last vestiges of sunlight from the street.

Chapter 29

The rest of the team hit the road for Woburn the morning after Jenn and Peter returned home. CJ left first with Mikol in her red Mercedes Coupe to open the house. Jules had agreed to drive the Pelling's Citroën with Arthur and Merlin. Eric rode with John and Danie in their rented Land Rover.

As the Citroën exited the M1 at Brogborough, Arthur could see the Land Rover a few car lengths ahead of them, but no sign of CJ's Merc. In a few minutes, the small convoy turned off the wider road onto a narrow country lane with increasing tree coverage. Arthur was looking off to the right when he heard Jules exclaim, "Cottage my ass!"

He caught glimpses of the manor house through the trees on the left before they pulled into the brick-paved driveway. Swafford House rose over the lawns as a monument to red brick and glass. Four white pillars fronted the two-story main building, flanked by symmetrical wings. The newcomers parked near CJ's convertible on the front drive. Looking every bit the 'Lady of the Manor', CJ stepped out of the imposing black front doors as bags were being extracted from the arriving vehicles, and welcomed her guests.

Arthur beamed. "Not even the Romans lived in such opulence."

Merlin, stone-faced as ever, hoisted his duffel bag onto his shoulder and marched past CJ mumbling, "I assume there's a room in this palace suitable for our base of operations?" He didn't wait for an answer.

CJ looked back at her gathering compatriots and gave a raised-brow eye roll before hurrying after the wizard.

Two smartly dressed septuagenarian servants met the travelers inside the door. CJ introduced them as Bob and Barb and assured the team that they'd take care of all their needs. "We have rooms ready for you, gentlemen. If you'll please follow us upstairs." The wizard wandered off, but the rest fell in behind the older couple on the carpeted stairway and saw Mikol waiting at the landing above them.

"I'm sure you'll find this to your liking, meine Freunde. The toilet in my room is larger than my whole flat in Innsbruck."

Merlin was peeking his head around corners and opening doors when CJ caught up with him. "Looking for a meeting room, Merlin?" she asked.

The old wizard grunted in affirmation and stopped. "Where would you suggest?"

"We have two likely options," CJ said. "The dining room is most like the conference room at the Temple. Natural lighting and space to spread out." She was walking as she talked and led Merlin to a set of white double doors. Pulling them open, she motioned him into a room with mint green walls surrounding a polished wood table and seating for ten. There was even a fireplace in the same relative location as in their first meeting space, but there, the similarities ended. To the right, past one end of the table, were glass doors that opened to a brick patio. Where the Committee Room felt like a conference center, this dining room spoke of elegant meals with tuxedoed aristocrats.

"This would do, yes," Merlin said. "What was your other option?"

CJ, still standing in the doorway, gestured back into the hallway with a nod of her head and guided Merlin twenty feet to an opening on the opposite side. There were no doors inhibiting access to a warm kitchen with walnut flooring and pale peach walls. In the center of the room was a white-painted island topped with polished cherry butcher's block. A row of windows in the back looked out at the garden behind the house. Stepping towards the windows, he took in an explosion of color, flowers in a multitude of varieties. His gaze tracked a manicured path through the foliage, which led to the Swathe Ford Pool, the small lake that gave the house its name.

Merlin leaned on his staff, lost in thought, then turned back to the room. Between the island and the windows were two square tables, each with seating for four. Backed barstools added capacity for three more at the island itself. "Lady Cynthia, we've got our new base of operations. Now, would you please show me where I can stow my things?"

Chapter 30

A buffet lunch of sandwiches, fruit, and pastries on the island greeted Arthur as he stepped into the kitchen. He was tossing a white and blue rugby ball that the twins had given him, and set it down on the table next to Jules.

A 65-inch flat-screen TV stood on a table in the corner opposite the entrance. Jules had taken the seat closest to the screen and plugged in his laptop, turning the TV into a wall-sized second monitor. He was whispering into his computer's microphone, but from the computer jargon he could hear but not understand, Arthur assumed he was talking to Peter. Happily leaving the new sorceries of this age to the others, Arthur moved to examine the lunch spread.

CJ had her laptop open. She'd spun her chair around and straddled it, resting her chin on the back of the seat while tapping away. "One would think nothing happened in Kabul without my say-so," she said to no one in particular.

As the rest of the team trickled in, Jenn and Peter appeared on the screen. Arthur asked Jules, "Can they see us as well?"

"Yes, Arthur. This camera," he pointed to a webcam mounted on top of the screen, "can pick up the entire room, and CJ has provided conference room quality audio, so it should be almost as if they're here with us."

He turned to the camera, then back to Jules to confirm he understood the gist of what he had been told. Facing the screen, Arthur said, "Jenn and Peter, how are you holding up? I know this is such a terrible time for your family, but thank you for staying connected to our quest while you grieve."

Merlin, who had no patience for matters of sentiment, brought the conversation back to the point from his seat at the island. "Jenn, Peter, as you've most likely heard, there were four more murders in and around London last night, each following the same pattern as those we've speculated Morgana had her hand in."

Jules glanced down at the notes on his laptop and said, "Ministers Armstrong and Balding were both poisoned at home, allegedly by their wives. Alfred Dunlop, Senior Director at Barclays Bank, had his throat cut by his mistress, a Priscilla Taylor, in the back seat of his limo as they were heading to dinner. Finally, Major-General Botting of MI6 Home Office was bludgeoned from behind in his study with a hefty brass candlestick. His wife, Gloria, hit him so many times that fingerprints were required to make a positive identification. Their teenage son walked in on the scene. He told police that his mother was sipping coffee in the chair she had beaten his father in, his body slumped on the floor at her feet. The major-general's blood covered both the chair and the suspect." Jules allowed all this to sink in.

"Jennifer, there would be no dishonor if you both disconnected from this meeting, or this quest for that matter. I hope you know that," Arthur said. "The same manipulative force behind Colin's murder had turned my own son, Mordred, into my would-be assassin. I have been pondering my last days before Camlann this morning, and what your father had said about the transience of kings in my age. And how only those I thought of as friends showed up for Myrddin's meeting. Now, their descendants are the only friends I have left. You've faithfully honored the role written for you so many years ago, and I am loath to see more tragedy befall your family."

Peter was staring at his camera, showing no emotion. Jenn was holding back tears, dabbing at her eyes with a tissue. "Go on," she said. "I'm OK." She glanced at Peter, then back to the camera. "We're OK and we're committed to seeing this through and taking that bitch down. The police have just left and, frankly, I need the distraction."

Arthur scanned the room for comment and then said, "Please continue, Jules."

"If there is a positive to last night, a fifth murder attempt failed through what appears to be luck," Jules said, then glanced back at his notes. "Roger McGovern, Special Envoy to the EU Defense Council, was changing into his pajamas last night when he heard a click. McGovern looked up and saw his wife pointing a handgun at him, pulling the trigger with no shot, a dry fire. McGovern dove through the bedroom door and crawled to the next room, where he locked himself in."

Jules paused the narrative again, scanning ahead in his report, lips moving as he digested the relevant information. He went on, "Then he heard the explosion of a single shot followed by the thump of a body hitting the ground. Being fully informed of the spree of wife-perpetrated killings, he stayed in the guest room and phoned Scotland Yard from his cell.

"The police reported that Mrs. McGovern had placed the pistol in her mouth and taken her own life. Investigators suspect the cartridge had jammed when she attempted the murder. Police are scratching their heads about why she would kill herself versus pursue her husband."

"She was more afraid of failing Morgana than dying, I'd suggest," said Arthur in a soft voice. He looked over at Merlin, who had remained standing by the buffet. Pushing his chair back from the table so he could pivot and face the wizard, he continued. "If you recall, Merlin, at Camlann, we witnessed many of Mordred's foot soldiers falling on their swords or cutting their own throats when defeat was imminent. It vexed me at the time, but they likely felt this death was preferable to Morgana's wrath. This fits the theory that Morgana is indeed behind the murders."

Eric, leaning against the window wall, lifted his glass of water towards Jules and asked, "Jules, are the authorities making any progress? This has to be driving them insane."

Jules glanced at Jenn via the camera and back at the room,

pausing before answering the question. "No, Eric. They are releasing sound bites claiming progress, but frankly, they have nothing."

CJ looked down at her laptop, and Eric turned toward the window. Otherwise, the room was still. Across the table from CJ, Danie turned in his chair and looked up at the screen. "Hello, Jenn, can you hear me OK?" She responded that she could. "Great. How about the investigation into your father's murder? Did anyone see anything we can use? We know these are related, even if the police don't."

John shot his brother a scowl. "Jenn, look, if it's too soon, you don't need to talk about this. We can reach out to the authorities." Despite his offer to put that conversation off, all eyes were on the screen, hopeful.

Peter spoke up. "Nobody saw or heard anything useful. Neighbors reported the shots but didn't investigate. And at that time on a weekday, all sorts of cars were coming in and out of town. Nobody noticed anything out of the ordinary." He paused and looked at Jenn, eyes asking permission to go on. She didn't respond.

Peter leaned into the camera. "Guys, I think Jenn might have something…"

She held his gaze for a moment before looking up at the camera. "It's probably nothing," she said. "However, Peter has spun up a tale that he wants me to share."

At this, Merlin stepped further into the room, towards the camera, with his untamed eyebrows lowered. "What did you learn, Jennifer? I sense this may be important."

Jenn looked back at Peter one more time. He encouraged her to continue with wide eyes and a nod. "As I said, it may not even be related, but I overheard locals talking about how Meghan Bonneville was spotted in town, at the Tor."

"Meghan Bonneville," Merlin repeated, his voice drifting off as he looked out the window, leaning on his ever-present staff.

Danie voiced what most of them were thinking: "Who is

Meghan Bonneville?"

CJ leaned back in her chair, crossing her arms over her head. "Some London posh who recently inherited a boatload of cash from her mom and dad, and is in the process of turning it into even more money. I recall meeting her at a party several years ago my parents dragged me to."

Jenn tried to dismiss the attention her gossip had generated. "This was most likely a case of mistaken identity. People like her don't wander the streets of a town like Glastonbury." To Peter, she said, "And I can't imagine she'd climb the Tor unless there was a gala at the summit. It just doesn't make sense."

Not convinced, Peter continued. "It's more than that, Arthur. I've done further research on her. Her inheritance followed the murder of her parents, right in front of her, a few weeks back. The killers kidnapped her and left her for dead in an old church three hours away. She escaped, or was let go, reports aren't too clear, and jumped back into the family business without so much as a nap, and went after the London finance world with a vengeance. I guess where she was aggressive before they took her, afterwards, she was driven, taking risks beyond reason, and winning. On top of empire building, she also funneled crazy amounts of money into an inner-city transitional program for first-time offenders, male offenders. Pretty busy for a traumatized heiress, don't you think?"

"Why do you think this is relevant, Peter?" Arthur asked.

"Well," the younger Pelling continued, "stories have popped up online about a change in her behavior. This coincides roughly with the start of the murders. She canceled appearances and declined invitations. The gossip columns were on fire for a day or so, but moved on to more lucrative prey. She came back up on social media and business blogs shortly after, as men in her inner circle were either cast out of Bonneville Partners or left of their own accord. It was called The Purge in one article, but nobody ever talked about why it was happening. Again, people lost interest, and the web went dark on Ms. Bonneville."

"So, she wanted to give women in the company more opportunities." This time, Jenn's opposition was less enthusiastic. "That's commendable, not villainous, isn't it?"

Peter interrupted, "And didn't you say the guy's dog started acting strange after meeting her? Possessed, he said?"

Jenn shot Peter a look but then turned back to the camera and nodded.

Arthur stood and slapped his hands on the table. "Yes! That must be her! Listen, we believe that if Morgana came back, it would likely be as a woman, correct? Morgana famously hated men of power, and this woman recently launched a campaign against men. And it seems she is well placed to know, at least socially, all the suspects in the recent murders. This is excellent! Well done, Peter! And Jennifer. Anything else?"

"Only that the socials say Bonneville has left London," Peter said. "Speculation about her absence has created a bit of a stir. What do you think, Merlin?"

Merlin hooked the leg of the high-top chair behind him with his left foot and spun it around. Sitting on the edge, then setting him? self back with a grunt, he popped the last bite of a sliced beef sandwich in his mouth and said, "In London, I shared that the king cast Morgana out of the family as a young girl to Exeter, where she was repeatedly abused."

"And she would empathize with a woman who had been through a similar trauma," Jules noted.

"Exactly, Sir Jules," Merlin said. "And vice versa. That commonality, combined with Ms. Bonneville's noted changes and her surprise appearance in Ynys Witrin, is too much of a coincidence to ignore."

"One more coincidence I can share then," Peter added. "I read the kidnappers released Meghan at an old church in Exeter, St. Olave's. Full circle, as they say?"

"And if I'm not mistaken," Merlin said, voice rising in excitement, "they built St. Olave's on the site of the same Christian community Morgana had been banished to. Excellent work, everyone!"

Still leaning over his laptop, forearms on his thighs, Jules looked up and pulled his cheaters to the end of his nose. "I've confirmed what Peter reported about Bonneville Partners." He looked back at the camera. "No offense, Peter, but I always look for multiple sources."

"None taken, sir," Peter replied with a smile and a glance at Jenn.

"I've also accessed CIA and MI5 databases. While there are plenty of references to Bonneville in unrelated inquiries, I find nothing that links her to the victims." At a loss for more, Jules sat back and crossed his arms.

CJ pivoted in her chair to face Jules. "But they had no reason to suspect her or look for connections, did they? If you provide them with the seed, they may find an entire forest of inferences. I saw this in the field all the time. We'd get the craziest, luckiest leads and take down a network that had been staring us in the face the whole time. Sometimes literally. I think this is it." She looked around the room, eyes wide with excitement that they could finally act. The energy level rose as the hunters caught the scent of their prey.

Arthur interrupted the revelry. "We may not want to show our cards yet, CJ, Jules. If the authorities were to pull in Morgana … Bonneville, we might not get access to her, despite Jules' connections. And she needs to die, not rot in prison."

Arthur sat and pounded his fist on the table. "But we can act, can't we, Merlin? I mean, we suspect, but don't know, that Miss Bonneville is Morgana. We can act! I can confront her and confirm. John and Danie can come along to back me up. Then we can take her out and end this."

"Hell yeah!" the twins barked in unison.

"Easy, boys," CJ said. "We still don't know where she is."

"And while we look for her, Jules, CJ, and Eric can head to London," Arthur said. "And speak to the families of the murderesses and the victims for links to Bonneville. They may find something the police wouldn't have thought to be relevant."

CJ reached out to Mikol's shoulder. "And you, sir, since we don't even know where to find the bitch, I'd suggest that you use the time we have to teach his highness how to shoot. Swords are dashing and all, but we don't live in that world anymore."

Arthur nodded like the birthday boy who'd been promised a pony. "Yes, I would love to learn how to shoot your guns. What amazing weapons! Armed with these, I could have built an empire to rival Alexander's. And frankly, Mikol, I'll need you to join us on the approach once we've located her. I'd often post archers out of sight for cover to neutralize unanticipated accomplices or movements."

CJ made eye contact with Mikol and winked.

Mikol crossed his arms over his chest. "Arthur, we will start training today. CJ, I assume there are suitable places on the property where we can work on handgun, and maybe longer-range, shooting?"

CJ smiled and nodded. "I'll show you." And stood.

Arthur stood as well. "Now we have a plan, but lack a location. Jules, Peter, can you use those miraculous machines to find where Miss Meghan Bonneville might be hiding?" He looked at the camera. "Peter, I know I ask too much, but we need your skills. Can you do this for us without neglecting your father? Your sister?"

Peter nodded.

Looking about the room, Arthur leaned forward, palms on the table. "We have a plan, gentlemen and ladies. Let us prepare ourselves, for shortly we will take the fight to Morgana."

Chapter 31

Cloudy skies threatened a wet Wednesday morning in downtown London. Meghan Bonneville kept her oversized sunglasses tight to her face as she hastened from the revolving door to the waiting car. The headquarters of Bonneville Partners was in a modern glass and concrete structure typical of the financial district. Word had gotten out that she was in town despite her telling only a select few. *Somebody has been indiscreet.* On her dash to the car, she saw a gaggle of reporters and their ever-attendant cameramen surrounding her, which drew a scowl. *Eliminating that weak link will be an amusing distraction.* Tossing her black handbag onto the back seat and climbing into the Mercedes after it, she mused about how little it would matter in a few weeks. By the time the door slammed behind her, she had turned her thoughts to the meeting set to convene at eleven o'clock that morning.

Arriving at a nondescript destination near the docks, the driver put the car in park and turned back to his passenger. "Are you sure you want to get out in this neighborhood, Mum?" he asked, sounding concerned. He glanced up and down the narrow street. An abandoned lot just ahead was the only break in the canyon of brick walls rising on each side of the cobblestone road.

"Is this the address I gave you?"

"Yes, Mum, but you don't see women of your class on these streets, if you'll pardon my sayin'."

"Duly noted," she snapped. *Like WE would need his help anyway. Men are so pathetic.*

The driver stepped out, came around the front of the car, and opened the door for his eccentric client. Meghan ignored his outstretched hand and exited without looking back.

Once the car had departed, Meghan doubled back two buildings. Pushing through a windowless door, she advanced down a dimly lit passage, the clicking of high heels announcing her approach. She smiled at two young men sharing a smoke and chatting outside the meeting room at the end of the hall; new recruits. They both dropped what was left of their cigarettes onto the cracked linoleum floor and extinguished them under the soles of expensive leather shoes with pointed toes.

"Morning, Mum," the men, boys really, said in unison. They both did their best to stand tall and stand out.

"Good morning, gentlemen." As she spoke, she reached out with both hands and cupped the boy's cheeks, one at a time. "Let's get on with it then," she said, smiling with a slight cock of her head. She hitched the strap of her bag higher on her shoulder, walked past the infatuated boys, and into the room where more than a dozen young men were waiting.

Folding chairs had been strewn about the open expanse, but most of the men were standing. Brick walls, painted institutional gray, enclosed a twenty-by-twenty-foot windowless space that smelled of stale cigarette smoke. A long folding table on Meghan's left as she walked in the door, sporting a stained wooden top on tan tubular steel legs, was the only other furniture. Behind the table, opposite the chairs now filling up, were Dylan, looking thinner and tired; spent, and Paul, in contrast, beaming with confidence.

They both snapped to attention, expectantly watching her walk in. She nodded to the leaders but walked among the men, offering and accepting embraces and kisses of various intensity. One towering, muscular black man slid his hands down to her backside and pulled her closer. Her playful eyes snapped to a dark intensity that he couldn't misread. The offender dropped his hands and stepped back, sudden fear in his eyes, but unable to look away. Meghan held his gaze with an icy stare, her hands on his upper arms. Then, as if it had never happened, her face warmed, and her hands

192

slid up to his cheeks. She pulled his head down and kissed him on the mouth. The room fell silent as all eyes, with a mix of desire and devotion, watched Meghan disengage, turn, and stride to the front of the room. *Animals, all of them. Filthy beasts.*

She stepped behind the table, ignoring Dylan's posturing for her attention. She turned to the room and addressed the gathering. "Boys, we're moving into the critical phase of this mission. Four of the five executions last night went flawlessly, so you can commend yourselves for the preparation and efforts you've put in. Even though Tammy failed to make the kill, her failsafe behavior kicked in, which eliminated all links back to us. Mrs. Botting understood the cost of failure and did what *she* needed to do." She gave Dylan a sideways glance as she placed her palms on the table and offered the room a nod and a smile. "Well done." A few boys clapped, unsure if that was appropriate. "No … please give yourselves a round of applause." She joined in with light clapping, first to the left side of the room, then the right. The men stopped when she stopped.

"I will deliver a note to the Prime Minister tonight with our payment demands. Either he agrees to our ransom in five days, or the killings will continue, and at a greater pace. None of his men are innocent, which means all will look at their wives, girlfriends, employees, and mistresses with fear. Believe me, they will pay, even if they must tear their sofas apart for pennies." She now turned back to make eye contact with Paul on her right, offering a smile. There was no smile for Dylan, and he noticed.

She faced the room and slid her bag off her shoulder, placing it on the table. "Once they agree to the payment, we must execute the next steps perfectly. We will not be unopposed, it seems. There is one who may have knowledge of our goals and who possesses the power to stop me. One that we didn't eliminate when we had the chance." She stepped back, motioning Dylan to the table. "It is critical that you all understand that failure is intolerable." She looked up at Dylan, who was fidgeting with a sheen of sweat.

The witch's voice rose as she turned to him and continued. "I identified the one man who threatens all we worked for, told you where he would be, and gave you specific instructions, didn't I, Dylan?"

He nodded and stammered. "Yes, Mum, but..."

"And didn't you say to me," lowering her voice mockingly to Dylan's inner-city drawl, "'Yes, luv, I understand'?"

"Yes, Mum, but..."

She cut him off again, face red, now screaming. "I will not tolerate failure! When I ask you, or any of you," she turned back to the room. "...any ONE of you to do something for me, I will not be ignored, I will not be second-guessed, I will accept nothing but perfection and," turning back to Dylan, stepping up, and placing her face inches from his, she hissed, "I WILL NOT TOLERATE FAILURE!" She punctuated that last statement by reaching her right hand up to Dylan's face and, with her index finger, pushing him backwards from the middle of his forehead.

The room watched this exchange in silence. The men had never seen the boss lose her temper like this, but were more surprised at the way she seemed to close the censure. Dylan simply stood there watching her. She was two to three inches shorter than he, but loomed large at that moment. Meghan took two small steps backward, maintaining eye contact with him. Her lips smiled, but her eyes retained the vengeful look from when she was calling Dylan out. She raised her hand, held it in front of his stunned face ... and snapped her fingers.

Dylan spun to his right and threw himself headfirst at the wall behind them. His skull hit with a wet thud, and he fell to his knees. Struggling to his feet, still crouched, he dove at the wall again. Men with experience inflicting head trauma would have recognized the sound of cracking bone. Several young men jumped to their feet in protest, and a few even made towards Dylan to intervene. Meghan stopped them with an outstretched hand, palm out, and cold eyes. Having no other option than to watch, they saw Dylan, now unable to even pull himself to his knees, pounding his forehead on the blood-covered floor again and again.

Meghan slid her hand into the bag she'd placed on the table and hissed at Dylan, "Stop." He collapsed in a heap. She pulled out a handgun, switched off the safety, and held it grip-first over Dylan's head. Like a drunken man, he rolled onto his back and reached for it. Meghan placed the gun in his hand, then took her bag from the table. She stepped away from the events playing out on the floor as the rest of the group watched Dylan lower his arm. He brought his free hand up to the gun, rotated it, thumb on the trigger, and placed it in his mouth. Some in the room would later comment on the dead look in his eyes, the whites glowing in his blood-covered face, while others would swear they could recognize terror, the look of someone who knew he'd die and was begging for a last-minute reprieve. All would remember the sound of the shot reverberating in the small cinderblock-walled room as Dylan fired a single round through the roof of his mouth, spraying bits of skull and brain across the floor. His body slumped forward, blood pooling beneath what was left of his head.

The expanding puddle of blood from Dylan's head stopped just short of her high-heeled black leather boots. Meghan stepped around to Dylan's left arm, which had fallen to his side, the gun still entangled in his dead fingers. She bent at the knees, pried the pistol from his grip, and wiped the handle on a clean spot of his shirt. Standing, she looked over at Paul, who was doing his best to be invisible, and handed him the gun. His face went white, eyes bulging, not blinking, but he accepted the pistol. "Paul," she hissed, "you are my right-hand man now." Pulling his face to hers, she kisses him on the mouth and whispered, "Don't fail me."

To the rest of the room, pacing like a general in front of assembled troops, she said, "Don't any of you fail me. I expect nothing but perfection from here on out." She paused for effect. "And when we succeed, you'll all have wealth and power beyond your wildest imagination. But if we fail…" She glanced back down at Dylan. "Well … you don't want to fail." This was a group of hardened young men who didn't take threats lightly. Meghan could see resistance and anger forming on some faces. Anticipating this, she reminded her army, "I know some of you may be thinking you want out. Some of you might be thinking," again lowering her voice to the tone she mocked Dylan in, "'Let's take the bitch out before she can do us!' Well, let me share that it's already been done. It only takes a touch, and I've touched each of you. Some more than others," she smiled at a few of the seated boys. "And I don't recall you complaining. Right, Leon?" She addressed the black man who had gotten too friendly when she'd entered. His hand rose to his lips.

"Now…" She pivoted and directed the finger at Paul. "Grab some boys and clean this mess up." She pointed to a man in the back and said, "Roddy, take me back to Exeter. We have work to do."

Chapter 32

Arthur lifted his Glock and took aim with a two-handed grip, shoulders square to the target and knees flexed to absorb the recoil. The hearing protection took getting used to, but between the previous afternoon and this morning, Arthur had fired over 500 rounds at improvised targets, making the earmuffs essential, despite making coaching problematic. And Arthur needed considerable coaching.

"It's OK, *Your Highness*," Mikol offered, handing Arthur another clip. "You aren't making any mistakes that every new shooter hasn't made … over and over again. Nice to know wobbly hands and poor aim are timeless traits."

"When this is over, Sir Mikol, maybe we'll spend an hour or two with swords to learn what other traits are timeless, eh?"

Mikol just chuckled. "Again."

By lunchtime, he was hitting head-size targets with 80% accuracy from twenty meters. After discussing likely fight scenarios and environments, Mikol decided not to waste time on rifle training. Arthur would be in the thick of things when they went down, so a light handgun with a high-capacity and easy-to-replace magazine would serve him best.

"These weapons are truly revolutionary," Arthur said after exhausting another magazine. "Fifty men armed as such could conquer all of Europe."

"Some from my country have tried in the past, *m'lord*. Unfortunately, there was always someone shooting back. It didn't end so well … for anyone."

They were in a brick-paved car park that once had served as the stables for the manor. The last exercise for the morning was a ninety-degree sweep. Mikol had placed targets at varying heights and distances, requiring Arthur to move and shoot. "Much as enemies in your day didn't have the manners to stand still and take it, expect that you'll be facing mobile and obscured opponents," Mikol coached. "You must keep your head and weapon constantly moving to ensure coverage. Move one without the other, and you're exposed. If we can get body armor for you, I'll be more comfortable, but let's assume the worst and compensate with more training."

"I was never fond of metal plate, anyway. Too constricting," Arthur said.

Ignoring that, Mikol said, "Now, remember, since you're new to this, take zwei schüsse, two shots, per target. If the trigger is worth pulling, it's worth pulling twice." Arthur performed the exercise from a standing position, hitting three of the five targets.

As Mikol was guiding him through the same exercise from a crouch, Merlin walked up, cell phone to his ear. Pulling the phone from his face and tapping the disconnect button, he looked up at the student and teacher. "We have news from the London team and would like to bring everyone in for an update. How is Arthur's training going?"

Arthur tore the ear protection off his head and looked at Mikol. He was growing more comfortable with the shift from leader to learner after a lifetime of command, although it had been a rough start. Mikol, face deadpan, said, "If the bad guys are slow, cocky, or we catch them off guard, his highness is likely to give as good as he gets. It'll be our job to keep them off guard, I guess."

Expecting a better review, Arthur opened his mouth to defend himself, looking at Mikol, then Merlin, but thought better of it. He was as ready as he was, and words wouldn't change anything. The three men stood in silence, letting the gravity of the moment hang above them.

Finally, with a nod to their shared thoughts, the wizard said, "Lunch is ready," and he turned back to the house.

Danie and John were already on their second plate of chicken and pasta by the time Arthur and Mikol had joined. Jules was in his usual spot next to the large screen and hooked up to Skype. Merlin was nibbling the crust off a slice of garlic bread in a highchair at the island. Mikol sat with the twins, offering a nod, not a smile.

Jules had his phone to his ear, head down. He lifted his eyes, noted that everyone was ready, and sat back up. "I'll need to get back to you, but this is great, really great. Thanks!" He reached over and tapped a green button on the conference phone. "Eric, CJ … are you still there?"

"Oui, Jules, and you are on speaker," Eric replied. "My apologies for the call quality, but the mademoiselle and I are in the car for more … privacy."

Jules looked up as he answered. "Yes. Great! Let's start at the beginning. Merlin knows a bit of what you shared, but John and Danie were out for a run, and Mikol and Arthur were making a shitload of noise out back. Please walk us through what you learned."

CJ's voice filled the room. "We spoke to Bridget Reynolds, the first killer, Jacquie Mattson, the restaurant shooter, and Priscilla Taylor, who knifed the banker in his car. The rest had lawyers blocking us, but I think we caught a reflective cross-section."

"Oui. I agree. And I doubt the others would have responded differently. We took turns leading to see who they'd be more responsive to. It didn't matter, mes amies. It was quite extraordinaire."

"Right, that," CJ said. "We secured a room without guards or video monitors. At our request, the killers weren't cuffed or restrained. We convinced the authorities that we could handle ourselves." The listeners in Woburn could hear muffled chuckles. "Anyway," CJ continued, "we asked them questions about the murders, and they showed no sign of recognition, as if they didn't remember. That was consistent with the reports we'd read."

"We then went through a list of names," Eric chimed in. "Some

199

nonsense, some from current events, and some celebrities, but inserted Meghan Bonneville in the middle." He fell silent, conferring offline with CJ on the right words to use.

CJ's voice came back on the speaker. "Each of the women flinched when we mentioned Bonneville. That was the only reaction to anything, really. And after that, they froze. They were done. That name, guys … that name freaked these ladies out."

Leaning into the microphone, Jules said, "I accessed the social media feeds - Facebook, Twitter, Instagram - of the victims using other names Jenn provided and saw a few intersections of the killers' activities with Bonneville's." Arthur looked at Jules, head cocked, as he tried to comprehend Twitter. "Sorry, Arthur," Jules said. "There are a variety of digital … digital?" he paused to make sure this term was familiar.

"Yes, Peter showed me the … Internet?" Arthur replied.

"Right, great," said Jules. "And on the Internet, there are places, message boards if you will, one can use to tell their friends where they're going, where they've been, or what they're thinking. Like this Facebook post after a fundraising event earlier this year. Mrs. Taylor shared that she sat with Bonneville. She even posted a picture of our suspect. We call this social media. In this age, it's like a trail of footprints that we can follow. Does this make sense?" Arthur nodded. "Bonneville had access and opportunity. Since we're operating outside normal legal and judicial channels, we don't need proof yet, but the response Eric and CJ got to her name, combined with the circumstantial relationships, suggests we're on the right path. We still lack a motive."

Arthur pushed his chair back from the table and dropped his hands to his lap, slapping his thighs. "Of course, this woman is Morgana. I said so before."

"CJ and Eric, can you jump to the last bit you learned?" Jules asked.

"Oui Jules. We couldn't locate or speak to many family members, but did talk to the sister of Jacquie Mattson, a Mrs.

Falwell. She met us in SoHo. Mrs. Falwell, Liz, recalls that Jacquie had recently been talking about her new best friend, Meghan."

"It was Bonneville," CJ added. "And Liz shared that Jacquie's husband demeaned her in front of clients and she was afraid he'd be pimping her sister out in a matter of time. What she hadn't told the police, because she didn't think it was relevant, was that Bonneville was helping her work through this, having been victimized herself recently."

"It fits, doesn't it?" John exclaimed. "Bonneville offers grief counseling that resulted in the elimination of the problem. I'm sold on the perp, Jules, but still wonder how she picked the vics?"

"We may figure that out once we know what her endgame is. However, we need to consider the possibility that it was random. Maybe only certain victims were relevant while the rest were smoke. Alternatively, maybe they were kills of convenience because of the abuse, and her only goal was chaos and fear."

Arthur stood up and paced the room. "It is time to act. We shall confront this Bonneville, and I will strike her down and end this reign of terror and exact justice for Colin, for all she's done."

Merlin stood as well, leaning on his staff. "And I must insist that once we confirm her modern identity, you must act with restraint. To end this quest, we must bring all the pieces together at the precise time. If you confirm it is Morgana, you must retreat. Do you understand?"

"Retreat? But I can end this, Merlin. We learned at Camlann that she has no power over me and, with Excalibur, I can send her back to hell. Merlin, I will not run from this conflict when I can smash it."

Pointing his staff at Arthur, Merlin said, "No, Arthur, I will not let your arrogance doom this quest."

Arthur stopped and pointed back at Merlin. "If anyone needs to curb their arrogance, it is you, wizard. Without your meddling, Morgana would never have achieved such power in the first place."

"And without my meddling, you would never have been born."

201

"Please! Both of you," CJ huffed.

Arthur turned to the window. A calmer Merlin leaned forward and said, "My point being, we can't risk her vacating Bonneville as she abandoned her form so many years ago. This will set us back to square one. There is much I haven't foreseen, but this I can say with certainty - this does not end with Arthur swooping in and claiming victory. If you attempt to slay this human vessel, she may simply hop to another, and we'll have lost all the progress we've made. There are other pieces we must put in place, rituals that must be respected, before we can set this right. May I have your word you won't attempt to slay her before the proper time?"

Red-faced, Arthur returned to his place at the table and kicked his seat forward. Leaning with his palms on the back of the chair, he said, "You have my word, Merlin, but I will defend myself if necessary. This oath will not render me helpless if threatened."

"I'd expect no less." His posture relaxed. "Now, Jules may have insight into her location. Is that correct, Sir Jules?"

Jules leaned back in his chair and took his reading glasses off, allowing the tension in the room to bleed off. "Yes, well, I give credit in this case to Peter, who sent me an e-mail this morning that broke it open. We learned yesterday that Bonneville had abandoned London about the same time the murders picked up. Peter hacked into databases of property sales and found that a corporation linked to Bonneville Partners purchased a flat in Exeter, a St. Nicholas Priory, which is attached to…" Jules paused for effect, "St. Olave's church, the same place both Bonneville and Morgana were taken to. I then got access to security camera footage in the area and had a few hits with image recognition, putting Bonneville in that vicinity, jogging, shopping, etc. I'd conclude that she has established a residency there. It would be my best recommendation for an approach."

"That location makes historical sense," Merlin said. "I believe, Arthur, that this is where you and your sister may finally be reunited."

Chapter 33

GPS brought the Land Rover bearing Arthur, John, and Danie to a car park just south of the church. Each of the men had press cards on lanyards around their necks, identifying them as BBC correspondents. John popped open the tailgate and handed Danie a weathered black camera bag and a Canon DSLR. For his cover, John tossed a tan cross-shoulder bag over his head and slipped his hand around a camcorder. Arthur's card identified him as Johnson Allen, a staff reporter. Bob and Barb had found him a tweed sport coat, a 1990s knit tie, and a pair of black-framed, flat-lens glasses to complete the look.

Before leaving Swafford House, a brief call confirmed Bonneville was still away from her London office and wouldn't be available for the foreseeable future. Climbing a short stairway, Arthur paused at the door and glanced back at the twins, his face set, and his eyes hard. With a nod from the ruggers, Arthur turned back to the door. He raised his right fist to pound when Danie stopped his wrist. Arthur snapped his head, adrenaline-fueled eyes demanding an explanation, but Danie just smiled and nodded back in reassurance. He released Arthur's hand and reached past him to push a white button on the door frame. They heard a soft chime through the closed door. Arthur took a deep breath, then resumed his professional look.

The door opened just enough to reveal a black man, close to the South Africans in height, in a white crew neck t-shirt under a thin, dark gray sport coat. His right arm spanned the opening, revealing heavy gold bracelets that matched the chain around his neck. "Whaddyou want?" he asked, blocking the visitors' view into the flat.

From within the flat, another male voice called out, "Leon, mate? Who is it?"

In response, Arthur jumped into the script they'd rehearsed on the drive. "Johnson Allen from the BBC. Ms. Bonneville's office should have phoned ahead to let you know we were coming."

Motionless, with eyes locked on Arthur's face, Leon replied, "Nobody's called. What's this about?"

Arthur said, "Look, pal, we've driven three hours from London and expected to have time with your boss. We're working on a story about under-thirty entrepreneurs and were told Ms. Bonneville would speak to us. Can you help, friend? At least ask her?"

The guard hesitated with uncertainty, then stepped from the door and looked to his right. Danie used this opportunity to step past Arthur and shoulder the door all the way open, practically knocking Leon off his feet. John followed him in, with Arthur at the rear. Leon regained his balance and reached to the small of his back. Danie removed that option with a crushing blow to the face. As Meghan's man crumbled to the ground, John and Danie pulled silenced handguns out of their respective bags.

"Who's at the door, bro?" mumbled another man as he stepped into the room, gnawing on a baguette. He froze mid-stride, mouth open, as he saw three pistols pointed at his head.

"Call her out," Arthur said quietly, stepping up and bringing his firearm to the man's head.

The newcomer's eyes moved from Arthur to Danie and then to John. Coming back to Arthur, his eyes were wide, almost pleading, as he began shaking his head. First haltingly, then with increasing speed and animation, he mouthed "No," then turned to the top of the steps behind him. He shouted, "Meghan … get…" but the handle of John's Beretta silenced him, sending him to the floor as well.

"What's going on down there?" a woman's voice called out. Danie confirmed to Arthur that it was Bonneville, based on the recorded interviews they'd listened to.

John and Danie trained their guns on the entry to the hallway at the top of the stairs when Danie caught movement in his peripheral vision. Arthur was slumping and clutching his chest. Her voice had triggered the centuries-old wound from his last encounter with his sister. The king saw Danie's concern and waved him off, gesturing with his head to the stairs. Danie looked up to see Meghan Bonneville staring down at them. Her black eyes were wide and fixed on Arthur's face, eyebrows raised.

Arthur straightened up, forcing the pain from his face. "Morgana," he said, meeting her gaze.

A mix of uncertainty and fear swept through Morgana and into Bonneville. She fled back down the hall, screaming to the unseen, "Get out here, now!"

Arthur started for the stairs, but the twins grabbed him, one per arm, and spun him towards the door. John said, "We got what we came for, Your Highness. It's her. We need to go." The ruggers hustled Arthur to the door while the king tried to spin back to the confrontation. John and Danie pushed him through the still-open door as pounding footsteps reached the room behind them.

They hit the bottom step at speed and ran to the left as the first of Meghan's guards got to the door. One man had just raised his gun when the door jamb to his left exploded, splinters stinging him in the face. A second and third shot slammed into the door to his right. The guards reacted to this attack by diving back into the flat.

Coming in a separate car, Mikol was covering their retreat from a window in a three-story building across the yard, giving him a view of both the entrance and the parking lot. By the time Meghan's men worked up the courage to venture out again, both cars were en route to the M5 and the safety of Woburn.

**

At the priory, a skinny, acne-faced youth with a wisp of beard on his chin and jeans that hung low on his hips broke away from the group at the door, leaving the intruders to his colleagues, and took the stairs two at a time to check on Bonneville. Flying splinters had torn his face in several places, and a trickle of blood stained his shirt. The door was open, and she was pacing in her suite, talking to herself, as she did more and more these days. He stopped at the entrance and waited to be acknowledged. She paused by the window and turned. "They got away, didn't they?" Before the man could respond, Meghan said, "Don't answer; I know. Shit … Shit."

"They had a sniper covering their getaway, Mum. Once they got outside, we had no chance."

"Are Roddy and Leon dead?" she asked.

"No, Mum, Roddy is still out, but alive. Leon is coming to." He paused, fearful of what he might hear, but asked anyway, stammering, "Are you going to … You know, like Dylan?"

She stepped towards her man, whose trembling made him look much younger. Meghan clenched her fists as she tried to control her rage. "You have all failed me today, but if Dylan had done what I asked, we wouldn't be in this position." She took another step towards the bearded young man and reached up to wipe away the bead of sweat on his temple that was mingling with the blood. At that, he lost control and started shaking, afraid to meet her gaze but more afraid to look away.

"No, my boy, you all will get a pass today, but we need to move. That son of a bitch found me too soon, and I'm not prepared to confront him yet."

His shaking slowed. "Beggin' your pardon, mum, but exactly who is that man?"

"That man is a ghost with no right to exist in our world. I need to finish this now."

***

At nine o'clock that evening, Prime Minister Andrew Hargrove received an ultimatum via e-mail on both his personal and his monitored government accounts. Subsequent analysis by the digital crimes unit at MI5 traced the origin across numerous IP hops until they hit a dead end at an Internet cafe in Antwerp. There was no closed-circuit or security camera footage in this cafe or directly out in front. Experts agreed that was unlikely the physical origin of the message, anyway.

The British government summoned academics from the top collegiate history departments to a second-floor conference room in the British Museum in London. Specialists in biblical lore, as well as British history and legend, convened to discuss the puzzling request and fill in the gaps for the military and political stakeholders in this crisis. What was the extortionist asking for? Where was it? And why would an unnamed perpetrator sacrifice a dozen prominent men's lives and threaten to increase the carnage exponentially to acquire it?

The e-mail gave them five days to answer these questions and deliver the ransom.

As a matter of procedure, Julius Ashton, the American liaison to the special task force investigating the murders, attended the meeting. The pieces were now falling into place, and he excused himself at the first opportunity to get back to his other team and start getting real answers.

Chapter 34

Thursday - Day One

Jules stepped through the front door of Swafford House and paused. Since the Keepers arrived, the noise and activity had been constant. This Thursday afternoon, the house was as silent as a mausoleum. He dropped his bag at the base of the stairs and crept down the main hall, conscious of his footsteps in the tomb-like quiet. Stepping into the drawing room, he paused. A fire was smoldering to his right, but it too seemed complicit in the silence, gently crackling and popping. Danie was teaching Arthur chess at a small, round table just past the hearth.

"Tell me again, why is the king so powerless in this game?" Arthur moaned.

CJ was reading in the armchair by the French doors that opened to the back lawn. She was wearing glasses, a first as far as Jules recalled. Through the doors, he could see Eric and Mikol on lawn chairs.

Arthur looked up and saw the questioning look on Jules' face. "Colin's funeral…" Arthur said. Jules nodded. In the excitement and activity of London, he'd forgotten.

CJ looked up at this exchange and offered a subdued smile. That's when Jules noticed she had a large glass of red wine in her hand, obscured by the book she was reading. "Is there another glass?" he asked her, stepping further into the room.

She nodded. "You betcha," and motioned to the long table behind the red sofa.

Setting his drink on the end table, he plopped into the couch, eyes fixed on a spot beyond the fireplace. That comparatively violent movement in an otherwise still room got everyone's attention. "So … before I start, anything new?"

Arthur pivoted towards him. "You've heard how the encounter with Bonneville went, I take it?"

Taking a sip of his wine, Jules replied, "Yes, and I'd like to get the details, but later. I'm not sure if your visit prompted it, but she has raised the stakes and made a ransom demand." Leaning forward and sweeping the room with his gaze, he said, "The clock is ticking." He had the room's attention.

Danie stood. "Hold that thought, mate. Let me call the others in so you don't have to repeat yourself." He stepped around Arthur to the glass door and pulled it open. Eric and Mikol started at the sound, and Danie waved them in. "Jules is back," he said. As they walked past him into the house, a colossal figure in a blue sweatsuit crossed in front of the lake at a slow jog. "Yo! John!" he bellowed.

Bob slipped into the room with a tray containing a pitcher of water, a glass, and a towel for John.

"Where's the wizard?" Jules asked. "He's got some explaining to do."

"With Jenn and Peter at the funeral," CJ said.

"This can't wait, and we'll just have to catch him up," Jules began. "After the confrontation yesterday, the Prime Minister received an email from an anonymous account. It was brief and to the point. The government has five days to locate an ancient relic and deliver it, or the killings of prominent men will escalate at an increasing rate." He let this sink in, then his eyes connected with Arthur's. "She demanded the Stone of Destiny."

209

Chapter 35

Friday - Day Two

Mid-morning the following day, a Friday, the Citroën bearing Jenn, Peter, and Merlin pulled into the brick driveway. The rest were waiting for them in the kitchen. Merlin stood by, stealing glances at the wall clock, while the team offered condolences to the Pellings. He was fidgeting and looking for a gap to bring the team back to order. Unable to control himself any longer, he spoke up. "Right, yes, please, we should get on with it. Can you all please sit down? Things must move quickly now. Our wait has ended."

Jenn, eyes still red and face blotched from tears, dropped her overnight bag and glared at the old man who had, just days ago, assured her she'd have time to grieve.

Arthur placed a gentle hand on her shoulder before she could respond. "Jenn and Peter will take the time they need. The only one who needs to 'get on with it' is you, Merlin. The stone! It's always been about the stone. You've deflected and yammered, having us believe there are multiple stones for multiple things, downplaying their importance, but there is only one stone, isn't there? And you knew that was what she sought."

Merlin set his jaw and tried to stare down the confrontation.

Arthur took another step forward, gesturing with his arms, volume rising, and persisted. "I…" then spread his arms and scanned the room inclusively, "**we** … know you've been holding back information we need. You knew the ONE stone was her goal the whole time, and we've lost weeks, maybe even…" He paused and looked at Jenn and Peter, but chose not to finish his thought. "Merlin, do we all have the same goals here, or do you have your own agenda, for which we are merely pawns?" Arthur placed his hands on his hips and locked eyes with the wizard. "You will tell us all you know. I will not tolerate your games any longer. We can end this. No more need die."

Merlin's face had turned red as he went through various combinations of brow furrows, eye rolls, and tight-lipped contortions. Standing to full height, he pointed his right index finger at Arthur, curled it back into a fist, then looked down at his hand.

Jenn stepped towards him, conciliatory versus confrontational. She put her hand on the wizard's arm and said, "Please ... what have you been holding back?"

The fight drained out of the wizard's face. His posture became less rigid, and his arm dropped. Looking past Arthur to the team, he nodded slowly and repeatedly as he pulled up his stool and sat down. "You are right to be angry, and you deserve the truth. I have kept this secret, planning and postulating this moment for centuries, fifteen centuries by my count, so I admit I've presumed an unfairly superior position on its resolution. I apologize for holding back and will try to be more forthcoming as we proceed."

Arthur nodded, still glowering at the old wizard, while Jenn urged Merlin to continue. "You deserve the truth," then with his best attempt at an American accent, "and nothing but the truth." He extended a hand to Jules' shoulder, then spoke to the room. "All these years, I suspected that the stone, THE Stone, was her goal. It was her obsession in Arthur's age and prompted much of what led to Arthur's near-death at the battle of Camlann. However, I didn't KNOW and hoped that it wasn't. You see, exposing the Stone, revealing its existence in this age, is dangerous. The reach of one ill-intentioned person is so much greater now than in Arthur's day. I couldn't trust that if I suggested it as a target, unfolding events wouldn't suggest it to her or her cohorts and make it her objective. If it wasn't her target, it should remain forgotten. That would be best." He walked towards the center of the group and continued. "I should have trusted you, but it's been countless lifetimes since I've trusted anyone … so I ask, I BEG your forgiveness. Your agenda, your goal, your quest, is my quest. There will be no more secrets," he said.

Mikol brought the group back to the point. "Merlin, do you know where this stone is?"

"Alas, Sir Mikol, I do not. I know where it went after Camlann, but don't know where it is now."

Arthur leaned back and crossed his arms. "Why would you have let it out of your sight, wizard, knowing how important it was?"

"Aye, a fair question. My powers were drained after I cast the spells to save you. They were old magic, powerful magic, and they left me hollow. It took many years to recover, and over that time, I made many mistakes."

With an outstretched, encouraging hand, Jenn said, "Please, Merlin, tell us everything you know."

Merlin laughed and said, "Lady Jennifer, there aren't enough years left in your life to hear everything I know." She rewarded the comment with a chuckle. "However, I can summarize what I know about the Stone." He had everyone's attention and began his story.

Chapter 36

"The first written reference to the Stone we're concerned with is actually in the Old Testament," Merlin began. "Your Christian Bible tells how when Jacob touched his head to a rock in a traveler's hostel, he experienced visions of the one true God. This year was 1,900 BC; remember this.

"The stone accompanied Jacob's family, the House of Israel, as they traveled the land. It found its way to Jerusalem and oversaw the crowning of the kings of Israel for over 1,000 years."

"The coronation stone!" Peter whispered.

"Correct, young Peter, but it's more complex than you believe. Many centuries later, in the year 625 BC, Jeremiah, a direct descendant of Jacob, prophesied that all of Israel would be laid waste since the people had strayed too far from God's message. He was imprisoned for these words. Then, as the armies of Babylon were on the verge of overwhelming Jerusalem's defenses in 589 BC, Jeremiah was released and charged to spirit Jacob's stone westward, far from the imminent destruction of Israel.

"Jeremiah fled with Baruch, his friend and scribe, on a merchant ship that plied the Mediterranean Sea routes of the tin trade. Scholars of the Stone accept the fact that it arrived in Britain around 586 BC. After this, the story becomes murkier."

Merlin paused and poured himself a fresh glass of iced tea. "They were greeted in Cornubia by early Druidic practitioners."

"Were you there, Merlin?" she asked.

"No, my dear. This was not yet my time, but these were my people, and oral traditions were sacred. They agreed to send the Stone of Destiny east while Baruch took a second cart, already loaded with another stone, a reddish one, north to Scotland, where it lay in hiding for a future deception."

"This became the Stone of Scone," Peter exclaimed. "It was all a ruse? So, where did the real Stone go?"

"To understand that, Peter, I must take you back a further 2,000 years. All across what is now modern Europe, disparate groups of men, with no means of communicating with each other, erected stone circles to honor the gods and provide a suitable place for blood sacrifice. In Britain, one massive stone ring was built to reign over all others - Stonehenge. They completed it in 1900 BC, the same year..."

Peter blurted out, "The same year Jacob found the Stone of Destiny!"

"Precisely, Peter. After this, the druids waited ... they waited for 1,300 years until that ship arrived in Cornwall bearing the talisman that was to complete the promise of Stonehenge."

Jules, who'd been trying to document this story on his laptop, was the first to speak. "586 BC is almost a millennium before Arthur's battle at Camlann. I can find stories of the Stone of Scone, but not Jacob's Stone beyond the Bible. Was it buried? Used but shrouded?"

"Ah, Sir Jules, this is where it gets relevant. Any other questions? No? So then let me take you back to Stonehenge and THE Stone.

"They placed the Stone on the long, flat sacrificial altar at the center of the henge. For ten days, druid leaders sacrificed slaves, beasts, and virgins over the smooth, black stone until the red speckles inherent in its surface were indistinguishable from the spattered blood. All manner of depravity was called upon to ensure they had the full attention of the gods."

Merlin noticed the incredulous look on Jenn's face. "Men worshipped cruel gods, my dear, then and at many times and places since. I'm not convinced much has changed. A conversation for another day."

214

"Torches illuminated the altar until an unnatural wind began circling inside the henge, reaching such a ferocity that it blew all the torches out. Then, all was still.

"When the fires were again lit, the form of a man became visible. He was lying with his head resting on the same stone that inspired Jacob to embrace the God of the Israelites."

Merlin had everyone's attention. The room was dead still until Danie blurted out, "So who did they find?"

The old wizard played out this drama with a long pause and a smile. "Who indeed, good knights. This was when yours truly arrived in Britain."

This revelation hung over the astonished group for what seemed an eternity. Jules was the first to find his voice. "So, the Stone didn't just supercharge your magic; it was your magic."

Merlin nodded. "In many respects, the Stone and I were one, yet separate. The nearer we were to each other, the stronger I became, and vice versa. It traveled with me as I wandered this island over centuries before Arthur and Morgana, searching for my purpose. I weathered countless storms of arrogance followed by black pits of despair in my quest. After all those years and all the miles, the only certainty was that I alone must protect this power from all who might misuse it. In my vanity, I didn't realize that those same dark forces would use my overconfidence against me, knowing that wherever Merlin the wizard went, the Stone wouldn't be far. When I ceased my roaming and settled in with Uther at Tintagel Castle, finally admitting to myself that forces rising against me might be a match for my tired powers, those most vested in possessing the Stone set events in motion. Tintagel was too defensible, so they manipulated the ongoing conflict with the Saxons to draw the seat of Dumnonian power from the coast ... to Camelot."

In a flat voice, Arthur whispered, "Camlann was about the Stone, not the kingdom."

"That is correct, Arthur. Morgana and her son were seeking

power, but not your power; at least not at first. Even though your army was victorious that fateful day in Camlann, I knew the Stone wasn't safe, for there would be other attempts to seize it. While it was in my possession, it was in danger. Hence, I returned to Camelot after sealing Arthur in Avalon to obtain the stone fragments needed to fashion your daggers. I then swore Guinevere to a quest."

Jenn examined Arthur's face at the mention of his lost queen. The king remained impassive, and Merlin continued. "I bade Guinevere escort the Stone to Lothian, Scotland, today, where I had alliances with men of my order who had fled north and survived the Roman purge under King Lot's protection. They were ready to conceal it. Scotland was far beyond the imagination of most Britons of the day and was the Stone's intended destination when Jeremiah left the Holy Land, anyway. As I told you back in Glastonbury, Arthur, your queen made it to Edinburgh and lived out the rest of her life as an honored guest of the landed families. She and your son Amhar were both laid to rest in that land. I visited the Stone twice after this. On my third trip to Edinburgh around 1100, coming back to Britain with William and the Normans, I learned the Stone had been moved. Nobody in my network had been informed of its destination, nor had they been able to trace it. This was when I lost track of it. I inquired and listened, unsuccessfully, for rumors but chose not to pursue it further. Today I wish it were not so, but I do not know where the Stone rests."

Danie leaned forward. "But Merlin, didn't you look for it? You must have been curious?"

John chimed in, "Right, I mean, how could you not search for it? As you've said, it was the source of your magic, your power."

"Did I look for it? As I said, I did for some years, but settled into relief that it was lost. First, you must understand, the Stone was like a drug to me. I was distraught when I lost access. I was diminished in its absence, so if I'd found it, I wouldn't simply be able to walk away. And believe me when I tell you, a character like me showing unexplainable interest in an artifact like that would have provoked suspicion. Second, I didn't trust that I could keep it from Morgana. I couldn't be sure where or when she'd return or who she might employ to do her bidding. In truth, of all mortals, I presumed only Arthur was truly immune to her powers, and I feared even the most loyal of my devotees could be corrupted. Lost to the world was the best place for it."

Jenn pushed her chair back from the table. "Well, that's changed, hasn't it? Not only does it need to be found, but it needs to be found by us, and quickly. Where should we start, Merlin?"

Peter was already working on his laptop, typing, scrolling, and typing some more.

"Understandably, where it might have ended up weighed heavily on my mind," the wizard said. "Especially in the darkest times of my despair. You must remember that this was an object of immense power and unknown origin. Did it come from God? Was it, itself, God?" He noted the expressions on John and Danie's faces, both devout Christians.

"God in a stone? As a stone? I can see you think it's incredulous, but your Bible tells you that the nature of God is unknowable. If true, assumptions about what God can or can't be are self-defeating, correct?" John and Danie had no response. "My point is that an object of such power leaves a trail. It impacts its surroundings, its age, and the people who encountered it." He stood again and started pacing the room in teacher mode. "Now I didn't have the benefit of the Internet," gesturing to Peter, "so I could only speculate about what that influence might look like. I do believe our information warriors should be able to uncover something with modern resources."

"But where should we start?" Jules asked. "The search parameters are still too broad."

"Yes, yes, I understand it might seem that way, but I believe those who moved it would not have wanted it to fade into oblivion. In fact, I'm certain that they never expected to lose track of it in the first place." Merlin smiled. "Maybe it isn't lost, and somebody knows where it is and what they have. Whether they'd surrender it for our cause is another story."

"That may explain the murders," CJ said. "Morgana would likely have assumed the same, that someone knew where the stone was. As I see it, most, if not all, of the victims were in positions that could have intersected with a relic like this. Wasn't the first guy in charge of antiquities or something?"

"Exactly," Merlin said. "But the fact that she needs us to find it means that didn't pan out. The next round of killings will be punitive." The wizard stepped up to stand behind Peter, hands on the young man's shoulders. Another smile crept across his face as he took in what Peter was searching for on his laptop. Looking up at the team, he said, "My advice to you would have been to look at the Arthurian legends, especially those that seem out of place or unexplainable in origin. However, it appears Sir Peter has beaten me to that conclusion."

"What have you found, Peter?" Jenn asked.

Peter held up his finger to request another minute, typed a bit more, rolled the wheel on his mouse to scroll down the page he was reading, then looked up. "Right, so there are a few stone legends that intersect with stories of King Arthur, even the Holy Grail. Each takes us in different directions, but one seems to be our best chance to pick up the trail if it had, in fact, been noticed." He then clicked through tabs on his Internet browser and shared what he had learned and where this information might take them.

The resulting conversation, bordering on debate, and often wonder, lasted for two hours. When concluded, Arthur stood. Action was imminent, and he doled out assignments.

CJ would leave first thing in the morning.

Jules would head back to London to liaise with MI5, stay on top of what they learned, and if necessary, run interference.

Eric, restless to get moving, was sitting on the back of his chair, rocking as he spoke. "But mes amis, we have a general description of the Stone - black with red flakes - but how will we know it is THE

218

Stone when or if we find it?"

"Excellent question, Sir Eric," Merlin answered. "The true Stone glows when addressed in ritual. It isn't like switching on a light bulb. It is subtle, but I promise you that if you see it, you'll know."

CJ, arms folded, asked, "OK, I'll bite. It glows in ritual, but how do we invoke the right ritual?"

"There are different forms, simple and grandiose," Merlin shared. "Having spent lifetimes with the Stone, I've learned that if one uses the phrase 'I submit to the wisdom and the power of the gods', or sentiments of that nature, the Stone responds. It seems to work in all languages. My guess is that it looks into your heart versus responding to the words. I'd suggest you own that phrase, internalize it, believe it."

Arthur placed his hands on the back of his chair and addressed the room. "Gentlemen, ladies, you know what you need to do. Please be careful, for we know not what Morgana has surmised, or if there are other forces aligned against our success. Let's stay in constant contact via phone or the Internet."

Mikol had been silent throughout the discussion. "If we find the Stone, Merlin, what then?"

Merlin replied with a mischievous smile, "Why, Sir Mikol, *when* we find the Stone … we give it to the bitch."

Chapter 37

Saturday - Day Three
     A bit of turbulence, followed by the captain's monotone announcing one hour to landing in Syria, brought CJ upright from her nap. Rule Number One of covert work (and they were all Rule Number Ones, she now realized) was to grab some sleep whenever you could because you didn't know when the next chance would be. She'd caught a Royal Air Force craft from Halton field, about thirty minutes south of Woburn. CJ looked around at all the empty seats in the transport plane and thought maybe knighthood had advantages after all.

     Her destination was the al-Tanf military base in southeastern Syria. It was a US facility in a highly contested region near the Iranian border. A skeleton team of British Special Forces was in residence. From al-Tanf, she'd transfer to a helicopter for the hop to the ancient town of Palmyra.

***

CJ wasn't initially sold on the justification for the trip, but the logical foundation Peter compiled had impressed her, and she agreed it was the best option they had. Peter had started by summing up the relevant Arthurian and Grail legends for the group.

     "The first recorded history that has a genuine connection to both the historical and the legendary Arthur was by Gildas. In 540 AD, he wrote about the Battle of Mount Badon. As Merlin shared with Jenn and me last week, he'd pressured Gildas to keep Arthur's name out of it." Peter looked at Arthur, then up at Merlin. "Gildas said this is where the Britons threw back the invading Saxons and reversed their momentum." Checking his growing enthusiasm, he asked, "Is this correct?"

Arthur nodded. "It was the first battle I led. My father was still king but wouldn't live much longer. It was a fierce battle, and our victory was costly. But yes, Badon Hill was historical." CJ chuckled as this conversation played back in her head because Merlin had called Gildas a 'bloated banquet pheasant.' She was sure this was scathing ridicule in a former age. After discussing Monmouth, De Troyes, and De Boron, the whiz kid got to the Grail story that impacted her.

That story turned out to be a compilation of two lesser-known Grail legends. "Has anyone ever heard of the Vulgate Cycle?" Peter asked.

Nobody other than Merlin had, so he continued. "The first section of this compilation was called the History of the Grail and took a unique deviation from prior norms." He shifted in his seat and scanned his notes before continuing.

"The Vulgate Cycle is a distinct document from the other Grail legends, and not simply because the author or authors are unknown. It was written in the early thirteenth century, around 1210, with heavy Christian themes. In fact, the manuscript suggests that Jesus himself instructed Galahad to take the Grail out of Britain and bring it to a spiritual palace in the city of Sarras. It said Galahad traveled with Percival and Bors ... and WE know Galahad DID travel with Percival and Bors to France, right?"

Merlin confirmed.

"Right," Peter continued. "So what if, as Merlin suggested, this is an attempt to document an oral tradition of moving something of power with a faint attachment to Arthurian Britain to Sarras? What I find interesting is that we not only know that Galahad and Bors traveled to France together, but that it is likely that both their descendants were Templars. The Templars are historically linked to the Grail legends, so the Grail may actually be the Stone. It's far-fetched..." He hesitated and looked at Jenn, then Jules for support, "but what if the Templars shipped the stone to Sarras at the end of the twelfth century?"

Mikol, never one to let facts get blurred by fantasy, joined in, waving his phone for emphasis. "Let's say we like the theory, OK. But where is Sarras then? I just Googled Sarras, and it appears mythical. How does that help us?"

"Right … well, I believe it's real and in Syria."

"Syria?" CJ asked.

Peter looked over at her again. He was an eager young man with eyes on fire. "Right, well, digging deeper into the Vulgate Cycle, we learn that Sarras was eleven walking days from Jerusalem. With some map math, the most likely city at that distance was Palmyra. Josephus also reported that upon entering Sarras, they went to the Temple of the Sun, which is an easy match for the Temple of Bel in Palmyra."

"Palmyra is still there," CJ said. "But ISIS targeted the Temple, and it would be hard to imagine anything of value surviving that or the centuries of regional conflict."

"Even if the Stone is gone," Merlin added. "Someone looking for the right clues might pick up its trail."

"That still seems like a stretch," Jenn said. "There were Crusader states still functioning north of Jerusalem, so why divert west to Muslim territory?"

"We may never know, Jennifer, but I believe had it remained in Christian hands, it probably wouldn't have been lost, and history may have played out differently," Merlin added.

"Or the Templars felt it was safer outside of the Crusader states," Jules said. "Sort of a misdirection move."

"Hiding in plain sight," John offered.

"Maybe, and that's where the second part of this story, from a writer named von Eschenbach, comes into play," Peter said. "Jules, you shot me that link. Do you want to take this?"

"Sure, Peter. The last connection is that, in the same period that produced the Vulgate Cycle, the early thirteenth century, Wolfram von Eschenbach in Germany wrote his Arthurian legend, Parzival, my new favorite, for obvious reasons," added Percival's descendant. "Interestingly, he stated explicitly that the Grail was a stone, breaking from prior traditions of it being a vessel, either a bowl, kettle, or cup. It's an odd coincidence that at the same time, one chronicler of Arthurian legend suggests the Grail is a stone, another says it went to Sarras. Neither story had a precedent or even a logical explanation for straying from the norm. Team, we should check out Palmyra."

Peter jumped in. "There's more. Von Eschenbach called the Grail Lapis Exilis, the Stone of the Exiles. I think that's a reference to the Israelites. Wolfram also said the Stone can bring the dead back to life and heal wounds. He then said knights defended it, and that it's heavy but portable."

CJ looked up from her notepad. "OK, hotshot, you've sold me on the mission. What else ya' got?"

Peter smiled at her, then turned to Merlin. "Do you recall how you said that the Stone could sort of, you know, tell if you weren't sincere when you recited the phrase about submitting to the gods?" Merlin nodded with a knowing smile. "Well, old Wolfram said that only the baptized can see the Grail." His looked around the room with a big grin. All were waiting. "Right, it's obvious. Only believers, the committed, can see it, which is consistent with what Merlin told us about the Stone. I think Wolfram knew."

Merlin clapped his hands. "Well done, Peter. He may have known, but he didn't learn it from me. Eschenbach was mistaken more often than not, but the things he got right were unique to his work. Well done indeed. I'd read all the same works but never connected them as you have. Bravo!"

And so it was that CJ found herself back in the Middle East, just days after being pulled back to England.

***

223

Dr. Ahmad Ali Hossam, Palmyran Minister of the Syrian Directorate of Excavations and Archaeological Studies, was waiting for CJ at the Museum of Palmyra. Once in his office and behind a closed door, he said, "Your government's requests were quite unusual, Miss Jones. Not the least of which was to work with yourself, an investigator, but not a historian or archivist." He motioned her to the chair across from his desk and logged into his PC. After scrolling and clicking, he spun the monitor so they could both see it. "I was asked to investigate lesser-known facts, legends, and stories that suggest the arrival or departure of persons or material out of the norm in the first two centuries of the second millennium. Is that consistent with your expectations?"

CJ nodded.

"OK then. I pulled together a handful of my most promising graduate students and directed them to focus on the arcane, cast-aside stories that were uncorroborated or thought too inconsequential to be included in official histories. To my surprise, we pulled in a few more than I expected." He slid a single sheet of paper with a bulleted list across the table to CJ. "We've summarized the topics, relevant facts, and keywords for you so you can focus your time on only stories that you deem important."

Four hours later, alone in the academic's office and hunched over his desk, CJ connected with the team in Woburn by phone. "Dr. Hossam wasted no time in telling me we'd asked for a miracle, and he'd risen to the occasion. His grad students unearthed ledgers from 1185. A local warlord was tasked with providing food and drink for a band of Templars coming from Jerusalem with a relic for the temple. That would be the Temple of Bel. This stuck out because Templars rarely ventured that far east. Does that trigger anything with you guys?"

"As we've noted," Peter said, "the Templars factor into most Grail stories and had an incredible influence over events of the age. Having the Stone in their possession again would tie up loose ends."

CJ leaned back and crossed her legs. "OK, there's more. So we know the Templars brought something important to Palmyra in 1185, but no other details were recorded. However, 125 years later, approximately 1310, Western European soldiers returned and took something out of the Temple. The diary of a certain well-placed woman recorded her fear of being taken by these barbarians. Her words describe them as dirty and desperate. And dozens of rats followed them into the city! Dr. Hossam translated her description of the men as Rat Kings. She said the vermin followed the wagons out of the city. There weren't any other rational details in this account. The rat thing caught someone's attention enough to file it away with the archives that stuck around." She paused for comments but heard only silence.

"CJ, this is Arthur. I think the rat references are important."

"Absolutely!" Jules said. "Great work, CJ. We have a lead to follow up on. We need to fast-track discovery on Templar activities after 1310. This was just three years after the French King Philip destroyed the Templar Order. We need to figure out where they took the Stone. Peter, can you connect us with an accessible expert on Templars?"

"Already on that," Peter said. "It looks like a leader in Templar history teaches at Cambridge, about 45 minutes from here. I'll try to reach her. Give me a minute." CJ heard the shuffling of chairs as Peter stepped into the hallway.

"Back to the thread, CJ," Merlin said. "The connection to rats is interesting in a few ways. In Exeter, I learned that Morgana had developed a certain affinity for rats and demonstrated a skill for bending them to her will. This relationship with the rodents was certainly evident at Camlann. As I'd suggested, she would have needed to cast her consciousness into a living being. While I assumed it would be a human, I suppose it could have been a rat, maybe many rats. Hypothetically, if the Templars brought the stone to Palmyra and Morgana's rats caught wind of it ... which is problematic but not impossible, she would have focused on that power. If she'd had direct access to the stone, as I suggested earlier, it would have been 'game over'. However, proximity still offers benefits and could explain how she lasted in this state for so long." He turned to the gardens outside. "Remarkable."

"I wasn't sure of the significance," CJ said, "but ancient records note a rat problem in the temple for the better part of the 13th century. Could she have been searching for a way to get to the stone with rat … scouts, I guess?"

"Quite possibly," Merlin responded.

A cough from Peter got the team's attention. "I connected with the Cambridge Templar expert's office," he said. "She is conducting research at the British Museum in London. Her assistant confirmed she'd be available to meet with us and is … get this… familiar with the reason for our request."

"That's a plus," Jules added. "I think we can kill two birds, or rats if you will, with a trip to London."

Chapter 38

Saturday - Day Three

Danie used the break in the meeting to grab some of the leftover chicken from the fridge. "Hey! With you!" his rugby-playing twin called out. John winked at Jenn when he caught her chuckling at that, still accepting a plate from his brother.

Arthur sat back in his chair. "OK, let's talk Templars and Stones. My suggestion is that John and Danie should meet up with Peter's Templar specialist. Their credentials as academics might put her at ease."

"While in London," John asked, "are there other leads we can follow up on? At the museum, maybe?"

"To be frank, I expect you boys can get more value from this trip to London outside the halls of knowledge and in the, well, halls of beer."

Smiling at the quizzical looks, Jules continued, "We know Bonneville poured cash into a program of sorts for the type of thugs you guys met in Exeter. This is probably just a cover. Anyway, the office for that is in the docks area. I'd suggest John and Danie head down there posing as new toughs in town and looking for work. There is a pub right across the street where you might learn something. Spread drinks around and ask pointed questions. Since you don't look official, you might attract the right attention. We don't have time to be subtle, and I would wager subtlety isn't your strong suit, anyway. I'd also wager that since you can out-eat any man I've ever met, you can out-drink most as well."

Fighting past a mouthful of beef sandwich, Arthur said, "That's brilliant, Jules. Career soldiers know the danger of idle talk in the company of strangers. Conscripts, however, were often so overwhelmed by the experience or the anticipation of battle that they would prattle on, revealing all sorts of intel we couldn't otherwise obtain."

Jules sat back in his chair. "Exactly! This whole thing went down rather quickly, over only a few weeks. The recruits she had access to were likely gang types who thrived as much on reputation as actual deeds. Talking about what they did or what they planned is second nature to these guys in their climb to the top of the heap, the rubbish heap in this case." He turned back to John and Danie. "I mean, call us with anything you find that can help on the Templars, but then head to the river. Find some of these guys and chat them up. There's no time for subtlety, so drop pointed references to, I don't know, magic, mind control … Guys, what else?"

Eric suggested bringing up the #HimToo murders.

Jenn offered they might drop references to her father's killing. Seeing Peter was uncomfortable with this, she said, "Peter, Dad would want us to use every tool we have at our disposal. If our boys happen to meet one of the killers this weekend, we might advance our plan and move a step closer to justice." Peter mumbled in agreement and buried his face in his laptop.

John and Danie were already up and heading to the door when Mikol sat forward and leaned his forearms on the table. "I don't want to throw a wrench in this otherwise lovely plan, but we exposed John and Danie to Bonneville's people in Exeter. Each on their own is notable; as a pair, unforgettable."

Arthur set his jaw and acknowledged Mikol's point with a nod. Then he looked at John and Danie. "Men, I thought about that, and here are two things I'd tell you. First, my gut tells me that nobody who might show up tomorrow night will recognize you. Only captains are invited to the king's … or queen's in this case … quarters, and any left hanging by the docks are foot soldiers."

"What is the second thing?"

"We really need information, gentlemen. We're blind." All eyes were on the twins as they turned to each other.

"I understand this is risky, men. I wish there…"

"We're in."

Arthur leaned back in his chair and said, "Thank you both. Please do me one favor, though? If you recognize a face or sense things turning, get the hell out of there. Go through the damn wall if you must. I…" He looked over at Merlin, who nodded almost imperceptibly. "We need you for the final encounter."

The wizard jumped in.. "We need ALL of you for that. Please be careful this weekend."

***

On the drive from the British Museum to the docks on the Thames, John and Danie reported back to the team. All, save the wizard were waiting for their call. "Merlin disappeared shortly after you left," Jenn said. "Maybe he called for a car when we were grabbing supper, I don't know, but this unpredictability is driving me nuts."

"No worries, mate," John replied. "We're on our way to the pub on Wapping. We didn't learn a ton at the museum, but did get one lead that warrants follow-up."

"CJ's story about the Templars removing something from Palmyra in 1310 triggered a connection," Danie said. "The last 'official crusade' was in 1330, led by Sir Henry St. Croix, a Baron of Rosslyn and a confidant of Robert the Bruce, King of Scotland. Legend has it that St. Croix went on a mission to exchange Bruce's heart for a relic of personal importance to the former king."

"Guys … Scotland and an important relic?" Jenn said. "This has to be what we were looking for."

"Well, was he successful?" Arthur asked. "What happened to the relic?"

"While St. Croix's battle is well documented," Danie answered, "we don't know much about St. Croix's success, or lack thereof, on Bruce's mission. The records say St. Croix refused to speak of it when he returned to Scotland in 1331. He died shortly after."

John leaned into the dashboard. "Our expert suggested we speak with a professor at the University of Edinburgh, a Dr. Ian Cockran. She believes he has access to records that haven't been published. We think, Danie and I, that sharing some of our inside knowledge with Cockran might open him up a bit."

"I think we're making progress, guys," Jenn said. "But the clock is ticking. I don't think we can afford to play coy any longer. If he can help us, let's not hold back."

"I think a trip to Edinburgh was inevitable," Peter said. "We know from Merlin that the Stone went there, but disappeared." Scanning his notes, he said, "Right, what I've learned is that in 1297, King Edward the First, after conquering the Highlands, demanded that the Scots surrender the Coronation Stone, the Stone of Scone, to the English. The large sand-colored block was carted off to Westminster Abbey. However, the following year, Edward came back with a force and ransacked the Scone Abbey … looking for what? Edward realized he'd been duped and went looking for the real Stone. There is no record, though, that he found anything of substance on that second try."

Jenn connected the dots. "Of course he wouldn't! The actual stone couldn't have made it back until at least 1331."

"Right, so in 1328," Peter added. "The English even offered to give the Stone they had back as part of a larger treaty, but the Scots passed. Why? Because the Scots knew it was a phony."

"Jules, I'd heard that the Templars re-formed in Scotland," Eric said. "What do you know about this? Can they help us?"

"Not likely. This is a loosely formed club of role-players. Harmless and irrelevant. I think a meeting with the good Dr. Cockran is our best next step."

"I would like to meet with Dr. Cockran," Peter said, quickly and earnestly. "It's research, and that's what I do on this team."

"I don't know, Peter," Jenn said. "If we could zero in on Edinburgh, it's conceivable Bonneville has too. I'd expect they are watching for anything suspicious there. They know who you are,

Peter; they came to our house. It's too dangerous."

"I think Peter makes a good point, Jenn," Jules said. "His research has been key to getting us this far. If we need to piece things together on the fly with the professor, it's got to be Peter or me. And I need to be working with the authorities in London."

"Eric, can you go with him?" Jenn asked. "Watch over him?"

"Oui. I will keep him safe, Jenn. You can count on me."

With nothing more, John and Danie dropped off the call and started looking for parking near their next mission.

***

Saturday - Day Three

Despite its austere facade, the interior of Black Bart's was well lit with colored trappings, almost festive. John and Danie grabbed stools at the bar. Samuel Smith Lager was the house favorite, served in response to Danie's generic request for two beers. The place was sparsely populated, with only a few older patrons sitting at the bar. They expected this, and it was per plan. They didn't want to be seen as intruding on established conversations. The prey needed to come to them.

As the clock above the bar struck five, a group matching the target persona entered the pub. These four young men were in their early twenties and dressed for the street. They were laughing and otherwise projected friendly, but John noticed how the locals quieted and eyed the newcomers with suspicion. The general atmosphere of the pub darkened as these rough-looking boys jostled chairs at a round table in a far corner and hunched forward to add an aura of conspiracy to their conversation. Bea, the girl behind the bar who had been all smiles with the gregarious South Africans, quickly grabbed a tray and pad and hustled over to take that table's order. All traces of joy were gone as she pulled her apron straight and her knee-length skirt down to cover as much of her legs as possible.

John leaned over to an older man with whom he'd been comparing notes on the state of international rugby and asked,

"Simon, what's the story on this lot? Seems like they sucked all the air out of the place."

Simon glanced over at the boys and whispered out of the corner of his mouth, "Them's a bad sort. Their type is growing bolder every day. It's best to stay out of their way and get out before they get too much to drinking."

"Or they look like an excellent group to have as friends, if you know what I mean," Danie replied.

Simon shook his head and said, "I'd advise against. You seem like fine boys. I wouldn't suggest having anything to do with them." John and Danie stood, prompting Simon to look up and shrug. "I suppose you fellas can take care of yourselves. Just watch it."

Danie thanked the old man with a brief squeeze of his shoulder while John caught Bea by the elbow and whispered in her ear. One tough caught this exchange and called their comrade's attention to the brothers. John and Danie turned their backs to the room and leaned across the bar. In minutes, Bea lined up six pints. The ruggers wrapped their large hands around three glasses each and began their recon mission.

"Gents," John began, "I couldn't help but notice you looked thirsty." They set the mugs on the table and said, "Our treat." They faced four young men in a hostile posture. This was the moment the play would either click or collapse.

Danie picked up the banter. "Trust is earned, right? If you gents would accept our hospitality and listen to our proposal, what's the worst that could happen? You get a few free beers, and life goes on. However, if we reach an accord and you like what you hear, this could be a profitable night for all involved." None of the men spoke. They remained motionless and defensive.

The young man to John's immediate right, in pointed snakeskin boots, tight black narrow-legged jeans, and a black t-shirt, held John's gaze, searching for falsehood or threat. He then broke into a smile, showing yellowed teeth with a flash of gold up front. He grabbed the closest beer and said, "Boys, it would be our pleasure to drink your drinks. M'name's Jeb, and on behalf of me mates, if you keep these beers coming, we'll listen to what you have to say. Iff'n we don't like where it's going, well, I reckon they'll hear the likes of you hittin' the ground on the other side of the river."

With the rules of engagement established, John and Danie pulled up two chairs and started into the role play they'd rehearsed in the car.

Five hours later, John, Danie, and their new best friends stumbled into the street and parted ways with a commitment to meet at the clubhouse on Monday morning. Jeb, being held upright by the still sober John, even banged on the outer door of the center to emphasize the location. John banged with him as they burst into laughter.

Striking a more solemn tone with a lowered voice, John asked, "So this is where it happened, Jeb? To that guy? Right here?"

Jeb spun his face up to John's and poked him in the chest. "This is the spot, my friend. And I told you this so you'd know, if you join us, if you have the guts to join us…" He accidentally spat in John's face as he forced the word 'guts' out. "That is what we're all dealing with. But the lady has promised wealth and women beyond our wildest dreams. The top guys are already getting the women, so they say. And we're taking down the aristoca … the aristos … the rich fucks!" He burst into laughter again, perceiving he had recovered gracefully.

John looked over at Danie, who nodded. They got what they came for. There would be no meeting on Monday.

Chapter 39

Saturday - Day Three

While Peter and Eric jetted north that evening, the ruggers gathered everyone in the living room for a recap.

"Mission accomplished, I guess, for inserting ourselves into a group of Bonneville's goons. These guys are scared shitless of her but believe she'll shower them with riches when all is said and done."

"Yes, scared, but they're all fucking in love with her, too," Danie added. "It sort of got uncomfortable as they sized each other, and US, up. Not out of fear, but jealousy. Fucking nuts!"

John nodded. "Nuts. Anyway, once you pour a few drinks into these clowns, they won't shut up. The two most important things we learned were that they expect a climax at Stonehenge and … the lady really is a witch. Where's the wizard, Jenn? I'd expect this is the shit he'd want to hear about."

"We don't know, John. Over the years in Glastonbury, he was always coming and going without notice or comment."

Danie jumped in, more buoyant than the conversation warranted. "A wizard is never late, Frodo Baggins. He arrives precisely when he means to."

John didn't rise to the levity, and Danie slumped. "First, the straightforward part. These boys have been prepping for security detail at Stonehenge. They think the government will hand over a ransom there; cash, gold, bearer bonds…" John's narrative paused. "A dragon's treasure?" he offered for Danie's benefit.

"Get on, John." The moment had passed.

"She's kept them in the dark about the actual business. We

234

dropped the word 'stone' a few times, and it didn't register. They know all about the murders, though. In fact, they were morosely excited about them. However, they're convinced it was part of a grand extortion scheme, and riches will soon follow."

"John, did they hint at numbers?" Arthur asked. "How many would be at Stonehenge, if that is indeed where the transfer is to take place?"

"I asked about the size of their team," Danie said. "OUR team, in the moment. Jeb, the leader of sorts, said the plan was to bring about a dozen men to the drop. Others were staying in London to prepare the route back. They think, as John said, it's cash, and it's coming back to the city."

"What about weaponry?" Arthur asked. "All we saw at Exeter were handguns. Any suggestion of bigger guns?"

"These guys think of themselves as gangsters," John said. "And arrogantly self-reliant ones at that. We didn't pick up anything to suggest they expected resistance, so personal weapons are probably the play."

"Guys like this," Jules added, "are mostly loners. These thugs have an over-inflated sense of self-worth, bordering on narcissism. This personality trait knows no fear, which makes them dangerous in uncontrolled, spontaneous scenarios. When you know what you're up against, these guys are predictable. We can expect small arms because they can't think past that."

"You said there were two things," Arthur said. "What was the second part about the witch?"

John recounted the story of Dylan, with his self-inflicted abuse and suicide. "It scared the boys shitless. As they tell it, she puts a suggestion…"

"Something like a computer virus," Danie added.

"Yeah, a virus in their heads which she can execute with a snap of her fingers. They said she transmits it with a touch, and most of the boys have had more than a touch from Her Wickedness. It sounds like she sexed them up to compliance and then locked them in with the threat of self-mutilation. Fucking freaky, if you ask me."

"Arthur," Jules said. "I recall you saying something about the battle at Camlann, that fighters in Mordred's army seemed more afraid of retreating than advancing into certain, albeit honorable, death. She may have perfected this curse by then."

Arthur nodded. "OK, we know she expects to take possession of the Stone at Stonehenge and that she can induce suicidal behavior with a touch. I wish Merlin were here, but he said that Morgana had no power over me. Something about being a blood relative. I expect we'd be able to confirm that with him … if he were here." He looked down and shook his head. Lifting back up, "John, Danie, anything else?"

"Nothing else … just some conjecture," John said. "After talking to the historians, learning of her, I guess, witchiness, and confirming Stonehenge as the drop point, we couldn't help but wonder if Stonehenge is more than just a meeting place. What if she needs it for some kind of ritual there, like Merlin said?"

"Without him to suggest an alternative," Arthur replied. "I'd say that if she had hidden something before I struck her down, the likely spot would have been Avalon, under the Glastonbury Tor. We should examine Morgana's Avalon lair for clues to her plans and what else she was capable of."

Jenn stood and stepped behind her chair. "She may have been scouting a way back in to secure it when she was spotted in Glastonbury last week. For all we know, she succeeded, and then, who knows what we'd face if we returned."

After an uncomfortable silence, Arthur spoke up. "I will go. I won't deny my uneasiness over descending back into the hole I'd been in for so many centuries. However, if I am to put it behind me, I must confront it."

Mikol spun the uneaten croissant he'd been examining in his hand. "That's all good and probably healthy, yes," he said. "My only concern is that, while Morgana may have a watch on likely Edinburgh locations, I think it's a foregone conclusion she has the

Tor under surveillance."

Arthur nodded as he responded. "Sir Mikol, if you will offer your protection, I'm quite sure we can handle anything Morgana and her ragged band can throw at us." The sniper leaned back in his chair, legs extended and crossed, and nodded.

Jenn grasped the back of her chair. "I'll go too," she announced, crossing her arms.

"No, Jenn, it's too soon. You're ... we're still grieving." Arthur looked at Jules for support, but the CIA man knew better than to get in the middle of it.

"I am no fragile flower, Arthur. You need another set of eyes in that cave, and I am the right person for the job." Arthur's eyes scanned the room, still looking for support. Finding none, he lowered his head with a nod.

Mikol broke the ensuing silence. "It's settled then. Is there a shop in town that sells hunting or camping equipment? I have some things I'll want to grab."

Chapter 40

Sunday - Day Four

S Mikol's Sunday morning began with a pre-dawn drive to the outskirts of Glastonbury, making the three-hour trip in just over two, thanks to CJ's Mercedes. He entered the town at 6 am. Arriving ahead of Arthur and Jenn was the plan; he needed time to get situated. With the ragtop up, trying to be as inconspicuous as possible, he took a few circles around the Tor. On the third circuit, he felt comfortable that the hill wasn't under surveillance from the street. Nobody looked out of place.

Minutes later, he crept into the Pelling's driveway, stopping just short of the house. With his personal Glock resting in his lap, safety off, Mikol ensured the house wasn't concealing a trap. No movement, no sounds, no confrontations. He pulled up alongside the dense foliage near the shed. As he exited the car, he popped the boot and hoisted out two unmarked black ballistic nylon bags, both about a meter long. With one in each hand, he walked back to the NPS gate Peter had told him to look for. He noted a new-looking rectangular red sign informing visitors that the park was closed for maintenance. Well done, Jules!

The sniper rested the two bags under bushes just outside the gate and covered them with leaves and branches, then headed back to the car.

He finally parked behind George and Pilgrims and started his trek to the Tor, thankful the early morning light was still grey. Mikol was wearing a black nylon jacket over his woodland camouflage blouse and pants. Camo was everyday fashion in the UK, but he didn't look like someone trying to make a statement with his outfit;

he looked like a soldier.

He approached the Tor on foot, using the park entrance off Wellhouse Lane. After jogging along the ring fence to the back of the Pelling house, he retrieved his bags and turned up the hill. The climb reminded him he'd neglected cardio. When he finally plopped down inside St. Michael's Chapel at the summit and caught his breath, he exhaled his gratitude through pursed lips. A vibration in his chest pocket cut short his rest. He pulled his cell phone out, saw Arthur's number, and answered, "I'm here."

"Good," Arthur replied. "We are just entering town, and about ten minutes from Jenn's house. How does it look?"

"Wait," Mikol said and went to the nearest bag and fished out binoculars. Risking an exposed silhouette against the morning sky, he circumnavigated the summit, scanning for signs of movement, surveillance at the base, or in the surrounding streets. Nothing. He retrieved the still-engaged phone from his pocket and informed the king, then hung up on Arthur's attempt at a pep talk. *The king talks too much.* Before putting the phone away, he set a timer. It had taken him fifteen minutes from base to summit. A full circle every ten should ensure nobody would surprise him.

As he rose for his first circuit, he spotted Jenn's blue Citroën pull into the Pelling's access drive. Foliage obscured his view of the car, but as per the plan, he knew they were pulling into the garage and would close the door behind them. Crouching down to his bags, he slipped out a Colt AR-15 semi-automatic rifle with a high-capacity magazine and fitted with a telescopic sight. Settling into the grass below the chapel, facing the house, Mikol pulled out a water bottle. He laid the gun and water on the grass to his right. Raising the glasses back to his eyes, he began his vigil.

***

At eight forty-five that morning, an electronic chirping disrupted the hushed conversation at an upscale coffee shop in London's West End. Paul reached for the phone with his free hand, the other still clutching his large, steaming mocha latte. He didn't recognize the number, so it wasn't Meghan. He wasn't sure how he felt about that. After what she did to Dylan, flying under the radar might be for the best. On the fourth ring, he realized the area code was Glastonbury. He swiped to answer. "It's Paul."

A hurried, breathless male voice responded. "Paul, this is Kenny T from Glastonbury. D'you recall our agreement?" Before Paul could respond, Kenny T continued, "Right, so you gave me fifty quid and told me there would be fifty more if I noticed something odd happening around town, d'you recall?"

"I do, Kenny, tell me what you know."

"Great! Great … so you were particularly interested in the Tor, d'you recall? So, this morning, government wankers put closed signs on all the gates into the Tor, maintenance or such. I never saw this before, Paul, highly irregular, wouldn't you say? I mean, there have been events and stuff, but…"

Paul cut him off. "Take a breath, Kenny. That's good. They closed the park. Anything else?"

"Well … I thought that was important, and that's why I called, but no … wait … yeah. Before I called, I went to make sure the signs were still there and saw a guy, a military-looking guy in camo, climbing up the hill. He was moving quickly and carrying bags. That's the other part, Paul. Highly irregular, right?"

"Describe the bags, Kenny," Paul said, trying to remain calm. Highly irregular indeed.

"One in each hand, dark, probably black, and long. Do you think they were guns, Paul? On the Tor?"

"Kenny, listen to me. I don't want you to tell anyone else what you saw. In fact, I want you to forget you even saw it. Whatever you do, don't stare at the hill. Better yet, do you have a car?"

Kenny said he did.

"Good, Kenny, get in your car, don't look at the Tor, and head out of town for the rest of the day. Have dinner and take your time. Am I clear?"

Kenny was responding to the calming authority in Paul's voice and said he was clear.

"That's good, Kenny. We'll get you your fifty pounds tonight or tomorrow. You did well. Now go." He hung up his cell and called Meghan's number at the backup flat in Hastings.

Leon answered and told Paul that the boss was on a run. She'd left her phone with him. Paul passed along the news from Glastonbury, and they both agreed that the team they'd left in Exeter at St. Nicholas Priory was the closest and should investigate. Paul disconnected and scrolled through his texts to see who he'd sent there after the mysterious attack. Found it. Chuck Yeardley and three other boys were camped out in Exeter. 'Chunky Chuck' answered on the first ring and promised the four of them would be on the road within ten minutes. The drive to Glastonbury would take them about an hour and a half.

Paul drained his coffee and smiled. "A well-oiled machine."

Chapter 41

Sunday - Day Four

It was a five-minute walk from their hotel on campus to the Old Medical Building, the current home of the School of History, Classics, and Archeology. As Peter and Eric crossed under an imposing sandstone archway, Dr. Cockran, whom they recognized from his staff bio on the school's webpage, caught up with them. He led them through a series of austere hallways and down a single flight of stairs to his office. He motioned for them to take the two chairs across from his desk and then sat in his cracked, red leather high-backed chair with several large rivets missing on each side. The moment he sat, he jumped back up. "Will you please pardon me? I fear my manners have fled. Would you like tea, coffee, or water perhaps?"

"We're fine, mon ami. Merci," Eric said.

Dr. Cockran settled into his chair this time, allowing the worn leather to crackle a welcome to its old friend. "I understand you have a letter for me?"

Peter and Eric exchanged questioning looks.

"Sorry," Dr. Cockran added. "He said it would be in the front pocket of your bag, young man."

Peter, who had dropped his backpack on the floor, leaned over and fumbled through the main compartments before pulling out a cream-colored envelope he hadn't put there, the initials 'IC' scrawled in elaborate script on its face. Wide-eyed, he passed it over the desk to the scholar. Dr. Cockran pushed his glasses up to the bridge of his nose, opened the letter, and read it twice.

They waited as he folded the note and slipped it back into the envelope. "Excellent. One can't be too careful in these matters, I believe. As requested in the letter, I'd like to offer a more meaningful introduction with a bit of background. The Fraser Chair, as it's come to be called, carries a solemn responsibility beyond our commitment to the university. So yes, I am familiar with your Mr. Wyse, as was my predecessor, and his predecessor." He took off his glasses and chewed on the end of the earpiece. "And so on and so on. We are among the few people in the world to know his, Merlin's, or Myrddin Emrys' secret. If he is telling me that now," tapping the letter, "is the time for this information to come to light, I'm inclined to comply."

"If you are so familiar with Merlin," Peter asked, "and what we're looking for, why haven't you come forward sooner?"

He slid his glasses back on as he bent forward to access a file drawer in his desk, ignoring the question. With a smooth motion, he unlocked and opened the bin. After flipping through several choices, he pulled a worn, coffee-colored folder out and laid it on the desk.

"First, I must tell you that this isn't the first request for this information in recent weeks … and it may not be the last. Hence the letter. You should also know that Merlin only shares what's necessary and precisely when necessary." He closed the drawer, locked it, and pocketed the key inside his jacket. "I would expect that had we spoken sooner, you might not have been prepared to ask the right questions or to make use of the answers." Elbows on the desk and fingers tented, he leaned in and said, "What I'm about to show you, Merlin himself has never seen. I assume he's explained why he hasn't undertaken a quest for the Stone?"

Eric nodded, but Peter, bursting with questions and the need for information, blurted out, "He told us he didn't trust himself with the knowledge."

Dr. Cockran grinned. "That's one way to explain it, I guess, Peter." He opened the folder, revealing photocopies of documents in different historic and forgotten languages. "Merlin's initial e-mail codified your expectations as hoping to find a clue as to the Stone's whereabouts, with no expectations that it is still in Scotland. Is that correct?" Peter and Eric nodded, although Merlin hadn't been part of the planning for this meeting. "Good, because I fear that's the best you're likely to get. I can tell you little-known details about the Stone and introduce you to Sir Henry St. Clair, as Merlin requested. I sincerely hope this information, along with the other lines of inquiry your team is making, will bring you success. However, don't expect a simple answer to that which you seek. The Stone is truly lost."

For the next hour, Dr. Cockran walked them through six hundred years of logs, diaries, and archives by the silent keepers of Britain's most venerable secret. He saved a few pages from a preserved diary from the mid-fourteenth century for last.

Dr. Cockran pushed his chair backwards and leaned into the desk as he slid a typewritten page out of the folder and squared it to his desk. With sparkling eyes, he looked up at his guests, took a breath, and began.

"Now for St. Clair. Sir Henry St. Clair was the seventh Baron of Rosslyn during the reign of Robert the Bruce. He chronicled what would become the last Crusade in 1330. His small army consisted of remnants of the once-mighty Knights Templar. St. Clair and his companions swore an oath to Bruce to fulfill his deathbed wish. While the king's body was to be buried at Dunfermline Abbey, he charged St. Clair to take his embalmed heart to Jerusalem and place it in the Church of the Holy Sepulchre.

"They never made it past Spain, you see. After routing the Moors at Teba, St. Clair's sons rode into a trap, and by the time St. Clair could reach them, his sons were dead. The Moors were so impressed by the courage of the Scottish knights that they allowed the survivors to take their dead home. This marked the end of the quest and a more personal failure for St. Clair, who, it seems, was oath-bound with an ulterior motive for the trip. He was on his journey home with his decimated host when fortunes turned."

Cockran pushed his readers high on his nose and picked up

another sheet. "Three horsemen, Templars from an earlier age, had been searching for Sinclair since learning that Robert had passed. In exchange for interring the king's heart in Jerusalem, he was to bring an unnamed artifact back to Scotland. The Templars gave Sinclair the relic but said they would not be returning to the Holy Land, so both the relic and the king's heart returned home."

Dr. Cockran's head remained bowed over the sheets he'd been reading from, lost in St. Clair's memories from a millennium past.

"Well, is that it?" Peter interrupted. "Did St. Clair bring the Stone back?"

"We don't know, Peter. We don't even know for sure it was the Stone or if what he acquired in Spain made it to Scotland. St. Clair died within a year after returning. There was no record of an unusual or historic artifact in his estate. He took all knowledge of this matter to the grave."

"And I assume, Dr. Cockran, that others of your, how do you say, organization, have searched for this cargo under the assumption it was the Stone to no avail?" Eric asked.

"That is correct. The fragment of St. Clair's diary that told this story didn't surface until the mid-seventeenth century, but periodically since then, or when some of the newer material or references I'd shared came to light, we'd have another go at it."

"But Merlin has not taken part in any of these … these Grail quests?"

"No, Eric, he hasn't. Until now, he steadfastly avoided any chance encounter with the Stone for the reasons he has shared with you."

Silence. Peter flexed his neck and cracked his knuckles after taking pages and pages of notes and walking the stories backward and forward to ensure there were no holes unfilled. He had nothing more to ask, so he closed his laptop and slid it into his backpack. "I think it's time Merlin came back to Scotland, to Dunfermline Abbey even, to see if he can pick up on something we mortals couldn't find."

Eric stood and adjusted his light blue sports coat.

Cockran remained seated. "So, it is true? The king has returned?" he whispered.

"Oui, monsieur, Arthur has returned." Peter stopped zipping his bag and looked up to catch this dialogue.

Dr. Cockran released Eric's hand and sat back down. "Then there is one more piece of information I would like to share with you. I'll let you decide what to do with it. But I don't think Merlin is the one who should come back here."

Chapter 42

Sunday - Day Four

Stepping up to her back door, Jenn promised herself she'd keep it together. They had a job to do and needed to be in and out before anyone knew they were there. She'd been home just days before, accepting condolences and thanking friends, neighbors, shop regulars, and town fixtures for their support. Duty kept her mind off the worst parts. Now, walking into the empty house, she felt overwhelmed. He was gone forever. Leaving Arthur standing in the kitchen doorway, she ran to the living room, where she could always find her father when he wasn't at the bookstore. She went right to her dad's recliner and collapsed into it, leaning forward with her face in her hands. She could still smell the lingering aroma of his pipe and imagined a half-full glass of scotch sitting on the table in front of her. At least she wasn't crying … yet.

She was thankful Arthur gave her a few minutes to compose herself. When he finally joined her, after a few uncomfortable coughs, the best he could offer was, "Jenn, are you alright?"

Jenn had a better sense of her own needs. She sprang off the chair and wrapped her arms around him, burying her head in his chest, and let the tears come. "I'm so glad he got to meet you before…"

Arthur returned the embrace and just waited.

"He always believed, but I … I could never accept it. Could never accept you were real."

Arthur looked around the room at all the books that captured the legends and myths of his fictionalized past and said, "I suspect the real me was a bit of a disappointment. A pompous ass, if you will."

Jenn stepped back, wiped her eyes with her sleeve, then looked up. Her vision was clear, and her will was hardened. "No, Arthur, that's not true. You were everything he hoped you would be. Now, let's get to work."

Arthur placed his hand on her arm and said, "Jenn, there is something I need to share with you. Now is probably the best time."

She took a half step backwards and looked up into Arthur's eyes.

"After you left London, Merlin pulled me aside and told me that my father hadn't simply fallen ill but that Morgana somehow had gotten to him and was responsible for his death. Revenge, I would assume."

Jenn's eyes welled with tears again, and she reached up to Arthur's face.

"I'm telling you this now, so you understand how committed I am to bringing the witch to justice. If this quest unfolds as Merlin believes it must, there may be a time when you'll question the decisions or actions I must take. Please know that I will avenge the death of both our fathers before retiring from the battle."

They stood for a moment, eyes locked. Then, without another word, she walked past him into the kitchen and opened the pantry door. Reaching in, she pulled out Colin's shotgun.

In a smooth, practiced movement, she broke the old weapon open. Confirming it was still unloaded, she pointed the over-under barrels at the window to check the condition of the bores, just as her father had taught her. Out of the corner of her eye, she saw Arthur reaching down to check the status of the Glock strapped to his thigh, as Mikol had instructed him. She used his moment of distraction to wipe the last puddles from her eyes with a sleeve. "Would you prefer a sword, Your Majesty?" she asked.

Arthur smiled and said, "I'd prefer that a sword would be all I'd need, but alas…"

Jenn pursed her lips in understanding, then reached up to the top shelf. After a few probing tries, she pulled down a box of cartridges. She shook it to see how full it was, then stepped out and placed it on the table. Popping a shell into each chamber, she snapped the gun closed and checked the safety. "We should get moving," she said as she filled the pockets of her denim jacket with ammunition. "If those sons of bitches who killed my father show their pathetic faces, I will send them to hell myself." Stepping to the door, she added, "There are torches, a shovel, a pry bar, and a tarp in the shed. Let's go." After a moment's pause, she could hear Arthur hustling to catch up with her.

After gathering the last batch of supplies from the shed, they made for the NPS gate and began their climb. Arthur stopped. He shielded his eyes and looked up at the summit. "There," he said.

Jenn saw two flashes of reflected light from the top. This was Mikol's signal that the coast was clear.

Following the same path that Colin and Peter had taken two weeks prior, the dry turf allowed them to reach the opening in minutes. Peter had done his best, but there was no mistaking that someone had turned the ground. Arthur took the shovel in both hands and began to dig.

Jenn and her flashlight descended first, leaving Arthur to pull the hatch closed. Following that ominous boom of closure, Jenn heard Arthur making his way down to the chamber. The steady beam of Arthur's torch told her he'd made it to the bottom.

In a slightly higher tone and speed than normal conversation, Arthur chuckled and said, "It already feels like ages since I left this place … and I should know…" prompting a second chuckle. Jenn wondered where he had picked that phrase up.

There was no time to ease into it, so she called, "Arthur, you need to see this." She flashed her light onto the floor to give him a target.

Arthur joined Jenn as she swung her flashlight in and painted light on a wall in an adjacent chamber. Bony forearms from the sixth century were still hanging in shackles bolted to the wall. These two pairs of skeletal arms were no larger than those of a child. Other remains of long-ago captives were on the floor beneath. As unnerving as that was, Jenn directed his attention using her light to dozens of rodent skeletons, tiny bones, and skulls that were on top of and alongside the human remains.

"What did she do?" Jenn whispered.

"My sister was morose after she returned from the Christians, but I swear I never heard tell of this level of depravity in her. She must … she must have been perfecting her control over the beasts and the minds of people. I would imagine that children would be more suggestible than adults."

"But who are they, Arthur?" She took a step closer to him but kept her light and her eyes on the fallen children.

"We'll never know, Jenn. From what I've learned, even in the short time I've been in your world, there are still countless young ones who get lost, wander off, or are taken and never found. I can't say how she might have procured these, or if they are the only ones."

After the initial shock dampened, they explored the rest of the room. To the right of the bones was a wooden table, somehow still standing, and the remains of a chair in pieces below it. Empty ceramic pots and vials were stacked both on and next to the table. Someone had embedded a rusted knife with a bone handle in the tabletop. There were loose sheets of parchment spread about the surface. Arthur pointed to the top of the page and read the Latin out loud, "Loudin principio creavit Deus caelum et terram. Does that mean anything to you?"

"That's Latin. I don't know Latin, Arthur."

"One upside of my antiquity, I guess. It translates to 'In the beginning, God created the heavens and the earth…'"

"That is the first line of Genesis, the first book of the Old Testament!" She looked up at Arthur. "This is the book that first spoke of Jacob's Stone."

She flipped through other pages of small Latin script, followed by entries filled with characters she didn't recognize. Overwhelmed with a sudden sense of urgency, she scooped them all up and shoved them in her bag.

"We should keep moving, Arthur," she said, then stepped off to her right. Her light picked up a half-barrel in their path, whose oiled wood had preserved its original shape and structure. She stepped forward and saw rodent bones filling the vessel. She shuddered and moved back into the main chamber.

***

When Arthur and Jenn had descended into the hill, Mikol settled back into his prone position. There was nothing untoward visible on any of the approaches to the Tor. He took another pull from the water bottle and trained his glasses on the hatch Jenn and Arthur had descended through. No change. He scanned up to the Pelling house and saw nothing out of the ordinary either. Looking up further, he marked a dark blue Ford entering the Pelling's neighborhood, the third car he'd spied coming or leaving the area. This one, however, turned onto the unmarked drive leading to the house. He could make out two figures, the driver and a passenger, in the front seat. Wait. There was a third person in the back.

Rolling to his right, he pulled the phone from his breast pocket and hit redial on Arthur's number. No answer. They speculated that there might not be reception under the hill, and now Mikol was cursing himself for not running a simple check to confirm. *I guess it's confirmed now.* He pulled his knees under him and leaned back. Gun across his lap, he pushed himself on his back up the six feet to the stone structure, which would provide some cover. His camo would stand out against the soft brown of the brick, but this would be less obvious than the silhouette of a man against a canvas of clouds behind the highest hill in the area. He snapped the glasses back up and confirmed his fears. The Ford must have pulled into the Pelling's car park at the front of the house, now hidden by tree coverage. He scanned the base of the hill. Nothing. Keeping his back to the stone, he sidestepped to his left, following the exterior of the chapel, looking for intrusion from a second or third location.

He was about to step around the corner to the east wall when he stopped. Instinct guided him back to the ground, where he pulled himself on his forearms to his bags. He unzipped the other bag and pulled out an identical black AR-15. He jammed three extra clips in his pockets and tossed this rifle over his shoulder as he crawled back. *Too slow.* Forsaking the binoculars for the more familiar rifle scope, he swept the eastern slope, alternating between the magnified detail of the scope and bare eyes. Moving to the north face, his peripheral vision caught movement. He could make out a handgun in the grip of a heavy, dark-haired, and bearded man making for the hill from a break in the encircling hedge.

Mikol tried the cell phone again. Still nothing. While his intruder was scrambling through the dense foliage at the bottom, he whipped around to the south side of the chapel to check on the status of the three passengers. He couldn't see anything, which meant they were either looking for a way into the house or had gained access. Moving back to the east, he stepped into the chapel and flattened himself against a wall. He shuffled to the entry, gun at the ready, stepped forward, and sighted down the hill. The big man had made good time, scrambling with hands and feet up the grassy hillside. As Mikol watched, the intruder snapped his head to the summit and their eyes met. The big man dropped to his stomach, and Mikol stepped forward, keeping his aim on the prone figure. No point in being subtle now. His opponent pushed up to his elbows, pointed his pistol up the hill, and started squeezing off shots. Having coached these habits out of recreational shooters and hopeful professionals, Mikol knew that being the object of his aim was the safest place to be. Still, the noise would attract attention. For the first time since his years in the Austrian army, Mikol targeted a man's head and squeezed the trigger once. He saw a brief flower of red appear above the man's nose before he slumped to the ground, his firearm now silent.

Mikol sprinted back to the south side of the hill, where he could

252

observe both the covered opening and the home. The unfriendlies must be inside by now. As quickly as possible and keeping his eyes on the back of the house, the sniper half-slid, half-crawled down the hill to the entrance Arthur had disappeared into. Upon reaching the passage, he pulled the rifle up and brought the scope to his eye. Still no sign of movement from the house. They would have a better view of him than he of them, but there was nothing he could do until he got his team out. He ripped the door open and leaned his head into the black hole. "Get out now! We have company!"

***

Silent and lost in their thoughts, both Arthur and Jenn broke into a run when they heard Mikol's voice from the stairway. Within seconds, they reached the opening and found Mikol, motionless except for small pivots of head, shoulders, and weapon, moving as one.

In a forced whisper, he said, "Come out and get on your stomachs, facing down to the gate. There are three of them in the house. I took out a fourth who was trying to get behind me on the north slope of the hill. I haven't seen anyone at the east or west entrances to the park."

As they scrambled into a prone position, Jenn pulled the shotgun up and laid it on the ground under her right arm, hand clutching the wooden pistol grip. Arthur reached his right hand down and pulled the Glock forward to clutch it with both hands, pointing downslope. Both waited for Mikol's next instruction.

Keeping his eyes on the tree line that blocked their view of the house, Arthur asked, "Jenn, is this spot visible from that upper window?"

"Yes," Jenn replied. "Just barely. Do you…" but a distant crash followed by two sharp cracks interrupted her. If they hadn't been focused on that window, the distance, and the reverberation across the field would have made it impossible to pinpoint the source of the sound. Before it had even registered with Arthur, Mikol had sighted the window and taken two shots.

With his eye still at the scope, Mikol said, "I saw a figure drop back, but there was no way to be sure if I'd hit him, so he may come back. Go now!" he said. "Go straight to the bushes below. Approach them from the street side, where you'll likely have the advantage of surprise. I'll cover from here. Go!"

Arthur and Jenn jumped to their feet. They ran, hopped, and stumbled down the remaining slope until they reached the trees. Looking back up at Mikol, Arthur saw he was still in position, his rifle swinging back and forth from window to gate. The sniper turned his head from the scope and motioned for them to move towards the front of the house. Arthur put his hand on Jenn's shoulder and pointed to a gap in the brush.

After stepping past the foliage, they heard two shots from the hillside and answering fire from the ground to their right. He had lost sight of Mikol and had to trust he had their backs. Jenn followed Arthur as he moved to his left to stay in the trees and headed for the road. When they reached it, they broke into a sprint. Jenn matched Arthur's pace step for step despite her shorter stride and bulkier weapon. Reaching the drive leading to the house, Arthur motioned for Jenn to hold up.

They moved back into the tree line to their right to get around a neighbor's house for fear of drawing attention. They approached the Pelling's carport cautiously. There had been no gunshots since they'd reached the bottom of the hill, nor could they see movement from the house. Jenn touched Arthur's shoulder and pointed at the dark blue Ford. It was empty. Arthur risked the cell phone and rang Mikol.

In a whisper, Arthur relayed they were in the trees to the right of the driveway, Mikol's left. There was no movement or visible enemy. "Mikol, they must have seen us vacating the hill and will be looking for us. But if they expected we'd make for the house, we'd have taken fire by now, so I think we still have the element of surprise. I need you to…" Arthur paused. "I would suggest that you draw their attention while Jenn and I break for the house. Do you agree?"

Mikol grunted his affirmation, and Arthur dropped the phone in his pocket. "Five seconds."

Jenn thumbed off her safety and confirmed her readiness with a nod. Arthur checked his mag and slammed it back home. They heard one, two, three shots from the hill. The thuds on the side of the house were unmistakable, as was the more primitive sound of large-bore handgun fire being directed back at Mikol. Arthur pointed Jenn toward the front of the house while he sprinted for the shed.

Stopping to catch his breath, Arthur peered around the corner and saw a pale, thin young man with shoulder-length, sand-colored hair on one knee, taking ineffective shots at the hill. Arthur stepped into the open, oddly conscious of the fact that there was no sword on his belt. Shaking that off, he trained the Glock on the boy's chest, coaching he hadn't needed. Targeting the torso was second nature.

Morgana's man looked up, and for a second, dropped his muzzle. Then his face hardened, and he snapped the gun towards the intruder. Without hesitation, Arthur placed four rounds into the assailant's chest. The younger man went down before he could get a shot off. Since Arthur had blown his element of surprise, he fell back to the tree line and took cover behind a large trunk that offered a view of the kitchen entrance. Within seconds, he saw a figure at the door, handgun drawn as he leaned against the glass. Arthur chose not to expose himself for a low-probability shot. He'd prefer to know where the third man was before engaging.

A shotgun blast from the front of the house brought that clarity. When he glanced back, his target had retreated into the kitchen.

He moved through the trees as quickly as possible towards the sound. Breaking for the corner of the house, he stopped short when he saw Jenn standing over a fallen combatant. With blood on his right shoulder, he was using his forearm to crawl towards a dropped gun. Before Arthur could raise his weapon in support, Jenn fired again, and all movement stopped.

"That was for my father, you asshole," she said in a forceful but breaking voice.

Arthur lowered his weapon and stepped out of the trees. Jenn caught the movement and jumped, snapping the Lincoln up in reaction. Arthur tried to calm her with a raised hand. Jenn's eyes were wide and watery. After a moment, she came back to the moment, wiped her eyes with her sleeve, and nodded back. Arthur motioned her towards the front door and then went back to cover the garden.

Arthur felt his phone vibrate in his pants pocket. It was Mikol. He answered and provided an update. One intruder was still in the house.

"I'm coming down to the gate," Mikol said. "Cover me as best you can." The connection severed, and Arthur alternated between watching the back of the house and the path to his right. Mikol was at his side within a minute.

"Jenn is still at the front of the house," Arthur whispered. "How do you suggest we proceed?"

"Let's see how stupid this guy is." Mikol started firing into the door, spreading his shots about the area of the opening. Another shotgun blast from the opposite side of the house joined in his provocation.

Expecting a surrender, Arthur moved up to the building where he could peek into the kitchen window. Before he could look in, he heard a shot from within the house and dropped to a knee. He waited, but nothing followed, so Arthur rose to the window. The third intruder was lying on his back, his legs and arms splayed in a growing puddle of blood spreading from a self-inflicted headshot. Arthur stood and motioned Mikol forward. The Battle of the Tor was over.

Chapter 43

Sunday - Day Four

S The blue Citroën pulled into the brick-paved drive of Swafford House around six o'clock on Sunday evening. Jenn saw CJ's Mercedes parked off to the side. Mikol was back already.

The new arrivals joined the rest of the team in the lounge. Jules rose and offered Jenn his place on the couch, but she smiled and waved him off. "I'm OK, but thank you. If this is where we're talking, I'll grab the chair by the fire."

Arthur accepted a drink from Bob, stepped over to the French doors, held his glass up, and cleared his throat to get everyone's attention. "Ladies and gentlemen, however this quest may end, I can say, with absolute sincerity, never was a group better suited to the task. To us and our success!"

Glasses were raised.

After taking a long sip, Arthur lowered his drink and said, "Now, my friends, we must get down to business. We've learned a lot over the past days, but we haven't yet found the Stone. We still have time, and maybe…"

"She was bluffing? Not a chance, mein Herr."

Of course, Mikol was right. But it was the wrong tone. Hoping his voice conveyed greater confidence, he went on. "I do believe we've made progress. I am told that dinner is being prepared, so let's use this time to summarize and brainstorm…" Looking at Jenn, he asked, "Brainstorm?"

She raised her head. "Aye, m'lord."

"OK, we know she expects to take the Stone at Stonehenge," Arthur said, "and that she can induce suicidal behavior with a touch.

I wish Merlin were here…"

"Where does he keep sneaking off to, anyway?" John asked.

"For the record, it's pissing me off," Mikol added.

"I've known him my whole life and sort of expect this from him," Jenn said.

"My friends, he was no better in my day. He often disappeared when I needed him most, but I couldn't get rid of him when I didn't need him," Arthur said. "He'll join us when it suits his needs. We should move on." Bourbon in hand, he said, "First, I'll share that we did come under attack at Jenn and Peter's home. We walked away unharmed thanks to Mikol." He raised his glass to Mikol, who accepted it with a nod. "You've proven to be as stalwart as any man in my service."

A cough from Jenn interrupted his narrative. "I'm sorry, was that out loud?" she murmured, head bowed over her drink.

CJ released a "Hah!" but kept her thoughts to herself.

Arthur continued without acknowledging the interruption. "We don't know how they knew we were there, but suspect the hill was being watched. It matters not. Four armed assailants arrived while Jenn and I were under the hill. Two things were evident. First, we confirmed Jules's supposition that these men will fight with small arms. All they possessed were pistols of similar size to mine and were easily taken down by Mikol's…" He looked at Jenn with admiration. "and Jenn's superior firepower. Since none lived to tell the tale, it isn't likely the others will learn from this. I expect that we'll be facing handguns at the stones. Mikol?"

"Perhaps," he said.

Shaking that off, Arthur continued. "Under the hill…" Yet Peter interrupted, mouth agape.

"Wait, there was a gunfight at the Tor? Jenn, you fought?" Jenn looked at Peter and was bolstered by his admiration. The celebratory feeling was short-lived. She had killed a man. Her head dropped towards her drink, wrapping her free hand around her opposite shoulder.

Arthur stepped back in. "Yes, Peter, team, there was a fight. Maybe this will be a sporting story for dinner, but now, let's focus on information that brings us closer to our goal. No ... No..." He pleaded as Peter, John, and Danie demanded details. "Let's wait on the fight. It didn't bring us closer to the Stone." He paused. "Other than that, when we had the last man trapped in the house, he chose to take his own life rather than surrender. It is consistent with the fear of failure we've observed previously. Not new information, but confirmation of what John and Danie learned. Bonneville, or, I guess, Morgana, has these men frightened. This may be useful as events unfold."

"We found a stash of documents under the hill," Jenn added. "We probably won't know if there's anything we can use until Merlin goes over them."

"And has the wizard explained why he didn't search the place when he checked Arthur into the Witch Hotel?" Mikol drained his beer and slammed the mug on the end table. "If I could see through birds' eyes and pop in and out at will, we'd all be headed home by now."

"Not constructive, Herr Mueller," CJ snapped. Their eyes locked and, after a few seconds, Mikol slumped back onto the couch. A curt wave signaled his surrender.

"OK, well, some pages were in Latin," Jenn said, "but a good deal of contained writing in some script I'd never seen. Hopefully, they shed some light on her plans or motives or something."

Stepping forward from his spot at the window, Eric said, "OK, here is what Peter and I have been talking about. 1307 is the year the Templars were crushed. I think it's important, then, that something of value was taken from Palmyra in 1310. If the Templar's power came from the Stone, it would make sense they'd have a plan to secure it in all cases. They might not have expected to be betrayed, but they had centuries to plan contingencies. Oui, Peter, c'est vrai?"

Peter stood. "Right, Eric. The fabled Templar treasure was

259

never found, which presents the possibility that nobody really knew what to look for. A few things jump out from the timeline. Dr. Cockran believes the Stone was in Edinburgh, thanks to Guinevere, until the French arrived in 1066. Shortly after that, a group of French monks, the precursors to the Templars in his opinion, came for it. He believes they took it to Paris, intending to continue to Jerusalem. This was conjecture from the writings of contemporaries because there was never any follow-up. Apparently, the French subjugation of a nation got in the way." He consulted his monitor for a few seconds. "So then, about 50 years later, the Templars formed, and they likely finished the job and took it to the Holy Land."

"Fast forward to 1185. That was about the time when Saladin," he looked at Arthur, who was likely the only person not familiar with the Crusades. "In the eleventh through thirteenth centuries, Christian armies battled Muslim…" Noting Arthur's second inquisitive look, he backtracked. "Muslim, an Eastern religion that claimed the Christian Holy Land as its own." Arthur indicated with his eyes that Peter should continue, and he'd catch up later. "Right, so in 1185, the Muslim armies under Saladin were at the walls of Jerusalem."

"If the Templars feared they'd lose Jerusalem, they'd want to get it out. The Vulgate Cycle, written about fifteen years later, records knights taking the Grail from Jerusalem to Sarras, which we have good reason to believe is Palmyra. Now, why Palmyra? I can't say, but let's assume they had their reasons. This is supported by documents in Palmyra that speak of western soldiers bringing something that was deemed important enough to store in the temple."

"And…" Mikol added, "The Vulgate document said that Percival, Bors, and Galahad accompanied the Grail. And we know that these knights of old existed, and at least two of their descendants were Templars. While their timelines are off by 800 years, it's an odd coincidence, wouldn't you say?" Possibly the longest sentence he'd uttered on this mission, Jenn thought, but it made sense.

Peter spoke up again. "And then..." he glanced at Eric. Jenn observed a question being negotiated. Peter chose not to finish that thought and turned back to the room. "We also learned from CJ that in about 1310, men who acted and looked like Templars returned to Palmyra and took something out of the temple."

"Chased by rats," CJ added.

"Right, and then Dr. Cockran shared that a Scottish noble, Henry St. Clair, acquired what was most likely the Stone after it left Jerusalem in 1330, intending to bring it back to Scotland. Well ... that's it, I guess," and sat.

"Dr. Cockran was apologétique that the Stone had vanished from his records."

Jules, who was typing on his laptop throughout the briefing, spoke up. "OK. Here is the timeline we've constructed. In approximately 540, Guinevere brought the Stone to Scotland. Sometime after 1066, we believe those who would become the Templars took it to Paris, and then in 1118, they likely took it to Jerusalem. In 1185, we believe the Stone was transported from Jerusalem to Palmyra, again by Templars. Finally, 125 years later, in 1310, as the Templar organization was being taken down, western warriors removed something important from Palmyra. Rats, which we now believe to be Morgana's calling card, were all over the outgoing convoy. It feels right, guys."

Peter jumped in, too excited to wait for Jules to get to it. "Then, twenty years later, in 1330, St. Clair meets up with Templars fleeing Jerusalem with what we believe is the Stone. He intended to return it to Scotland, but we have no record that it ever made it." His volume rose, and his face showed a desire to continue, but after looking at Jules, then Jenn, his eyes dropped. He had nothing more to add.

"Thank you, Jules and Peter, for the summary. We have learned much. Much more than modern scholars appear to have pieced together. However, we lost track of the Stone in 1330, yet suspect it returned to Scotland. While we know more about Morgana's tactics, preferences, and plans, we are no closer to a conclusion than we were on Friday. Think … what are we missing?"

"For what it's worth," Jules said, "my report is that the government has nothing. Everyone is finger-pointing and arguing, but they have no idea where to go. That I've hinted at inside knowledge has raised my status on the team and given me certain privileges. However, I've got nothing else of value."

Arthur stood tall and stepped into the center of the room. "We must have some actionable insights from all our efforts." Arms spread, hands and face pleading, "Please, anyone, what is our next move? Where should we look next?" Silence. His arms dropped to his side, and his gaze went to the window and the gardens beyond.

The energy in the room seemed to deflate as all looked down at their phones or laptops. It seemed they were back at square one. "Peter?" Jenn said softly. Her brother looked at Eric, who now nodded in agreement.

"Arthur," Peter said, almost in a whisper. "We learned something else in Scotland. It won't bring us closer to the Stone, but Eric and I think you should know." He had everyone's attention. "Arthur, we know where Guinevere was laid to rest."

Chapter 44

M *onday - Day Five*

The next morning, Jenn and Arthur parked their rented Mercedes sedan in the angled spaces outside Dunfermline Abbey, a historic Scottish landmark north of Edinburgh. Jenn tried to imagine what must be going through Arthur's mind. To wake up after centuries and learn that everything you loved is gone must have been hard enough to process. Then to discover that something you lost, the thing you cherished the most in the world, had been found, in a physical form you can experience, must have strained his fragile grasp on sanity. How could Guinevere's tomb have survived intact for 1,500 years when most things, man-made or otherwise, including the abbey itself, had fallen into ruin or the shadows of history? To travel in a flying steel tube to see her should have terrified the once king. Jenn and CJ tried to prep Arthur for the experience of flying, and then, on the way out to the car, John and Danie took a turn. Whatever they said, it must have worked, because he seemed to feel comfortable with the adventure. Jenn watched for signs of panic, but there were none.

Built in the eleventh century, the abbey suffered the same fate as Glastonbury during the 16th-century Reformation purge of Henry the Eighth. Fortunately, they spared a small portion of the church, likely out of respect for the Scottish monarchs who had been laid to rest there. These included Robert the Bruce, who passed away in 1329. They walked under a time-worn arched passage and found themselves in a bright garden of green grass and half-barrel planters bursting with red, white, and pink flowers. An energetic and impatient academic was waiting on the steps of the west entrance.

Coming down the path to meet Arthur and Jenn, he stopped short, unsure of how to proceed. He stood there motionless, staring at Arthur and grinning. Jenn came to his rescue. "Dr. Cockran, I presume?"

He snapped back into the moment and turned to Jenn. "Yes … Yes … Thank you. I am Ian Cockran." He accepted Jenn's extended hand while still staring at Arthur.

"Dr. Cockran, I'm Jenn Pelling, and pleased to introduce you to Arthur Pendragon." She tried to release his grip, but he was back in the throes of awe. Arthur could no longer restrain his smile at this exchange.

He grasped the academic's shoulder. "Dr. Cockran, I must thank you for the courtesy you showed my colleagues over the weekend and the unexpected information you shared with us. I will forever be in your debt."

With this, Dr. Cockran released Jenn and, unsure of the protocol, reached up and reciprocated the grasp to Arthur's shoulder, then thought better of this and dropped to a knee. "Your Highness, King Arthur, I…"

Arthur laughed. "Please, none of that now. Totally unnecessary." He guided the professor back to his feet and offered a handshake. "Please, just call me Arthur."

Dr. Cockran accepted the gesture. "Yes, Arthur. Well … I can't tell you what an honor … a shock, yes, but an honor to meet you. We, my order, my predecessors, were told that this day might come by our mutual friend, Mr. Wyse, but it is extraordinary that I should be the one to welcome you…"

Arthur nodded. "Please, I don't mean to appear impatient, but…"

Jenn noted that Arthur's eyes were sparkling a bit, and he was shifting his weight from leg to leg.

"Of course!" Dr. Cockran replied. "Would you like a bit of background first? It's a fascinating story. Or should I just bring you to her?"

"Maybe we can talk as we walk, doctor," Jenn said. "Are there privacy concerns?"

Dr. Cockran assured them he'd arranged for the old part of the church to be closed to the public that day. "I informed the church's minister that a VIP would be visiting. She may introduce herself in the main body of the church, but that's the only encounter I would expect."

"What was she told about this VIP?" Jenn asked, smiling up at Arthur, wondering if that term translated for him.

"Only that our VIP, a Mr. King…" he pursed his lips sideways and nodded an apology. "I know … anyway, Mr. King is an important benefactor to my college and is interested in all things British Antiquity. I didn't reference you, Ms. Pelling, so you can identify yourself as best you see fit; his assistant, his daughter, or not at all, if you'd prefer."

Daughter! she thought. Let that pass, Jenn. "Thank you, doctor. If asked, let's go with his assistant, shall we?"

Dr. Cockran pivoted and encouraged them forward. "Please."

At the top of the stone stairs, he pulled on an iron handle to open the large wooden door, nested in a stone archway, then escorted them inside. The church itself was much like others in Britain from the past few centuries. Rich polished wood, sandstone walls, and marble pillars greeted the pair as they walked down the center, flanking their host. In this historical environment, Dr. Cockran began his story.

"The original occupation of this property dates back to before your time, Arthur. A wealthy local landowner, whose name has been lost, was said to have welcomed your Guinevere to his home."

Arthur stopped and turned to Cockran. "She wasn't welcome at the castle?"

"The accounts from that age suggest that she decided to live among the people so as not to draw attention to herself and her, well, mission. She was well cared for and well-loved among the townspeople. It was said she died peacefully in her sleep, seven years to the day after Camlann."

"Seven years?" The words came with a sigh. "She had so much life in her when we parted before…"

Jenn squeezed Arthur's arm, but Cockran moved on, oblivious to the emotion playing out in front of him, and guided them to a door at the side of the church. Passing through what appeared to be a storage space, he ushered them out a second door on the opposite side of the room. Jenn sensed they had entered the church office wing and couldn't help but wonder if they'd tucked Guinevere's tomb away amid desks and file cabinets.

Walking down a hall flanked with windowed offices and meeting rooms, Dr. Cockran continued. "Her benefactor spared no expense to prepare a tomb fit for her stature, but, per her wishes, it was unmarked and unheralded. Arthur, this may come as a surprise to you, but Guinevere accepted Christ in her dying years and was a powerful supporter of the local churches."

Arthur shared that he might have expected this. "The message of Jesus always fascinated Guinevere; he preached tolerance, forgiveness, and love for other people. Her choice certainly doesn't surprise me, Doctor. Although I truly wouldn't have guessed that cult could have survived the centuries."

"In the end, it worked out well for her and us. The local clergy and the established nobility took great pride in caring for and protecting her tomb. As the centuries passed, they'd lost track of Guinevere's identity, and various rumors arose. Over time, she was called the mother of Scotland or the mother of the Church. For a brief period, some thought she might be Saint Margaret or even the Magdalene. Anyway, she remained in relative peace as the world around her was thrown into upheaval. The first parish church on this site was built in 1061. They built an underground crypt specifically for Guinevere. Interestingly enough, records surfaced as to her identity around that time. My predecessors sequestered these documents as quickly as they were able, but somehow word got out. Soon after, the abbey became the preferred burial site for Scottish monarchs. After a few decades, I doubt anyone recalled why they buried their fallen kings and queens here, but it caught on."

Dr. Cockran paused in front of a nondescript door, differing only from the others by the deadbolt locks. They were imposing and serious compared to the simple doorknob locks on the others. He inserted a heavy brass key and turned it with a loud clunk.

Pulling the door open, cool, musty air assailed them. Dr. Cockran reached in and flipped a switch. The stone-walled and worn stairway revealed by the light surprised Jenn. This was in shocking contrast to the modernity of the hall they would leave behind.

"Please watch your step." He let them start down and pulled the door closed behind him, relocking the deadbolt.

"Please watch your step and hold on to the railing," he warned again. "The steps are uneven, and you might not get the footing you expect." When he was confident his guests were stable, he continued. "Yes, where were we? Right. One king in particular, Robert the Bruce, went to great lengths to identify the Lady of the Abbey, as she was called, and it validated, at least for him, his place in history. Bards and royals in those years had rewritten King Arthur of the Britons as a king of Scotland or from Scotland. I suspect the tribal knowledge of Guinevere, or the memory that an important part of your story resided here, created this feeling of ownership, of possessing rights to your legend. Robert fashioned himself to be a modern-day Arthur. If not directly related to you," Cockran winked, "as far as we know, he felt the comparison was otherwise his birthright. Your legacy fascinated him, as misconstrued as it was in those days. His passion for all things Arthur brought him into contact with the Knights Templar and my order, the descendants of the Highland druids who'd escaped Rome's purge. And then, with us, guess who?" He paused and waited. Jenn and Arthur, intent on their foot placement, didn't acknowledge he'd asked them a question.

Stepping onto the floor, Jenn turned back up to Dr. Cockran, who had paused on the third step up, and said, "Merlin. He met

Merlin."

"Right, Merlin. He visited my predecessors frequently to ensure your Queen was well cared for and occasionally inquired about the Stone, but it had been stolen away ages before Robert's reign." He stepped past Arthur and reached to his right. Another wall switch fired up electric lanterns that were mounted about the crypt. These were well-made imitations of oil lamps, flickering a yellow-orange glow on the glossy stone floor.

As her eyes adjusted to the flame-like quality of the light in the small, square room, twenty feet per side at the most, Jenn could make out two slabs. They were about three feet tall, parallel, and separated just enough to pass between. The left stone was bare, but an effigy of a female figure, lying with her arms crossed over her chest, was on the right one. Her head was resting on a rectangular stone pillow. The king took tentative steps towards it. Jenn gave him space.

Dr. Cockran dropped his voice to a loud whisper. "King Robert had the uncommon luxury of dying from natural causes in the care of loved ones. This was in 1329. He made two deathbed requests. The first was that he be entombed alongside Guinevere in this crypt with the perpetual stipulation that any memorial for him suggest he was laid to rest in the main part of the church so she wouldn't be disturbed."

Arthur, lingering in his approach, was halfway to his queen. He turned around to face the professor after that statement. "I would have liked to have known King Robert," he said.

"Of that, I am sure, Arthur. They say he stood out in his day by ruling with a significant amount of humanity and compassion. He was well-loved, as we understood you were, Arthur."

"You said he made two deathbed requests?"

"Yes, and the second was stranger than the first. As I shared with your colleagues, Henry St. Croix wrote of a secret mission to exchange his heart for an important relic."

"They told us this story, Doctor," Jenn said.

268

"Sadly, the outcome of this quest is unknown." He paused. Arthur had reached the stone effigy of his beloved queen and was kneeling before it. "Perhaps we will never know," Dr. Cockran said, mostly to Jenn, who was still standing beside him. "I'll leave you now. This room is yours for as long as you need it. I'll be upstairs if you require anything." With a nod of his head to Jenn, he took a step back towards the exit, then watched Arthur's bowed back and head in front of the carved memorial for several seconds. He then turned and walked up the stairs.

Jenn watched Cockran disappear into the darkness, then went to Arthur, who was now kneeling. She stood behind him for a moment and noticed that his upper body was shaking. *What were you thinking, Jenn? He is still in love with his wife.*

She rubbed the welling moisture out of her eyes with the palms of her hands, then knelt at his side. Arthur acknowledged her presence with a slight turn of his head and a smile. The low light masked the tears she knew were there. Neither spoke for several minutes.

Looking at the face of the effigy, Arthur said in a low voice, "The figure bears some resemblance, but then no artist could ever capture her radiance, certainly not in stone. Maybe burning coals, but not cold stone." Jenn remained silent. This wasn't about her.

Arthur's hands were on his thighs, oblivious to the hard floor. Jenn looked about the room, taking in the crisscrossed archways and raised crucifixes placed on the walls. Arthur was looking at the crucifix above Guinevere's tomb when he said, "In my day, we weren't so vain as to fashion gods in our image, you know. Merlin might have even gotten away with calling himself a god, but he chose not to. He felt that was a Roman affectation. Ironically, the depictions of your god actually look a bit like Merlin." He allowed himself a small chuckle. "That Guinevere came to your Jesus in her last days doesn't surprise me, but I sorely wish I could have talked to her about it. After all that we'd seen - the joys, the tragedies … the magic … How did she reconcile all that? How did she fit it into this religion of the Christ?" They both pondered this in silence.

Turning to Jenn, he said, "I know your priests say God created man in his image, but that doesn't make sense, either. Could anything in human form rule over all the world at once? Could one being nurture growing trees and forest animals while devastating those same creations with floods and lightning? Jenn, our gods didn't create the lightning and the trees. They WERE the lightning and the trees, the wind, and the rain, the stone. The gods did what they did, and we learned to live within their rules. Gods didn't command us to obey. They didn't care. Some people tried to curry favor or influence them, but I never held much stock in that. What care should gods have for our wants or needs?"

Jenn was now seeing Arthur in a different light. This was the King of the Britons, a man others died for. She could see it now. When he turned to her, she dropped her eyes back to the reclined figure on the stone bed. "This is so similar to how you spent the very same centuries, Arthur. It breaks my heart."

"Yes, but why was I allowed to lie on a stone bed for a thousand years yet walk away when she must lie here for eternity? How can your god explain this?" Arthur wasn't looking for an answer. Jenn offered none. She just watched and listened, knowing he'd need to get this out.

He continued in an almost pleading voice. "Our gods were hard. Hard to understand, hard on the people, hard on everything. But it was a hard world, and the minute you let your guard down, the world would smash you. We understood such things in our age. The old gods were fair, and they didn't lie to us. They made no promises and left us to carve our own destinies. Your religion of Jesus is much easier. Do as you're told, submit. God and Jesus will take care of you. Beg forgiveness, and he will grant you a reprieve. Why then be accountable or responsible? Cruel kings and landowners had the same message, you know. Do as you're told, and we'll take care of you. Step out of line, and we'll crush you. This religion feels to me like another way to force people to do the bidding of the powerful.

270

If you open your eyes, you'll see that your god isn't telling you what to do, is he? The church leaders are. And who are the church leaders? Mostly men?"

Jenn whispered back, "Yes. Mostly men."

"So, what's changed? Men of power are still ruling the people as men of power always have. Maybe this is what Morgana is fighting against. I used to see the world with clarity. I don't any longer."

He pushed to his feet. Jenn leaned back and rose with him. "I prefer the old gods better," Arthur said. "Submitting was easier to comprehend when you knew you couldn't stop the rain or the wind." He reached out for the first time and touched the cheek of the stone face in front of him. "What were Merlin's words for the Stone? I submit to the wisdom and the power of the gods…"

As he uttered those words, Guinevere's pillow glowed. It was a yellow-green light, contrasting with the flickering orange of the electric flames surrounding them. Jenn, mouth agape, looked up at Arthur. He'd fixed his eyes on the block under his queen's head. Guinevere had kept the Stone safe … for all these centuries.

Chapter 45

Arthur and Jenn arrived back in Woburn on Tuesday afternoon as lunch dishes were being cleared. CJ and Mikol met them in the front hall. "Merlin is back," CJ said. "No explanation or apologies. He simply told us he was 'eager to speak with Arthur.' He's out in the back garden with John and Danie."

At this news, Arthur's face dropped.

"What's wrong?" Jenn asked.

Arthur brushed that off. "I should find them. CJ, can you try to pull everyone together in the kitchen in forty-five minutes? Please see if we can get Jules on the line. Thank you." Then, without another word, he deliberately walked to the rear garden doors and slipped outside.

As the door closed, Jenn queried CJ with a cocked head. "Don't look at me," CJ said.

Thirty minutes later, Jenn and Peter were the first down to the kitchen. Eric, fresh from the shower, followed.

"Peter," the Frenchman called out. "You should join me next time. You need to exercise both your mind and your body." CJ had installed a punching bag in one of the carports for Eric's workouts. Peter smiled sheepishly and buried his head back in his laptop.

Mikol and CJ drifted in as Barb and Bob laid out biscuits with pitchers of iced tea and lemonade. Peter, with his back to the glass doors, pulled his head away from his screen and asked if he should get Jules online. There was no response; everyone was looking out the windows.

"What gives, guys?" he asked, but again, no response. He spun his chair around and saw what had captured their attention.

272

Out by the pond, John and Danie flanked Merlin as they walked. Arthur was walking backwards, facing them. Distance obscured their expressions, but Arthur's gestures were animated, and the brothers' postures suggested they weren't happy with what they were hearing. If Merlin was speaking, he did so without body language.

As if the old wizard had sensed an audience, he motioned for the hulking South Africans to stop. They all looked simultaneously at the house. Jenn instinctively turned from the window, feeling guilty for having been caught. The foursome by the water huddled, and the watchers could see Merlin emphasizing some point now by waving his arms and pounding his staff into the turf. They saw Arthur embrace each of the boys, then the small group headed up the greenway to the house.

Five pairs of eyes followed them in. The room was in total silence as the last arrivals moved to their usual seats. Jenn verbalized what they were all thinking. "Are you going to tell us what that was all about?"

John and Danie looked down at their table. Arthur shifted in his seat, looking at Merlin.

Merlin dodged the question. "Peter, were you able to get Sir Julius on that big tele?"

Peter stammered something that sounded like 'Yes' and connected the second monitor to his laptop.

The video feed to Jules appeared on the wide-screen, and all could see him shifting in his chair and nudging his laptop screen to center his image. "Hi, everyone."

Jenn leaned forward and got things started. "What was the reaction in London to the news we found the Stone?"

"Well," Jules smirked as he responded, "disbelief, mostly. Most had convinced themselves that the demand for a fictional paranormal artifact was a wild-goose chase concocted by a psychopath to justify an ongoing murder spree. I shared a bit of the backstory, leaving out the fact that King Arthur and Merlin are

273

sitting in Milton Keynes drinking…" He leaned forward, forehead growing large as he squinted at his monitor. "What is it you all are drinking?"

"Iced tea, Sir Julius," Merlin answered from his usual stool by the island, that day covered in assorted fruits, cheeses, and crackers. "Now, if you please, stay focused and don't worry about our refreshments."

Jules sat back and stretched his arms high before dropping them onto the top of his head. "OK, that's the mood we're in today. Fine." He was smiling, but his voice was low and raspy. "They wanted to send an expert to validate the authenticity of the Stone, and I convinced them this wasn't necessary. 'Hey,' I said, 'it's a magic stone. What experts do YOU have in that field?' That sort of reset our relationship, and they have been receptive ever since." He sat up straight again and dropped his hands to the arms of his chair. "I expect they will pull in Ian Cockran to consult, but Jenn, you didn't tell him you'd found the Stone, right?"

"That's right, Jules. Although he probably knows about the armed presence that showed up at Dunfermline following our visit, so I'm sure he's been asking questions."

"Sir Julius," Merlin asked. "Do you think things will go smoother if we fill him in on the full story?"

"I've been thinking about that myself, Merlin, and think we should bring the professor into the inner circle. We're mostly unknown, unvetted faces to the establishment. He's got credibility. If he supports moving the Stone, it will go much more smoothly."

Merlin stood from his barstool and excused himself. Pulling his iPhone from the front pocket of his brown corduroy pants, he stepped out of the room.

Arthur turned back to the webcam and asked, "Jules, have you worked out the logistics for transporting the Stone to the circle?"

"We're looking to airlift it by chopper to Boscombe Down, about twenty minutes east of Stonehenge," Jules said. "There's an old Ministry of Defense training site there with an airfield, which was used for pilot training back to World War I. It's still secure and only about fifteen minutes from Stonehenge. We'll load the Stone into a van or truck for the approach to the site and have a small utility vehicle in place for transport from the ... hold on. Peter, can you make me a presenter?"

With a few mouse clicks, Jules' face contracted to a small rectangle in the corner of the screen. An aerial view of Stonehenge filled their view. "If you can see my pointer, there is a turnaround for buses about 400-500 feet to the northeast and up here." He sketched a circle around a service pull-off fifty feet past a bus stop. "Up here is a more secluded service area. I've got people reconning that as we speak. High level, we'll truck the Stone to one of these two spots and transfer it to a UTV for the final approach."

Arthur stood to get a closer look at the view Jules was showing. He stepped back and looked up at the cam. "This is good, Jules, an excellent start in such a brief time." Turning to the room, he continued. "I'd like you all to work out the details, but after discussing options with Merlin ... well, we don't have options. We can't take her out before she receives the Stone because we can't have her vacating Bonneville and inhabiting another. However, we can't give her too much time with the Stone either, because we don't know what she can achieve with it. I don't like it, but we think our window of opportunity is narrow."

"We'll have minutes from the time we deliver the Stone to isolate and apprehend her. Merlin will then use the power of the Stone either to contain ... or evict ... I guess I'm not sure what this spell will do..." He gave Merlin a chance to clarify; Merlin said nothing. Arthur, uncomfortable with this crucial aspect of the plan, stammered on, "Well, our job will be to get the Stone there, take out her protection, and immobilize her. I'll need to own that last piece." His voice fell as his eyes locked onto the aerial image of Stonehenge. Snapping back to the room, he added, "Due to the mind control thing, of course. Questions?"

"What do we do with her once you've immobilized her and

Merlin has, well, un-magicked her?" Jenn asked. All followed the turn of Arthur's head to Merlin.

Merlin turned a small bunch of green grapes around in his hands, scrutinizing his options, then picked one and popped it into his mouth. Looking up to Jenn, he said, "For reasons that will later become clear, you are just going to have to trust I'll handle this next step." He looked back to his grapes and said, "Please move along."

With no further questions and wanting to keep the pace up, Arthur continued, "OK. How do we get to this point? I'd suggest that Jules and Eric stick with the Stone, from its removal in Dunfermline to the bus lot. John and Danie, I'd like you to wait at Stonehenge and take ownership of the transfer to the smaller vehicle. You two should be able to lift it where we'd need four normal-sized men."

John and Danie nodded.

"Eric, I'm thinking then that you and I take the vehicle with the Stone to the handoff, likely to the center of the ring. We'll have to improvise from there, as we won't know how Morgana's men will be arrayed until that day."

Eric, standing and leaning against the window wall and carving off bite-sized chunks of an apple with a small knife, nodded his understanding.

"I can't imagine you'll be allowed to approach the lady without being searched," Mikol added. "But without a gun, you'll be sitting ducks if all hell breaks loose."

Eric popped an apple chunk into his mouth. "I'll be fine."

Mikol, whose life and livelihood revolved around guns, pushed himself back from the table and fixed Eric with a mocking look, dark brows lowered. "Help me understand then. What do you intend to do? Dance about and kick everybody when they aren't looking?"

Eric smiled then, without taking his eyes off Mikol, flicked his wrist. All heads reacted to the sound of his knife embedding itself in the center of the backrest of the chair directly across from Mikol. As the team turned back to Eric, he took another bite out of the apple in his hand. "As I said, I'll be fine."

Arthur broke into a grin. "All right then. Sir Mikol the Gun Master, I'd like you to examine the ground and do what you do best from an appropriate distance. CJ and Jules, you'll stay close to offer support as the situation unfolds. You are both trained for these scenarios, and I'd feel safer knowing you had my back."

Jules nodded; his face was still displayed in the small inset window on the screen.

CJ grunted more than spoke affirmation.

Arthur then turned to Peter and Jenn. "My friends, I cannot ask you to take part in this battle. You aren't warriors, and there would be no dishonor if you stayed at a safe distance until the danger has passed. What say you?"

Jenn saw the conflict in her brother's eyes. Peter was many things, but a fighter wasn't one of them. However, the team had relied on his intellect to get to this point. He should be part of the resolution. Thinking fast, she said, "Jules, will you be able to get live satellite coverage of the exchange?"

Jules switched the display back to the camera feed and, with his head once again filling the screen, said, "A satellite is out of the question, but I could probably get video using a drone. What are you thinking, Jenn?"

She stood up and put her palms on the table. "We don't know what Morgana, Bonneville, whatever, is capable of. It might be helpful to have Peter sit with a remote team watching the scene from above. He will know more about the true situation and might respond more appropriately if something, I don't know, sorcerous? If something otherworldly took shape. People who don't know what we know won't understand what they're seeing … Does this make sense?"

"It does make sense. Peter, if you'd do us the honor?" Arthur said. "Be our eyes in the sky, if that saying fits?"

Peter accepted the role and beamed at his older sister. She knew he wasn't a coward, but what could he do among these accomplished fighters?

"Jenn," Merlin asked, "will you be in the monitoring center as well?"

Jenn hesitated and looked at Arthur then Peter before responding. "It's probably for the best." The king bowed his head in agreement.

Once dinner had been cleared, Arthur transformed the Woburn dining room into a war room. Printouts and laptops covered the table. Their ultimate confrontation was imminent. They knew their objectives and the field of battle.

The sun had dropped, but dusky light was still hanging in the sky. Everyone was dragging, the stress of the day, of the past week, taking its toll. Arthur was standing by the glass doors, lost in thought and staring at reflections in the rippling pool across the gardens, when Peter called from the far side of the dining room. "Arthur, you should see this." All heads turned.

"What is it, Peter?" Arthur asked.

"I think it's her," he responded, eyes wide with disbelief, fingers hanging motionless over mouse and keyboard. Arthur ran to Peter's side. The others crowded in behind them. With a smile, Eric hip-checked Danie, who had crowded up close. Danie guided him up front.

Peter scratched his head. "So out of the blue, my Skype app popped up a connection request from 'M'. Now I don't know an 'M', so I chatted back a request for more information and got this response…" He leaned back to show everyone his screen.

Jenn read it out loud. *"Bring Arthur to the camera. I wish to speak with him."*

Merlin, who had hung back, unfazed by this turn of events, said, "May I suggest that you all come around the table with me? We don't know what she knows, but I doubt a team photo at this juncture would be in our best interests."

When the group had settled into listen-only mode, Peter looked over at Arthur, now in a chair to the younger man's left, where he could share the camera. Arthur nodded, and Peter clicked into the connection. Before them, the face of their quest, of their study and consternation for the past few weeks, filled the screen.

"Hello, Arthur," she said.

Arthur leaned forward. This wasn't Morgana, but somehow it was. Her eyes told the story; dark, bottomless, joyless. "Who am I speaking with? Bonneville or Morgana?"

She laughed, her amusement seeming genuine. "You are as dim as she said you'd be. I didn't expect we would need introductions after all we've been through, but I'll play your game. My name is Meghan Bonneville, and I am honored to make your acquaintance, Lord, His Highness, King Arthur Pendragon."

Arthur ignored the provocation in her voice and asked, "Is Morgana there as well?"

The face on the monitor lost all pretense of mirth. "Morgana is here with me, but she prefers me to speak for her on this plane." Her smile returned. "I called to congratulate you, Arthur. We knew that once you set your mind to it, you would find the Stone for us. Bravo."

Peter leaned into the laptop camera. "You will not speak to us like that, you … you monster. You don't know what we've been through, and you can rot in…"

Arthur saw Peter's eyes widen, his complexion go pale, and his fighting posture slip into submission. His gaze never wavered from the laptop monitor.

"First, young man," Bonneville said, "you will speak when spoken to, not before. Is that clear?" Without waiting for an answer, she went on. "Next, we don't answer to you, to anyone. We know what we know, and we'd lose the little respect we grudgingly have for your misfit band of merry knights if you were so thick as to deny it. We know what we know." As she made that statement, Peter clutched his arms across his chest. Tears welled in his unblinking eyes. Jenn rushed over to pull him away from the laptop and held him until the shaking stopped.

Through the speaker, they all heard Bonneville laugh. It was a high-pitched laugh, bordering on a cackle. "Big sister to the rescue, I see. Jennifer…" she called.

Jenn was far from the camera with her arms around her brother. Her only response was a look of raw hatred at the back of Peter's laptop.

"Jennifer, sweet, tragic Jennifer. I do believe we're even now. A life for a life, they say. Frankly, I never would have thought you had the balls to pull the trigger, but also to you, I say, Bravo."

"We're far from even, you bitch!" Jenn snarled over her brother's shoulder.

Arthur pulled the laptop to him and lowered the volume. "You have my attention, whatever you call yourself. What do you want?"

"Straight to business, is it? Fine." Meghan froze on the screen, falling silent with eyes closed. Arthur looked up, fearing they'd lost the connection. Before he could comment on this, her eyes opened, and a faint, tight-lipped smile spread across the face that filled the screen. Arthur knew in an instant he was now talking to Morgana.

"You listen to me, Son of Uther. You will deliver the Stone to me at Stonehenge on Thursday at dusk. I will be waiting. I'm sure you have grand delusions of stopping me, maybe killing my dear host while we stand defenseless in the open. Your shooter would make easy work of it. Let me save you and all of England a great deal of pain, brother. If you kill Bonneville, I'll find another host, maybe not right away, but I am patient. Ask yourself, does Myrddin have the strength to put you down and bring you back a second time? Can you survive another long sleep? It must have been icy and dark…" Her attention drifted off. Arthur remained silent.

Her eyes snapped back to the camera, now focused, and she said, "Do you want to know why I did what I did? Why I took those men's lives by turning their concubines into weapons? I'll tell you, so you understand who you're dealing with. I killed them partly because they deserved it, but mostly, dear brother, I did it because I wanted to. You have NO idea how I've suffered over the centuries while you slept in relative comfort and Myrddin traipsed about the world like a celebrity. I almost hope you try to stop me. The alternative for me is killing; more killing and that will be satisfying as well."

"Yet what will you do when you have the Stone, sister? You'll continue the killing. Only your reach will be farther. Why should we believe otherwise?"

"Do you think I care what you believe or don't believe? I speak now to the lady warriors in your band. It has always been my intention to use this power to raise the feminine to an equal place in this world. I seek to explore the mysteries of this and other universes for truths that can empower our race to live in peace, not this one-sided power grab where women are objects and weak."

Still cradling her brother, Jenn said, "You're a murderer! Nobody in this age will ever support you and whatever twisted plan you think you're pursuing."

With head still bowed, face behind her hand, she said, "Enough. I've said enough." She stared through digital space into Arthur's eyes. "You know where and you know when-we are done here. And dear brother, please leave that rusty old sword at home, will you? I'm afraid that's a deal-breaker."

"But wait, Morgana, sister, if we have questions or need to coordinate, where can we find you?" The video went black. Arthur looked up at Peter, who was now standing apart but near Jenn.

Morgana's voice called out from the laptop speakers one last time. "Peter can find me." Then, she was gone.

Jenn stepped forward, face set and eyes burning. "Arthur, I've changed my mind. I want to fight this devil."

As the others let this exclamation sink in, CJ stepped into the hall and called for Bob. "Get an exterminator out here … for rodents. No … tonight. Now!"

Chapter 46

At ten o'clock on Thursday morning, Jules watched a team of archaeologists emerge from Dunfermline Abbey into the misty, gray drizzle. They had spent two long days debating the best tactics to remove a stone that was integral to the sixth-century tomb of Queen Guinevere of Dumnonia. Eric was leaning with his back against the brick sentry box to the right of the door, and Jules was watching from a few steps below. They were both dressed in black tactical gear, but they were not what caused the scientists to pause at the top of the stone steps. Though they entered the Abbey alone on Tuesday morning, armed with lights, tools, tarps, and photographic equipment, a small army greeted them on their exit. Sixteen helmeted Special Forces troops arrayed themselves around a black Mercedes van, armed not with tripods but with assault rifles. Eric and Jules were underdressed in comparison.

The scientists had wrapped the Stone in a green canvas tarp and strapped it to a stretcher-like pallet. Four of the scientists, one per handle, carried it. Dr. Cockran was a few steps in front of the stretcher-bearers, leading them out of the church. The two remaining members of the research group followed the relic. A fine layer of dust coated all the scientists. Sweat tracks washed lines down the cheeks of some. *Or are those tears?* Jules thought to himself. He understood that this was an emotional experience for specialists trained to preserve monuments, not tear them apart. The silent, somber looks of the six men and one woman, eyes forward, mouths set, spoke volumes. These middle-aged-to-senior academics had insisted on carrying their burden to the waiting van themselves, despite having some of the fittest soldiers in the realm ready to accept the hand-off. That was a condition of their participation. Even Eric, Jules noticed, was standing straight out of respect and watching these brilliant scientists move as if they were bearing one of their own to their last resting place.

They shuffled, as much a tribute to the solemnity of the moment as to the weight of the stone. They would need to take it down over twenty steps. The delivery took fifteen minutes to complete. After the academics slid the stretcher into the van, Jules took charge of the situation. He and Eric moved to the still-open back doors of the vehicle and asked both the protection detail and the scientists to step back. Eric, then Jules, climbed into the windowless van and closed the doors behind them. Eric reached up and switched on a ceiling light as Jules unwrapped the unremarkable-looking, chipped and scratched block.

"It's not what I expected," Eric whispered as he and Jules got their first look at the prize they had been searching for.

Jules' response was to reach out and grasp Eric's shoulder. "Let's get this over with," he said.

By prior agreement, Jules would attempt to invoke the ritual that verified this stone was still the Stone of Destiny. Eric acknowledged that his lack of belief in any higher power than the individual, while recently challenged, might cast doubt on a negative response from the Stone. As Merlin had told them, sincerity appeared to be a vital component of the ritual. Taking several deep breaths to clear his mind, Jules closed his eyes and breathed, "I submit to the power and the wisdom of the gods." His eyes remained closed, fearful that if he were overanxious, the Stone might not react. However, the sound of Eric pulling the canvas back up over the Stone snapped him back into the moment. He could see a soft yellow-green glow leaking from the folds of the cloth as Eric hurried to ready the package for delivery.

"It worked, let's go," was all Eric said to Jules, wide-eyed at the results.

The thirty-minute drive from Dunfermline Abbey to the RAF

airfield in Kirknewton, twelve miles southwest of Edinburgh, was uneventful, although they took nothing for granted. Two armed troops were in the cab, while two more joined Eric and Jules in the back. Two Land Rover Wolf 90 tactical vehicles led the way. A third followed. Each Wolf had four armed soldiers watching for threats to the convoy. Teams of special forces guarded both sides of the Queensferry Crossing Bridge, which had been shut down to civilian traffic hours earlier. Crowds of the curious and inconvenienced conjectured potential explanations for the cloak-and-dagger activity. Below the bridge and circling in the Firth of Forth, rigid-hulled inflatable boats, courtesy of Her Majesty's Coastguard, ensured the delivery was safe from water-borne attacks.

Jules could hear the pulsations of a helicopter's blades as the convoy roared across the airfield, coming to what he thought was an unnecessarily abrupt stop. They waited in the soft glow of the interior lights until support personnel pulled open the double doors. The gray glow of a cloudy sky and a pulsating, unnatural breeze from the chopper greeted them.

"At least the rain stopped," Jules said as he shielded his eyes from the light, still oppressive after thirty minutes of near darkness. They were about forty feet from the helicopter. Jules squinted at the markings on the long, olive-green aircraft and burst into laughter.

"What is so funny, mon amie?" yelled Eric over the sound of the rotors and engine.

Jules put his arm around Eric's shoulder and leaned towards his ear. "Someone in London has a strange sense of humor. This is an AgustaWestland AW101." He watched his friend's face for a sign of recognition. Seeing nothing but a blank stare, he leaned back in and yelled, "The nickname for this bird is 'Merlin'."

Chapter 47

As Jules and Eric were loading the Stone into the Merlin outside Edinburgh, the rest of the team arrived at Stonehenge to take position and set the scene. Peter remained at the Visitor Center to get the drone feed set up, and Mikol split off from the team to find a secure spot to monitor the remote access areas while the rest took two green UTVs for the final one-mile stretch to the bus lot.

Jenn and CJ were in black tactical gear with bulletproof vests matching Jules and Eric. Against Jenn's objections, Arthur refused to show any acknowledgement of fear and would meet the moment in street clothes: blue jeans, his Columbia boots, and a heavy, gray wool fisherman's sweater with three open bone buttons at the neck. Finding gear for John and Danie was a challenge the Special Forces liaison struggled with. They found vests that the immense men could squeeze into providing at least partial coverage, but they still had to wear their own sweatpants and running shoes.

Bonneville's instructions were that only Arthur's team could come within a mile of the drop, and they must come unarmed. There was no response to Arthur's request for reciprocity. As a tactical compromise, Arthur and Eric would deliver the Stone unarmed, as asked. The rest of the team would not be so compliant. Jenn carried the same model Glock that Arthur had trained on, receiving a crash course before leaving Woburn. CJ and Jules chose Colt Carbines with a short barrel, laser pointer, and flash suppressor. All members of the task force wore transparent earbuds and wireless microphones clipped to their vests, plus infrared beacons to make them more visible to Peter's drone.

Arriving at the bus turnaround, the two Gators circled to the right and stopped, facing the stone ring. Arthur jumped out of the lead vehicle and offered Jenn his hand. "Shall we?" he said, then hitched up the leather belt of Excalibur's scabbard, purchased from a novelty antique shop on High Street in Glastonbury.

CJ grunted as she climbed out on her own. John and Danie remained seated, both staring blank-faced at the ring of rocks.

Jenn walked over, put a hand on John's shoulder, and said, "C'mon, guys, let's walk the scene." John smiled at her, and Jenn noticed a tear in his eye. Speechless, he nodded and stepped out of the Gator. Danie followed, his gaze still fixed on the site.

As a group, they walked to the center of the structure. Jenn looked southwest, to the patch of trees near Normanton Down, a three-thousand-year-old grouping of barrows. These were the burial grounds of the long-forgotten tribe that built Stonehenge. She knew Mikol was in those trees, waiting for Bonneville's men to establish their position. She didn't expect to see him, but felt better knowing he was watching. Turning back to the team, she saw CJ looking towards the trees as well, her hair pulled back in a tight ponytail. Uncharacteristically, a soft smile softened the agent's normally hard face. CJ looked up, and Jenn winked. CJ held eye contact for a moment and then, with sideways nods, they rejoined the others.

Another black, windowless van received the Stone when the chopper landed at Boscombe Down airfield. Jules took the wheel for the twenty-minute drive to Stonehenge. They arrived at three o'clock, leaving a little over two hours until sundown.

Arthur waved them up and said, "The stone is here, everyone. Take your positions. John and Danie, let's get back to the lot."

Jenn turned and jogged back to a storage shed she'd use as cover near the bus lot, nodding at Jules, who had wasted no time exiting the van, then hustled past her to a rise about ninety degrees around the monument near the ring road.

She took a knee and tried hard to remember her training as Arthur asked, "Everybody set?"

"Yes," she said, echoing the responses of the rest.

Mikol followed with, "Perfect timing. The witch is pulling in from the south."

"Roger that," Peter returned. "We'll launch the drone." Their eye-in-the-sky captured three Jeeps turning right from the access road and bouncing across the field before coming to a sliding stop, side by side, at the tourist sidewalk facing the rocks.

Jenn turned away from the Jeeps and tried to see CJ and Jules, by now under tarps designed for camouflage and taking advantage of the fading light.

Turning her attention back to the new arrivals, she saw three to four men jump out of each Jeep with an armload of oil-fed torches. She watched the men hustle their loads into the ring and plant the lights in a circle around the center. Jenn thought of Merlin's description of the last ceremony for this artifact so many centuries ago. The symmetry was appropriate.

Chapter 48

Arthur also watched the activity with interest. He'd built a plan based on the information available, but couldn't know if Morgana had any surprises in store. They'd have to wait and react to what happens next, which was all the more frustrating because his plan required perfect timing. But this was his burden to bear since only he could guess when that perfect time came. As he recalled their last conversation back at the base, he wished Merlin could have prepared him better. *'I don't know'* was not the answer he'd hoped for.

***

The prior morning at Swafford House, Arthur rose before the sun and shuffled downstairs to the kitchen. Following the aroma of freshly baked rolls, his eyes were open, but he wasn't yet seeing. He was a few steps into the kitchen before he realized he wasn't the first one awake that morning. Sitting at the island on his usual stool was the old wizard.

"I thought you were going to sleep the day away," Merlin commented as he blew a puff of steam off his fresh mug of coffee.

Massaging his eyes with the heels of his hands, Arthur shook his head a few times before responding. "When did you get back, Merlin? And how did you get back?" The wizard had disappeared after Morgana's contact via Peter's laptop the day before. Arthur crossed his arms as he waited for a response. He didn't expect Merlin to explain himself, but he wasn't alert enough to know what else to say.

"I've only just arrived, Arthur. Come sit and have some coffee.

We still have much to talk about." Bob appeared and placed a steaming mug of coffee in front of Arthur alongside trays of rolls, assorted jams, and butter. The king accepted the hot beverage, waiting for Merlin to continue.

"Arthur, my boy, are you sure you are prepared to go through with the plan we discussed?"

"You said it's the only way, Merlin. Right?"

"I'm afraid so," Merlin responded. "Especially after poring over the documents that you retrieved from Avalon."

"Then this is how it must end. And the team will do as we've asked." Arthur reached across Merlin's cup and picked up a pitcher of cream. A short pour brought the color and temperature to the desired ranges, and he took a longer drink.

"I share your assessment, and they aren't my concern. You are, Arthur. I am amazed at how quickly you've adapted to this age. You have embraced this team, and they've accepted you, befriended you. To be a king is to be alone. You've changed, softened maybe. Will this be a problem?"

Arthur didn't respond. He would do what he needed to when the time came. He communicated this with a slow shake of his head.

"Good. Moving on," Merlin said, "I need to revisit the timing with you. From what I learned in Morgana's documents, I now believe that our window will be tighter than we'd discussed." He picked up his mug and drained it, wiping his mouth, beard, and mustache with the sleeve of his tan cotton shirt. "If you recall, I told you that Morgana would need to merge all the bits of her consciousness she may have placed in the minds of those she needed to control before invoking the Stone. She'll need all her strength, and that's when she'll be vulnerable. It's why I insisted we deliver the Stone to her since it's the only time we could be sure she was, well, all there."

"I recall," Arthur said, clutching his warm mug with both hands as he took another sip.

"Yes, well," Merlin continued. "Her research was impressive, and I hope to find her sources … I picked up Egyptian, even Babylonian, influences…"

"Merlin, please…"

"Yes, right. What I'm trying to say is that we'll need to be more precise than I previously suggested. I'm confident she can't begin to extract the Stone's power until she's collected all the fragments of her consciousness. You know, she's likely distributed pieces of herself into the men that surround her and any rodents she deemed useful. That's how she controls them. She'll need to consolidate those before destroying what remains of the Bonneville woman. That's the part I've been dwelling on. I am now convinced we'll need to ensure she has fully expelled Ms. Bonneville and is fully present in that body before we make our move. Do you understand?"

"Does this mean she'll kill Bonneville? I doubt she'd consent to that and would likely resist if she could see it coming, for all the good it will do her. Maybe we can use this."

"It's not black and white, Arthur. Bonneville's body will continue, but the person that was Bonneville will cease to exist. Some resistance may work in our favor. It may distract Morgana for a moment."

"A moment may be all we need." Pivoting to face the wizard, Arthur asked, "So how can you be so sure she hasn't fully possessed the girl already?"

"Because, my boy, Bonneville still has a voice. Didn't she reprimand you Tuesday night for calling her Morgana? It may help if you understood what is happening right now with your dear sister." He didn't finish that thought, eyeing the motion to his left.

Peter shuffled into the kitchen, dressed in baggy faded jeans and a plain red t-shirt. "Hullo, Merlin," he said and stopped behind the island across from the men.

Arthur reached out and gave Peter's arm a reassuring squeeze. "Morning."

Merlin grunted. "Until she has access to the stone, Morgana won't have the strength to possess another human, only to be … a

290

guest. Make no mistake, we don't become the host. We merely co-exist, share experiences, make suggestions. This is easy in a less complex life form because they can't grasp what was happening or differentiate our thoughts from their own. Humans are much more difficult because once they understand they have a guest, they have free will to decide its fate. You see, young Meghan could have thrown Morgana out if she wished. Instead, she agreed to share her mind, her fate. We can assume she is sympathetic to Morgana's mission. This is likely why it took centuries for your sister to show herself. She needed to find a willing host, one who was receptive to her story; a damaged psyche who would be open to her manipulations yet properly placed socially to enable the events we'd witnessed. We may never know how many attempts she'd made."

"What about the women who killed their husbands?" Arthur asked. "Or the man at the Tor who shot himself? Couldn't they have simply said no?"

"That's where the art of reading your hosts, the gift of manipulation, comes in. Those women were assuredly predisposed to the actions Morgana compelled them to perform."

Arthur remained unconvinced. "What about her man who tortured and killed himself? You aren't suggesting that he wanted to do … well, that?"

Merlin, in full teacher mode, sat straighter and used his hand for emphasis. "Remember, they have to acknowledge the guest to know the thoughts aren't their own. They wouldn't know to resist if they didn't realize the suggestion or command wasn't independent thought. Most likely, the instruction came so rapidly and powerfully, he didn't even see it coming. With a weak mind, these sorts of suggestions are fairly easy."

Merlin leaned down and blew across the top of his coffee again. "As I was saying, I am now convinced that we cannot strike until Morgana has recovered all the fragments of her being and absorbed enough of the Stone's energy to completely displace Bonneville. However, from what her notes suggest, we can't allow her to continue past that point and finish the ritual. To my knowledge, no one has ever completed this successfully, but if she succeeds, she may travel beyond our ability to stop her. In effect…" He paused to ensure his audience was hanging on this next bit, "…she will have become a god."

Peter had frozen, mouth agape, and a croissant-laden hand hovering inches from his face. He was staring at Merlin in disbelief.

Arthur focused more on the tactical aspects of this revelation. "We need to strike her down after she has fully possessed Bonneville, but we need to do it before she goes any further with the ritual, since we can't know what makes her invulnerable. How will we know when one ends and the other starts?"

Merlin took another gulp of his hot coffee and turned to look out the window at the gray morning light, a shallow mist rising from the Swath Ford Pool. After a moment, he lowered his cup to his lap and looked first at Peter, then at Arthur. Arthur saw what might have been the most genuine concern he'd ever seen on Merlin's face. "I don't know, son. Nobody has ever been so arrogant, so careless, as to attempt what Morgana is going to attempt." Peter had placed his uneaten croissant back on the counter as he waited. Merlin set his jaw, then said, "I don't know. I simply don't know."

Chapter 49

I don't know," the old wizard had told him.

This was not something a leader said to his men on the cusp of battle, and Arthur would not share his uncertainty with the rest of the team. There's nothing they could do to help, and he needed them focused on their tasks. He turned to look at Eric, leaning against the hood of a Gator, legs crossed and hands in his pockets. His self-confidence was limitless. This was the man he needed at his side.

In contrast, he saw Danie was sweating, and John was pacing. "Boys," Arthur said, "let's move the Stone to the Gator. It appears our exchange is imminent."

The twins slid the stretcher bearing the Stone out of the van and carried it to the waiting utility vehicle. Arthur tucked the green tarp in at the corners of the stone, and they turned back to the monument. About a dozen torches had been lit, and the center altar glowed in the flickering orange light. Arthur caught movement at the Jeeps. At the fringes of the fire's light, he could see another figure moving into place. As tall, if not taller, than those preparing the scene, the flowing movement of fabric confirmed that Morgana was joining her men. It was time.

Arthur unbuckled the leather strap of Excalibur's sheath and pulled it off his waist. He held it for a moment, looking up at John. "If there were another way, we'd take it, son." He extended his arms and presented the long sword to the South African. "Please keep it safe and out of sight."

John hesitated; his eyes locked on Arthur's. He reached out with both hands and accepted the weapon.

"Thank you, John … and Danie. I know what I'm asking you to

do is difficult, but it's the only way."

John didn't respond. He slung the strap over his head and adjusted the sheath, making the pommel accessible with his right arm over his left shoulder. The belt wouldn't fit around his waist.

Arthur stepped forward and placed a hand on each of the young men's shoulders, then stepped back and turned to Eric. The Frenchman was watching, with no emotion or curiosity showing on his face. "Eric," Arthur said, "if you've changed your mind about a firearm, best to tuck it away in the vehicle."

Eric patted the empty holster on his thigh and said, "I am ready when you are, my liege. It will be fine." The once-king smiled at the jest. Eric's unflappable attitude was not the only reason Arthur had chosen him to accompany the Stone. Of all the Keepers, he knew Eric could do as much damage without a gun as others could with, thinking back to Eric's impromptu exhibition at Swafford House the prior evening.

As the light faded on Stonehenge, Eric nodded towards the monument. "Arthur, it's time."

Arthur followed Eric's gaze and saw a figure silhouetted by the flames, with his arms outstretched, waving up and down. They were ready. Eric climbed in behind the wheel of the Gator. Arthur sat next to him. John and Danie climbed into the second Gator and followed as Eric pulled onto the paved road.

Eric veered their Gator off the sidewalk, stopping in full view of Morgana, who was flanked by two men. Leon, whom they recognized from the confrontation in Exeter, had waved them up and stepped forward. The sky had turned a deep blue; the only light was now the array of torches, blazing in two concentric rings around the flat stone where the sorceress waited. The closest torch was on Leon's right, presenting an eerie, half-lit facade.

Arthur led Eric forward and felt a slight increase in the breeze. The stabbing pain from his ancient wound caused a misstep before he could suppress it. If Eric noticed, it didn't show.

Leon motioned for them to stop. "Cheers, gentlemen." Sizing

up Arthur, he said, "And nice to see you again, Your Highness. Can I assume you followed the rules like the fine gentlemen you appear to be? No weapons … no sword…? Come a few steps forward, mates, into the light." He beckoned them forward with flexing fingers.

They closed the gap and noted he'd left his weapon holstered across his chest. Leon saw what Eric was looking at and said, "Don't get any funny ideas, mates. My pals can protect my lady and me." He gestured back towards Meghan. "You've been in their sights since you turned off the walk."

Arthur could make out dark shapes near most of the standing stones. They'd expected this. In his left ear, he heard Peter's calm voice.

"Right, I've marked seven bad guys around the outer ring, besides the three with Bonneville. There is a guy to Arthur's left. The next is a few stones around, and a third, a few more stones after him. Jules, a fourth is in the center of the capped pillars, and the fifth is two stones to his left. Mikol, six and seven should be in your line of fire."

John whispered into his mic, "There's an eighth guy in the inner ring, between the second and third. That's it, though."

Leon signaled with a twirl of his finger that they should now spin so he could confirm they were unarmed. Satisfied they had no weapons tucked away in their dark clothing; he motioned his men to step forward.

Turning to Arthur, Leon said, "We're going to bring the treasure to the lady now. Don't forget that you are still standing only by her good graces."

"You may want to find more hands, monsieur. We can help, as can our friends, if it is too much for you." Eric pointed over at the twins.

Leon smiled, his white teeth glowing in the dancing light against his dark skin. "Well, thank you for that, *Mon Sewer.* Since we're all friends now, why don't you two chaps lend my mates a hand? The boss lady wants to speak to the big guy, anyway. Those other fellas can stay right where they are." Arthur was relieved to see that at least this went as planned. Falling in behind, they walked to the back of the Gator and each chose a handle.

Peter's voice informed the field team that now was the time to move up. All focus was on the Stone. Arthur knew Mikol was moving out of the trees on the ATV. CJ, Jules, and Jenn must also be creeping closer.

The four pallet bearers shuffled the Stone to the center of the ring, between flanking torches. They placed it on a fallen stone, where the original altar had been. The sorceress maintained eye contact with Arthur as the Stone progressed.

Leon grabbed a corner of the tarp and pulled. "Let's see what you gents have brought us … What the hell is this?" He looked up at Arthur, eyes dark and mouth set as he snapped his weapon out.

"Leon, dear, it's OK. This is what we were looking for. Put your gun away."

The tall man hesitated, looking from Morgana to the Stone and back. He holstered his gun but fixed a glare on Arthur.

The sorceress looked over at Eric, then smiled. "Ahh, the Fighter! It's Galahad! We didn't foresee this. YOU are a son of Galahad! Still fighting Arthur's battles after all these centuries? I expect that the others are also descendants of your precious guard. The soldier, the shooter, the spy, the giants?" Noting a momentary lowering of Arthur's brow, she added, "Yes, I know of them, and I'm sure they're all here. But it won't matter." She held her hands over the Stone, palms down, about six inches above the surface. She took a deep breath, then exhaled at a measured pace, eyes closed and face down. The surface of the stone flickered.

Arthur spoke in a measured tone, trying not to increase tension levels. "Morgana, you don't need to do this. Let's leave this age to survive or fail on its own, you and I."

The dark lady laughed, and as on the first web call, it was more of a shriek. "You still think I'm Morgana? She is with me, but I am my own woman. We choose to act as one."

"Then you must understand, Miss Bonneville, Morgana doesn't share power. Once she gets what she wants, my sister will possess you and erase you. She's only using you, but you can cast her out. You simply need to choose it."

Jenn's voice in his ear, "Arthur, what are you doing?"

He ignored her. There still may be a peaceful solution.

Meghan leaned forward, and her smile disappeared. "We expected something like this. Men only understand power and control. It is inconceivable to men that we can work together. Someone doesn't need to be in charge. I am honored that she chose me, and I look forward to seeing this through to the end. However, if you foolishly strike down this body, Morgana will just befriend another. We aren't sure how you found me, but know this: you won't be so lucky the next time. She can outlast you, Arthur; you, the druid, all of them." She waved her arms to the darkness beyond the light of the torches. "Where is the old fool, anyway? It doesn't matter. The revolution has begun. Our enjoyable experiment with the sad women of those arrogant men only proved that the city, the country, is teeming with willing collaborators." She finished the gesture with a stroke of Arthur's cheek. He remained steadfast. "Worth a try," she said with a pout.

"Now that we understand each other, let me get a better look at lovely Galahad." Meghan moved towards Eric, but Arthur stepped in between.

"You will not have this man. As you suspected, there are as many guns trained on you right now as there are on me. I will suffer another age of waiting, if need be, to find you, but this I will not allow."

Leon stepped up, hand back on his holstered weapon. Her two other men shot their hands out, ready to restrain Arthur if he'd continued. There was a collective exhalation as Meghan held her hands up in faux surrender.

"Fine," she said. "There will be time for fun later." She winked at Eric as she moved back to her position in front of the Stone. She placed her hands on the scratched black surface and closed her eyes. "And we'll need blood to complete the transformation. There's poetry in spilling Morgana's little brother's blood instead of someone loyal to us."

Eric returned the gesture with a bow, then reached his right hand up to a pocket on his vest in a measured movement. Leon noted the change, snapped his weapon up, and pointed it at Eric's head. "Stop right there. Put your hand back down … slowly."

Eric responded with a peaceful look and pulled out a tin of cough drops, pinched between his thumb and index finger. "It's OK, my friend; the damp air is getting to me. It's OK." Keeping the tin in clear view, he opened it and pulled a single lozenge out. Showing it to Leon, and then to the others, he popped it into his mouth. He saw the gunman relax, so he extended his hand out, tin open. With raised eyebrows, he offered to share.

Leon glowered back and shook his head. The gun tip dropped but remained at the ready. Eric let his hands fall and clasped them together in front as he sucked on the drop.

Meghan tossed her black hair behind her neck with both hands and then brought them back down to the surface of the Stone. It glowed beneath her fingertips. She closed her eyes and dropped her head.

Arthur could see her lips moving, but couldn't hear the words over the strengthening wind. The flames on the torches were snapping in the gusts, showing a circular pattern. This was not a natural breeze, he thought.

Seconds passed, then minutes before anything changed. When it started, it started with Leon. Both hands flew to his temples, fingertips trying to crush the pain. His eyes were wide, and his mouth dropped open as he stared at Meghan. John whispered, "Something's happening. The frontman looks like his head's exploding."

Arthur risked a glance to his left when the two closer men, then

298

all the gunmen, spread out around the ring, clutching their heads. Recalling Merlin's prediction, Arthur presumed this was Morgana calling the pieces of her consciousness back, consolidating her being. Rats, too many to count, fled the shadows for the open fields. He glanced over at Eric, who understood the sequence of events.—

Peter's voice rang in Arthur's ear. "Hold on. Where did he come from? Jenn, Jules, between the two of you to the north, somebody else is out there. Can you see anything?"

"I see him … hold," Jules said. A few seconds passed, then he came back online. "Shit. It's Merlin. When did he get here?"

"Right! It's about time," Peter said. "Copy that. Merlin is walking in from the north, about 500 feet out now." Still with a hot mic, the team heard Peter say to the team in the Command Center, "I'll explain later."

Arthur struggled not to look. Merlin had said he'd be there when he needed to be there, but was circumspect about details. He noted from the posture of the men surrounding him that the headaches must be subsiding.

Bonneville's eyes snapped open, her pupils darting side to side. A pained cry, "Nooooo," emitted from her open mouth and faded to silence. She met Arthur's stare with a pleading look, as she realized the magnitude of Morgana's deception. There was nothing he could do.

Her eyes and mouth crushed closed. Her hands had dropped, and her palms lay flat on the cold stone. Time stopped as the woman's face relaxed, and her eyes opened. The difference in her visage was shocking. Looking over the Stone at him, younger than he remembered, but with that unmistakable icy rage emitting from coal-black eyes, was his half-sister, Morgana.

Arthur said, "Now."

Chapter 50

Eric's hands flew. The men alongside Morgana clutched their throats, surprised by the sudden pain. Eric's tin had held a few cough drops and four throwing stars. As blood seeped through their fingers and their knees buckled, Eric spun. He threw a sidekick to Leon's throat, followed by two strikes with his fist to the bridge of the man's nose. Leon crumpled and hit the ground as his comrades did.

Wasting no time, with a step and a leap, Arthur was over the Stone, tackling Morgana, who hadn't had time to react.

From the field, shots rang out. "Dammit, I missed," Jenn cursed into her mic as she flung herself to the ground. "I think I got the guy to my right, but I'm taking return fire from the guy on my left."

"Jenn, are you OK?" Her brother's reply was a whisper in her headset.

"I'm OK. I may have clipped him. Not sure. He's firing wildly, but he crawled behind a stone, so I've got no shot. I need help!"

Jules came on, "Stay calm and keep him pinned down, Jenn. I've got line of sight but want to get a little closer. I took out his buddy right in front of me, so I should be clear."

"The hostile to Arthur's right dropped behind a stone when the shooting started and is still active," Mikol said. "I'm keeping him engaged, but does anyone else have eyes on him?"

"Negative," CJ said, "but my two targets are down. I'm advancing slowly."

"Not to worry, mon ami," Eric whispered. "I brought your utensils from dinner last night, but fear they may get a bit soiled before I can return them. Can you keep his attention for another

300

moment, s'il vous plaît?"

Mikol's response was three shots into the sarsen their foe was hiding behind. When the gunman leaned right to return fire, Eric launched a blade.

Jenn heard metal striking stone, followed by a rifle crack from the dark.

"You missed, hotshot," Mikol said, "but he was dumb enough to look for you. Threat eliminated, and don't sweat the tableware."

"Merci, mon ami."

Peter's voice came back on the comms. "Jules, I see you moving up, but be careful. Merlin is approaching from your right."

Merlin had reached the access road north of the monument. He maintained his pace towards the fight, unconcerned that bullets were flying in every direction. Jenn blinked hard but could swear he glowed; arms raised, palms forward.

"What's that old man doing?" Mikol asked. "Surrendering?"

Merlin stretched his arms up and towards the center of the ring as he advanced. "The Stone ... he's trying to control the Stone," Jenn yelled.

Morgana's scream punctuated Jenn's exclamation. "No! NO!! This is foolish, you bastard, you failure of a magus! I'll just come back stronger, and the vengeance I'll wreak will be tenfold!" she thrashed from side to side.

Leaning forward, Jenn could see that Arthur was grappling with Morgana on the ground. *She should be no match for him!* He had one arm wrapped around the witch, pinning her left hand to her body, and was struggling to get a grip on her right. *She must be getting strength from the stone.*

A bullet struck the corner of Jenn's shed, and she jumped back. Another crack followed.

"He's neutralized, Jenn," Jules said.

"I think that's all of them," Peter said, "but please be careful and do not approach Morgana without Arthur's go-ahead. Remember, we only *think* she needs to touch you to control you."

Jenn rose and pulled a pair of binoculars from her belt to get a better look at Arthur's struggle. She had an unimpeded view through the stones.

Morgana's foot found a hold, and she used it for leverage to thrust into her larger brother with enough force to roll on top of him. Arthur's grip slipped as he let out an anguished howl. Morgana had pulled out a knife of her own, and it found his right thigh. Pushing the pain away, he pulled his leg up and tried to trap her with his knee. Another stab drew a more controlled response. Morgana, swinging wildly, had embedded her knife in Arthur's right foot through the side of his boot. He shot his leg straight, which wrenched the weapon out of her hand. A punch to Morgana's face followed, catching her cheekbone below her left eye. She slackened, and he seized the moment. The king wrapped his arms around her waist, spun so they both faced the center of the henge, and fought to get his feet under him. With his back against the altar rock, the wound in his thigh bleeding profusely, he propelled them up and backwards onto the Stone.

The entire team heard Morgana screaming, her face next to Arthur's ear, "Ypovállo sti sofía kai ti dýnami ton theón!" The language was unimportant; the Stone reacted with the yellow-green glow.

Lifting his head high, Arthur called over the wind, "JOHN! NOW! She's getting stronger!"

The giants leapt off the Gator and ran towards the king. John pulled Excalibur from its sheath as he ran. Danie was one step behind him. They were both yelling what Arthur would have recognized as a war cry. Jenn could see the Stone behind Arthur shimmer in the middle of the black rocks. Time was running out.

Arthur's call in Jenn's earpiece was barely audible over the wind noise, but when she saw John and Danie break from the Gator, she asked, "What the hell is going on?" but got no response. She rose to her feet, crouching low, and watched the twins' progress, and moved forward cautiously.

***

Fear had paralyzed Jeb from Black Bart's pub, and he lay curled up on the ground behind an inner stone after the first shot, watching his mates drop left and right. The boss had promised this wouldn't happen. She assured them they would not dare to start a fight after the ransom was delivered. He wasn't sure why, but he was told never to ask questions. *Well, I'm asking them now, goddammit!* It had been several moments since the last gunshot, but he knew it wasn't over yet. The boss was wrestling with the big guy ten to fifteen feet in front of him, but he was helpless. A shot was out of the question because he might hit her, and physically involving himself would expose him to their guns. *Helpless.* Breathing heavily, he called out, hoping to be heard over the wind screaming through the rocks. "Mikey, Pete? Mates, you still there? Anyone?" Nothing.

He heard loud voices from outside the ring. Hoping some of the boys were still giving them hell, he rose a bit to get a look. Instead of his mates, he saw two of the largest men he'd ever seen running from the walkway. The first man was waving a big-ass sword! Recognition rolled in slowly. These were the guys he'd chatted up at the pub. *Those assholes played me!* His sense of betrayal pushed aside his fear and uncertainty. Stepping out from his cover, he aimed and fired. The shot went wide, but the guy waving the sword slowed down.

***

"JOHN," Jenn screamed. "DANIE! There's still an active shooter!"

Danie hadn't heard the shot but pulled up at Jenn's warning. John wasn't at his side. He whipped around and saw John had stopped, several steps back. Danie yelled, "Go, John, you have to go!" John didn't move and looked lost as the sword tip dropped. "Go, John! Go!"

Looking back at the stones, Danie could see Arthur was struggling. In his earpiece, Morgana continued her recitation in languages that he couldn't place, and the Stone was glowing brighter. Their window was closing. "John, move!"

At that, John snapped back to the moment and launched another primeval scream. He swung the sword in a large circle over his head, but on his next step forward, a crack rang out, Excalibur flew out of his hands, and he clutched his chest. The sword sailed, end over end, embedding itself in the turf halfway between the brothers. John's legs failed him, and he fell to his knees, then to the ground, bouncing forward on his chest once before stopping, motionless. The next few moments seemed to creep forward in slow motion.

While the focus was on John, Eric screamed into the feed, "NO! I will not!" Then, "She's trying to get in my head!"

Ignoring the growing urgency, reaching his fallen brother became Danie's sole purpose. He turned fast, lost his footing, and went down to his hands and knees, scrambling back those precious steps to where John lay. Arthur was struggling; Eric might succumb. He'd seen the Stone glowing and heard the wind whipping, but could only act for his brother. As he reached out to John, movement to his right caught his attention. Merlin stood beside him, the wind whipping his gray cloak, hair, and beard. He had both hands on the staff, planted firmly. A vision of stability in an otherwise deteriorating situation. His eyes were on Danie, only for Danie. The wizard's calming voice came into his head. *That's why we needed two of you, dear boy. You must finish this.*

Arthur cried out, "Danie!" over the howling of the winds.

Eric was on his feet, hands clutching his head, but shuffling towards one of the fallen men's handguns, repeating "Je ne vais pas!" but with less and less authority.

The rugger looked one last time at his brother, lying motionless in the grass beneath him, then sprang to his feet. He reached the sword in two giant strides and grasped Excalibur's handle. He pulled it from the ground, spun off his planted left foot, and charged towards Arthur with the same yell his brother had called, seconds before.

More gunfire. He couldn't tell if it was friend or foe. He just kept running.

"I took him out, Danie," Jenn screamed. "You're clear! GO… GO… GO… Kill that bitch!" Then she weaved her way through the scattered rocks within the circle towards Arthur.

Danie stumbled as he jumped over a rock, then side-stepped another. Arthur saw him coming and hauled Morgana to her feet, his arms clutching her shoulders and waist.

Eric turned to face the charging giant, expressionless, with black eyes and outstretched arms. He stepped in Danie's path, but the rugger's mass cleared the Frenchman with no loss to his momentum.

Danie adjusted his hands, spinning the sword as if he'd been born to wield that weapon. As he secured a plunging grip and lifted Excalibur over his head, Arthur pushed up and backward, launching him and Morgana onto the Stone of Destiny. His back slammed into it, taking Morgana's full weight on top of him. In a single movement, Danie leapt towards Arthur and used his momentum to plunge the sword at Morgana's heart, driving it through Arthur's and into the Stone. An explosion of sound and light climaxed the drama and obscured the next moments. For Danie, the silhouette of Merlin, arms and staff raised above his head, had imprinted on his mind but was instantly lost in the blinding white light. His consciousness faded as Jenn cried, "NO! What have you done?"

***

The wind circling the stones stopped, and the clouds covering the moon parted. Jenn ran to the center, stumbling over rocks and fallen bodies to reach Arthur. *Maybe it wasn't what it looked like. Maybe he's OK.*

Her heart stopped when she reached the altar. He was gone. They were gone. Only Arthur's sword remained, embedded in the black stone. "Where is he?" she yelled to the night sky, spinning erratically. She exploded into motion, frantically searching the rocks for the king. *Where is he!?*

Coming full circle, back to the center, mouth agape and eyes welling with tears, firm hands grasped her shoulders. She looked up to see Danie now standing. He pulled her close and said, "He's gone, Jenn. They're both gone."

"He can't be! No … that's not… He's not…"

"Jenn, this was the plan all along. He had to go back with her. I'm sorry." He pulled Jenn close and wrapped his enormous arms around her tiny body. Danie said softly, "I'm sorry, Jenn. He said there was no other way."

Jenn gave herself over to his embrace and the grief of another loss. None of it made any sense any longer. Her mind went black.

Chapter 51

The government went into spin mode. Within minutes of the flash when the sword penetrated the Stone, or the Event, as it was later called, they swept in and removed all evidence of an otherworldly occurrence. Ambulances came for John and Danie while the rest were whisked away in the same windowless black van that had brought the Stone earlier that afternoon, save Merlin. Officials swept the scene, and he was nowhere to be found. Nobody had seen him since.

Jules helped complete a confidential report detailing the paranormal nature of the story. The contributions of Arthur and Merlin, who Jules had kept out of external conversations from the beginning of the planning, were similarly absent from the official transcript. A cover story would inform the public that conventional British forces thwarted a terrorist threat.

***

The team regrouped at Swafford House two days later. There were no clouds to filter the afternoon light illuminating the living room as Jenn stepped in, nursing an oversized glass of chardonnay. CJ was on the couch next to Mikol, not attempting to hide their fresh couple status. Jenn smiled as CJ met her gaze before glancing at the unlikely, and still unsmiling, Austrian. A shared nod spoke volumes.

Eric sat in CJ's recliner, fully extended, legs crossed. He planned to leave the following morning. The brief exposure to Morgana's possession compelled him back to his former life, to reassert control over his fate. The Frenchman tipped his glass to Jenn as he scrolled through his phone.

Peter was sitting with Jules at the small table Arthur had played chess with the brothers on. She noticed her brother was joining in the type of small talk he had always avoided; a laptop 'shield' no longer needed. Jules had convinced Peter to accept an exclusive internship at MI5 in the Digital Crimes Task Force. In this exchange program with the CIA, he'd have his university paid for while working with the latest technology. Jules saw a bright future for her brother and promised Jenn he'd look after him during his time in the States.

Jenn leaned her back against the French doors, conscious that this was the spot Arthur preferred to address his team from. She cleared her throat to get the room's attention. Struggling to find her voice, she managed to say, "I'd like to … I…" Her head dropped, and she swirled the contents of her glass, lost in the gentle movement of the wine. After a few imperceptible nods, she lifted her face, drained the remaining wine, then forced a smile as her eyes swept the room.

Jules rose and grabbed a bottle of Jenn's favorite from a bucket of ice. He topped her off with a bow and a flourish. "M'lady…" he said.

"Cheers, Sir Julius," she said, attempting to mimic Merlin's raspy grumble. "Right. Now…"

A commotion at the front door and the booming voices of the South African twins interrupted her address for a second time. Jenn exhaled and turned as their entrance captured everyone's attention.

"Are we late for dinner?" Danie had a backpack slung over his shoulder and a grin that spoke volumes of his relief that his brother was OK. Stepping in behind Danie was John with his left arm in a black nylon sling. Otherwise, nothing in his demeanor hinted at any concerns.

"A Swanepoel is never late for dinner," Peter said. "Dinner is served precisely when they arrive."

Danie dropped his head in mock shame. "It was funnier the first time," he mumbled.

"Excuse me … all … ladies and gentlemen," Jenn said as the South Africans settled in. "Now that we're all here … or, all that remain are here," she corrected herself with a catch in her voice. "A toast to those we lost. We don't know where they are, or when they are … but…" She choked on the thought and wiped a welling tear from her right eye.

CJ noticed Jenn's losing battle with tears and stood up. "To Arthur Pendragon, High King of the Britons!" Glasses were raised, and cheers were exclaimed.

John added, looking to Jenn and Peter, "And to Sir Colin Pelling, I wish he could have been here to share this moment with us. From all I've heard, he truly was a great man."

Jenn wrapped herself in a hug, wiping a tear with the index finger of the hand holding the wineglass. She offered John the most appreciative smile she could muster.

Jules then raised his glass. "And to the wizard, Merlin…" He dropped his head, shook it slightly, then glanced over at Jenn. "OK … to Merlin, the biggest pain in our respective asses … but the most extraordinary man to ever walk this planet." He nodded to his glass and his team. This toast was quieter, but with enormous respect.

Jenn cleared her throat again and said, "I guess now is the best time to share what Merlin entrusted me with since Eric is leaving tomorrow. I'll be putting my move to London off indefinitely. I won't be returning to teaching either. Our quest's epilogue of sorts will consume my life for the foreseeable future. Let me back up a bit. When I returned yesterday, I found a thick envelope with my name written in Merlin's unmistakable scrawl. First, this note confirmed that he's gone as well. He didn't say where he went, or *when,* for that matter, but I don't think we'll see him again.

"Merlin has instructed the firm that has been managing the business aspects of this endeavor to disburse the remaining funds to this team. I haven't delved into the specifics, but the investments Merlin made over the centuries did well, very well."

Jules grinned. "I'd expect that his investment strategies

wouldn't pass ethical scrutiny, having that special relationship with time and space, you know."

Jenn chuckled. "I guess we'll never know about that. Nevertheless, the money is ours, all of ours," gesturing with her wineglass, a sweep of the room. "That is, all minus certain gifts and grants. He designated me to be the executor of the disbursement.

"One particular initiative he's encouraged me to pursue is a global foundation to study and support victims of domestic abuse. He and I had discussed how Morgana was driven to madness by the pressures of the society she grew up in. While her response to it was horrifically medieval, she did illuminate that we haven't come as far to balance the scales as progress, as civilization, would rightly warrant. The willing participants in her search for the Stone alone speak to how far we still need to go. I'll be managing this from Glastonbury."

CJ uncrossed her legs and leaned forward. "I think that's a brilliant way to make all this seem less senseless. Money isn't an issue for me and my family - I mean, just look at *this* place. I'll be OK. I'd like to donate my share of the funds to your foundation."

"Thank you so much, CJ," Jenn said, eyes welling up again. CJ crossed the room and hugged Jenn until she got control of herself.

"I'm sorry about that ... again!" Jenn said, chuckling wetly. She cleared her eyes with the heel of her hand. "There's one more thing. Merlin revealed that he'd kept an extensive journal, some of it digital, but mostly scribbled notes and clippings; *crates of them*. The disbursement plan includes a sizable grant to the University of Edinburgh, specifically to Dr. Cockran, to organize and archive all this information. He'll make sure that we all have unfettered access, and I'm confident he'd welcome your involvement."

"Will this effort set the record straight on the historic King Arthur?" Danie asked.

Peter stood up and said, "I think that the world is a richer place with the stories as they are. Maybe the greatest gift we can offer Arthur is to let him remain a legend." He glanced over at Jenn, who encouraged him to continue with a smile.

"I mean, I grew up sort of knowing there was another history obscured by all the stories, but … but it was the legends, the sword in the stone, the quest for the Grail, Lancelot and Guinevere, that kept me passionate and motivated for what might come next. Maybe people need more wonderment these days than less. I don't know…" He looked around the room.

Jenn beamed and said, "We don't know where Merlin's journals will lead us, but I, for one, would hate to be responsible for depriving future generations of King Arthur and his Knights of the Round Table. I agree with Peter. Anyone else?"

This question set the group to discuss the possibilities such a journal might offer, but they were enthusiastically in favor of Peter's proposal. Turning her back to the room, she glimpsed movement through the glass, a charging horse and a glint of sunlight off shining armor. *No*, she realized, a breeze had brushed the tall grass and rippled the surface of the water. Then, as suddenly as it came, the wind was still. *He's gone.* Raising her glass to the wind, she whispered, "Cheers, your highness." She pivoted back to the buzz, crossed her arms, and dabbed her eyes again. It would fall upon her shoulders to memorialize and safeguard the true story, and the new story, of Arthur, Merlin, Morgana, and this extraordinary team - the Soldier, the Shooter, the Spy, the Giants, and the Fighter.

Epilogue

An explosion of light awakened him.

His arm snapped up to cover his eyes. Pivoting away from the offending glare, he realized he had been sleeping. The feather pillow, the blankets - they all felt familiar, smelled familiar. Pulling his arm up a small bit, he ventured a look. Tapestry over stone walls? Paintings of dark-suited men on horseback hunting pheasant hung on the papered walls in his room at Swafford House.

"Arthur, wake up!" He flipped around to face the voice, arm back over his eyes to shield them from the sunshine. "We let you sleep in since it's your birthday, but the sun is high and, like it or not, we do need you."

He saw a figure silhouetted by the daylight pouring in from a large window, heavy drapes pulled to each side. He could make out long hair and a woman's curves behind the flowing, translucent fabric of her outer gown, playing and swaying in the breeze. As his vision came into focus and his eyes could finally provide details to his brain, he saw auburn hair loosely tied and hanging over her left shoulder. He recognized the intense eyes and the provocative smile. *Guinevere! But how?*

She sat on the bed next to him and cupped his left cheek in her hand. "There you are. Happy birthday, my lord ... my love." She kissed him on the top of his head.

He sat himself up and took her hands in his. "Is this a dream? Are you really here?"

"If only this day were a dream, Arthur, but preparations for your celebration are well underway, and I need your help ... soon, please." She had just gotten those last words out when Arthur smothered her in a bear hug and buried his face in her hair.

"I've had the most horrible nightmare, my love. I can't even begin to know where to start." He pulled his head back and kissed his wife deeply, gently urging her down onto the bed.

"No, you don't, *Your Highness*!" She placed her hands on his chest and pushed him away. "Maybe we'll have time for that later, but I do doubt it will be today. Messengers from your sisters came in the middle of the night, and they'll ALL be arriving together with the high sun. If the shock of your awakening didn't make it clear, that time is near."

Arthur dropped his hands to her waist, not yet prepared to break their touch. "ALL my sisters are coming for my birthday? Even Morgana?"

The queen, not liking the look on Arthur's face when he said that, placed her hand on his forehead to check for fever as she mouthed back at him, *Morgana*? "You mean Morgan, don't you? *Morgana*? Of course, Morgan is coming. I mean, she and her young hellion Ywain practically live here at Camelot. I think our children prefer her to us, frankly."

Arthur took her hand from his head and looked at her with his eyes tight, brow furrowed. "Morgana, who has vowed to kill me - that Morgana has been with our children?"

"Now you have me worried, Arthur." She sat back to get a better look at his face. "Kill you?! She has done no such thing, and I can't imagine why you'd call her Morgana. Aunt Morgan, your sister, your hunting companion, your partner in annoying pranks? That Morgan? Please, Arthur, get up and let the ladies dress you. You'll feel better once you get food in your stomach." She stood up, smoothed her thin cloak over her more substantial red felted dress, and stepped back.

"Oh, and you-know-who has been pacing outside our door. He has something quite urgent to share with you and won't leave until he does."

Arthur cocked his head as he swung his legs over the side of the bed; his bed … at Camelot. He patted the stuffed feather mattress in disbelief with both hands as he took in the room. He looked from side to side, as much to loosen his neck after a long sleep as to reassure himself he was in his chambers in his own home. "I'm sorry, my love. I'm feeling disoriented this morning."

"Maybe because it's practically afternoon," said Guinevere, arms crossed over her chest and left hip jutting out in her *we're-done-playing* look.

"Fine, it's late," Arthur said, smiling, missing that look terribly. "Who exactly is waiting outside?"

"Your pet, your loyal hound, '*Sir*' Bedivere. So, if you have your wits about you, may I allow him an audience?"

"Of course," said Arthur, standing and pulling a blanket over his shoulders, noting he was still in his thin bedclothes. He was unsure whether he should move or what to expect.

Guinevere paused, trying to read the look on her husband's face and wondering if she should be concerned. With a small half-shake of her head, she dropped her arms and strode to the door, eyes lingering on his face for a moment longer. Pulling it open, she thrust her head through and stated, "The King is awake. You may…" but the flurry of movement as the overly eager Bedivere pushed past her into the room cut her off. He was carrying a parcel wrapped in plain white cloth.

He bowed to the king. Then, remembering his manners, turned and bowed even lower to the Queen and stumbled, his backside bumping the frame of the door. Guinevere fought to constrain the smile that broke out every time this knight, hardly old enough to warrant that title and the responsibilities it entailed, attempted to look older than his years.

"Your Highness," he said, turning back to Arthur. "Myrddin bade me bring this to you the minute you woke." He handed the bundle to the curious king.

"A birthday present from the old wizard?" Arthur asked as he unwrapped the parcel. He froze. His face paled, and his mouth dropped. He held in his hands a pair of worn Columbia leather hiking boots. He looked up, speechless, at Bedivere, then at Guinevere.

Not sure what to make of this response, the squire continued, "He insisted I clean them up and present them to you as new. Now I've seen nothing like them before, so I don't actually know what new looked like, but you know … wizards, right? Anyway, they are clean and in good repair except for that tear on the side of … that one." He pointed to the right boot. "Old Myrddin told me he'd 'curse my progeny to be dim-witted like me if I failed him.' Now, sire, I don't know where my progeny is, but I certainly don't want it cursed." Then, realizing he might have used an improper phrase in front of the queen, he stammered, "Beg your pardon, m'lady."

This time, Arthur laughed with Guinevere. He placed the boots on the floor next to him and embraced his young protégé. "Progeny refers to your children and their children, Bedivere. I am uniquely qualified to affirm that your progeny will do nothing but honor their forefather. You'd be proud of who they'll become."

Bedivere, unaccustomed to physical contact with the king, glanced over at the queen with pleading eyes, looking for an explanation. She shrugged and smiled, then turned to the window to gaze down the hill at the woods below, the River Cam in the distance. Townspeople and servants were busy completing preparations for the grand celebration.

Merlin, who had been in the hallway listening to this exchange, chuckled. He closed the game he was playing on his iPhone, slipped it into a deep pocket, and ambled to the stairs.

***

Deep beneath the British Museum, behind two security doors, one requiring a key card and the second, biometrics, was a lab reserved for confidential research. Few knew of its existence, and even fewer would ever have access.

A scientist and an archaeologist hovered over a binder of bound, torn, and worn parchment mixed with more modern photocopies. They were working in a dark room with a cantilevered, scissor-arm can light illuminating the text and nothing else. In hushed voices, they argued and negotiated various passages, each written in a different forgotten language. Agreeing at last on a passage in Latin, the archaeologist spoke the words.

Both men's breathing stopped as the yellow-green glow from the stone, reflecting off the tarnished blade protruding toward the ceiling, cast an eerie halo around the table they were observing.

A table containing the legendary Sword and the Stone.

Thee End

www.ingramcontent.com/pod-product-compliance
Lightning Source LLC
Chambersburg PA
CBHW070549260626
47161CB00002B/554